The Bird of Bedford Manor

MICHELLE GRIEP

YOU are the reason we do what we do here at Barbour Publishing. We promise that we will always use our God-given talents to produce content with you in mind—and that we will remain biblically faithful, no matter what.

Thank you for being the heart of our business.

Print ISBN 979-8-89151-241-2

Adobe Digital Edition (.epub) 979-8-89151-242-9

Scripture quotations are taken from the King James Version of the Bible.

Cover Design: Kirk DouPonce, DogEared Design

Published in association with the Books & Such Literary Management, 52 Mission Circle, Suite 122, PMB 170, Santa Rosa, CA 95409-5370, www.booksandsuch.com.

Published by Barbour Publishing, Inc., 1810 Barbour Drive, Uhrichsville, Ohio 44683, www.barbourbooks.com

Our mission is to inspire the world with the life-changing message of the Bible.

Printed in the United States of America.

Dedication

This one is for you, dear reader, because without you I'd be muttering plot twists to myself and stress-eating deadline snacks for no good reason, and—as always—to God who gets all the glory, the credit, and the frantic midnight prayers when chapter 12 won't behave.

Chapter 1

Bedfordshire, England, 1820

She was reborn that day of dust and wind, with tangles in her hair and a hard cracked soul. Who knew such a transformation could come from something as simple as the snaring of a rabbit? Her first kill. The vanguard moment of self-reliance—and she'd sworn it wouldn't be her last. Not if she could help it. But now, despite the skill her brother would have been proud of, game was scarce, and Juliet Finch wondered how much longer the stretch of wood and field beyond their mean cottage would sustain her and Aunt Margaret. She just might have to trust in God to provide. . .though she wasn't quite sure she was ready to talk to Him again.

Not yet.

Bleary-eyed and yawning, she silently closed the gate in the thick darkness before dawn, then tucked the empty burlap sack more snugly into her belt. It'd felt strange that first time she'd donned men's garments. Now, more than a year later, the trousers and scratchy woolen tunic were as much a part of her as the ball gowns and riding habits she'd once worn. If Colin Chamberlain could see her in her current state. . .he'd be glad he'd spurned her.

She kept to the worn rut winding through the trees, her steps sure and steady on a trail she could walk with her eyes closed—and they might as well have been. Beneath the canopy of fat oak leaves and clouded sky, not a star shone so much as a snippet of light. The first few times she'd ventured out like this, such blackness had been paralyzing. At least once, she'd run back to the cottage and bolted the door. A week of nothing but watery gruel had cured that ailment. Now? The witching hours were her dearest friend, for therein did she find sanctuary.

The woods ended abruptly, an unnaturally straight edge. The groundskeeper at Bedford Manor took his job seriously, keeping the lichen-covered stone fence free of growth for a good ten paces on either side. Easier to catch poachers that way.

Easier to catch her.

Juliet scanned the chest-high barrier one way then the other, squinting to detect movement. Granted, the task was nearly impossible in this darkness, but that could work to her advantage. If she couldn't see anyone, then neither could anyone see her. She hoped.

Satisfied, she sprinted ahead and heaved herself up and over, landing on light feet. Now that she was on Russell property, all her senses heightened as she dashed into the woods on the other side. An owl hooted at her arrival, its eerie call indicting her for disturbing its domain. Ignoring the night bird, she caught her breath before padding onwards. There was no path here. She didn't dare travel the same way twice on this land. Marking a predictable route would get her killed, and worse, be the end of Aunt Margaret. There was no way the old dear could manage for herself, not after the accident.

Near the base of a large beech tree, she carefully parted the undergrowth, then frowned. The horsehair loop she'd so carefully crafted sat empty, still attached to the peg she'd secured into the loamy ground. No small game had passed this way, but that didn't mean her other snares held no prizes.

One by one, she checked her woodland traps, frustration rising with each barren noose. By the time she reached the end of the trees, her sack hung at her hip without a morsel of meat in it. Her stomach growled. So did she. But no sense wasting time in lament. Already some of the blackness in the sky leached into more of a charcoal hue. Day would soon break.

Leaving behind the safety of the trees, she darted across the field to the dark line of a hedgerow. She dropped to her knees and crawled until finding an opening wide enough to shimmy through. Her sleeve snagged. Fabric ripped. And skin. Bother. She ignored the sting as she broke through the other side, then crouch-ran along the edge of the row until it ended in a small patch of brambles. She had set only one snare here, yet a grin broke as she pushed the growth aside. A fat grouse lay on its side.

Her smile faded, though, as she set about loosening the bird. It always pained her, this taking of life for life. A blessing for her and Aunt, but a curse on the little fowl. Ending one life to nourish another felt like a sin.

"I pray you forgive me, little creature," she whispered as she laid it inside her sack.

She reset the snare, a bitter laugh rising in her throat. What use was praying for pardon from a dead bird when her belly cramped? She could barely keep enough meat in the house to feed two mouths. Was it God's design to test her very soul to death? Rising, she glanced at the ever-lightening sky. No, she would not cower. She would survive—no matter what it took.

She slung the bag over her shoulder and tromped back along the hedgerow, then veered towards the manor itself, making good time until the sharp report of a snapped stick cut through the air like a gunshot.

She tore back to the hedgerow, diving into the base of it for protection and nearly losing her hat—which was better than losing her head. There, on the other side of the hawthorns, the dark figure of a man strode out from the woods, a rifle cradled in the crook of his arm. Another poacher? No. Not with that sure gait. This was a man who belonged here. Knew the grounds. Maybe even knew where she now scrunched into a ball, for he strode right towards her.

Sweat wept hot on her brow in the cool air. Surely he would hear the rush of her breathing, the dead giveaway of her heart banging against her ribs.

Thud.

Thud.

Thud!

Her pulse kept time with the tromp of his footsteps—footsteps that were now so close the ground vibrated with each step. Should he find her...no. Better not to think of the noose tightening around her own neck as it had the little grouse's. Poaching carried the death penalty—or banishment to Van Diemen's Land, which would be just as fatal. Or so she'd heard.

The feet stopped right in front of her. If she reached out, she could touch the wet hem of the man's trousers. If he squatted...oh Lord, if he squatted!

She scrunched her eyes shut, throat closing. She could not stand to think of suffering such an ignominious death.

And all because of her father.

The man's coat rustled. Then came a metallic click—the cocking of that terrible gun. She squeezed her eyes tighter, sickened by the cold, hard promise of violence. This was it. Retribution. How much would it hurt? How quickly before her heart stopped? How—

The world exploded.

Chapter 2

So, it came to this. Henry Russell gripped his pistol with a steady hand as he stalked through the woods on silent feet. After eight weeks of his sister's tears and fright, sleepless nights, and far too many threats from the shadows, he would avenge the terrors Charity had suffered—or die in the trying. . .an outcome Carver the groundskeeper had warned him against. But so be it. It was too important *he* be the one to settle this, to manage things with his own two hands.

He crept from tree to tree, scanning the darkness, listening so hard it hurt his ears. An owl called. Mice scurried in the underbrush. Overhead, leaves rustled faintly from a whisper of breeze. And through it all, he could yet hear Charity's fists pounding on his bedroom door, hardly a quarter of an hour ago. Her voice choked with horror. Her body shaking. She'd flung herself against him, panicked because that man—the fiendish phantom who'd plagued her these past two months—had stood outside her window. She was sure she'd seen him.

Henry barely took the time to put on his trousers and hadn't bothered with shoes. Yet now his bare feet served him well, save for the occasional sharp piece of gravel that dug into tender skin. Even so, he relished the pain. Better that than calling for help when he ought to stand firm on his own. He'd done that once, as a boy. Never again.

Circling back to where he'd started, Henry blew out a disgusted breath. It appeared Charity's tormentor was not in this stand of trees.

There was no telltale snap of twigs, no hasty breathing, not even a single footfall. Blast! He'd thought for certain the scoundrel would flee through this stretch of woods. Hopefully Carver was having better luck on his end. His groundskeeper knew this land better than anyone.

Once again Henry gazed into the darkness—though the sky wasn't nearly as black as when he'd first dashed outside. Perhaps it would be best to check the hedgerow or—

Crack!

A shot rang out, violating the predawn quiet. The sharp report echoed through the trees, ruffling the feathers of birds in their roosts. His heart lurched, blood surging through his veins. Clearly Carver had sighted the man or maybe even taken him down. Victory!

Henry took off in the direction of the sound, pulse pounding in his ears. Branches whipped against him as he sprinted, but he paid them no mind. The thrill of the chase urged him onwards.

Nearing the edge of the trees, something caught his eye—a dark shape racing across the lawn between shrubbery and woods. He skidded to a stop, breath stuck in his throat. The man was moving quickly.

Straight towards him.

He froze. Had Carver missed his shot? Or had he hit his mark and wounded the blackguard, who was now trying to escape? Henry squinted, straining to make out details in the dim light. Something wasn't quite right about that figure.

And where was his groundskeeper?

Unease prickled down Henry's spine. He shifted back a step, eyes darting for a hiding place from which to spring. And...there. A cluster of holly bushes. Without another thought, he dove into the spiky foliage. The pointed ends of the leaves scratched sharp against his arms and legs where he crouched. Annoying, but necessary. The dense foliage provided excellent cover.

He tucked tightly into the crevice, musty earth and crushed leaves filling his nostrils. Forcing his breathing to steady, he prepared to launch.

Footsteps pounded. Closer. Urgent.

Henry tensed. The man was near. Just a few strides away. Breath heavy in the damp air. Once the fellow passed by, he'd pounce, swing one arm around the villain's neck, and dig the muzzle of the gun into his back.

But then the footsteps quieted. Barely two paces beyond his hiding place, the fellow stopped, leaning heavily against a tree.

Henry's eyes narrowed. What was this? Why would the scoundrel pause, hanging his head like a man in despair? Carry a sack slung over his back? And was that a sigh? The longer Henry stared, the more a brick sank in his gut.

This wasn't danger cloaked in dark.

He wasn't even sure this was a man.

As the person shifted slightly, a too-large tunic and baggy trousers came into clearer focus, confirming Henry's worst suspicions. It was a mere boy, clothed in garments two sizes too large. Carver had been grumbling about a poacher the past few months. Apparently, Henry had found him. Not the criminal he was after—but a criminal, nonetheless.

The lad stepped away.

Henry sprang, grabbing one of his slim shoulders. "Hold it right there."

He spun the boy around, leveling the flintlock pistol at his chest. Not that he'd shoot the lad, but a gun had a way of putting the fear of God into anyone.

Impossibly large eyes peered up into his own. Hard to say what colour they were in this dim light, but one thing was for certain . . .fear swam in those pools, the same fear he'd witnessed in his sister's eyes. One giveaway curl sprang out from a patched flatcap, the tendril brushing against the curve of a delicate cheek. Thunder and turf! This wasn't even a lad, but a woman, barely a slip of a thing. The desperation vivid on her face twisted something deep in his chest. Something dire must have driven her to play such a dangerous charade.

"Who are you?" he demanded. "What the deuce are you doing on my land?"

A visible tremble rippled the fabric across her shoulders. "I am someone who is merely trying to survive, sir."

Her dulcet tone and clear diction labeled her a lady. But that was impossible. No lady he knew would deign to set foot in the woods at night—and dressed as a poor boy no less. An act, then? Appear his equal to garner sympathy? He studied her face, the high cheekbones, the full lips, but she was a closed book.

"Survival or not," he clipped, "stealing is a crime. You do realize what happens to poachers, do you not? I should have you arrested here and now."

Her mouth flattened to a grim line. "Yes, I know. Had I any other choice, I would not be here." She glanced at the sack on her shoulder. "My aunt and I have nothing but what I catch, for the harvest this year was bad. There is no work for me in town, as you well know the economy is particularly troublesome for everyone—save, perhaps, for you."

His grip on her shoulder lightened. Truth ripened her words, bitter as it was. The countryside was full of desperate people these days, yet that did not excuse theft.

He uncocked his gun, though he did not release her. She held his gaze, sparks of pride and strength flashing. She was a brave one, he'd give her that. "What if I were to—"

She twisted from his grasp, ducking low, darting aside, fast as the wind.

Hang it all!

The chase was on.

He tore after her, gained ground, lunged and—

His foot snagged. Something bit into his bare ankle, jerking him off balance.

He went down hard, pain shooting up his leg as he hit the ground. His pistol skidded from his hand, disappearing into the underbrush beyond his reach. Henry grabbed for his foot, trying to free himself, but the horsehair snare might as well have been a solid cable of wire. His ankle throbbed white hot, and he suspected at best it was badly bruised. At worst, broken.

Meanwhile the girl didn't waste a moment. Her lithe figure sprinted through the woods, and a breath later, she vanished into the trees.

Disgusted with himself for letting her give him the slip, he struggled against the snare, but the blasted thing was well set. The more he pulled, the tighter it cinched. Frustration boiled over. There was no way now he could give chase. Not like this.

Several grunts and winces later, he managed to free his foot and stagger up to stand. Gingerly, he tested his weight, clenching his jaw at the fiery pain. It was sharp, but bearable, yet the joint was not hale enough to endure the strain of a dash through the woods. Leaning against a tree, he squinted into the oncoming dawn.

The woman was long gone.

He limped over to retrieve his pistol, supporting himself heavily on his uninjured leg. As he pocketed the weapon, he couldn't help but feel a reluctant admiration for the girl. She was resilient. Intriguing. And—hang it all—quite comely.

But she only doubled the trouble. Unless Carver had cornered the tormentor, now Henry had two rogues to find.

Chapter 3

Her lungs burned. And her thighs. Even so, Juliet pressed on, flinging herself over Bedford Manor's rock wall and scraping her face in the process. She landed hard on her forearm and then rolled to her feet, all the while expecting a shot between the shoulder blades to take her down. Now would be a good time to pray.

But what would be the point? God hadn't answered when she'd pleaded for her brother's life as he lay dying from consumption. The great Creator hadn't responded when she'd wept out her very soul at the injustice she'd suffered by her father's own doing. And where had God been when Aunt Margaret had teetered at the edge of death, her body frail and fevered?

Juliet sprinted through the trees, fighting branches, rocks, roots. She tried to listen for footsteps at her back, but her own breathing and the rush of blood in her ears made that impossible. She didn't slow a whit until she caught sight of the ramshackle cottage she shared with Aunt Margaret. The prayer she refused to utter had been answered anyway.

Why did some prayers merit favour and others did not? Why did God always seem to turn away His face when she needed Him most? And yet. . .here she walked, still alive, the danger past. Maybe—perhaps—God was still there, watching, waiting for her to acknowledge the thin thread of grace woven through her life. But how could she when He had let so much be torn away?

Sucking in great gulps of air, Juliet shook off the jittery feeling in her arms and legs as she crunched along the gravel path. When Uncle William had been alive, this small structure of stone and timber had been a cozy home. He had purchased it from the manor soon after marrying Aunt Margaret, a blessing that now spared her from paying rent. But with him gone, things had fallen into disrepair at an alarming rate. And since it belonged to her, she couldn't turn to the manor for any help—help that it desperately needed.

Ivy had overtaken two of the walls and half the eastern side of the roof. The wooden shingles on the corner of the west side were rotted, a drift of bird down filling the depression. Rising sunlight glinted off the two front windows, highlighting gaps where the glazing had fallen away. Juliet took great care in pushing open the door, for an abrupt move could take the rickety thing clean off its worn hinges. This place needed a man's touch, sure enough.

She crept inside, hoping to make it past the small bedroom without disturbing her aunt. Let her sleep. Hopefully a good rest would ease the sting of her censure when the woman found out Juliet had been poaching despite being cautioned against doing so.

"You've been out again."

Juliet whirled, slapping her free hand against her chest. Aunt Margaret sat at the big table that dominated the only other room in the cottage, her leg propped on a barrel. Beyond her sallow complexion and deep-set eyes, intelligence glinted in her gaze. The woman was far too keen. There would be no use in denying her.

But diversion might work.

"Aunt, what are you doing up?" Juliet grabbed a shawl from the back of the chair near the hearth and draped it over the woman's shoulders. "You know you should not leave the bed on your own. You could have fallen." She pressed a light kiss to her aunt's parchment brow.

Aunt Margaret patted her cheek, her fingers cold against Juliet's skin. "Someone's got to keep an eye on you. I've been asking for God's favour the whole time you've been out."

"Well then, it is a good thing He listens to you. And being that you already know where I have been, perhaps you would like to clean this bird while I get a pot ready." She dropped the bag onto the table.

"Oh, Juliet." Aunt Margaret shook her head. "This poaching has got to stop. It's too dangerous. If the groundskeeper were to catch you—"

"Please do not fret. I am very careful."

"Oh?" She aimed her bony finger like a dagger. "That scrape on your jaw says otherwise. How did you come by it?"

"It is merely a scratch." Absently, she pressed a light touch to the injury, her hasty retreat still fresh in her mind. . .the all-consuming intensity of the man who'd held her captive even more real. What was the fellow doing in the woods in what was clearly his nightshirt, bare of feet, and trousers riding low on his hips from lack of braces? There was no way he could have heard or seen her from the manor, so there'd been no reason whatsoever for him to have raced from his bed with a pistol in hand. No, he'd not been looking for her, that much was obvious. But he had looked *at* her. And despite the fear of that moment, the threat of her very life, those grey-green eyes and husky voice of his had done strange things inside her chest.

"—then God was surely looking out for you."

She startled at Aunt's voice, pulled back to the present. "I beg your pardon?"

"I said God was surely looking out for you, for I suspect there is more to your adventure than a run-in with a sharp branch." Aunt Margaret narrowed her eyes. "Promise me you will not go out again."

"I will do no such thing. We need to eat."

"There are still jars of ointments and bottles of tinctures to sell." Aunt Margaret fluttered her hand towards the shelves behind her. "I know hawking wares is quite a fall from grace for you, but it is a respectable business and far less hazardous than bagging fowl from Bedford Manor."

A sigh deflated her. "Not anymore," she murmured.

Aunt Margaret angled her head, concern etching lines at the sides of her mouth. "What do you mean?"

Juliet bit her lip. She didn't want to worry her aunt more than she already did, but there would be no hiding the truth from the woman. Aunt Margaret was as good at snaring one in a lie as Juliet was at poaching prey. She sank into a chair across from her aunt. "I did not wish to upset you, but. . .last time I went to town and set up a sales crate, that pompous new apothecary, Mr. Scather, and I had a row. He threatened me, said if I did not move on, he would get the constable involved unless I could produce a license. And without a license, I would be arrested."

"Arrested!" Aunt Margaret slapped the tabletop, rattling the salt cellar. "The women of our family have been herbalists for generations. None of them needed to purchase a paper to sell their goods! What does he know of tradition, of local medicinals being passed down through the ages?"

"See? This is why I did not tell you. Times have changed, Aunt. There are new laws, different regulations. And Mr. Scather seems determined to make his mark by seeing them enforced—particularly the Apothecaries Act. But do not let this trouble you. I will see to it that we manage despite him." Juliet patted her aunt's hand, then filled the teapot with water before setting it on the grate. "I think a spot of chamomile will be just the thing for now."

"This is outrageous." Anger shook her aunt's voice. "The remedies I make are just as good, if not better, than anything that pretentious peacock Mr. Scather can concoct in his fancy apothecary shop. The people of Bedford ought to know that. They've trusted me for years."

"I know but Mr. Scather has connections, and he has already begun spreading rumours about our remedies being unsafe. Last week, Mrs. Cunningham refused to buy her usual lavender salve from me, claiming she heard it might cause a rash. It is only a matter of time before others believe such hearsay as well."

"So that's why sales have dwindled." Frustration leeched from her aunt's words, replaced now by concern. "And that's why you've reset your snares, risking your life."

Juliet faced her aunt, curving her lips into a reassuring smile. "All is not lost. I fully intend to visit your past customers and try selling to them directly. It may take more effort, but it is safer than setting up a stall in the market."

"A good plan—until we run out of stock." She frowned. "And now is such a good time to collect plants. I wish I could venture into the woods to teach you what to harvest. A pox on this leg!"

"Give it time." She squeezed her aunt's shoulder. The woman had nearly died from blood loss and then from fever, not to mention she'd broken more than one bone in her leg when she'd tumbled into that rocky ravine. Juliet pushed down a shiver just thinking about it. "I am grateful you are alive, Aunt."

A small smile replaced her aunt's frown. "And I am thankful you are here, though I know you miss your old life."

Juliet couldn't deny it. She did miss her old life, with an ache that sometimes kept her awake long into the night. How weary she was of scraping and clawing, wondering where their next meal would come from, and from the ever-present burden of keeping them both alive. She wandered to the window, watching green leaves flirt with gold and rust. Winter would soon be here, making birds scarce, though she had a good eye for tracking larger game.

She pressed her fingers to the glass. If only she could get her hands on a bow and an arrow or two, she could take down a deer. She was sure of it. After her brother had trained her, she'd learned to outshoot him back in the day. Much to his chagrin. And a buck or a doe would last them for weeks, longer if they dried the meat. But where on earth would she get a bow?

And even more daunting, how could she risk hauling such a big animal off the Bedford estate without getting caught? Was she even strong enough? The danger would be tremendous, but the reward... oh, what a reward.

She let out a long breath, fogging the glass. It was a temptation she could hardly afford to ignore.

Defeat never came easy. Never had. In all his twenty-eight years, Henry could count on one hand the number of times he'd given up—and this would not be one of them. Wincing at the fiery pain burning a line all the way to his kneecap, he clutched the banister and hobbled up the first few steps of the grand stair in the front hall.

His father had left him in charge, and he would not fail. Not because of an injury. Not because of anything. If he couldn't manage his responsibilities until his father's return, what did that say about his ability to one day shoulder them permanently? To be the man his father believed he could be?

The man he needed to be.

"Henry!"

His sister descended in a flurry, her silk robe billowing ghostly white in the spare light of dawn. The fear on her face vanished as she gaped at his bruised ankle. "You are hurt. Here, lean on me." She flung her arm around his shoulders. "I shall settle you in the sitting room and send word for the doctor at once."

He pulled away, taking care to keep his full weight on his uninjured foot. "I made it this far on my own, Sister. There is no need to pester Dr. Branch. It is Carver's opinion my ankle is not broken."

She popped her fists on her hips, a pout to her bow-like lips. Golden curls framed her face, leastwise those not caught up in the full braid hanging down her back. She was a summer sun, this younger sister of his. Her eyes blue as freshly budded cornflowers, but her tone was an August storm. "Mr. Carver is a groundskeeper! Not a physician."

"Yet he knows animals and has plenty of experience with injuries, both in the field and around the estate. You forget he's seen more sprains and broken bones than most. Do you not remember how he nursed the hounds back to health after their skirmish with that badger last spring?"

"You are not a hound, stubborn man." With a toss of her head, she once again reached for his shoulder. "And so you must at least allow me to see you to your room and get that foot propped up while I ring for tea. Furthermore, if the pain worsens or I find there is much swelling, I am calling Dr. Branch. Agreed?"

"I hardly think I have a choice, Sister dear, for you are every bit as stubborn as you claim I am." He smirked, then stifled a sharp inhale as they climbed the stairs. For all of Charity's help, he would have done better on his own, yet he couldn't refuse his younger sister. He never had been able to. By the time they reached the first-floor landing, sweat dotted his brow. Thank heaven his was the nearest chamber on the left.

As they moved towards the door, his ankle afire, his mind wandered back to the woods. He'd underestimated that pixie—whoever she was. The memory of her flashed vividly, the defiant gleam in her eye, the dark wild of her hair that escaped her hat, the lightness and speed of her feet as she'd flown like a bird in the breaking dawn. She'd paused for the briefest of moments when he'd fallen, a flash of concern on her face just before she'd disappeared into the thicket. He winced again, this time not just from the pain, but from the frustration of knowing she'd bested him.

His sister shoved open the door while glancing at him sideways. "I am assuming you did not catch the scoundrel."

Hah. Which one?

"Not yet," he said simply.

"Hmm." Her brow bunched as she grabbed a pillow off his bed. "I thought I heard a gunshot."

"You did. Carver saw a shadow move on the far side of the hedgerow, but when he investigated, there were no tracks." He eased into the chair, allowing Charity to elevate his leg on a pillow. "Neither did he spy anything to indicate someone had stood beneath your bedroom window. No footprints. No crushed grass."

Charity folded her arms, a distinct jut to her jaw. "I saw someone, Henry. I did not imagine it. Furthermore—"

He shot up his hand, staving her off. "I believe you." And he did. No doubt she saw something, but a human? The dark before dawn had a way of playing tricks on the eyes of a woman already skittish from previous scares. "This will soon be over, Charity. I vow I shall find whoever it is that frightens you so."

"I just hope you find him before someone really gets hurt." She knelt at his feet, gently pushing up the ruined hem of his trouser leg and frowning at the angry red line on his skin. "This is bad enough. You should have thought to put on shoes."

"You came to my door weeping and incoherent. Shoes were not of foremost importance at the time."

She crossed to the washbasin and moistened a cloth. Returning to his side, she cleaned off the grass stains and smudges of dirt from both feet. A fresh wave of tears glistened in her eyes. "Oh, Henry," she murmured. "What are we to do?"

We?

He plowed his fingers through his hair. His father had entrusted him with the household, with Charity's care, with everything that mattered in his absence. And now—game stolen, a trespasser haunting the grounds, his sister trembling in the night. He was supposed to shield her from this. Be the man who could stand firm against trouble just as his father would have were he here.

So he hadn't written. Hadn't summoned his father's help. And wouldn't. He'd cried wolf once before and vowed never to do so again.

But Charity wasn't bound by that vow. She shouldn't have to live in fear while he wrestled with doubt.

He shifted in the chair, bracing for resistance. "This situation is not your responsibility, Sister. I cannot track down this harasser of yours if I am constantly worried about your well-being. That being said, I believe it is time you join Father in Italy. A holiday would be just the thing to put you in a better frame of mind, and I know Father would love to have your company."

She sank back on her haunches, head shaking vehemently. "You know I cannot leave."

"Yet it is safer for you to be far from this madness. I will find out who your tormentor is and put a stop to it while you are sampling

Italian society and cuisine. Who knows? Perhaps you shall be swept off your feet by a dashing young gentleman." He winked. "And about time for such an event, I'd say."

She scowled, rebuffing his attempt at levity. "The women at the parish depend upon me to help with the widows. Then there's the Harvest Festival, and Clara and I still need to gather donations for the charity ball. That silent auction won't run itself, you know. No. I cannot—will not—abandon the people of Bedford."

"I admire your devotion, I truly do. With each passing day, you become as gracious as Mother ever was, God rest her. But your safety is more important than gathering used garments or serving on a food line. There are others who can take on such obligations. Let them."

"It's more than that, Brother." She twisted the cloth in her hands. "I have a place here, a role to play. I am doing something meaningful, something that makes a difference in people's lives. There is nothing for me in Italy other than sheltering under Father's wings."

"I am not asking you to live there forever, only for as long as it takes me to find the fiend who plagues you."

She strode to the washbasin, the thud of her slippers surprisingly loud on the rug. "I will not run away."

"I will not risk your life."

She whirled. "Henry—"

"Not another word on the matter. I will arrange passage for you and a chaperone today."

"But—"

A sharp rap on the door cut her off. "Master Henry?"

"Come in, Carver." Despite the throb in his ankle, Henry lowered his foot to the floor and straightened his spine. Appearing weak in front of the staff was an inexcusable blunder.

The groundskeeper entered, still garbed in his mud-splattered coat and a soiled kerchief around his neck. He brought with him the musty scent of damp dirt, a leftover hint of gunpowder, and a folded strip of linen, damp from dew and darkened by the grime of his hands. "I decided to take one more turn about the property and found this."

Henry stood, keeping his weight on his unscathed foot. Carefully, he unfolded the material. A single pearl earbob rested against the cloth. He passed it on to Charity. "Does this look familiar?"

She gasped. "I've been missing this for days. Why, I thought I'd lost it for good."

Cold unease settled like fog in his lungs as he faced Carver. "Where did you find it?"

"Near the hedgerow where I suggested we put out a mantrap."

Henry bristled. "You know my thoughts on such a vulgar contraption."

Carver held up his hand. "I do, sir. I merely mention it because of the location. I swear it wasn't there when I first searched the area. It's almost as if someone deliberately placed it in that spot so I'd find it on a second look, toying with me—toying with us."

Wrapping her fingers into a fist around the little bundle, Charity shook the earbob in the air. "Why play such wicked tricks? Why try to scare me away?"

Henry stifled a growl, as disturbed as his sister. "Whoever we are dealing with is closer than we thought. . .close enough to enter your bedroom and pilfer a piece of your jewelry."

Lifting his hat brim, Carver swiped his brow and then reset the old felt cap. "Someone on staff, sir?"

Henry hesitated, the implication stabbing as sharply as the pain in his ankle. Most had been with the family for decades, making them more than mere employees. It was no small thing, after all, to send their butler to Brighton to winter by the sea in effort to ease his rheumatism. Mrs. Biggs, the cook, had nursed him through childhood fevers with her bone broths. Jack, the stable hand, had taught him to ride. Even Woodley, the footman and newest member of the staff, never murmured against his unending duties—or so he was told. Mrs. Hamby, the housekeeper, would never allow such an impropriety under her expert eye.

He searched the groundskeeper's eyes for any sign of doubt. "I have already questioned the staff extensively about the recent unwelcome notes to my sister and the anonymous flowers that have been sent with such threatening prose. All claim innocence, and I am inclined to believe them. The servants of Bedford Manor are fiercely loyal."

Carver nodded, though the lines on his brow remained troubled. "Aye, sir. Loyal they are, as far as I know."

"Then who is it that torments me like this?" Charity cried.

Henry removed the earbob from his sister's hand and eyed it with thoughts aswirl. The sound of distant thunder rumbled outside the manor. A storm was coming. He rolled the pearl between his fingers.

Then again, it appeared the storm was already here.

He turned away, closing his eyes. He would *not* call his father back from Italy, but that didn't mean he couldn't seek higher help.

Oh, God. He pressed his thumb into the pearl. *If You are near, speak. If You are willing, guide. And if You are merciful—send help. I shall take it however You choose to send it.*

Chapter 4

It had been an odd experience the first time Juliet stepped foot in Craft's Milled Goods. She'd never had need to run household errands before. That's what servants did—and the way she used to disregard such service shamed her now as she waited for Mrs. Craft to package a pound of flour. The nutty scent of freshly ground grain was oddly satisfying, as was the anticipation of the bread it would make. A simple pleasure, one she'd taken for granted in the past. My, how the mere passing of a twelvemonth had transformed her in ways she never could have imagined. Though she resented the upheaval her father had caused in her life, she was grateful for the newfound humility and appreciation for hard work she had once overlooked.

But oh, how she wished those changes could have been wrought in a less painful fashion.

She pressed her fingers to her rumbling belly, glad for the grind of the large millstone out back masking the ghastly noise. That single grouse yesterday had been tasty, but she'd given the bulk of the small bird to Aunt Margaret. Today they would have bread to go along with the thin broth she'd made from the bones. Tomorrow and the next day, she would stretch that loaf and soup as far as humanly possible.

But then what?

Mrs. Craft set a small cotton sack on the flour-dusted counter. Her dark little eyes were like two currants pushed into a circle of dough. "That will be a penny, Miss Finch."

Stars above! So much? Juliet set her basket on the counter then tugged open the drawstrings of her reticule. She poked about with one finger, jingling the last three coins to her name. Two farthings and a ha'penny. Just enough to make the purchase, yet it would leave her with nothing.

She cinched the pouch tight then pulled out an amber bottle from her basket. "I'd not part with this lightly, but perhaps you might take this by way of payment—with a bit more flour added in to make it a fair trade."

She pushed the bottle across the counter and pulled the bag of flour towards her.

Mrs. Craft shoved the bottle back. "Mr. Scather says his new stock of laudanum is more effective than yarrow for lady problems, so I am giving that a try. Just bought a bottle yesterday." She held out her palm. "So, that will be one penny, if you please."

Drat that Mr. Scather! Was he to steal every last one of her aunt's customers? Irritation burned in her throat, making it hard to force a pleasant smile. "I understand the new apothecary may seem to bring innovative ideas and novel cures, but my aunt's remedies are tried and true, the recipes handed down through the generations. Have you not been satisfied?"

"I have, actually, but Mr. Scather says his laudanum works faster and more effectively for my cramps and headaches. He claims it not only alleviates pain but also soothes nerves and enables a restful sleep. I can't argue with promises such as that." She shoved her palm closer. "And you still owe me a penny."

Juliet's smile wavered as she painstakingly fished out the last of her coins and laid them on the woman's flour-dusted hand. "There you are, Mrs. Craft, but remember this. New does not necessarily mean better. Laudanum may ease your symptoms as Mr. Scather suggests, but it will do so at a cost. That medication is highly addictive. In the long run, you will spend more money, for you shall find the desire for such a drug will overpower your common sense." Juliet picked up the bottle and jiggled it. "I will save this yarrow for when your laudanum runs out."

Mrs. Craft pursed her lips but nodded. "Thank you for your concern, Miss Finch. I will keep that in mind. Good day."

Juliet tucked the tincture and the flour sack into her basket, then stepped into the cool of the early-September morn. A slight breeze carried a mouthwatering aroma of bread from the nearby bakery. The loaf she'd be able to make when she returned home would be mean indeed compared to the golden-crusted loaves in the window of Mrs. Flanagan's bakeshop. She glanced at the limp reticule dangling empty from her wrist. No sense desiring such an extravagance. She might not have the funds for a tasty treat, but at least she had flour.

She tossed back her shoulders and strode past the delicious scent. Beyond Mrs. Flanagan's, the striped awning of the greengrocer rippled in the wind. She couldn't afford anything in there either, but that didn't stop her from pushing open the door and setting off a tinkling bell.

"Good morning, Miss Finch!" Mr. Walton wiped his palms on his white apron as he sidestepped a barrel of apples. "What will it be today?"

"Actually, I was about to ask you that same question, sir." She smiled as she pulled off the cloth covering she'd tucked over the tinctures. "What interests you on this fine morning? I have brought some of my aunt's finest extracts."

He rubbed his hip as he peered into the basket. "Well, I can't deny that rain yesterday crawled right into my bones. What do you have for that?"

"Step into my office." Her grin grew as she beckoned him to the counter with a tip of her head. One by one, she pulled out a few bottles. "I recommend the willow bark, which is good for easing joint pain and inflammation. Or you could try this ginger extract. It is wonderful for warming the body and alleviating rheumatic aches."

"Hmm," he murmured as he picked up the ginger.

The door bell jingled merrily behind them, followed by a man's low voice. "Good morning, Mr. Walton. I find I am in need of some—Miss Finch. What are you doing?"

She turned at the man's approach, her stomach tightening as she gazed at a horse-faced fellow, long in the nose and with a dense mane of dark hair. He smelled of vinegar and the metallic scent that tarnished the skin after holding on to a handful of copper pennies for too long. His calculating eyes, hooded with heavy lids, peered at her from behind wire spectacles.

Juliet narrowed her own eyes. What was Mr. Scather doing here? Did he not have a shop to attend? She lifted her chin, refusing to be cowed. "Good day to you too, Mr. Scather."

He scowled at her basket. "Surely you are not selling your concoctions to our good grocer here. We have already had this discussion, miss, unless you should like to do so again with the constable? Or have you somehow acquired a license to peddle your wares? If so, I should like to see it. Now."

She plucked the bottle from Mr. Walton's hand and gathered the other as well, then covered the entire basket with the cloth. She'd visited her father in gaol and swore never again to set foot in such a foul place, so a constable was the last person she wanted to see. "If you will pardon me, Mr. Scather, I do not have time for a lengthy conversation, nor do you. After all, do you not have a business to mind? Or are you too busy minding the business of others?"

Red crawled up the apothecary's neck. "You will regret this impudence, Miss Finch. Mark my words."

Mr. Walton chuckled. "She's got you there, Scather. Seems to me she's just trying to help folks in need."

Juliet turned back to Mr. Walton, heart swelling at his defense. "Thank you, sir. I appreciate your understanding."

Mr. Scather stepped toe to toe with her, fury blooming purple against the white of his collar. "If I hear you've sold so much as one flower petal to anyone in town, I will have you locked up, young lady."

"Do not trouble yourself, Mr. Scather. I am fresh out of petals." She grabbed her basket. "Good day, sirs."

She swept past him, the hem of her pelisse whapping against his shins. Odious man. She yanked open the door, practically unseating the bell, so wildly did it clatter, then crossed the road with determined steps. No way would she continue down Mr. Scather's side of the street. Why couldn't he leave her alone? Surely one little basket of tonics wouldn't put a dent into his daily profits. Nor would—

"Oh!" she cried.

Juliet stumbled sideways, bottles rattling, while simultaneously reaching to right Miss Potter. Clearly the woman had barreled out of the milliner's shop without a care. Then again, had her own mind not been on rotten old Mr. Scather, the collision wouldn't have happened in the first place.

Miss Potter's hands flew to her head, fingers fussing with an outlandish nest of feathers that had likely left a very naked bird out in the cold somewhere. "Miss Finch, I do apologize. I fear my new hat has bewitched me body and soul."

"No, no, Miss Potter. It is I who should have been more attentive." Juliet swiped up the hatbox that'd flown from Miss Potter's grasp. "Are you quite all right?"

"Never better." She hugged the round case to her chest. "I find a new hat cures any ill that may plague a woman."

Well. So much for trying to sell an elixir to a person without a complaint. Juliet gripped her basket with both hands. "I am happy to hear it."

"And how is that dear aunt of yours? I truly ought to make the effort of getting out to see the poor dear. You know how I—"

Miss Potter rambled on about her full schedule and all the various charities she took part in, but Juliet paid scant attention. She couldn't. Trotting down the road on a sleek black horse was an imposing man with a rather wide set of shoulders—a very masculine torso that was now clad in a tailed riding coat with a white linen stock wound around his throat and tied in a bulky bow. Tight breeches clung to muscular thighs above shiny black riding boots, and he wore a tall black hat with a curled brim. Quite the change from a fellow in a nightshirt with a flash of chest peeking through, but it was him. She was sure of it. The man in the woods. The one who—if he recognized her—could summon a constable and have her tossed into prison.

In a flash, she ducked behind Miss Potter, pulling the woman around as a human shield and eternally grateful for her bodacious hat, which would block the man's view of her face. Her heart raced, not just from the fear of being caught, but from the memory of his intense gaze and his strong grip on her shoulder.

"I say. Miss Finch!" Once again Miss Potter resettled her hat. "What has gotten into you?"

"I—em—well, there is a horse coming down the road at quite a clip. I did not wish to risk you getting a face full of dust."

"But it rained only yesterday. There is more danger of kicked-up mud than dust."

"Yes, that too." She surreptitiously glanced past Miss Potter's shoulder. His horse clopped by with a regal step, every bit as compelling as his master. "Do you happen to know who that man is? I mean, if the gentleman had managed to splatter you, we ought to know who to blame, hmm?"

Miss Potter glanced backwards, then chuckled merrily. "Don't be absurd, Miss Finch. Mr. Russell would never do such a thing. I've never met a more civil man in my life."

A swirl of thoughts left her unbalanced, and she widened her stance to keep from tottering. The *heir* of Bedford Manor? La! What in all of God's green earth had he been doing outside in the darkest of night hunting for her? And in naught but shirtsleeves? Was he so consumed with protecting his game that he'd not leave the task to his groundskeeper? She nibbled on her lower lip. This added a whole new depth of danger to her poaching predicament. If he discovered her true identity, the consequences would be more than dire.

They'd be deadly.

The fine hairs at the nape of Henry's neck bristled. Someone stared at him. He'd wager on it. He jerked a glance over his shoulder, every nerve on alert.

The carriage he'd just passed ambled down the road, not a soul looking back at him. Two women stood in conversation on the pavement, one sporting a ridiculously feathered hat. Two lads played a game of kick-a-rock on the other side of the lane, and a shopkeeper in a blue apron swept away dirt in front of the tobacco shop. None of them paid him any heed.

But the man in the bakery doorway surely did. That fellow stared at him from beneath the wide brim of a black hat. Henry narrowed his eyes, studying the figure. He was tall, broad shouldered, and leaning heavily on a cane. Strain showed in his clenched jaw, the rock-hard line of it visible even from this distance. His dark coat pulled tightly around him, either warding off a chill or perhaps concealing something. And those eyes...deeply set, dark as midnight, and fixed on him with disturbing intensity.

Henry's breath caught as recognition seeped in. Edwin Parker. My, how the man had changed. Gone was the jovial young fellow whose suit Charity had rejected over a year ago now. If memory served correctly, the man had joined the military after leaving town. So, what was he doing back in Bedford? And why such a venomous stare?

Before Henry could call out, a cart rumbled down the lane, obscuring his view. When it passed, the doorway stood empty, leaving behind nothing but an echo of Parker's unsettling presence. Unless, of course, he'd read far too much into the fellow's expression. Perhaps the man was simply trying to remember who Henry was.

He faced forwards, urging his horse onwards with a slight pressure of his heels to the animal's sides—then winced from the leftover ache in his ankle. This sordid affair with his sister's tormentor had him wound far too tightly. He'd spent the better part of yesterday relentlessly questioning each staff member, but to no avail. None offered any intelligence on the matter, though the footman's reticence lingered in his mind longer than the others. Woodley, the most recent hire—three years ago, now. The man had been agitated and tight lipped, but was such reserve really an indictment? Perhaps he simply feared for his position.

At the next corner, Henry headed east, forcing his mind to the tasks of the morning. A stop at the George Hotel to arrange a coach to London and hopefully attain a shipping schedule for passage to Italy. Then town hall for travel documents and a visit to the bank for some lire. Charity would fuss, but knowing the villain had been in her room had sealed his resolve. She must leave the area, and the sooner the better.

He guided his horse to a stop at the front entrance to the George and dismounted, taking care to land on his stronger foot.

"See to yer mount, sir?" A young stable lad looked up at him, hope for a fat coin shining in his eyes.

"Yes, please." He flipped the boy a ha'penny while striding to the door where a porter nodded a greeting. Henry tipped his hat, then pulled it off completely as he entered. Once inside, he scanned the room out of a newly acquired habit birthed from the past weeks of heightened vigilance.

To his right, the clink of teacups and low murmur of patrons drifted from the dining room. A polished mahogany reception desk sat on the far side of the lobby. Beyond that was a maze of plush chairs and low tea tables where guests gathered in pairs. Nearby, two women bid farewell to a smartly dressed gent, and when they turned, the younger lady's blue eyes lit.

"Henry!"

Clara Whitmore and her mother approached, old family friends, their presence as familiar as a warm glass of brandy by the hearth.

He greeted them with a bow and a grin. "Good morning, ladies."

"What an unexpected pleasure." Clara beamed as she curtseyed, the very picture of poise and refinement. Her hair was drawn up in a perfect chignon, the colour of polished walnuts. Pink tinged her cheeks, her heart-shaped face and slender form the sort that turned men's heads.

Mrs. Whitmore dipped her own curtsey, chandelier light

gleaming off the silver strands in her hair. "It is always good to see you, Master Henry."

He smiled. Clara's mother would ever think of him as a lad in breeches. He gestured towards the dining room. "Are you here for a morning tea?"

"No." Clara folded her hands in front of her, flashing a gold bracelet on the curve of her wrist. "Mother and I stopped in for a meeting with a potential speaker for the upcoming charity ball."

"Ahh, yes." He tapped his hat against his thigh. "I nearly forgot, though Charity mentions it frequently. I understand she is working on the silent auction for the event."

"Yes. She is such a dear. Always so involved."

Mrs. Whitmore held up a gloved finger. "Pardon me, you two. I see Miss Henning near the potted fern over there and wish a quick word with her, if you don't mind."

"Not at all, Mrs. Whitmore. Good day." Once again Henry bowed.

"I will join you shortly, Mother." Clara smiled sweetly at the woman and then faced him. "So, what brings you to town this morning?"

"My sister, actually."

"Oh? Where is she?" Clara glanced around the lobby as if Charity might be about.

"She is at home."

Clara turned back to him with an arch to one brow. "How mysterious."

"None of it." He chuckled. Leave it to Clara to imagine an intrigue. She was always the one to dream up theatrics when they were children, forcing their abysmal playacting skills upon their parents. "I am merely enquiring about coach schedules for her."

Clara's smile faltered. "Is she going somewhere? We were supposed to work on the details for the ball together."

"Yes, well. . ." He gave a sheepish grin. Clara would not like the news one bit, for she and Charity were fast friends. "My sister will be joining my father in Italy soon."

For the briefest moment, Clara's lips parted in surprise before she recovered with a little laugh. "Italy? How. . .lovely." Her bracelet jangled as she clasped her hands too tightly. "What fortune to have such a caring brother arranging it all."

He stifled a snort. "Unfortunately, my sister does not share your opinion."

"I see. But if she's so reluctant, why go to so much trouble?"

His eyes dropped to the carpet. No lady should hear the real reason. "I may not actually purchase the tickets today. I am just gathering information."

"And yet you did not answer my question."

He grinned. "It is complicated, and we shall leave it at that."

"Very well. I suppose you know best, and if it is truly that important, maybe I could stop by and encourage her towards the idea. Does tomorrow after church suit?"

His brows lifted. "That would be kind, Clara. She might benefit from hearing it from someone else."

"Oh, it's not kindness, truly. Visiting the manor spares me lunch with Grace Woolcott and her matchmaking schemes. You see, you're doing me the favour." With a nod, she turned. "I shall see you then."

"Oh, Clara, one more thing."

"Yes?" She glanced back.

"Do you know anything about Edwin Parker returning to town?"

"Mr. Parker?" She shook her head slowly. "Not much. I heard he'd returned some months ago. Word is he suffered a nasty injury—something to do with his regiment being ambushed. Poor man. I suppose that's why we haven't seen him about. I imagine he's not quite the same."

"Likely not," Henry murmured.

She angled her head. "Why do you ask?"

"I passed him earlier. Thought I recognized him but wasn't certain. Just curious."

Clara smiled, bright and untroubled. "Ah. Well, I can't imagine he means to cause any stir. Men like that tend to disappear into their own troubles. Still"—she shrugged—"I shall keep my ear open for news, if you like."

"That's kind of you. No need, though."

"Nonsense. We old friends must look out for one another." She grinned. "Now, I best be off before Mother sends out a search party."

Henry chuckled. "Of course. Good day, Clara."

"Good day, Henry." With a graceful swish of skirts, she was gone.

He approached the front desk, Parker's return still weighing on his mind. If the man had been back several months, could he be the one tormenting his sister? Would Parker truly lash out merely because his life appeared to be unraveling? He would have no cause to wish to drive Charity away. None—unless by some twisted reasoning such an act might soothe his own crushed ego. A stretch, that. Leastwise for a sane mind.

Even so, the thought gnawed at Henry, adding to his unease.

Honestly, the sooner Charity sailed, the better. Hopefully Clara could convince her of that tomorrow.

Chapter 5

"Thou shalt not steal."

The words were a canker in Juliet's soul. Of all the scripture the reverend could have selected to expound upon today, he had to choose the eighth commandment? She fidgeted on the unforgiving pew, the wood as hard as her resolve not to speak with God. . .which was probably the reason for this morning's message. Retribution for her stubborn silence, no doubt. A divine reprimand for disobedience.

But shouldn't her father have faced such a reckoning instead of her? Was it not his failings that had destroyed the Finch family? Yet she was the one to bear the disgrace, suffer the consequences, feel the weight of God's frown.

And still the reverend droned on. "Remember, brethren, sin is never the answer, even when desperation whispers otherwise. Taking what is not yours strikes at the very heart of our Creator's providence, rejecting His will and inviting further hardship. To turn from God's provision is to welcome ruin."

Provision? Hah! Juliet bit the inside of her cheek to keep from scoffing aloud. That was entirely the problem. What provision had there been for her and her aunt? Where was the divine providence the reverend promised? For it surely could not be found in the empty cupboards at home or in the churn of her even emptier belly.

She pulled at a thread on the hem of her sleeve, the once-fine fabric now fraying. She should have stayed home today. Should stay home every Sunday morn, and yet that wouldn't do, not if she hoped to build trust amongst the community in order to sell her aunt's remedies. Whether one openly admitted it or not, appearance mattered. No one would purchase from a heathen.

An eternity later, the Reverend Mr. St. John bid the congregation to stand. An uncomfortable twinge of hypocrisy nipped Juliet as she rose. Was it right to accept a blessing when she wasn't currently speaking to the blesser?

"And now, may the peace of God, which passeth all understanding, keep your hearts and minds in the knowledge and love of God, and of His Son Jesus Christ our Lord; and the blessing of God Almighty, the Father, the Son, and the Holy Ghost, be amongst you and remain with you always. Amen."

The low drone of a corresponding amen followed as Mr. St. John strode up the aisle, his black cassock swinging about his legs. Juliet's feet itched to run out the side door, but that would be unseemly. So, she suffered in silence as she lined up with the other parishioners to be individually greeted as they exited.

The reverend dipped his head at her approach, his long nose practically sloping down to his chest. "Good day, Miss Finch. I trust you took today's sermon to heart."

"Yes." She bit her lip. It wasn't a lie, for she had listened to the man. She simply hadn't liked what he'd said.

His pale blue eyes searched her face. There was no hiding from that gaze, no matter how much she wished to escape it. Were all clergymen taught such a technique?

"I couldn't help but notice, Miss Finch, that you seemed a bit... distracted during the service. I hope all is well."

Hmm. That depended upon the definition. Even so, she nodded. "I am quite well, thank you. Just...a lot on my mind."

"Understandable, given the circumstances. I know things have been difficult for you and your aunt, but I encourage you to remember that even in your darkest moments, God's hand is always there to guide you."

She clenched her teeth, looking away lest he see the doubt in her eyes. Naturally, he meant kindness in his words, but in truth, God's hand had done nothing but take. "Of course, Mr. St. John." The words came out tight. Would he notice?

He frowned.

Drat.

He had.

"I realize you have had your share of struggles, but turning away from God will only lead to more pain. The Lord's mercy is boundless, and His forgiveness is always within reach."

Anger burned in her chest. "What if I am not the one in need of forgiveness? What if it is God who has turned His back on me?"

Mr. St. John's nostrils flared, but to his credit, his tone remained calm. "God's ways are not ours to understand, Miss Finch. It is most often trials that strengthen our faith, that draw us closer to our Creator, even when it feels as if He is out of reach. Such tribulations are ultimately a blessing, moulding our character, perfecting us for eternity."

She clenched her hands, heart pounding with frustration. All she wanted was food in her belly. Was that too much to ask? "Thank you for your concern, Mr. St. John, but I hate to hold up the line any longer. And so I bid you good day."

The reverend nodded, his expression inscrutable. "Just remember, Miss Finch, the church is always here for you, as am I, and so is God . . .whether you feel His presence or not. I shall keep you and your aunt in my prayers. Good day."

"Thank you." The words barely made it past her tight jaw. She didn't want the man's prayers. Such platitudes would not put food on the table, not as tangibly as a snare line. "Good day."

She stepped away from the receiving line, biting back the rest of her ire, only to face Miss Potter, who stood fanning herself beneath a monument of millinery caprice. Today's hat—an architectural marvel of velvet bows and what might have once been a stuffed partridge—teetered as she leaned in with a conspiratorial whisper. "What a sermon, eh? Far too much conviction for a Sunday morn, if you ask me." Without waiting for a response, the woman swanned off down the lane, the crooked bird bobbing in rhythm with her gait.

Juliet couldn't decide if she ought to applaud the woman's bravery for championing such eccentric headwear without a wink towards conformity—or send a discreet note to the milliner on behalf of Miss Potter's outlandish taste.

She settled on neither and instead set off down the path leading to home.

When she rounded the first bend, she nearly collided with Mr. Dankworth, her aunt's neighbour.

His podgy fingers grabbed hold of her arm, righting her before she could stumble. The roughness of his grip matched the coarseness of his coat. "Pardon me, Miss Finch. Didn't mean to scare you. Foxes don't mean to frighten chickens neither, but it happens all the same."

"Mr. Dankworth?" The man adhered to a hermetic lifestyle. What was he doing out in public? Unless. . . Alarm prickled at the back of her neck. "Is my aunt all right?"

"Far as I know. But it's not her I've come to speak about." He scratched the stubble on his jaw. "It's you."

She uncoiled slightly. "Me?"

He leaned in, his voice lowering. "What can be seen but not touched, heard but never caught?"

"I beg your pardon?"

"Your footsteps, miss." He curled his fingers around his lapels, proud as a prancing pony. "But I've seen them. Heard them in the woods. At night. Might be you chasing after herbs, or might be something's chasing you."

Her heart stalled. Sweet blessed mercy! Had he seen her setting snares? Or worse, hauling home a sack of game? She swallowed past the lump rising in her throat. "I do gather ingredients for my aunt. Harmless things. Nothing of note."

"Harmless as a sleeping bear—until it wakes." He nodded slowly, one eye twitching with suspicion, the movement dragging his thick eyebrow along in a jerky arc. "I've seen you near the manor at odd hours. The woods have long memories and short patience. So do constables."

Her heart banged against her ribs. Word was out about her nighttime escapades. No wonder since she'd run into the master of the manor himself—and his presence had lingered in her thoughts ever since. The way he moved. How he spoke. The grey-green velvet of his eyes that had, in that brief moment, held hers with an intensity she hadn't been able to shake. She couldn't afford to get caught—not by him. Not by anyone.

And yet now Mr. Dankworth knew.

She regarded him warily. "I assure you I only take what I need."

"Sheep nibble," he muttered, more to himself than to her. "But the fence needs mending all the same. And a sheep like Miss Russell ought to be tended to very carefully."

She stared, thoroughly confused. "I shall be careful, Mr. Dankworth."

"See that you are. Once a whisper grows legs, it don't stop till it trips someone." He reset his hat with a wag to his head. "Remember, people notice things. It would be a shame for anyone to get the wrong idea about your ramblings."

He strode off without another word, leaving behind the odour of sweat and the fear that he might know more than he was letting on. Was he truly warning her, or had he meant his words as a veiled accusation? Either way, he'd taken the trouble to seek her out and would no doubt be keeping an eye on her. As would that enigmatic master of Bedford Manor.

She set off briskly down the trail. So be it. She would not shrink from the challenge.

She didn't have a choice.

Henry stood by the sitting room window, half listening to his sister and Clara's conversation. Too many choices weighed on his mind to give the ladies his full attention. Should he put out a discreet watch on Edwin Parker or confront the man himself? Yet what did he really have to say to him other than question why he'd skulked about yesterday in the bakery doorway? That was no crime. And then there was the matter of the enigmatic poacher. He would speak with Carver today about intensifying security, but how to go about that? A snare for the setter of snares? Armed men? A concealed spring gun? Pah! None seemed right for a slip of a woman toting a game bag over her shoulder. There was also the matter of Charity. Was sending her to Italy truly the best option? Father would be sure to question her sudden arrival, and she was certainly giving Clara a stalwart defense for remaining at home.

A flicker of movement snagged his attention outside, and he brushed the curtain aside with his finger. Woodley, the footman, darted past the stables. What the deuce was he doing out there? A frown tightened his brow. Perhaps it was time to discuss with Mrs. Hamby about keeping a closer eye on the man.

"Isn't that right, Henry?"

He let the curtain fall as he turned back to the women perched on the settee. Clara's head angled like a curious robin. Clearly she waited for an answer.

"Whatever it is," he drawled, "I am sure you are right."

"There, you see?" She leaned towards Charity, patting her knee. "Your brother is nothing if not agreeable."

His sister cast him a malignant glance. "I doubt he was even listening."

"Tsk." Clara clucked her tongue. "Of course he was. Your brother has always had your best interests at heart—anyone can see that. Truly, darling, I think this trip could be good for you. I've heard Italy is breathtaking in the autumn."

Henry lowered himself into the chair across from his sister, glad for the gentle push. "She's right. Father would be glad of your company."

Charity sighed but said nothing.

Clara leaned forwards. "I haven't said it before, but you do seem pale lately. Tired. A change of scenery might be just the thing. I would miss you at the ball, of course—but your health comes first."

Henry gave her a grateful look, only for Clara to wave it off. "You'll come back refreshed and ready to conquer every last social engagement. Though I'll have to fend off that dreadful Grace Woolcott by myself in your absence. You must repay me for that one day."

Charity let out a weak laugh, though it sounded more weary than amused. "You make it sound as though I'm a grand lady off to the Continent for a season of leisure, rather than being shuffled about like a piece on a chessboard."

"Nonsense," Clara said, tone light. "You'd be the queen, not the pawn. And I daresay Italy will suit you. Sun, vineyards, handsome gentlemen. . . If Mother did not need me here for her megrim attacks, I could easily be persuaded to join you."

"I wish you could." Charity gave Henry a sidelong glance, her lips pressing tight. "Because nothing about this seems much like a holiday."

Henry straightened. "Holiday. A visit to Father. Surrendering to your brother's concerns. Call it what you will."

Clara nodded earnestly. "I agree. And since we are airing concerns, I have another one, this time for you, Henry. On my way in I noticed that new footman of yours skulking about near the stables. He looked positively shifty." She wrinkled her nose. "You might have Mrs. Hamby speak to him."

Exactly what he'd been thinking. "Thank you," he said. "I shall see to it."

Clara brightened as her gaze settled on Charity. "Then it's settled. You'll think about Italy, will you not?"

Charity exhaled, shoulders slumping. "Yes. . .I'll think about it."

"Good." Clara stood, smoothing her gloves. "Now, I must go. Mother's determined to rehearse our Sunday duets and heaven help me if I miss a note. Until later, my friends."

"Until then," Henry and Charity echoed together.

She glided from the room, skirts whispering against the floor.

Henry watched her go, the weight in his chest lighter than before. At least Clara suspected nothing. . .and she'd left him with one more reason to keep an eye on Woodley. Strolling to the tea table, he poured a cup of stout black. By the time he reclaimed his seat, his sister smirked at him with a knowing arch to her brow.

He eyed her over the rim of his cup. "What?"

She blew a disgusted huff. "She is sweet on you, Brother. Anyone can see that."

"How absurd. She cares for you as much as she does me."

"Perhaps," Charity agreed, though her tone suggested otherwise. "But in a far different manner. She would like more than friendship with you."

Hmm. Did she? He ran his finger around the top of the cup, pondering. If what his sister said was true, he surely hadn't noticed. "She has never said as much. She has never even hinted at anything else."

"Oh, Henry." Charity rolled her eyes. "She is a lady, not a trollop." His sister angled her head, lips pursing for a long moment. "Tell me, Brother, why have you never pursued her? Clara Whitmore is lovely, well connected, and takes interest in you. You could do worse, and you're not getting any younger, you know."

"Neither are you." He waggled his eyebrows.

Leaning forwards, she swatted his arm. "Brat!"

"Hey!" He chuckled as he set down his cup and dabbed away the few dribbles of tea that'd dripped onto his trousers. "I concede Clara is lovely and charming, and also a dear friend, but she is not really what I am looking for."

Charity spread her hands. "Then what are you looking for?"

What a loaded question that was, and something he didn't usually take the time to ponder. He had a household to maintain. Tenants to manage. Paperwork to see to in a timely fashion in his father's absence. And somewhere deep down, the quiet drive to be enough on his own—to hold steady without calling for reinforcements. Though it was now empty, he reached for his cup, giving his fingers something to do while composing some sort of an answer—for her question would not be blown away so easily.

"I suppose. . ." He hesitated, collecting words that would suit both his sister and him. "I want someone who is more than a pretty face or a familiar name. A woman who is not enamored with titles or status. Someone with spirit, resilience, one who faces challenges head-on and does not shy away from difficult situations."

Charity cooed. "That sounds very much like Clara. She is all those things—save for the familiarity."

"Yes. . ." He flipped the cup round and round, searching for the right words. "I admit Clara has many fine qualities, but she is predictable. Adept at the usual female pastimes—needlework, household management, knowing all the steps to the latest dances. I want more than that. Someone who surprises me. Someone who knows her own mind but is not overbearing about it. I want a woman who stands tall when the world tries to knock her down."

"My!" Charity snorted. "Are you sure such a woman exists?"

"I hope so, though I have not found her yet." The words barely passed his lips when his mind betrayed him, flitting to the image of a lithe figure moving swiftly through the woods—the poacher who'd eluded him. A woman who had the nerve and skill to get by on her own, without the protection of any man or title.

"And if you did find her?" Charity coaxed.

"Well then." He set the cup down and stood, staring down his nose at his sister. "I would not hesitate to make her my own."

He spoke with certainty, but as he strode towards the door, doubt crept in, unbidden and unwelcome. Could he even recognize such a woman if she stood before him? He'd spent the past years so deeply entrenched in furthering his father's fine wine business that he'd scarcely given thought to women or marriage. His life had been a sequence of duties and obligations, each more pressing than the last.

But his sister was right. He wasn't getting any younger. And while he had always assumed there would be time later for matrimony and family, now he wondered. . .had he waited too long?

Chapter 6

The black of night ought to be spent in dreamland, not snugging a rope on borrowed trousers. Juliet gave the makeshift belt a final tug, then shrugged into a patched coat reeking of moss and manure. No matter how many times she'd washed and hung the thing out to dry, she had yet to rid that lingering odour from the worn fabric. Then again, ought a poacher really be prancing about the woods smelling of lavender and roses?

Yawning wide and long, she swiped up her bag and left behind her curtained-off alcove of a bedroom. It was cozy enough, if not cramped—and to prove it, she had a perpetual bruise on her elbow from hitting the wall.

She tiptoed into the big room, taking care to avoid the third plank to the left side of the table lest it creak and wake Aunt Margaret. Her aunt need never know she'd been out tonight, leastwise not until Juliet presented her with a big bowl of rabbit stew. . .hopefully, anyway.

"Juliet, this has to stop." Her aunt's voice cut through the blackness like a thrown dagger.

Sucking in air, Juliet whirled. Across the room, in the darkest corner near the hearth, nothing but the whites of Aunt Margaret's eyes shone, two sad beacons in the gloom.

"Oh, Aunt, you scared the breath from me." Juliet swooped to the older woman, pulse erratic. "What are you doing up? Here, let me help you back to bed."

"No, I will not be deterred so easily this time." Aunt Margaret batted away her hand with a frail touch. Her voice—while weak—held a steely authority Juliet couldn't ignore. "I forbid you to leave this cottage. You are playing with fire, child."

Did her aunt seriously think she didn't know that? Juliet bit back a snort, though the sound caught in her throat and threatened to turn into a sob. They were barely scraping by as is. Every snare she set was a small—yet very needed—step towards staying alive.

She dropped to her aunt's side, the cold stone floor biting her knees as she peered up into her wrinkled face. "I know you are worried, but I am careful, and we need the food. If I do not go, then what will become of us? You know as well as I the cupboard shelves are empty."

"There will be no food if you are caught. I would rather die of starvation with you at my side than alone, bearing the guilt of knowing you were hanged for thievery." Her aunt pressed her palm against Juliet's cheek, fingers trembling, her touch both tender and desperate. "You are all I have left."

A tear traveled like a lone vagabond down her aunt's cheek, weakening Juliet's resolve. It wasn't fair of her to worry this frail woman. Yet what else was she to do? Watch her starve to death?

No. Though it killed her in every possible way, she couldn't afford to give in to her aunt's distress, not when their next meal depended upon her. She pulled away, forcing a smile, though the action made her heart squeeze all the more. "Then I shall not be caught. There. Problem solved."

Aunt Margaret wagged her head slowly. "Oh, my dear girl, this isn't just about getting caught. It's about the taut line you're walking between right and wrong."

"But—"

"Hear me out." Aunt Margaret lifted a skeletal finger. "While I agree with you it is reprehensible for Mr. Scather to have damaged our means of income—"

"Obliterated, more like." She scowled. Horrid man.

"Yes, if you will." A small smile ghosted her aunt's lips for a brief moment before fading into the night. "Yet it is just as wrong for you to take what is not yours."

"It would be if the residents needed that food as desperately as we do, but Bedford Manor has more than enough game to feed half the town. They will not miss a rabbit or two. Poaching laws are archaic, a leftover evil from the times of overbearing nobles and greedy men." She clenched her jaw, ruing her knowledge of just how far a greedy man would go. Had her father not been so covetous, she wouldn't be in this predicament.

A cough rattled in her aunt's throat, pulling Juliet from her bitter musing. Alarm prickled down her arms. This was new. A lung infection would easily do her aunt in.

As quickly as it came, the cough disappeared, relieving some of Juliet's worry.

But not all.

Aunt Margaret produced a kerchief from her sleeve and dabbed the corner of her mouth. "Regardless of excess or greed, the fact remains *you* are not the master of that parcel of land."

Ahh, yes. The master. The man with those piercing grey-green eyes and heated touch she could still feel burning on her arm. She wanted to hate him. To despise him for his wealth and status, for denying her and her aunt a measly partridge or quail that he'd never miss.

And yet, though she'd outwardly deny it on pain of death, he'd intrigued her. His commanding presence, the way he'd looked at her with such intensity.

She sank back on her haunches, disgusted with him and herself. "What you say is true, Aunt, but I will not let us starve. And if that means setting a few snares, then so be it. Please, try to understand. I am going, and that is all there is to it."

Her aunt sighed, the whoosh of it laden with resignation. "You are just like your father, headstrong to a fault."

Every one of Juliet's muscles clenched. "Do *not* compare me to that man."

Her aunt reached for her, the tip of her fingers falling short. "I beg your pardon, Juliet. I didn't mean to bring him up. I'm just so—overwrought. I worry about you. I want to protect you."

Her aunt's voice broke, cutting Juliet to the core. This was too much. All of it—her aunt's fear, the gnawing hunger, the precariousness of their situation. Leaning forwards, she pressed a kiss to her aunt's palm. "I know you wish the best for me. But I am no child, and I cannot stand by doing nothing while we waste away."

"If you would but join me in praying for God's help then—"

She shot to her feet, unwilling to get pulled into yet another exhortation on the virtues of prayer. How could her aunt's faith remain so solid when they faced starvation? "We have been over this too many times. I am not ready."

Aunt Margaret's shoulders slumped. "Oh, my misguided, brave young lady. You take on too much, yet I can see you will not be dissuaded. Please, vow to me you will be on guard. Stay vigilant. The woods are not safe, and for a comely woman such as yourself, there are more dangers out there than just the law."

An ugly truth, that. She flashed a reassuring smile that was a lie. "I promise. I shall take extra cautions. Do not fret yourself into a frenzy. In fact, allow me to lead you back to bed now, hmm?"

Without waiting for an answer, Juliet guided her aunt to her feet, then with slow shuffling, led her to her bed. She tucked her in, smoothing the thin blanket over her aunt's frail form, and pressed a tender kiss to her paper-thin brow. "Sleep sweetly, Aunt."

"Thank you," she murmured, exhaustion already closing her eyes.

"Good night," Juliet whispered, then slipped out of the room.

Outside, she eased the cottage door shut, then paused to inhale the brisk air of the September evening. The chill of it revived her, cooling some of the hot emotions from the confrontation with her aunt. Despite the wrongness of what she was about to do—for yes, deep down she knew she ought not take what did not belong to her—there was still something about being out alone and free that invigorated her. Made her feel alive. Master of her own fate—and doing something constructive to fill the emptiness not only in her belly but in Aunt Margaret's.

The moon hung low in the sky, a quarter-crescent, which didn't do much to light her path through the trees. This time of year, a few leaves were already carpeting the ground. The rest traded whispers in the light breath of a breeze. All in all, it was a peaceful trek, though the closer she drew to Bedford Manor, the more her nerves wound into a tight ball.

She scaled the rock wall with practiced ease, landing lightly on her feet, then dashed into the thicket of trees where she'd been detained last time. Treading carefully, she peered into the darkness, spying for the grey-eyed master himself. What would he do if he caught her again—*really* caught her? The thought thrilled *and* terrified.

Forcing her mind to the task at hand, she traveled from one snare to the next, heart swelling when she found two partridges, and the trap by the hedge offered up a fat hare. What a banner night! She'd not have to reset her snares until at least the end of the week, especially if the next trap held a prize as well.

She glanced about before crossing the lawn. Nothing in front of her.

But something rustled behind.

She spun, staring so hard into the darkness her eyes hurt. Could have been a stoat. A hedgehog. A groundskeeper.

Yet the black line of woods appeared as it always did. Choked with secrets and peril, but without the skulking silhouette of a man with a gun.

She let out a long breath. Maybe she'd taken her aunt's warning too much to heart.

Resettling the bag over her shoulder, she turned back to the hedgerow when a sudden movement to her right caught her eye.

She bolted, racing for the safety of the trees, unsure of what she'd seen. Better to err on the side of safety than to—

She flew forwards, hitting the ground hard.

"Thievin' cully!" a man's voice growled behind her.

Instinctively, she rolled to her side. Or tried to. The hold on the hem of her coat was a steel bond, pinning her in place, yanking her back.

No! This couldn't be happening.

With all her might, she shimmied out of her coat, leaving her assailant with a handful of fabric.

Bagless, coatless, hopeless, she scrambled to her feet and sprinted once again. Panic charged through her veins. The cold air sliced through her thin shirt. Heavy footsteps dogged behind. Fear drove her on.

She plunged into the woods, branches clawing, pulling her hair, tearing her shirt. She dove into the underbrush, spikes of holly ripping sharp along her back, exposing her skin. Even so, she rolled into a tight ball, nearly crying out to God for deliverance.

Nearly.

She scrunched her eyes tight. If she couldn't see the man, then he wouldn't see her—a falsehood from childhood she'd never discarded.

Sticks cracked. Boots thudded.

Run past. Just run past!

Then. . .

Blessed silence.

Her eyes flew open. Had the man truly sped by?

Metal clicked. A rifle cocked. And a gruff voice boomed in the night. "I know you're there. Don't make me flush you out with a shot."

Her heart pounded in her ears, breath all but forgotten. Could she still fly away? But how when fear paralyzed her limbs?

A shot rang out.

Dirt, leaves, gravel flew into her face. She flinched, a yelp strangling in her throat.

"Out!" he bellowed. "You're only making it worse for yourself."

Slowly, she uncurled from her ball, trembling as she pushed up to all fours. Her breath came in shaky gasps, tears running cold on her cheeks. Blood and sweat stung her back as she peered up through the holly branches that concealed her.

The man's boots appeared first, crushing the earth beneath them, a mere ten paces from her hidey-hole. Tree trunks for legs came into view next. Then a rifle barrel. Long. Black. Unforgiving and aimed right at her. Juliet's throat closed, her gaze fixed on that terrible weapon. No matter how hard she tried, she was unable to look anywhere else, anticipating the fire of a shot to her head.

"There you are," he muttered, voice as rough as the gravel. "Come on. Move it—an' keep your hands where I can see 'em."

Her limbs felt like lead, but somehow she managed to crawl out, arms scratched raw from the spiky branches, hoping to God the man would show her enough leniency that she might be able to escape as she had before. But when the older man's dark eyes bored into hers and his fingers bit into her arm, she knew. This was it. There would be no escape.

Not this time.

Coffee and toast. The quintessential breakfast—especially if that toast involved a healthy slathering of apple butter. Henry bit into a thick slice of deliciousness, savouring the sweetness with a hint of tart lemon just as Carver swung into the breakfast room.

The groundskeeper pulled off his hat and ran his fingers through greying locks of wiry hair. He smelled of crushed leaves and the dampness of a root cellar—and no wonder. He looked as if he wore half the grounds of Bedford Manor on his coat. "Sorry to disturb ye, Master Henry, but I've got something ye'd like to hear, I think."

Brilliant. He could use some good news right about now. Henry set down his toast and picked up his coffee—the rich scent of which usually earned him a cancerous eye from Charity. In her words, only barbarians drank such a brew. But she'd not come down for breakfast yet. Thankfully.

He leaned back in his chair, leveling Carver with a look. "What I would like to hear is that you have caught my sister's tormentor and we are finished with such dastardly business."

A wry smile tipped one side of the groundskeeper's lips. "I have bagged a scoundrel of sorts, leastwise as it pertains to game."

Henry's pulse galloped. "The poacher?"

"One and the same." He shook his head, a sheepish dip to his shoulders. "I can scarcely believe that slip of a woman has given me the run for so long."

Henry set his cup down without so much as a sip. "Where is she?"

"In the toolshed out back. What would you have me do with her?"

"You? Nothing. I will see her for myself." He pushed back his chair.

"Don't know as I'd advise that, sir. She's a fiery one, and I've got the teeth marks to prove it." Shoving up his sleeve, he held out his forearm.

A distinct curve of angry red indented the flesh.

Henry's brow raised, though admittedly such a wound didn't surprise him overmuch, not after his encounter with the woman. "I appreciate the warning, Carver, but I think I can handle myself."

"That's what I thought too, but the little nipper caught me off guard." He tugged back the fabric to his wrist. "If you don't mind me askin', what do you mean to do with her? Poachin' is a serious offense."

True. And yet it didn't seem right, somehow, to completely ruin the woman's life. He rubbed the back of his neck. "I am not entirely certain yet." Dropping his hand, he faced the groundskeeper. "Feel free to come along and keep an eye on the yard while I have a word with our. . .guest, though I trust you have secured her well?"

"Aye. Tied her hands to an eyehook. She's not going anywhere unless you say so."

"Good. I shall decide what happens next once I assess the situation." He strode from the room, Carver's boots echoing on the floorboards behind him.

Outside, the first fallen leaves of autumn swirled in eddies as he crossed the gravel yard. He wasn't sure how to feel about capturing the woman. Yes, a poacher ought to be prosecuted, especially one that bit like a dog off a lead. And yet something in his spirit gave him pause. He glanced at the morning sky, where thin white clouds stretched like cotton against the blue.

Give me wisdom, Lord.

At the shed door, Carver pulled out a ring of keys and opened the padlock, casting him a sideways glance. "Sure you don't want me to go in with you?"

Henry shook his head. "With two of us, she might feel like a cornered animal, and as you know, those are the most dangerous sort. Just lay hold of her if she happens to escape."

He stepped into the small outbuilding, the faint creak of the wooden door breaking the silence inside. Dank air met his nose, tinged with the earthy scent of dirt and rusting metal. Various tools hung from the walls—shovels, a rake with bent prongs, a pitchfork, some hoes—their shapes dull in the thin morning light filtering through the wall slats. When his eyes adjusted fully on the slender form strung up on the farthest wall, he stopped dead in his tracks.

Her back was towards him. Through the torn fabric of her shirt, pale skin streaked with blood peeked out. So did the knobs of her spine. He ought not be witnessing this, for it was far too intimate of a sight, and yet he could not pull away his gaze. She was thin, painfully so. When was the last time she'd eaten a full meal?

Her hair, perhaps once the vibrancy of roasted chestnuts, now lay in wild tangles around her shoulders, a braid that had obviously lost its tether. Her head hung forwards, her slender arms dangling from Carver's bindings.

A wave of unexpected sympathy clamped tight around his heart. He wasn't prepared for this—a poacher, yes, but not a woman so beaten down by ill circumstance. Still, he held his emotions in check, remembering this was no small offense she'd committed. She'd been stealing from his land for over a year now.

He planted his feet. "Turn around, if you would, miss. I should like to speak with you."

Ever so slowly she pivoted, and when her face came into view, he inhaled sharply—not due to her disheveled appearance, but by the untamed beauty beneath the grime. Her cheekbones were sharp, yet the curve full and pleasing. Her hair cascaded around her face like the mane of a feral creature. And her eyes—sage with a ring of amber. Fear and boldness flickered simultaneously there, and something more. . . He cocked his head. Remorse. That was it. But for what? Being caught or for the desperate acts that had led her to be trussed up in his toolshed? Hard to tell. But of one thing he was certain. She was terrified. The threadbare fabric of her torn shirt rippled with her trembling, barely offering any protection against the cold air seeping through the shed's walls.

He frowned. Did he frighten her so? Or was it the inevitable punishment she feared most? Regardless, he couldn't very well leave her standing there, shivering in such a state. Poacher or not, she was still human, still a woman—and one who had suffered enough.

Without another word, Henry shrugged off his frock coat and draped the wool around her shoulders as best he could, his fingers brushing against her cold skin for the briefest moment.

Her wide eyes darted to his face. She blinked several times, her lips parting as if to say something, but no words came, and in that moment, he saw her vulnerability.

He retreated several steps, giving her space. "This is the second time we meet." The indictment came out huskier than intended, and he cleared his throat. "What have you to say for yourself?"

She glanced down at the coat, then back at him, tears welling in her eyes. "If you let me go, sir, I vow I will not set foot on your land ever again."

He swallowed, fighting to keep his composure. Weeping women were ever his downfall. "I was expecting an apology, not a plea bargain."

White teeth toyed with her lower lip. "I know it was wrong of me to take your game, yet I had no other choice."

Judging by her hollow cheeks and sharp lines of her frame, he could easily see the truth of that. Curious, he cocked his head. "What has brought you to such dire straits? Have you no father? No brother or husband to provide? What about seeking aid from the church or a charity?"

Her chin came up then, eyes gleaming. "I will not beg. Not while I still have hands to work and legs to walk. I've lost enough—I will not surrender my pride as well. As for family, I have no one but my aunt, and she lies abed."

"Who is this aunt?" He dared a step closer, studying her face. "Who are you?"

"I am Juliet Finch, niece to Margaret Brewster."

"Brewster." He rolled the name off his tongue, and the moment it flew free, recognition settled in. "The name is familiar. A neighbour, I think."

"Yes. To the east."

For a long moment he said nothing, trying to dredge up any and every memory he owned of Margaret Brewster. His father might have mentioned the widow once or twice, but other than that, he had no personal experience with the woman. And he'd never heard of Juliet Finch.

"You realize," he drawled, "that I would be well within my rights to turn you over to the magistrate."

"I know." She looked away, her jaw quivering. "Do what you will, then. Just. . .my aunt, she—"

"Would starve without you," Henry finished for her. "You have made your point clear, for you are very well spoken. You do not come from poverty."

She said nothing. Nor would she look at him.

Reaching ever so gingerly, he turned her face back to his with a light touch of his finger to her jaw. "There are stories in your eyes, Miss Finch. Tragedies, I believe."

"Please." Her voice broke. "If you would but let me go, I will trouble you no longer."

Hah! He suspected this woman would be troubling his dreams for days to come. He turned away, pacing the small space of the shed. It would be a shame to see that lovely neck of hers snapped, and yet there ought to be some semblance of justice for the game she'd stolen over the seasons. For indeed, she had stolen—and quite successfully up to now.

He stopped in front of her. "How is it you managed to evade my groundskeeper for over a year?"

"I merely did what I had to," she said simply.

"Yes, and you did it quite well. Too well, in fact. It seems you have skills most women would fear to acquire."

"Of necessity, not by design."

He narrowed his eyes. "I wonder what other skills you possess."

Her nostrils flared like a spooked filly's. "What do you mean?"

"You have proven yourself adept at moving through these woods unseen, and you have a knack for snaring game." She did. She had. Until now, the woman was every bit as keen at remaining undetected as his sister's tormentor.

And that's when a perfectly mad idea took root. Who better to hunt for a man than a hunter? And a female one at that? No one would suspect such a thing. She might be able to uncover information that as a man he would have a hard time getting at. Once again, he took to pacing. This was either a clever notion or the most absurd thought he'd ever had.

Well, Lord? Which is it?

And just like that, he remembered the night Charity had come to him, scared—thunder crashing, desperation choking him—and he'd begged heaven for help. He hadn't expected the answer to arrive in the form of a mud-splattered poacher. Then again, God's ways were ever mysterious. And what did he really have to lose if he made a bargain with this woman and it proved fruitless? It wasn't as if he'd be any further behind on figuring out who troubled his sister.

"Tell me, Miss Finch, how are you at tracking prey?"

She blinked. "What sort of prey?"

"Of the two-legged variety."

Confusion rippled across her brow. "Speak plainly, sir."

Henry stepped closer. "There is someone—an unwanted someone—lurking near my home. A tormentor who has yet to reveal himself. You have demonstrated a knack for. . .navigating the shadows, shall we say. If you should like to avoid an intimate rendezvous with the hangman's noose, I would make use of that knack."

Her jaw dropped, her words a whisper. "What exactly are you proposing?"

"I mean," he said firmly, "I will not have you arrested. Instead, I offer you the chance to help me catch this villain. If you do so, your slate will be clean. You will be free to go—provided you do not return to poaching on my lands. Or anyone else's, for that matter."

She was quiet for a long moment, her nose scrunching ever so slightly, before she said at length, "And if I refuse?"

"Then I shall call in the law. That could be avoided, however, if you repay your debt to me. Think of it as restitution. Service rendered in place of all the pheasant and hares that have mysteriously vanished from my woods."

Her lips parted slightly, maybe with a protest. Maybe not.

So he pressed on. "If you are not a thief at heart, then this is the easiest way to prove it."

An uncertain silence lingered. Was it so hard a decision?

Finally, the woman lifted her face, meeting his gaze with fierce determination. "Very well, then. I accept."

Chapter 7

Trussed. Trapped. Terrified. Not to mention torn over what she just agreed to do with a man who did all sorts of strange things to her insides—good and bad. Juliet leaned her shoulder against the rough planks of the shed, arms practically dead from being over her head for so long. Her body ached from the chase and subsequent hours she'd spent locked in this chilly outbuilding. Yet that was nothing compared to the degradation of having been caught like a bird in one of her snares. How foolish she'd been!

And how foolish she was for having agreed to partner with a man who stole her breath.

After what seemed an eternity since the enigmatic master of Bedford Manor had taken his leave, footsteps crunched against gravel, slow, deliberate, growing louder. Keys jingled. A lock clicked. The door opened with a creak. Juliet blinked against the brilliant sunlight pouring in, wrapping itself around the black figure of a muscular man with a bucket in one hand, a cloth bundle in the other, and a long knife hanging off his hip.

The groundskeeper.

The one she'd bitten in the arm.

Her heart raced as he set down the items and slowly pulled the blade from the sheath. Stubble covered his jaw. Crescents the colour of bruises hung beneath his eyes. He'd not slept because of her. The hard set to his jaw silently accused her for such a crime. His dark gaze—cold and sharp—locked onto hers as he approached. He could do as he wished behind these walls and lay the blame for what she suffered at her feet. No one would ever know.

Her pulse thudded in her ears as he stopped a breath away, the smell of a grave about him, all damp dirt and foreboding. "Ye don't deserve the master's mercy."

The growl of a tiger in the dark couldn't be more threatening.

Worse, he was right.

"No, I do not," she whispered.

He raised the knife, and she couldn't help but wonder if he'd cut more than just the rope. A man humiliated was a treacherous animal, for she had disgraced him by stealing game right out from under his nose.

She squeezed her eyes closed, a long-forgotten inkling of a prayer begging to be released past her lips—but she clamped them tight. Pleading for forgiveness now was the coward's way out.

Cold metal dug into the tender skin of her wrists, yet not the sharp edge. The rope fell to the ground. Her arms felt lifeless as they dropped like anchors. Absently, she rubbed where the bindings had nipped her flesh raw. The master of Bedford Manor's frock coat lay in the dirt at her feet, for it had fallen as well.

She braved a glance up at the man, then wished she hadn't. So much vitriol was hard to digest. "What happens now?" she peeped in a voice she could hardly believe belonged to her.

So much for bravery.

"Mr. Russell and his sister await you. Clean yerself up and put on that gown." He tipped his head towards the bundle he'd dropped atop a barrel. "And if ye so much as think of making a run for it, this blade o' mine won't be nearly as lenient as the master's."

He slapped the flat of it against his palm, making her flinch.

His mouth curved in satisfaction; then he wheeled about and called over his shoulder, "I'll be waitin' outside."

It took her several deep breaths before she could coax her feet to move. Fingers still tingling from being overhead so long, she fumbled with unwrapping the cloth bundle. Inside was a blue silk gown—a very fine one—a sliver of soap, a cloth for washing, and a comb. Turning her back to the door, she made quick work of peeling out of her ruined shirt and filthy trousers. Many winces and a few groans later, she retrieved Mr. Russell's coat and set it on the barrel, then stepped outside, feeling somewhat better—physically, leastwise.

The groundskeeper graced her with naught but a scowl, then strode across the backyard. She scurried to keep up with his long legs. They entered the manor's rear door, the corridors a blur as she sped double-time to follow him—and she nearly crashed into his back when he swung into a sitting room and abruptly stopped.

"Here's the girl, as you asked, sir," he grumbled.

"The *girl* has a name, Carver. Miss Finch, and as she will be part of the household for the foreseeable future, you shall address her as such."

Juliet's brows rose at Henry Russell's voice. Standing so closely behind the big groundskeeper, she couldn't see him, but the censure in his tone was undeniable. Which was surprising. Why extend her such a courtesy? She'd done nothing but steal from him.

The groundskeeper gave a sharp nod. "As you wish."

"Thank you, Carver. You are dismissed."

Her nemesis bypassed her, rumbling beneath his breath, "Softhearted fool—won't last a week with the likes o' her."

A lifetime ago it would have grieved her to be thought of as such a ne'er-do-well. And it still stung a little. Yet there was nothing she could do about others' opinions—a bitter lesson she'd learned like a slap in the face when her father had been tossed in gaol.

And there she stood. Alone. Exposed. Trying desperately not to give in to the quake of her knees as Mr. Russell and a woman with burnt-honey curls regarded her like a rare bird to be cautiously studied. While different in colour, their eyes shared the same intensity, as if well versed in summing up the worth of a person without asking a single question.

Mr. Russell lifted a hand towards his sister, where she perched on a burgundy velvet settee near the fire. "I thought it best if you met my sister right away and learn what you are up against. Charity, meet Miss Juliet Finch. Miss Finch, my sister, Miss Charity Russell."

Juliet curtseyed as gracefully as her legs allowed, her heart beating fast. One wrong move or word, and the man might think better of his offer. "I am pleased to meet you, Miss Russell," she murmured.

"Thank you, Miss Finch." The woman had a lovely voice, bright as a May morn. Her features were delicate and not nearly as angular as her brother's. "I must say my brother and I were both astonished to find a female poaching on our family land."

Heat flamed up Juliet's neck, spreading to her cheeks. She lowered her face, hoping to hide such a reaction. Hoping to hide period. Deep down she'd known a day of reckoning would come, but that didn't make it easier to bear. She swallowed hard. "I would not have done so had I any other choice, Miss Russell."

The lines around the lady's mouth softened a little. "I suppose desperation drives people to do things they otherwise wouldn't. But you are here now, and my brother tells me you will be helping us with a different kind of hunt. Please, have a seat."

Juliet crossed to a chair adjacent to Miss Russell and sank onto the cushion, a hush threading the air. She hadn't suffered such a precarious meeting since the day the solicitor informed her that her family's fortune was gone.

Mr. Russell leaned against the mantel, arms crossed, exuding an effortless confidence. His swept-back hair caught the late-morning light streaming in through the window, setting off a deep golden fire. Every inch of him radiated the authority of a man accustomed to control, his broad shoulders and strong jawline adding to his commanding presence. This was the sort of man whose appearance could inspire a deep-set trust or a cold-sweat fear, dependent solely upon how his gaze landed on you.

And when he looked at her, she was glad to be sitting, for her legs would not have held her.

"The short of it, Miss Finch," he rumbled, "is that my sister has been tormented by someone who clearly means to frighten her away, if not worse. This is no small matter. In return for your own freedom, you shall help me catch whoever is responsible."

Juliet nodded slowly, the weight of the situation feeling like a wet woolen blanket pressing her down, chilling her to the bone. She snared animals, not humans. "If that is so, then why not get the law involved?"

His jaw tightened. "The law has little patience for whispers in the dark. Evidence would be required—irrefutable evidence. Besides, I would rather not have the entire town knowing my sister is being harassed by an unknown lunatic. The gossip alone could ruin her reputation and possibly make her more vulnerable than she already is."

"I see." Juliet shifted uncomfortably on the chair. This was a tenuous situation, for well did she know how completely—and how quickly—misplaced words could decimate a woman's character. "How long has this been going on?"

Mr. Russell scowled. "Too long."

"What my brother means to say," Miss Russell cut in, "is two months."

Juliet cocked her head. "And what exactly has been done in that time?"

The siblings exchanged a glance, and at length, Mr. Russell gave his sister a sharp nod. The woman pulled several papers from her pocket, then handed them to Juliet. "It began with these."

Juliet unfolded the first note. The handwriting was bold and deliberate, each letter formed with the measured precision of a man unused to wasting ink or words.

My dearest Charity,

You are such a precious flower, too ephemeral for the troubles of this world. Consider seeking peace elsewhere, for the countryside is rife with dangers, and a lady of your grace deserves safety and serenity.

With kindest regards,
A friend

A chill crept down Juliet's spine, for she doubted very much a friend would send such an ominous message. She tucked that paper behind the rest and opened the next.

My dearest Charity,

It must be exhausting, always looking over your shoulder. Perhaps it is time you find refuge elsewhere. The world can be unpredictable, and it is wise to remove oneself from its hazards before they draw too near.

Take care,
A well-wisher

Juliet frowned as she quickly opened the third note.

My dearest Charity,

I see you every day, walking the halls of Bedford Manor. There are shadows around you, darker than you think. You cannot stay here forever. The wise know when to leave.

Do not wait until it is too late.
A concerned soul

That did it for the notes, save for a single penned bit of poetry on what appeared to be an enclosure card—no doubt for flowers, for the faint scent of roses yet clung to the paper.

The roses bloom with crimson grace,
Yet petals fall in death's embrace.
Beware the thorns that lie in wait,
Lest you, dear Charity, meet your fate.
So flee, little bird, while you may.

Juliet's blood ran cold at the words. Whoever this person was, they weren't merely playing games. There was something far more dangerous at play here, something sinister. No wonder Mr. Russell had made such a bargain with her.

She shuffled the papers back into order. "Have you any idea who is responsible for the letters or why you are specifically being targeted?"

Miss Russell shook her head, a sad tilt to her brow. "I do not."

Mr. Russell strode over to Juliet, collected the notes, then sat next to his sister. "Whoever it is, the fellow is clever, leaving no trace of his identity, no return address. To make matters worse, my sister is certain she's spied someone outside watching her at various times. My groundskeeper Mr. Carver and I have found a scant amount of footprints. Whoever it is takes great care in hiding their trail. So, that is where you come in, Miss Finch. I suspect you know these grounds better than I do."

Guilt tightened her stomach, and she pressed her fingers against her belly. Of course she knew the land—she had poached on it for long enough. But the thought of using those same skills to catch a human only made that cramp twist tighter. She eyed Mr. Russell. "What exactly do you expect from me?"

Mr. Russell rested his elbows on his knees, his hands clasped together as if considering his next words carefully. His eyes narrowed a fraction. "I expect you to use whatever abilities you have to find this person before he harms my sister. You will watch, you will track, and you will let me know when you sense something amiss."

On the surface, such a task didn't sound too hard. She had the knowledge of how to skulk about at night and look for anything unusual, but this was no ordinary hunt. Who knew how dangerous this elusive fellow might be? Yet truly she had no choice.

But Miss Russell certainly did.

She speared the blue-eyed woman with a direct stare. "Forgive me, Miss Russell, but why do you not simply go away for a while until this whole thing blows over?"

The lady tossed back her shoulders, a fierce determination in the purse of her lips. "I will not run from my own home, Miss Finch," she clipped.

Admiration blossomed warm in Juliet's chest. She knew firsthand how hard it was to leave behind a childhood home. Had she not been forced to leave hers, she'd be just as adamant as this woman.

"Very well. I will find whoever it is that torments you so cruelly." Juliet rose from her seat, her own resolve hardening as she spoke. At least her poaching talents could be put to use in service of a noble cause. "What time shall I return?"

To her surprise, Mr. Russell stood as well, his towering presence suddenly more imposing. His voice turned steely, every word cutting through the air with unmistakable authority. "You misunderstand, Miss Finch. This is your home for the duration of our arrangement."

Her stomach dropped. Stay here? She had thought she would return to her aunt's cottage and come back when needed, though now that she truly considered, she realized this was an impractical plan, given her task. Still, the idea of living under the same roof as this man and his sister—surrounded by the very people she had stolen from—drove the air from her lungs. She gripped the back of the chair, fighting panic. "What, exactly, do you mean?"

Planting his feet wide, he folded his arms, a mountain not to be moved. "You will remain on the estate until the matter is settled. Should anything occur, I'll need you here to answer for it. Besides, I intend to keep a close watch on you, both to ensure your safety and to make certain you fulfill your part of the bargain."

Juliet went still, her heart thudding in her chest. He didn't trust her. Logical, but it still stung. "So, I am to be your prisoner, then?"

"La, Miss Finch!" Despite the gravity of the conversation, Miss Russell laughed. "That is rather theatrical. Bedford Manor is hardly Newgate."

But Juliet didn't so much as glance at her. Though she dearly wished to, she could not pull her gaze away from the man in front of her.

"Surely you must realize," he drawled, "what a privilege I am extending to you, Miss Finch. Until you prove your loyalty, I can hardly depend upon the word of a poacher."

Of course. He had every reason to be wary. He was the master of the house. She, nothing but a thief. The very idea that he should trust her at all was laughable. Still, despite all reason, there was something about this man—something that made her yearn for more than just his cautious regard.

"I understand," she murmured, though it wasn't true. Not really. She didn't comprehend the first thing about all the ways this man unsettled her.

But one thing she did understand—her aunt.

She drew in a shaky breath, her heart weighted by duty and a decision already made. "Be that as it may, I cannot simply stay. My aunt relies on me. She is not well, and the cottage does not run itself. I should not have even been gone this long."

Mr. Russell's expression didn't change. Not at all—then all at once. He gave a sharp, single nod. "Take a few moments to collect yourself in your new quarters; then I shall drive you to your aunt's myself. You can explain the situation to her and gather what you need."

That stopped her. The offer wasn't cruel, nor begrudging—but it was controlled, calculated, like everything else about him.

She dipped her chin, the lump in her throat too large to speak around.

At least now she'd have one more hour to think how to soften the blow when she told her aunt her worst fear had come true.

Afternoon sunlight filtered through the trees, weaving intricate patterns across the winding road leading from Bedford Manor to the outskirts of the estate. Henry sat in the driver's seat of the open carriage, reins in hand, his thoughts snarled as he glanced at Miss Finch sitting silent beside him.

His sister's gown, while elegant, seemed out of place on the young woman. It hung too loose on her frame. Her dark hair, hastily pinned up, had already begun to escape in tendrils, catching the light and framing her face in a way that made him want to study her more closely. She was like a caged falcon, barely restrained, her sharp green eyes always moving, calculating, waiting for the right moment to fly away.

He'd have done the same were he in her position.

He eased the carriage around a bend. Juliet Finch hadn't said more than two words since they set off, her face fixed on the road ahead, her hands clenched tightly in her lap. The unease of her rigid posture was palpable—the same guarded stillness he'd noted when he and his sister had interviewed her that morning. The girl had spirit, that much was evident, but so much more was going on beneath the surface. Something he couldn't quite identify.

Or could he? For surely she fretted about being caught and forced into tracking a man who might potentially threaten her own neck—and that thought chafed. He didn't wish her to be in danger any more than he did his sister. Yet with her hunting skills, Miss Finch was a necessary asset. No scoundrel would expect a woman to be on the prowl for him. Henry would simply have to keep an eye out for her safety while also assuring she would not bolt at the first chance.

He flicked the reins with practiced ease, urging the horses forwards as the road narrowed, the trees closing in on either side. He hadn't expected to be driving Juliet Finch anywhere today, let alone offering to escort her to her aunt's cottage. Yet the look in her eyes earlier—the unwavering loyalty to someone who clearly depended on her—had caught him off guard, and he'd yielded. Not because she pleaded. She hadn't. In fact, she'd seemed more resigned than hopeful, but her concern had been real—a concern that had driven her to breaking the law.

He glanced at her sideways. "So, how did you learn to set a snare so handily? My sister is proficient at many things, but not in bagging a quail. I daresay not many women are."

She reached for the sidewall, gripping it as the wheels jolted over a rut in the road. "My elder brother never wanted a sister, so he made a tomboy of me." A smile lit her face, softening her usually guarded expression. "Philip was an avid outdoorsman and a very good teacher."

"Was?" He angled his head.

"Yes." She turned away, her next words coming out strained. "He died of consumption."

"I am sorry to hear it." The words were entirely inadequate, but it was the best he could offer. He could only imagine what it would be like to lose a sibling—how it might break him were he to lose Charity. His heart squeezed, a small pain compared to the grief Miss Finch clearly shouldered.

He studied the road in front of them, but his mind was entirely on the woman beside him. She'd lost a brother—and apparently the rest of her family save for the aunt she lived with. Her manner of speech, the grace of her movements, how she'd properly greeted his sister, all led him to believe she was a lady of some social standing. Yet there she sat in one of his sister's old gowns after having been caught red-handed with stolen game in her sack.

"Tell me, how is it"—he slipped her a glance—"that you have left behind a life of refinement for that of a thief?"

"Perhaps you can first tell me, Mr. Russell, how it is you mistake desperation for thievery?"

He faced her full on, admiring the lift of her jaw and appreciating even more that she would not be cowed by him. There was strength in this woman, and that he could respect. "Desperation, you say? I suppose that is one way to justify your actions. Yet that does not explain how a woman with your poise and breeding finds herself in such a predicament."

"Sometimes life has a way of falling apart without a written invitation to do so."

Defiance crackled in her tone, a layer above bitterness. He didn't like the idea that misfortune had touched her in ways he couldn't yet understand, and he gripped the reins all the tighter. "What happened? What was it that caused your life to come undone?"

She focused on the horizon as if the answer to his question might be found in dirt and gravel. "I mean no disrespect, Mr. Russell, but I do not wish to speak of it."

Frustration twisted in his gut. He wasn't accustomed to being shut out, especially not by someone under his care—or scrutiny. For reasons he couldn't quite articulate, it mattered to him, her story, her pain. Yet Juliet Finch seemed determined to keep him at arm's length, and while that infuriated him, it also attracted him.

Bah. What was he thinking? He urged the horses onwards with another flick to the reins. She was here for one reason only—to help catch Charity's tormentor.

An uncomfortable silence stretched between them, broken only by the sound of air hissing in through his teeth as he rounded a bend in the road and the cottage she shared with her aunt came into view. Sweet mercy! He pulled the horses to a stop in front of a broken gate hanging onto a rotted post like a crooked tooth. *This* was where the woman and her elderly aunt lived? The place was naught but a collection of boards leaning against one another like drunkards, each seeming to hold up the other by sheer accident. The roof buckled in places, and the rest looked ready to give way to the next gust of wind. Patches of moss and rot covered the walls, creeping like a cancer, while the few windows were blocked by threadbare curtains.

His jaw tightened. The contrast between Juliet's resilience and her circumstances was a testament to the steel in her spine. He had seen women of means wilt under far less. And yet here she was—thin, hungry, a thief by circumstance—and still, she held her head high. It unnerved him how much he admired that.

Juliet climbed down before he could set the brake. "I will not be long."

"I will go with you." He pulled on the brake and jumped to the gravel.

"No." She shook her head so sharply, a curl broke loose and dangled against her cheek. "My aunt is frail. It would not do to startle her."

Cornering the carriage, he strode up to her. "And yet I will not have you slipping out a back door."

"There is none. That"—she tipped her head towards the front door—"is the only entrance."

"A window, then."

"Neither are there any windows on the back side. I assure you, Mr. Russell, I am no liar."

"But you are a poacher."

A rugged sigh whooshed from her. "I am also a woman of my word. I will not run. I shall merely see that aunt has a pot of tea at the ready and the last slice of bread to go along with it. Then I shall pack up my belongings and return to you. It will not take long."

His gaze flicked between her and the dilapidated cottage. His instincts urged him to go with her, to make sure she didn't run off. And yet, there was something in her eyes—an honesty, bravery perhaps, but sincerity nonetheless—that gave him pause. She had every opportunity to lie, to spin some tale, and yet she hadn't. She'd faced him head-on.

"Very well." He ground his teeth, hardly believing he'd give her such a freedom. "But if you are not back in five minutes, I will come in after you."

She nodded, though he could tell by the way her lips pinched his words had stung. She walked towards the warped door with steady steps, leaving him standing by the carriage, hands clenched at his sides.

As the door creaked shut behind her, he let out a long breath and leaned against the carriage, eyes fixed on the cottage, thoughts churning. Had he made a mistake? Should he have gone with her? His instincts said yes, but his gut also told him that she wasn't the type to run. Not now. Not after she'd made a deal with him. And yet, the nagging doubt remained.

She could still surprise him.

A few minutes later, the door creaked open again and Juliet reappeared, approaching him with a wary look in her eyes. "My aunt would like a word with you."

He quirked a brow. "Would she?"

"She. . .insists."

Intrigued, he followed her inside. Despite the general shabbiness of the place, it was a tidy home, smelling of herbs he couldn't begin to name. Across the room, a small woman with steel-grey hair and a keen gaze sat propped up in a chair, fingers twitching as she gestured to the other chair. She didn't speak until he and Juliet sat. "You're the master of Bedford Manor."

He inclined his head. "I am, madam."

"I suppose that makes you responsible."

"For Miss Finch?" he asked, unsure where this was going.

"Indeed. I want to know what sort of man you are, Mr. Russell, before I entrust my girl to your fine estate."

So, this was to be a reckoning. Not of title or means—but of character. He hid a smile. She reminded him of Juliet, only older, frailer, and twice as immovable. That same fire in the eyes, the same iron will wrapped in politeness. No wonder Juliet was the way she was. The pair of them could stare down a magistrate without blinking.

And somehow, an hour later, he found himself promising to see the roof mended before the first frost.

Chapter 8

There was safety in a moonless night. Black crevices to hide in. No light to betray her. Even the wind was hardly more than a secret, as if it held its breath. The scent of moist earth lingered in the cool air, leaves rustling softly with each tread of Juliet's horse. These were the best sort of evenings to lay a snare, trap a quail, bag a feast. Even so, she frowned as she guided her mount through a maze of trees. Such darkness wasn't helpful at all when following a man in a black coat riding on an inky stallion.

She squinted ahead to make out Mr. Russell's imposing figure atop his horse, familiar now with his broad shoulders and regal posture. She knew the trail well enough, but not the man. If he turned and she wasn't paying attention, she'd lose him. And that was the sum of the entire past week, tagging Henry Russell's heels around Bedford Manor. Together they'd explored potential weaknesses where an intruder might breach the security of the house and scouted for signs of any recent ill-intentioned activity—the very purpose of this late-evening ride.

She ducked beneath a low-hanging branch. Then again, he'd shadowed her as much as she had him. Yes, he'd allowed her to gather her belongings unhindered at Aunt Margaret's last week. He'd even shown much generosity by hiring a nurse to attend her aunt and sending over baskets of food. But those good actions were offset by the uncertain gleam in his eye every time he looked at her—and he did look. He watched her unceasingly.

She adjusted her grip on the reins, her pulse quickening. His wary scrutiny chafed, yet it also stirred an attraction to the very man she'd stolen from.

And she wasn't quite sure what to do with that.

Juliet shifted uneasily in the saddle, her thoughts tangling with each step through the darkened woods. So much had changed in the past week she hardly knew what to think anymore—which meant it would probably be better to simply focus on the task at hand. Upping her horse's pace, she strained to see ahead.

A sudden whinny broke the stillness.

Something hit the ground. Hard.

Then a grunt, a groan, and hooves pounding against the earth, growing more distant with each passing second.

Her heart lurched. "Mr. Russell?"

Nothing but the hoot of an owl answered.

She dug in her heels, urging her mount around the next bend, then pulled up short. Five paces off lay a dark figure in the dirt with no horse in sight. Panic bubbled at the back of her throat as she dismounted. What was she to do if Mr. Russell had snapped his neck? "Mr. Russell!"

Kneeling at his side, she pressed her hand to his shoulder, bracing for the worst. For an agonizing eternity, he didn't move, the silence louder than the thudding of her own heart.

"Henry?" Her voice was a shiver in the darkness.

This would be a good time to pray, to plead for this man's life. She'd seen enough death and felt the stab of it too keenly when she'd lost her brother. But her lips remained sealed, trapping the prayer on her tongue. Would it really do any good to beg for mercy now, when her past prayers had fallen on deaf ears?

Then again, could it hurt?

With a jolt, he sucked in air, eyes flying open. "What—what happened?"

Shaking his head slightly, he pushed up to his elbows.

She drew back, relieved beyond measure. "You were thrown. You could have split your skull."

His white teeth flashed in the dark, a devilishly handsome smile. "You underestimate how hard my head is." He sat up fully then, brushing away leaves and dirt from his trousers.

"Are you sure you are all right? Perhaps you ought to take it easy for a moment."

"I am fine. The only thing damaged is my pride." After a roll of his shoulders, he held out his hand. "Though I wouldn't mind a shoulder to lean on as I stand."

Still jittery from the whole affair, she steeled herself and helped him to his feet. His fingers wrapped around hers, and despite the thin leather of his gloves, something sparked between them—warm, steady, real. Not at all like Colin Chamberlain's touch, which had always felt like a performance meant to charm but never truly reached her.

When Henry pulled away, he teetered a moment before regaining his usual confident stance.

"So." She cleared her throat. "What spooked your horse?"

"I do not know. I came wide around the bend, yet I saw nothing." He rubbed his temple, wincing slightly. Evidently he was not quite as fine as he claimed to be.

"I'll take a look." She retraced her steps towards the curve, scanning the brush. That's when she spotted it—a thin, frayed line hanging from a trunk, tied at chest height for a horse. She crouched, fingering the dangling twine now broken.

"Over here," she called. "Looks like someone rigged a snagline. Wouldn't hurt a horse—but enough to spook it."

"No wonder Apollo bolted."

She straightened. "It is fresh, barely weathered. Someone was here not long ago."

Henry planted his hands on his hips. "Who the devil would set something like this?"

"Good question." Juliet scanned the darkened woods—eyes more than adjusted to the lack of light. "Whoever did it might still be nearby."

Henry caught up to Juliet as she mounted her horse, unease churning in his gut. The woman's determination both impressed and concerned him. She was fearless—too fearless—but now that true danger might be afoot, ought he really subject her to such a threat? What had at first seemed like providence when she'd been caught poaching—an answer delivered at just the right moment—now felt dangerously close to presumption. Had he mistaken a convenience for a godsend? Had he foolishly leaned on human help rather than waiting for a wiser course? And if he had. . .would she be the one to pay the price for it? Thank God he'd been in the lead instead of her! If she'd been thrown. . .well, he would not even think of it.

"Perhaps you ought to wait here while I ride on ahead." He offered his hand to help her down.

She glanced from his fingers to his face, a slight shake to her head. "I am no wilting flower, Mr. Russell, and I intend to keep my end of the bargain. I will help you find this villain." Instead of accepting his hand, she held out her own. "We will make better time if you ride behind me. I realize it will not be proper nor comfortable. . .that is, unless you prefer to wait here while I go?"

A wry smile tugged his lips. Stubborn, unconventional woman! He accepted her steadying grip and swung up behind her.

The moment he did so, he realized what a grave mistake he'd made.

She smelled of the air just before a rain, hinting at storms and life and promise. Though she kept a rigid back, there was softness beneath that woolen coat—more than he might have expected. A week of steady meals had already begun to fill out the angles left by too many months of hardship. His hands barely touched her waist, but even that light contact was dangerous.

And far too memorable.

She urged the horse into motion, and Henry sucked in a breath. Each stride rocked her body against his, the rise and fall maddening in its rhythm, intoxicating in its innocence. Heaven help him, but he could not help wondering if she felt it too.

Bah! Banish the thought. This was a woman of wind and steel. She'd said herself her brother had made her into a tomboy. She probably thought of him as nothing other than a sibling seated behind her.

Yet. . .had she not called him by his given name when he'd fallen from his horse? True, it was a small thing, but it had stuck with him. And it might do him a world of good to think of her as simply a sister.

He leaned forwards a bit, speaking quietly. "You called me Henry earlier."

She tensed. "I. . .I meant no disrespect, Mr. Russell."

"None was taken. In fact, given the circumstances, I think it only appropriate we dispense with formalities. You are already on a first-name basis with my sister. May I call you Juliet?"

Hooves thunked steadily against dirt and undergrowth, the only answer to his question. At length, she glanced over her shoulder, her expression quite unreadable in the dark. "I am a poacher. You are my employer, or a redeemer, if you will. Do you really think such a leniency is advisable?"

"No—and yes. We are allies, are we not? Working together, living under the same roof, I believe there should be some measure of trust between us."

"Trust?" She laughed, the sound light as a summer breeze. "This coming from the man who watches my every move?"

He shifted uncomfortably. Now there was a truth he wasn't eager to acknowledge. He did keep a close eye on her—he had to. At least that's what he told himself. "It is an obligatory evil. For now, at any rate. But using our Christian names might help build a bridge between us."

Had he truly just said that? Is that really what he wanted?

Unwilling to battle that particular demon tonight, he pressed on.

"The thing is I am not a man who revels in keeping my distance. At least, not from those I work closely with. And we cannot very well get any closer than we are now, eh?"

"I suppose I am practically sitting in your lap, Mr. Russell." Once again she glanced back, this time with an arch to her brow. "Or shall I say, Henry? And yes, you may call me Juliet since your sister already does so. Now then, to the matter at hand. I have found the best way to snare prey is silence—and this horse is loud enough."

She faced forwards, which felt like a loss. He wasn't sure if he ought to be irritated by her obvious censure or applaud her spunk. Still, he had gained a victory, which was enough for now.

As they rode on, he scanned the darkness, the woods black as a crypt. It was hard to detect anything other than shadow upon shadow.

Until one moved.

"Look to your left," he whispered. "Beyond that white oak. What do you think?"

Her head swiveled, followed by a sharp inhale. "That is no animal."

She nudged the horse into action, and he nearly fell off for the second time that night. Trees blurred as he fought to hold on to her slim form but not too tightly. A branch snagged his sleeve; holly tore at his trousers. Eventually they closed the gap, and she tugged on the reins.

But the figure was gone.

"He cannot have gotten far," she breathed. "Hold on."

They pounded away, then slowed as they reached the end of the tree line. Keeping them in the cover of the woods' darkness, she stopped. He slid to the ground, boots landing with a thud, crushing leaves and sticks.

Which earned him a frown.

He stared into the dark as she dismounted, then slowly turned in a circle, straining to see.

Juliet crouched, pressing her fingers into the dirt. "Stay still."

"What are you doing?" he whispered.

"Feeling for any kind of vibration. If he is nearby and makes a move, I will know." She closed her eyes as if she might become one with the earth herself.

His breath hitched slightly at the sight. There was something primal about this woman and the way the forest spoke to her. Something he might never achieve.

Eventually she rose, a sad shake to her head. "Nothing," she murmured. "If he was here, he is long gone by now."

While he admired her ability to read the land like a novel, frustration nipped at him. They'd been so close! "You are certain?"

"I know what I am about, sir. I have been doing this for a year now."

He sighed, running a hand through his hair. Of course she knew what she was about. She navigated this land as if she were the master. "I do not doubt your skills, Juliet. I just. . .well, I had hoped we could put an end to this tonight. It is as if we are chasing a ghost."

She dusted off her hands, shoulders straightening. "Sometimes all we have are ghosts. I understand your frustration, but that is where perseverance comes in."

He blinked, once again taken aback. She pulled no punches, this one. "So, what now?"

"We try again in the morning, when the light is better, and I shall see if there is anything left to track. Whoever was here likely left behind some sign. They always do."

He cocked his head. "You did not."

A grin spread as she pulled herself up into the saddle, yet she said nothing. Which was a blessing in disguise as far as he was concerned, for the way his thoughts mired in a muddle, conversation was out of the question.

They might have foiled the tormentor's attempt to unseat Charity on a ride, but that didn't negate the fact that the villain had been here and slipped from his grasp. How was he to protect his sister—and now Juliet—if he didn't know who he was up against or when the cad might strike again? Now that he'd actually spotted the man, the danger felt all the more real.

Juliet shifted in the saddle, and he could sense the tension still radiating from her. He should say something. Anything. But what? That he regretted this? That he didn't want her in harm's way? That he was starting to care for her in ways that complicated this entire situation?

No, he couldn't afford to think like that. Not now. He wasn't a man prone to sentimentality and he must foremost think of his sister. She was his first concern.

But the night's ride had made one thing all too clear. Juliet was becoming a close second. . .a complication he hadn't anticipated.

Chapter 9

Cloudy mornings were meant for lolling about beneath a downy counterpane, surrendering to heavy eyelids and the cozy softness of a feather bed. . .especially when true sleep hadn't arrived until just before dawn. Juliet yawned as she trod the corridor, feeling a little guilty that Charity and Henry would likely be finishing up their tea and toast by now. But after last night's fruitless ride, she'd stared up at the lacy bed curtains, puzzling over the figure she'd barely caught a glimpse of. There was no way to identify who it had been, but circumstantially, Mr. Dankworth's land did neighbour Bedford Manor in that particular corner of the estate. Maybe a visit to the hermit was in order—especially since the last nameless bouquet of flowers left on the manor's front stoop had been a collection of wildflowers.

Flowers she knew grew on the man's grounds.

Stifling one more yawn, she entered the breakfast room, then stopped, surprised to see another lady seated next to Charity. And what a lady. Her rich brown hair twisted into a lovely coil atop her head. Her skin was flawless on her heart-shaped face, highlighting dainty rose-red lips and eyes the blue of which could occupy a poet for years. Maybe decades. She was the kind of woman whose beauty might invite envy, a perfection that could easily spark rivalry amongst other ladies.

Henry stood. "Good morning, Miss Finch." He dipped his head. "May I introduce a dear family friend, Miss Clara Whitmore. Clara, meet our houseguest, Miss Juliet Finch."

Juliet dipped a curtsey. "Pleased to meet you, Miss Whitmore."

"You as well, Miss Finch." The woman nodded her greeting and then turned to Henry. "You are full of surprises, Henry. I wasn't aware you were hosting a houseguest, especially now with Charity potentially traveling to Italy."

He waited until Juliet sank into her seat, then reached for another piece of toast before he sat as well. "Miss Finch's visit is rather unplanned, though her presence has been a great help to me."

Clara's eyebrows arched ever so slightly, though to her credit, her tone remained light. "How intriguing. You've never mentioned her before."

Henry's gaze flickered to Juliet, his face unreadable. "Miss Finch has been kind enough to lend her assistance in a. . .delicate matter involving the estate—one in which she is well versed."

"Mmm." Clara tilted her head as if deep in thought. "Between overseeing the estate and watching out for your sister's well-being, I wager you'll barely have a moment to yourself. Then again, you've always been rather adept at juggling multiple responsibilities." She took a slow sip, her gaze sliding to Juliet with pointed interest. "But I admit it does make me wonder what could possibly demand so much of your attention that you've called in reinforcements."

Juliet fought the urge to squirm on her chair. The woman's unspoken question hung in the air like a noose waiting for a neck.

Time to steer the conversation onto safer ground. "I must say, Miss Whitmore, the view from Bedford Manor is quite stunning this time of year. You are blessed indeed to have such friends. It must be wonderful to visit whenever you like."

"Yes, I've always loved coming here." She sipped her tea. "There's a peace to this place, the sort that makes one feel they belong here."

Charity patted Clara's arm. "Of course you do. Our families have been intertwined for generations."

"And hopefully for many more generations to come." She lifted her cup high. "To good friends."

"Hear, hear!" Henry grinned, the clink of his cup along with Charity's and Clara's a cheerful sound for such a dreary morning.

It was an intimate exchange, wholly natural of course, and yet a bittersweet pang sank deep in Juliet's chest. This was something she couldn't be a part of. Could never be part of again. She busied herself with buttering a piece of toast, hoping to ease the uncomfortable knot in her stomach.

Clara set down her cup. "So, Miss Finch, have you been enjoying your stay?"

"Very much." She smiled, astonished at the truth in her words. Though she'd been here little more than a week—and she missed her aunt—somehow she'd settled right into manor life, albeit not in a role she would have chosen.

"I would expect as much." Clara dabbed her lips with the corner of a linen serviette. "It is serene here, tucked away in the countryside. I find there's something about these quieter places that soothes the soul, don't you think?"

"I could not agree more." And she couldn't. Life at Bedford Manor was much less stressful than scrapping about for her next meal in the dark of night.

"I always breathe a little easier when I come for a visit. Oh, Charity, your cup is empty, dearest." Clara reached for the teapot and poured some of the tepid brew, then turned back to Juliet. "I hope you've had the chance to enjoy the grounds. I find a good walk through the gardens or a ride across the fields is so invigorating."

Juliet took a bite of her toast, hardly tasting the creaminess of the butter. It had been so long since she had been able to stroll through manicured gardens without a care or ride a horse simply for the pleasure of it.

She set down her toast, appetite fleeing. "I have not had the time yet, but I should like to."

"I am afraid I have kept Miss Finch quite busy," Henry cut in.

Clara's gaze bounced between them, finally landing on Juliet.

"Well, if you ever tire of Henry's company and Charity is unavailable, do let me know. I'm always happy to take a stroll with new friends."

New friends. The words struck a chord inside more deeply than they should have. How long had it been since someone had spoken to her with such kindness, as though she was someone worth knowing? And just how quickly would that sentiment change if this woman learned the truth of her situation?

"That's very generous of you, Miss Whitmore," she murmured.

Clara waved a hand dismissively, the gold bracelet on her wrist catching the light of the oil lamps. "Oh, please, do call me Clara. I daresay we'll all be on first-name terms soon enough."

Her throat closed. Juliet couldn't help but miss the ease with which women of means like Clara moved through life, their days filled with tea and companionship. The type of life that had been snatched away from her thanks to her father. And it was moments like these that brought that loss into sharp focus.

"How long will you be staying, Miss Finch?" Clara asked.

She fought the urge to glance at Henry. Doing so would be a dead giveaway that her presence relied solely on his command. "It is hard to say, but I do not think it will be very long."

Clara smiled. "Very practical of you. As my mother always says, houseguests and fish are best enjoyed while still fresh. Anything longer leaves a bad smell instead of good memories." She laughed merrily, then engaged Henry in a conversation about some mutual friend on a neighbouring estate. She drew both her and Charity into the conversation every now and then with a comment or a question. And the tightness in Juliet's throat turned into an ache. How lovely it was to relive her former life, if only for a few fleeting moments. How kind it was of Clara to include her.

Charity leaned close to Juliet and whispered, "She would make a fine sister-in-law, wouldn't she?"

Juliet's heart twisted painfully. Clara had warmth, charm, connections. As Juliet studied the easy rapport between them, she could only agree.

"Yes," she whispered back, the word catching just slightly. "She would."

Yet in that moment, she couldn't help but wonder what her life would have been like if her circumstances had been different. Once upon a time, she might have had a chance to marry a gentleman like Henry. A sigh leaked out of her. That was not her life anymore.

Clara turned back to them. "Charity, are you ready for our ride?"

Henry's jaw hardened. "I regret to say your ride has been postponed. . .indefinitely."

"Oh?" Clara's smile faltered. "Why? Is something amiss?"

He flashed a smile of his own. "Nothing to concern you."

"Too late." She frowned. "I am already concerned."

Oh dear. It wouldn't do to have this woman know about the trapline that'd thrown Henry from his horse. Juliet forced a light laugh. "You know men. Always fretting about some small thing. Would you not agree, Charity?"

"My brother is rather overprotective." She shrugged one slim shoulder.

"There is no question that you are his pet, darling." Clara leaned back in her chair, cocking her head at Henry. "But as I have come all the way here, I think it only fair to know why I am to be deprived of riding with your sister."

A muscle near his eye twitched as he exchanged a glance with Juliet. She gave him a subtle shake of her head, trying to warn him of the dangers of giving too much information. A seemingly innocent conversation could turn into an unintentional weapon in circles where gossip and curiosity were constant companions.

Even so, he pressed on. "There was an incident in the woods last night. Something spooked my horse."

Clara's eyes widened. "What do you mean?"

Juliet's stomach clenched. He should not have said anything. Revealing such a thing might cause more problems than it solved.

"Nothing to be overly troubled about." He stretched out his legs, crossing one ankle over the other as if he hadn't a care in the world.

"But I think it best to avoid the woods for now."

Clara's porcelain brow furrowed, and Juliet could see the wheels turning behind those brilliant blue eyes. "Well then, if we cannot ride, perhaps a walk in the garden instead?" She turned to Juliet. "And naturally you must join us, Miss Finch."

Juliet froze. The invitation had been so unexpectedly kind that she was momentarily at a loss for the words to turn down the woman. How exactly did one navigate the delicate balance between being a houseguest and a disgraced poacher? She looked to Henry for guidance, but before he could say anything, the door to the breakfast room opened and Mrs. Hamby, the housekeeper, stepped inside.

"Pardon me, sir, Miss Finch." She nodded at them in turn. "There is something I believe you both ought to see."

Henry exchanged a glance with Juliet as he rose. "It appears you will be unable to take that walk after all, Miss Finch. If you two ladies would please excuse us?" He clipped them a polite bow as he strode to the door.

Juliet stood, the shift in the room as dense as an October fog. "It was a pleasure to meet you, Clara. Until later, Charity."

Clara tilted her head slightly, interest deepening the blue in her eyes. "I hope we shall see you again soon, Juliet. Perhaps at the Harvest Festival on Saturday?"

Before she could formulate a reply, Henry called over his shoulder, "Of course, Clara. We shall all see you then."

Juliet followed Henry out of the room, and with every step, she felt the inquisitive gaze of Clara Whitmore burning between her shoulder blades.

~

Mrs. Hamby stopped in the front hall, pivoting to peer around him and Juliet. Did she seriously think someone else would creep up behind them to listen in on whatever she had to say?

Henry frowned. "What is this about, Mrs. Hamby?"

Lips pinched, she produced a ripped piece of paper from her

pocket. "One of the maids found this in the footman's livery while doing laundry. I thought you and Miss Finch ought to be privy to it."

Collecting the small slip, he held it up to eye height.

She doesn't know yet, but she will. Soon. Unless. . .

What the deuce? He glanced at Mrs. Hamby. "What does this mean?"

She shook her head, expression grim. Not one of her gunmetal-grey locks dared to break rank from the coil of hair atop her head. "I don't know, sir, but with all the. . .happenings around here, I hate to imagine."

Juliet held out her palm. "May I see it?"

Henry passed her the paper but kept his eye on Mrs. Hamby. "You found this in Woodley's pocket, you say?"

"The laundry maid did, yes, sir."

Suspicion warred with disbelief and a fair amount of caution. The note was vague. It could mean nothing. Then again, this might be the clue he needed. He glanced at Juliet, her teeth grazing her lower lip a moment before she offered back the note.

Her fingers brushed against his, her nostrils flaring at the contact. Even so, her tone remained as even as ever. "I suspect this is no coincidence."

Perhaps. Perhaps not. He ran his thumb over the hastily scribbled words. As master of the manor, he had to be prudent, and yet it was hard to deny that something sinister was taking root deep in his thoughts. "I should like to speak with Woodley," he said at length.

Juliet's gaze darted to his. "So would I."

He turned back to Mrs. Hamby. "Where is he?"

"Last I saw, sir, he was attending to the silver in the pantry."

He nodded curtly. "Tell him to meet me in the study once he is finished."

Juliet laid a light touch on his sleeve. "Perhaps it would be better if we spoke with him straightaway."

True. The element of surprise could be an ally. "Agreed." He cast a final glance at the housekeeper. "Thank you, Mrs. Hamby."

He guided Juliet down a side passage leading to the back of the house. The air turned cooler as they left the family-used portion of the manor to descend wooden steps, clean and tidy but decidedly less polished.

Juliet glanced at him from the corner of her eye. "We shall have to tread carefully when we speak to Mr. Woodley."

"Carefully?"

She nodded while gripping the handrail. "It is easy to say too much when you are trying to get answers." She paused, then added, "People can take even the smallest detail and turn it into something more."

His eyebrows shot to the rafters. "Are you accusing me of something, Miss Finch?"

"Not necessarily." She traversed the final step to the tiled landing of the servants' floor, then faced him, an enigmatic smile quirking the corners of her mouth. "It is just that earlier, with Miss Whitmore... well, I think it is possible she perceived more than you intended."

"How absurd. Clara is an old friend, not given to wagging her tongue in public."

"I meant no disrespect. She seems a lovely lady. I simply think there is wisdom in being cautious—even with friends. I have learned the hard way that those you think are constant companions can turn out to be rabid dogs."

He wrestled with her words while directing her into the left-hand corridor. Matching her stride, he mulled over all she'd said—and hadn't said. He didn't appreciate the implication he might have provided Clara with too much information. Clara was no stranger, no frivolous gossip. Still, Juliet's insight gave him pause. There was something unnerving about the way Miss Finch was always so aware, always watching, calculating, as though she saw through layers others missed. Was such a suspicious mien born of necessity, the by-product of a life where caution was the only way to stay alive? Or was her caution nothing more than an overactive nerve he'd accidentally struck?

He pressed his fingers to the base of his neck, easing the lingering tension. Then again, she wasn't wrong to be cautious. Women often reveled in a tale, no matter how innocent it began. And Clara...well, Clara was a good friend, but that didn't make her immune to curiosity.

"Is that how you have learned to get by, then?" he mused outwardly. "By leashing every word and reading every room?"

She licked her lips before answering. "I suppose you could say that."

He paused several steps shy of the pantry. "You never told me what it was that has brought you so low."

"No, I have not." Her eyes flashed with a now-familiar fire.

Insolent little sprite. And yet there was something thrilling in her refusal to yield, something that resonated deep inside him. Not only did this woman know her mind, she was determined to keep her dignity intact, no matter the cost. Such a fierce resolve demanded respect, even admiration, despite himself.

"Very well," he murmured. "You may keep your secrets...for now."

She raised an eyebrow, challenging him without a word—and it took every ounce of restraint not to reach out and brush a stray curl from her cheek.

Instead, he indicated the door ahead. "After you."

He followed her inside the small room, his nose immediately struck with the acrid reek of hartshorn and tarnished metal. An array of silverware was laid out meticulously on a black cloth with William Woodley seated in front of the lineup. He was a wiry young man, with dark hair clinging in wisps to his forehead. His shoulders bowed over his work like a prayer, as though some unseen weight pressed him down. Scullery maids might find him handsome, as he was pleasant of face, skin unmarred by blemishes or pockmarks. He glanced up at their arrival, the cloth in his hand stilling. Immediately he stood. A cornered hare couldn't look more panicked.

Henry halted a few steps past the threshold. No sense in giving the man an apoplexy. "We would have a word with you, Woodley."

The knob of the man's throat bobbed, but to his credit, his voice did not quaver. "Yes, sir?"

Henry set the note on the table and, stabbing it with his index finger, slid the paper towards the footman. "I would have you explain this."

Woodley collected the scrap, his eyes widening as he silently mouthed the words. Colour drained from his face. "I—I don't know, sir."

Juliet stepped closer to the man. "It was found in your pocket, Mr. Woodley."

He shook his head wildly. "I swear I never seen it before."

Henry studied the fellow carefully, eyes narrowing as he took in every detail. The footman's once-ruddy cheeks turned ashen. His posture was rigid with a slight tremor in his hands, the paper quivering noticeably. Either the man had been caught in a lie, or the terror of being falsely accused was too much for him to bear.

"Who is the 'she' implied in this note?" Henry pressed.

Woodley cleared his throat, that knob at his neck once again bobbing. "I have no idea, sir."

"And yet," Juliet drawled, "the fact remains that the note was found in your pocket. Surely you must have some explanation."

His brow furrowed as he fidgeted with the hem of his waistcoat. "I swear, I don't know how it got there, miss. I wouldn't. . .I mean, I'd *never* have anything to do with—"

Without warning, he clammed up.

Henry stepped closer, folding his arms. "It seems someone thought your pocket a convenient hiding place for such a message. Tell me, Woodley—if as you say this is the first time you've laid eyes on that note—then how do you think it came to be in your pocket?"

"I—I don't know, sir. It—it must've been slipped in when I wasn't looking. I swear it." Lamplight glinted off a moist sheen on his brow. "Am I in trouble?"

Juliet glanced at Henry, then back at Woodley. "I assure you, Mr. Woodley, we are accusing you of nothing. We are merely gathering information. Now then, that note implies someone, this mysterious 'she,' will find out about something soon. Is there anyone in the household who might have reason to believe you have been involved in anything. . .improper? Is there some untoward behaviour into which you are being coerced?"

His face flushed a deep crimson. "I do my duties and keep to myself. That's all. Ask Mrs. Hamby. She'll tell ye."

Henry aimed a finger towards the note, now crumpled in the man's hand. "That little missive implies otherwise."

Woodley's hands clenched into fists at his sides, his voice tight. "I didn't do anything wrong, sir."

Juliet stepped closer to the footman, graceful yet with a certain measure of authority in her stride. "Have you noticed anything strange around the manor? Something—or someone—out of place?"

Woodley hesitated, then slowly shook his head. "Not really, miss. But. . ." His jaw moved as if he chewed on something. "Well, it's likely nothing, but I did think I saw someone lingering near the stables a few days ago. Could have been one of the grooms, but I wasn't sure. I took a look myself, but I didn't see anything."

Henry lifted a brow. "And you did not think to mention this before?"

Woodley's chin dipped to his chest. "I didn't think it was important. People are always about. . . I didn't want to cause concern."

Henry's temper flared, and it was a fight to keep his voice steady. "Whether you intended to or not, you have already caused concern by keeping silent. I expect you to come forward with anything else you might recall. No matter how insignificant."

Woodley nodded hastily. "Yes, sir."

Henry exchanged a look with Juliet, his suspicion deepening. "I hope you understand the seriousness of the situation, Woodley. If we find out you have been keeping something from us, the consequences will be severe."

The footman drew in a shaky breath, then squared his shoulders. "I swear, sir, I'm telling you everything I know. I've no idea about that note. I don't know who 'she' is. I swear on my mother's grave."

"No need for swearing, Mr. Woodley." Juliet smiled. "Merely tell the truth, for if you do not, there will be nowhere for you to hide once we find out who has been plaguing Miss Russell."

"Of course, miss," he mumbled. "I wish Miss Russell only the best."

"Very well, Woodley. Carry on with your cleaning, though I will take custody of that note." Henry stretched his palm over the table and retrieved the damp ball of paper from the footman. "For now we will take our leave, but rest assured I—and Miss Finch—will be watching you closely. *Very* closely. Is that understood?"

Woodley nodded fervently. "Yes, sir."

Once he and Juliet cleared the room, she leaned close to him, her words barely a whisper. "Though he seems more afraid than suspicious—which admittedly could be a ruse—still, I cannot say I trust him."

"Nor do I," he muttered darkly, casting a glance back at the pantry door. "He is definitely hiding something. The question is what."

Chapter 10

Four days passed without incident. Woodley was a model footman. No more shadow figures appeared on Mr. Dankworth's side of the estate. Neither had there been any notes delivered—save for a cheery greeting from Aunt Margaret, which had put Juliet's heart at ease. But even so, as Juliet strolled next to Charity and Henry through the merrymakers at the Bedford Harvest Festival, she kept her gaze sharp.

Torchlight painted the mowed field in soft shades of golden orange. Booths stood in rows, selling everything from sheaves of wheat tied with ribbons to apple fritters. Hay bales and pumpkins added to the autumn feel in the air, as did the spicy scent of nutmeg and cinnamon. Even Miss Potter added to the seasonal ambience where she stood near the cider booth, wearing a hat plastered with fall leaves, sprigs of wheat, and a squirrel figurine perched at the very top. Juliet suppressed a grin. The woman possessed more confidence than a battalion of soldiers—and twice the nerve.

Juliet shifted her weight, shoulders easing—just a little. Being that nothing whatsoever appeared to be perilous, perhaps she could let down her guard, just for a moment. After all, Charity was nestled between her and Henry, so no harm could befall the woman here. Would it truly hurt to share in some of the smiles around her?

"Charity! Over here."

Juliet snapped her attention to the left where a few ladies

congregated near a seller of painted fans. One of the women—a buxom brunette with overlarge teeth—waggled her fingers, beckoning Charity to her side.

Charity upped her pace, breaking away from Juliet and her brother. "I'll catch up with you two later."

"Not so fast." Henry pulled her back with a touch to her shoulder. "I cannot keep you safe if you do not stay with me."

"Henry, really. I haven't seen Mary and Catherine for weeks, and I miss them."

He shook his head. "If companionship is what you seek, then invite them to the house."

"But they are right there." She flailed a hand towards them, her gaze drifting to Juliet's. "Tell him. You understand what it's like to be in the company of ladies you've not chatted with for so long. A little time with them will be harmless."

Charity's words struck a minor chord in her heart. She did know what it was like to be kept away from friends, for she dearly missed her former companionship with the ladies of Cheltenham. . .even if they had shunned her after her father's dastardly deed had come to light. She glanced at Henry. "It is a valid request. We can keep an eye on her from a short distance."

His jaw hardened, and for a moment she thought he'd deny her; then surprisingly, he gave a sharp nod. "Very well. But do not stray too far with your friends."

"I promise." Charity grinned as she scampered away.

A bittersweet sight, that. Juliet had once been so blithe. . .and now look at her. She blew out a long breath, releasing the jealousy building in her lungs. It was good for Charity to have such a small freedom, considering her recent troubles.

She gazed up at Henry. "I think it sweet how you look out for your sister."

"Some would say I am overbearing," he murmured, his eyes fixed on Charity.

"I say it shows you love her."

"It is only right I remain vigilant with my father away. I am responsible for her, and I take that charge to heart."

"Would that everyone took their obligations so seriously." Her father certainly hadn't. This time an angry huff came out.

Henry's brows drew into a straight line. . .the same protective expression he used when regarding his sister. "You have been hurt—deeply, I suspect—and by someone very dear to you."

Her breath stalled, those green-grey eyes of his penetrating beyond her carefully fashioned facade. Though couched as a statement, there would be no shrinking from such a direct query.

"Yes," she whispered.

A breeze whipped down the lane, tinkling a string of bells on the nearest booth and coaxing loose a wave of her hair. Good. She shoved it back, giving her fingers something to do other than relent to the scandalous urge to touch his sleeve and pretend to once again be a lady, one whom this man might cherish.

"I am sorry to hear it." Sincerity ran thick in his voice. "God never intends for us to carry our burdens alone. Sometimes it helps to have a confidant, and my sister tells me I have a good listening ear."

Longing welled, so tangible she tasted the sweetness of it on her tongue. How good it would be to share her woes with someone other than Aunt Margaret. To be met with compassion instead of derision. But could she trust him? *Should* she?

And if she did, would he discard her as easily as had Colin Chamberlain?

"Anything you tell me will remain with me. I vow it. Besides"—a slow smile spread across his full lips—"I have already seen you at your worst." He elbowed her shoulder playfully.

How true that was. He could have had her arrested, sent her away, and yet he'd taken her into his home to work alongside him. Though she'd known him scarcely over a fortnight, he'd been nothing but the portrait of integrity.

"But come." With a light touch to her arm, he guided her into the fray of pedestrians. "My sister is on the move."

Sure enough, Charity and her friends had strayed several booths down the lane. Juliet fell into step with Henry, casting him a sideways glance. "I suppose it is no secret to you that I come from a family of some standing, leastwise I used to."

"I knew you were a lady that first night we met."

Her brows shot to the torchlit sky. "In the woods?"

He chuckled, the happy sound blending with the giggles of small children gathered around a brightly lit puppet show, Punch going after Judy with a papier-mâché club. "Yes, even when you had mud on your boots and leaves in your hair, you carried yourself with a grace that could not be hidden. A true lady does not need fine clothes or jewels to be recognized, and you, Juliet Finch, are every bit a lady." Admiration warmed his tone as he steered her around the cluster of show gawkers. "But back to your tale of woe."

Indeed. Woeful it was.

"My father"—she nearly choked on the word—"was a man of affairs. A high-ranking one, to be exact. He managed the dealings of some of the finest families in England, not only overseeing their financial matters but also acting as a trusted adviser to very powerful men. This position afforded us a comfortable life. But that did not satisfy him. He always strived for more, reaching for things he ought not to have touched. As I understand it, he started small, shifting insignificant sums into his own account. At first, I believe he thought he could set things right should anyone find out, but eventually everything spiraled out of control."

Henry stopped dead in his tracks, a mix of horror and compassion chasing across his face. "Are you saying he embezzled money?"

She nodded, lips flat. "More than any of us suspected. He was caught, of course, for such a crime cannot go on forever without being discovered. There was trial, a very public trial in which our assets were seized to repay the families he wronged. My mother could not bear the disgrace when Father was hauled off to gaol. She had already lost my brother two years prior to consumption. The doctor said she died of a broken heart—and that nearly broke mine."

"Oh, Juliet, I am so sorry." There was a husky—almost vulnerable—rawness to his sentiment, which did much to begin healing some of the shame and contempt she'd suffered from her former so-called friends. Would that they'd been as understanding as this man.

Yet understanding did not fill a belly, as she well knew. "I appreciate your sympathy, Mr. Russell—"

"Henry," he interrupted.

"Henry," she conceded with a small smile. "But I have learned that 'sorry' changes nothing."

"And yet sometimes it changes us."

"How so?"

He was quiet for a moment, then said, "When I was a boy, I once thought my sister and I were in grave danger. Our father had gone to France on business—and that time, he'd taken our mother with him. Charity and I were left behind with only the governess and the household staff. My sister and I were convinced the house was haunted, that some malevolent spirit meant us harm. So, I sent a letter—panicked, begging my father to come home. He did. Dropped everything. Packed himself and Mother up and sped home. . .only to find nothing more than creaking shutters, a loose hedgehog, and two frightened children." A muscle ticked in his jaw. "I apologized, of course. Said I was sorry for drawing him away."

"A hedgehog? Creaking shutters?"

"Long story. The point is my father just pulled us into his arms and said, 'I will always come when you call—but make certain it's truly time.'" Henry exhaled slowly. "That 'sorry'. . .it didn't change the fact that I ruined a very important trip for my father, but it changed me. Taught me not to ask for help unless I was sure. Dead sure."

Ahh. Now she understood. Henry Russell wasn't cold—he was carrying a self-imposed weight.

Charity and her friends paused only for a moment at the farthest booth in the aisle, then rounded the corner, disappearing from sight.

Henry pulled her along, his long legs eating up the ground until they spied the ladies in the next lane over. He stopped at the end of the booths, allowing his sister space to shop in peace, and gave Juliet's hand a little squeeze before pulling away. "So, what about your father? Is he still in gaol?"

She shook her head. "He died in prison three months after my mother passed, whether from the abysmal conditions or the cancerous guilt eating his soul, I do not know. I had already gone to live with my aunt, as she was my only means of shelter, pitiful as it is." She turned away her face, unwilling to read his response. "So, there you have it. I am a poacher with a tarnished name. Are you so certain you still wish to keep me in your employ?"

Laughter rumbled in his chest. "More certain than ever."

She spun back to him. "How can you say that?"

"Your past—no matter how tragic—does not define who you are. In the short time I have known you, you have shown more strength and integrity than many in the highest of society ever could. If anything, your resilience makes me respect you all the more."

What?

Her breath caught. For the first time since the whole tragic event, she might believe—just maybe—that her worth wasn't entirely lost.

"Do you truly think so?" she couldn't help but ask.

"I do." He grinned, so irresistibly charming that her knees weakened. "And if you will trust me, I shall prove to you that you are more than the sum of your father's mistakes."

What a balm that would be. Why, she might even consider there could be hope in this bleak situation after all.

"Henry!" Charity flew towards them, barely stopping before crashing into her brother's broad chest. "Someone is watching me. I know it."

All his mirth fled. "Where?"

"Over there." Charity tipped her head towards the stretch of field before a long line of woods.

Juliet squinted into the dark, where a man-sized shape stood immobile near a stack of hay. "You go one way. I will go the other.

We shall flank him."

She didn't wait for a reply. Using all the skills she'd honed over the past year, she quickly crept towards the east, keeping to the deepest patches of night, drawing ever closer to the man who clearly kept watch on the festival. That wouldn't last long, though. As quiet as she might be, he would surely detect the rustle of her hem in the long grass.

So, she'd just have to use that to her advantage.

"Pardon me, sir." She waved a hand over her head as she advanced, hoping to hold his attention until Henry could come up from behind the fellow.

The man turned her way. So far, so good. She could already make out the silhouette of Henry stalking closer to him.

"Please, sir." She waved again.

He kept staring.

Henry drew nearer.

"I seem to have lost my way," she called all the louder.

The man stood rock still, clearly not the chivalrous sort.

Ten paces more now. Maybe nine, as Henry's stride was so long.

"Could you help—"

Crack!

A stick broke like a gunshot beneath Henry's heel.

The man bolted towards the tree line, a distinct limp hampering his speed.

Juliet's gaze shot to Henry, who stood rigid for barely a beat—but in that beat, there was an unmistakable fury hardening his face and his fists. A rage she'd never dare to stand against. May heaven help the man who'd presumed to stare across that field at Henry's sister. He'd need all the help he could get.

For without a word, Henry tore after him.

White-hot fury pumped through his veins as Henry sprinted across the dark field. Parker! He might've known.

"Hold it right there!" Lunging, he grabbed a handful of Parker's coat and spun him around.

Parker leaned heavily on his cane, the only thing keeping him upright besides Henry's death grip. "Unhand me this instant, Russell."

The words were calm—eerily so—which only validated Henry's initial suspicions. He gave the man a jaw-rattling shake. "This stops here and now. Do you understand me? I ought to haul you off to the constable this instant."

Parker wrenched violently, breaking loose and stumbling backwards—then planted his feet, gripping the ebony cane with both hands. With a twist and pull, he unsheathed a hidden rapier from within the shaft. The slender blade caught the festival's spare light as he leveled its tip at Henry's chest, his dark eyes twin voids in a skull-like face. "I have no idea what you're talking about. Now back off."

Despite the threat, Henry stood his ground. "Do not play the innocent with me. Clearly some sort of guilt is involved here, else you'd not have run from me."

Parker's gaze was sharp as a dagger. "When a man is flanked, it is only natural to flee."

He had a point. Barely. "And yet why would you be standing out here in the dark?"

"Not that it is any of your business, but since my service, crowds have a way of inciting anxiety."

Plausible.

But far too convenient, particularly since the man had been staring at Charity. Henry grunted. "Listen, Parker, I know you nurse a grudge against my sister for rejecting your hand, and I saw you lurking about in town. You cannot deny this."

"I do not answer to you. If you have a valid legal complaint against me, I shall happily see you in court. Until then, stay away from me."

"*You* stay away from my sister!"

"Hah! That's the problem with you Russells. Always thinking you are the center of attention." He flicked the tip of the rapier, slicing off one of Henry's coat buttons before sheathing the thing. Once again he used the implement as a cane instead of a weapon as he pivoted into the dark with a lurching grace, the kind nightmares favoured.

Henry narrowed his eyes on Parker's retreating form, barely keeping from charging after the miscreant and knocking him to the ground.

"Who was that?" Juliet's voice floated over his shoulder. "And why did you let him go?"

"Edwin Parker." He spit the name out like a mouthful of soured milk. "Charity's former beau."

"Former? Who scorned whom? What is the history here?"

After a last lip-snarling look at the man, he turned to Juliet. "Parker used to be a familiar figure in the Bedford social circle, a frequent visitor to the manor. It was no secret he admired my sister. Initially, my father and I were open to the match. He was a respectable candidate, and if Charity married him, she would remain close to home."

"Hmm." Juliet crossed her arms, one finger tapping the crook of her elbow. "Clearly that is not how it played out. What happened?"

"When Parker finally proposed, Charity declined. She told him she valued his friendship—but nothing more. She did not harbour any romantic feelings for him and refused to marry without love. He took it hard. Too hard. For months he wallowed in shame and resentment. We were all glad when his brother persuaded him to join the military, and he left home."

"Yet now he is back." Juliet's gaze slid to where the man's dark shape struggled over a great hump of field grass and disappeared into the fray of the festival. "And he is likely even more bitter as he has clearly suffered some sort of life-altering injury during his service."

Indeed. Did the man account that pain to Charity as well?

"So"—Juliet turned back to Henry—"why did you not collar him tonight and press charges?"

He snorted. "Trust me, I wanted to, more than you can possibly know. But what solid evidence do we have against him?"

"Point taken." She sighed. "So, now what?"

"He knows I am onto him, and I warned him off. Hopefully that is enough to stop him from continuing his devilish deeds." And if it wasn't, next time he'd make sure to meet the villain armed as well.

"I suppose time will tell if that is so."

A breeze rattled the line of trees behind them like bones clacking in the wind. A visible tremor rippled across Juliet's shoulders, though he doubted very much it was from fear.

In a trice, he loosened the buttons that remained and swung his coat around her shoulders. "You are cold."

"And now you are as well. There is no sense in both of us shivering. I shall be fine once we return to the festival, especially after a stop by the bonfire." She fingered the lapels.

But before she could pull it off, he stayed her hands with a gentle—yet firm—touch. "Until then, I insist. I will not have you taking ill."

A slow smile curved her lips. "I suppose I cannot refuse my employer. Though if you have intimidated this Mr. Parker well enough, you may not need to keep me on any longer."

The thought was a punch in the gut. Oh, he'd be glad enough to be rid of his sister's tormentor, that was for certain, but that very same blessing would mean a goodbye to Juliet. Bedford Manor would not be the same without this little bird flitting about the passageways, riding out in the dark next to him to scout for threat, gracing the breakfast room each morn. And more than that—he'd seen her with Charity. Heard their laughter dancing through the halls, glimpsed them bent together over a game of draughts or sharing quiet duets at the pianoforte. Those moments spoke of genuine care. Not obligation. Not pretense. But a tenderness for his sister that touched him deeper than words could say.

And he wasn't quite sure what to do about that.

So he grinned to mask his foolish feelings. "When I release you from our bargain, how am I to be certain you will not return to your former habit of relieving me of my game? For a lady of your talents will not be satisfied to sit in front of a fire with a lapful of needlepoint."

"Ahh, but you underestimate me, sir. Given the right company, I could be convinced to stay indoors—though I prefer a bit more excitement than needlework." An impish twinkle sparked in her eyes.

Which delighted him most absurdly. "The poacher knows how to flirt, does she?"

She gathered his coat tighter at her throat, a rakish tilt to her head. "I have more skills than bagging quail."

"Yes, I believe you do." Unbidden, his gaze fixed on her lips. A mistake, that, for his heart took off at full gallop. One step—just one—and he could pull her into his arms. Feel her softness. Taste her—

Great heavens! What was he thinking?

He pivoted, offering his arm without making eye contact. "As you suggested, we ought to return to the festival."

He guided her across the field, her fingers barely a whisper on his sleeve, and yet that touch became his sole focus. Which was a danger. His sister's welfare had to be first and foremost in his mind, not how the nearness of Juliet Finch made him feel.

Giving himself a mental shake, he pulled away the moment they spanned the last hump of grass and pointed to where Charity conversed with Clara Whitmore near a booth of ribbons and lace. "Over there."

Scanning the nearby crowd for any sign of Parker, he stopped at Charity's side. "Where are the rest of your friends? You told me you would stay with them."

Clara arched a brow, dipping a graceful curtsey. "Good evening to you too, Henry. And to you, Juliet." Her glance skimmed the coat draped over Juliet's shoulders. "I must say, that is quite the look. If you're not careful, Juliet, you'll start a trend."

Juliet's cheeks flushed. "I doubt I'll cause such a stir."

Henry took the opportunity to retrieve his coat, shrugging it on and breathing in the faintest trace of her wild scent—rosemary and crushed leaves.

Charity leaned in. "Did you find him?"

"I did," he murmured.

Clara glanced between them, brows furrowing. "Find who?"

Henry hesitated, but Clara's question was earnest, her blue eyes filled only with curiosity. "Nothing to bother yourself about. It was just a misunderstanding, that's all."

"Ah, you do like your little adventures, don't you?" Clara teased. "I hope it's nothing that will end up in the gossip pages."

"Nothing worth a whisper, I promise."

"Good." Clara's eyes twinkled. "Because I came tonight for merriment, not scandal."

"Then merriment it is," he said. "Shall we?"

He swept his hand towards the festivities, trying to muster some gratitude that after his words with Parker, the whole charade should be at an end.

So why the niggling feeling in his gut that it was not?

Chapter 11

Contrary to last evening's chill, a breath of summer revisited Bedford the next day as Juliet left Sunday service. And what a service it was. Reverend St. John's message had been more an accusation than a sermon. No doubt she'd be hearing his voice in her sleep tonight.

"The fatal wound of bitterness is borne by the one who allows it to fester in his bosom, not by the one who caused the initial injury."

She loosened the fichu at her neck, perspiration dampening her palms beneath her gloves. Naturally she knew forgiveness was good and bitterness bad. Didn't everyone? And yet how did one go about absolving the closest person in her life when he had caused such ruination? Still, at this moment, she really couldn't complain about her situation. She had plenty of food to eat, as did Aunt Margaret. She lived in a lovely manor home, complete with servants to cater to any need, leastwise for the time being.

And then there was Henry.

Absently, she rubbed her arms where his coat had embraced her last evening and inhaled deeply, remembering his scent of leather-bound books and bay leaves. A fragrance uniquely his. She hadn't wanted to surrender that coat, but the questions in Clara Whitmore's eyes were too many to name. . .not that she had any answers. Henry Russell rattled her composure in the most maddening ways, especially when he'd sat near her at the bonfire, firelight burnishing the gold streaks in his hair. And that knowing grin of his when he'd caught her studying his profile—oh my. She fanned herself, more uncomfortably hot than ever.

And yet for all his charm, it was what he'd said—almost absently—that had truly stayed with her. That story of a boy who once cried wolf and vowed never to do it again. There was something in that memory, in the burden he still bore, that explained so much about him. His restraint. His protectiveness. His deep-seated need to solve every problem himself. He hadn't just learned responsibility from that incident. He'd learned to carry it alone.

"Miss Finch? A word, if ye don't mind."

She turned at the sound of her name. Pale-faced Mrs. Craft scurried past the milliner's to catch up to her.

While concerned—for surely something fretted the woman—Juliet smiled. "I don't mind at all, Mrs. Craft. How are you?"

"Not good. Not a bit." She stepped close, lowering her voice. "I'm bound up on one end and spewing out t'other. My cramps ain't gone like Mr. Scather promised, neither. I've got poundin' in my head and in my heart. Worse, I'm seein' things ne'er meant for human eyes. Oh, miss, I'm worse off than before, that's what."

"I am so sorry to hear that." Gently, she squeezed Mrs. Craft's arm. "Laudanum has its place, of course, but not for your condition."

"I know that now, which is why I must ask for that yarrow ye set aside. Ye still have it, don't ye?"

"I do—or rather, Aunt Margaret does." Her fingers curled around the edge of her sleeve as she calculated how long it would take to walk to her aunt's, return to Mrs. Craft's here in town, and then make the trek out to Bedford Manor. It had been concession enough that Henry allowed her to attend church on her own. Straying so far without his knowledge or permission would be a strain on his trust. Then again, if he truly believed he had scared off Mr. Parker last night, he might very well dismiss her altogether upon her return. So, perhaps it would be best to stop at the manor before going to her aunt's.

She patted the lady's arm. "How about I bring you some later this afternoon? Will that suit?"

"Aye, miss. God bless ye. And here's a farthing for yer trouble." She pressed a coin into Juliet's palm before waving farewell.

Juliet ran her thumb over the warm metal. Only a few weeks ago, she'd been desperate for money, and now here she was, being handed a coin without even angling for it. She glanced at the sky, a thank-you on her tongue. . .until she remembered she still wasn't talking to God.

A strange melancholy draped over her shoulders as she tucked the farthing into her reticule and set off down the street.

Moments later, wheels rumbled against cobblestones, and a fine white carriage with polished brass fittings came into view. Two black horses—manes and tails braided with green ribbons—strutted along, proud as the September sun. An embellished *W* graced the side door, painted with gold leaf, and the emerald curtains were drawn back. Clara Whitmore gave a small wave, then ordered her driver to stop just past where Juliet stood.

"Juliet!" Clara leaned out, her expression bright with genuine surprise. "What a delight to see you. I confess, I half expected you to be at Bedford Manor as I didn't spot you at church this morning."

"I do not attend the same church as the Russells."

"Oh?" Clara's brows rose in mild surprise, her smile remaining easy. "I assumed you all worshipped together."

"Henry did ask," Juliet admitted, "but I prefer the quiet of Harpur. It suits me better."

"Quite understandable. St. Paul's is always so dreadfully crowded. I imagine Harpur must be a pleasant change." Clara waved her fan lazily. "Will you be much longer at the manor? I only ask because I'd hoped to invite you for tea and Henry seems to be keeping you on a short lead."

Good question. And when Henry did finally release her from their bargain, then what? She couldn't very well go back to poaching on his land. If only there were a legal way to sell her aunt's medicinals without having to pay for licensure. Mrs. Craft had shown there certainly remained a need for them, as well as for her aunt's wisdom.

"I'm not entirely sure how long I will be there," Juliet hedged.

"Well, if you are free tomorrow, you must join me. I've a fitting in town for the charity ball, but afterwards, we could sit and chat. I'd love to hear more about your time here." Clara smiled, warm and open. "Henry's always so careful with his words, and a woman's perspective is much more interesting."

Juliet forced a smile of her own, scrambling for something vague. "Perhaps. If schedules align."

"I do hope so. It's such a rare pleasure to meet someone new in Bedford." She rapped her fan against the door. "Well, I won't keep you. Mother's waiting. Until tomorrow, perhaps?" Clara gave a cheery wave. "Drive on."

As the carriage rolled away, Juliet let out a slow breath. If Clara suspected anything, she didn't show it. Only a woman curious about a newcomer—and possibly protective of a man she cared for.

Juliet strolled onwards, turning onto the lane leading to the manor. It was cooler here, beneath a canopy of coloured leaves. The loamy fragrance of autumn was magical in its scent. She wouldn't be surprised in the least to come across a fairy or woodland nymph on such an enchanted morn.

But all those charming notions flew from her head the moment she heard a low moan from the side of the road. Alarmed, she veered aside and peered into the undergrowth, only to spy Mr. Dankworth pressing his fingers against a rather nasty goose egg on his head. "Mr. Dankworth! Are you all right?"

His brows drew into a dark scowl. "Eh?"

She edged closer, cautious. "Do you need help? That is quite a bump you have suffered."

"No," he growled, lumbering upright with a sway that flattened the bracken beneath him. "I'm fine."

"You do not look it." She scanned the woods beyond him, an uneasy prickle rising along her spine. "What happened?"

"I was out walking. There's no law against it." He jerked his head towards the trees. "Ran afoul of some fearsome roots on those alders, blasted things."

Juliet looked hard at the spot. Sure enough, there were roots. . .and also the perfect vantage point to spy on the lane to the manor—the very lane Charity would travel along on her way home from church.

"You were off the road, then?" Juliet asked.

He sniffed, a sly grin twisting his mouth. "Sometimes the crow flies where the fox won't tread. And a man, well. . .a man's feet follow his secrets."

Her stomach tightened.

"I haven't seen you in the woods lately," Mr. Dankworth went on, eyes narrowing. "Though I hear you've been cozy with the Russells."

She stiffened. "How would you know about that?"

"I may keep to myself, but I am not blind," he muttered. "A man notices things. Especially when someone new strays into places they don't belong. The owl sees by night what the day won't tell. A girl as lovely as sunshine."

A girl?

She squared her shoulders. "Are you watching me, Mr. Dankworth? Or Charity Russell?"

His laugh came sudden and loud, sending the crows screaming skyward. But the humour died quick as he stabbed a finger her way. "You'd be wise to watch yourself. Not everything hiding in these woods means you well. The tree that looks sound may be hollow inside."

And with that cryptic warning, he staggered off, melting into the greenery like he'd never been there at all.

Gnawing the inside of her cheek, she continued on her way. Henry had seemed certain his stern warning to Mr. Parker last evening would put a stop to his sister's torment, but after this odd encounter, she wasn't quite as sure. There was something off about Mr. Dankworth—and always had been. He was a shadow gatherer. A lurker. The reclusive sort who might fixate on a woman with only heaven knew what going on in his mind. And he certainly paid close attention to the manor.

She glanced over her shoulder, half expecting to catch sight of his dark eyes peering at her from the foliage at the side of the road.

Perhaps Henry had been wrong. Perhaps it wasn't a jilted suitor who plagued his sister, but a rambling, unhinged man who hid away in his house in the woods.

The moment Henry stepped through the doors of Bedford Manor, he doffed his hat and set it on the entry table, then immediately loosened his cravat. Ahh, that felt better. Naturally it was right to dress smartly for Sunday services, but there was nothing like peeling off starched garments for something more comfortable.

Charity untied her bonnet ribbons as the footman approached, his footsteps muted against the Turkish runner. "A delivery arrived during your absence, sir. I left it on the salver in the drawing room."

"Thank you, Woodley." His gaze flicked to the stairs, the temptation strong to first go change into his worn linen shirt and woolen banyan—a perfect ensemble for a lazy Sunday afternoon. . .one well deserved after all the stress of late.

But curiosity won out.

He strode down the corridor, Charity on his heels. His lips slanted into a smirk. "I thought your shoes were too tight." After entering the drawing room, he swiped up a thick packet.

"I thought your frock coat was too stiff. We are a pair, are we not?" She smiled. "But a delivery on Sunday morning is too unique to pass up. I'm just glad for once it is you to receive a mysterious post."

"Hopefully last evening will stop any further posts for you."

He hesitated, knife in hand as his thoughts rolled back to the previous night, to how Juliet had looked wrapped in his coat. She'd been small yet fierce as ever in that oversize garment, clutching the lapels close at her neck. Her scent of rosemary and leaves, feminine and fragrant, had pleased him all the way to church and back this morn. There was something fundamentally intimate in knowing she'd taken his warmth as her own as she'd snugged the fabric tight against her body.

And that was a thought he ought not linger on.

With relish, he broke the seal on the envelope then pulled out two tickets stamped for Italy and waved them in the air. "But even if I have put a stop to Parker's nefarious dealings, that does not mean you cannot still take a holiday. I have arranged for you and Miss Potter to travel next Friday and will send a message for Father tomorrow."

"Miss Potter? Really, Henry. Even were I to consent to go—which I have not—I could hardly do so with Miss Potter's hats taking up the bulk of our luggage allowance." She folded her arms, a perfect little pout sketched on her lips. "Besides, as you've said yourself, you took care of things last night."

"I believe I did, but it might take some time for Parker to cool down. It is still a good idea for you to leave."

"I will not be shipped off like a troublesome child. Besides, the ball is next Saturday. Everyone expects me, and I will not miss it."

He tucked the ship vouchers back into the envelope, a glower of his own tugging at his brow. "It is a silly social event. I will make your excuses, and no one will think anything of it."

"*I* will think much of it!"

He slammed the envelope onto the salver, rattling the water carafe. "This is your welfare we are talking about. Do not be so vain."

"Vanity has nothing to do with this. After weeks of living in fear, hiding away behind the walls of this house"—she flailed her arms, nostrils flaring—"I finally have the chance to emerge freely back into society. I need this, Henry. I need this more than an unwanted Italian holiday."

He blew out a long breath, the desperation in her voice nearly unraveling his resolve. "Look, Charity, I understand your frustration. It has been a trial indeed. But please, at least consider the ramifications. Parker will be at that ball. There is no sense in enticing him back into his nefarious dealings."

"Oh, Henry." Rising to her toes, she pressed her palm to his cheek. "My sweet elder brother. You cannot protect me forever, you know."

"True, but as long as you are my charge—and you are until Father returns—then I will make sure no harm befalls you."

"I don't see how it can when you are on watch."

Ahh, victory. He grinned. "So, you will go to Italy?"

She pulled away her hand. "I did not say that. I—"

Crash!

Charity gasped. "What on earth?"

Henry charged into the corridor, boots striking hard against the flooring, his pulse hammering.

There lay Great-Grandmother Catherine's portrait—the gilded frame split in two, the proud matriarch's face marred by a jagged rip through her painted cheek.

Woodley stood nearby, white as chalk, his hands wringing like a guilty schoolboy's.

"What the devil happened?" Henry barked.

Woodley flinched. "I—I never meant—"

"What's this?" Mrs. Hamby stormed up to them, face pinched into horror at the damaged heirloom. "Oh no. That portrait's been there since your grandfather's time."

"I. . ." Woodley's Adam's apple bobbed several times. "I don't know, ma'am. I swear, it seemed off. I thought. . .I thought I'd fix it."

Henry stared hard at the man. "Fix it?" he echoed, voice low. "Such a task is not your place. You know this. Or were you perhaps loitering to hear the conversation in the drawing room and stood a little too close to the portrait?"

"No! I was only—" Woodley broke off, swallowing hard.

The lie hung there—thin and weak.

Henry let the moment stretch until Woodley's gaze dropped. "See that you do not overstep again. You have duties enough without turning your hand where it is not wanted. Next time I catch you sniffing around what's not yours, you'll be off these grounds before the dust settles."

"Yes, sir." He hung his head.

Mrs. Hamby sniffed. "I'll tend to this. You needn't worry yourself, sir. I shall see about repairing the damage." She paused, producing a slip of paper. "This came a few minutes ago. A village lad brought it for Miss Charity—bolted before I could ask who sent him."

Charity glanced at him as she held out trembling fingers.

He stayed her hand with a gentle touch. "How about if I glance at it first?"

Her shoulders sagged as she nodded.

"Thank you, Mrs. Hamby." He collected the note, then once again returned to the drawing room, Charity's steps not quite so eager this time as she followed.

He strolled to the window, his back towards his sister, and shook open the paper in a stream of sunshine.

Beware those you trust
And more those you doubt.
What seems at an end
Has yet to play out.
Fly away, little bird
Fly away while you can.
Fly away far and fast
Fly away or. . .

Henry's jaw locked. And from the corner of his eye, he swore—just for a second—he saw Woodley's pale face peeking in from the hall.

Chapter 12

A few spare crickets chirruped in the gathering dark of Bedford Manor's woods, welcoming Juliet back to her old haunt. The familiar rush of possible danger pulsed through her veins. She'd missed this thrill of the hunt. The hush between the trees. The eerie screech of a barn owl calling like an old friend.

And yet this time was also distinctly different.

She dared another peek at the master of the estate, walking several paces to her right. He was a distraction, this man, but it was not to be helped. Henry's dark form stalked like a panther, determined, stealthy, a predator to be feared. . .but what she really ought to fear was the growing admiration for him she could no longer deny.

She blew a quiet sigh. It had been with mixed feelings she'd returned from church earlier that afternoon, fully expecting him to release her from their bargain. To pack up and go back to Aunt Margaret's and resume her former life. Instead, with great surprise—and alarm—she'd listened as he'd read her the threatening letter that had been delivered for Charity. Apparently Mr. Parker had ignored Henry's warning of last night. . .unless Mr. Parker wasn't the one responsible for the harassment. And Mr. Dankworth had clearly been on the road to town, so it wasn't out of the realm of possibility that he'd hired a village lad to deliver that dastardly note.

Henry's gaze sought hers, his voice not much above a whisper.

"I trust you found your aunt well today."

"Yes, thank you very much. I appreciate you allowing me to visit her. It was quite kind of you." Guilt nipped her conscience. Her aunt hadn't been her only stop, for after that she'd delivered the requested yarrow tincture to Mrs. Craft.

"All I did was grant you permission. Hardly the makings of a hero," he murmured.

"That's a lie." She smirked.

He stopped, head cocked. "What do you mean?"

And that, right there, was one of the very things that drew her to him. The man had no idea how much his generosity benefited those around him.

"It is heroic what you have done—what you *are* doing, I should say. You could have had me arrested, sent me to my death, yet you did not. And now my aunt is flourishing in the care of the nurse you hired. She is well fed and not fretting anymore about the roof falling in on her head, for the repairs on her cottage are coming along quite nicely. Not many men are as generous, leastwise not those I have known, and those who are seldom let the world forget it."

"So"—a slow smile lifted his lips—"you think me a hero, do you?"

"Careful." She snorted. "Pride goes before a fall."

A light chuckle rumbled in his chest, competing with the snuffling of a nearby hedgehog. "You sound as dour as your Reverend Mr. St. John. No doubt he gave the parish a blistering this morning. Why are you drawn to such bleak services?"

A valid question, one not even she was sure how to answer, so she simply shrugged. "I suppose there is truth to what he says. Or maybe I am a morbid soul given to self-flagellation."

"No. You are no cowering hen. As much as I do not like Mr. St. John's style, I imagine he tries to impart truth, and I concede that it is sometimes the harsher words of wisdom that keep us grounded, so to speak. The book of Proverbs certainly is blunt. Perhaps, at times, such abrasiveness is what is needed to break down the walls we build around our hearts."

She shook her head. She'd had enough abrasiveness in the past year to last a lifetime. "Sometimes a barrier serves a noble purpose."

"And yet if those walls are built too high, light cannot penetrate. Nor can love."

Pah. Such words were the privilege of a heart exempt from life's cruelties. She had cut herself off on purpose—to survive. She *needed* to be a fortress against vulnerability. She would never allow herself to be as exposed and helpless as she'd felt when her father's greed destroyed their family. His weakness had condemned him to suffer a miserable death alone in a gaol cell. That would not be her fate. She would make certain of it.

Yet deep in a dark corner of her soul, Henry's words struck a chime. One she hadn't heard in years. The faint echo whispered of a time when she'd held firm to her faith. A time when she'd been innocent enough to trust in someone she'd loved.

She shoved the memory aside, aiming an accusing finger at Henry instead. "You, sir, sound as if you ought to be in a pulpit."

His teeth flashed white in the scant light remaining before dark. "I think I shall stick to being a hero instead of a preacher. I fear I lack the necessary patience to sway hearts."

"Oh, I think not. You have clearly swayed Clara Whitmore to your side."

"Clara and I have known each other since childhood. I am no more than a fixture in her life, like a favourite book on her shelf or a comfortable chair in the sitting room. We are friends, nothing more."

Relief loosened the tightness in her shoulders. A ridiculous response, of course, but one she could not stop. She peered past him, unwilling to let him see just how much his words affected her. "At any rate, it is no business of mine."

"Would that it were," he said under his breath.

At least it sounded like it. She snapped her gaze back to him. "What was that?"

"Hmm? Oh. Nothing." He swept out his arm. "But we did not come out here to while away the time in conversation, did we?"

She eyed him a moment more before she resumed scouting the trail. He was hiding something. Did he harbour some admiration for her? She blinked to keep from rolling her eyes. What a ludicrous imagining. A wealthy gentleman would not look twice at a woman who'd poached on his land.

They walked in silence, the crush of leaves and occasional creak of branches their only accompaniment—until she let out an *oomph* as she stumbled over a root. She shot out her hand to grasp a nearby sapling for balance.

"Are you all right?" Henry's footsteps quickened behind her.

"I am—" The rest of the words lay fallow on her tongue. A small slip of cloth snagged on one of the spindly twigs. She freed the fabric, running her thumb along the length of it. Muslin. *Fine* muslin. With a lacy hem. The sort only a woman of means would own.

And the only one of such stature residing at Bedford Manor was Charity.

"What have you found?" Henry's breath warmed the nape of her neck.

She turned, surprised at his nearness, and handed over the fabric.

The moment he lifted it to eye level, his jaw hardened. "This is my sister's. She trims most of her garments with this custom lace."

"Then either your sister has been running about in these trees, snagging her gown, or someone has left behind a very bold statement." Juliet crouched, studying the ground, annoyed with herself for having disturbed the area where she'd tripped, but then thrilled to see that a snapped stick lay perpendicular to the route they'd taken. She rose with a tip of her head. "The trail leads that way."

Without waiting for a response, she set off, traveling from mossy depressions imprinted with half-heel marks, to rocks disturbed by the same foot that had passed this way. The prints were large but unevenly depressed. Either the man walked with a limp or he'd been carrying something heavy that offset his balance. Or the fellow's boots were simply too big. Whatever, it was too hard to tell in the coming dark of night. Yet with each broken stick or swirl of leaves pushed aside, the more her heart raced with the thought of where this might lead.

Or not—for suddenly all the clues ended.

Slowly, she spun in a circle, studying the ground.

"Why are you stopping?" Henry whispered.

Failure tasted sour at the back of her throat. "I lost the trail."

He glanced around, a slight shake to his head. "Why would it end here? Whoever came this way could not have simply vanished into thin air."

"True, unless they went airborne." She glanced up at the maze of black branches.

"A flying scoundrel?"

"No, just one adept at climbing trees." Though judging by the distance between alders, that wasn't really a possibility. She pressed two fingers to her temple, rubbing little circles to ward off a headache. "Or it could be someone who knew where to step to avoid leaving a trace from this point on, and they are baiting us, drawing us to this dead end on purpose."

"Blast!" Henry growled.

She felt the same way, but even so, she tossed back her shoulders. "The game is not over yet. We will return to the tree where we found the fabric and follow the opposite end of this trail. Perhaps that will give us more clues."

Henry followed Juliet, annoyed that the cad he sought always seemed to be one step beyond his reach. . .and yet he couldn't help but also be grateful for the woman's honesty. It took fortitude to admit she'd lost the trail. Something to be admired.

And he would, if he weren't so frustrated by this fruitless chase. It was his duty to find the man responsible for putting his sister through such anguish, but thus far he'd turned up no solid evidence against any one person. Not even when he'd tracked down the lad who'd delivered the note the other day had he been satisfied. The boy had claimed he'd been in the market when someone pressed a coin and a folded paper into his hand, whispered quick instructions, and vanished into the crowd before he'd even gotten a proper look. Just a voice, a hand, and then nothing. No face. No clues.

Which was no help at all.

Henry clenched his fists as he tromped through dampened leaves, fury competing with a strong wave of helplessness. How many times had he sworn never to feel this powerless again?

At the sapling where Juliet had first found the fabric, she crouched, her keen eye seeking clues. She was a hound on the hunt, determined despite the fact that he'd basically coerced her into this arrangement. This was not her battle, yet here she was, giving it her all. If only he had met her at another time, in another place, with no dire distractions or societal expectations to keep them apart.

But that was an irrelevant thought here in the thick of night, pursuing a ruthless villain with the woman who'd stolen his game.

Juliet faced him with a grim set to her jaw. "We may not know where the man went, but we can trace these tracks to the part of the manor he visited—and I highly suspect it will lead us to your sister's window."

A growl ripped out of him. "Heaven help the rogue when I do catch up to him."

"Yes, I suspect he shall need it." With a faint smile, she pivoted, carefully picking her way through the trees.

And once again he followed, trusting her instinct yet scanning for any signs she might miss—not that he could see as well as she in the growing dark. Her keen senses continued to astound, truly.

Once they cleared the tree line, she picked up speed. Bedford Manor loomed ahead, black against the coming night. On this back side of the house, no warm light glowed behind the windowpanes, making it appear lifeless. Cold. Empty.

Almost like an omen.

Ten paces from the western wall, Juliet turned left. He stopped her with a touch to her shoulder. "My sister's chamber is the other way."

"That may be, but I am following the tracks. They are faint, but deep enough to distinguish where a heel has disturbed the soil."

He ground his teeth. Hopefully this route wouldn't end as abruptly as the last one. For now, he had to trust her. But in the morning, by the light of day, he would ask Carver to do his own search of the grounds for anything she might miss.

"Very well." He dropped his hand. "Lead on."

She turned back to the task at hand, skirting along the edge of sculpted boxwoods moulded against the manor's stone wall. Twenty paces more and she stopped, her face lifting, her lips parting, yet no sound came out.

He followed her gaze, and his blood turned to ice. "Do not tell me this is where the trail ends."

"Very well. I shall not tell you."

"Then I am right. This is where the man stood, is it not?"

She remained silent, but the dark gleam in her eyes told him everything he needed to know.

For a long moment, he pinched the bridge of his nose and closed his eyes. That patch of flattened grass sat directly below the window belonging to Juliet's bedchamber.

And now she was in peril as well.

"It is dark, Henry." Her voice traveled soft and brave on the night air. "I am a simple poacher, not a man hunter. I could be wrong."

"I never should have brought you into my world of troubles. Now *you* are in danger." He flung out his hand.

"I highly doubt that. This is a mind game. Nothing more than to scare me off."

"Perhaps it should."

She planted her fists on her hips. "I do not scare so easily, sir."

"I am aware of that." She truly was a remarkable woman. Still, did he really have the right to allow her to share his burdens at the cost of possible harm to herself? If he suggested ending their bargain here and now, would her pride allow her to retreat, or would she refuse him? The thought twisted his lips into a smirk. He could already imagine that stubborn tilt to her head.

But he had to try.

"Juliet, this threat is getting worse. There is no telling what the man might do to you or my sister. I will have her sent away to safety, and I will have you—"

"What? Thrown into prison?" Dry laughter rattled out of her. "The vaporous threats of an anonymous man are far more innocuous than the hangman's noose."

His chest tightened. Whether the law allowed it or not, did she really think he would stoop to such a violent act? "I would not have you hanged."

"And yet that is the price for poaching," she parried.

"I will not press charges." Widening his stance, he folded his arms, a rock not to be moved. "Besides, you have served me for a fortnight now. I should say that more than covers the game you bagged, hence we are even. I release you from our agreement."

Confusion rippled across her face. "You are an anomaly, sir. Why such mercy for a woman you barely know?"

"Let us simply say I should like to get to know you better and leave it at that." The words tumbled out before he could stop them, yet what was the point in even thinking of taking them back?

For they were true.

She blinked, apparently speechless, and she had every right to be. What sort of man said such a thing when standing beneath a woman's bedchamber window?

She blinked again, but this time it wasn't shock—it was resolve hardening behind her eyes. "No," she said simply.

His brow lifted. "No?"

"I will not walk away. Not while your sister is still in danger."

"But I just released you—"

"You cannot release me from my conscience." Her voice quivered with quiet conviction. "Charity is kind. Brave. She treats me like a person, not a criminal. I won't abandon her. You may have hired me for my skills, but I stay because I care. Do not make me leave."

Her loyalty shook him more than if she'd run. Wasn't this what he'd asked God for? Help? Wisdom? But now, staring at Juliet beneath the very window of her room, he wasn't sure if this was provision. . .or another test. Was he stewarding it rightly? Or simply dragging another soul into danger? Either way, the determined set of the woman's jaw signified she'd brook no further argument on the matter, leastwise for now.

He forced a nonchalant tone. "Look, it is late. I highly doubt anything more will happen tonight, and we are both tired. I shall have Carver inspect the grounds in the morning. In the meantime, I will see you to your room."

"Thank you, but I am quite capable. There is no need to accompany me as if I were a tot afraid of the dark. Good night, Henry." She stepped around him.

"Not so fast." He caught up to her, matching her stride. "I do not deny your courage, Juliet. Please, just humour me. I will not forgive myself if anything happens to you or my sister."

She cast him a sideways glance as if to deny him, yet finally relented with a slight nod of her head.

They walked in silence, more awkward than companionable, and he cursed himself for letting things grow so strained between them. What a fool.

Into the manor, along the corridor, up the stairs, every single step, he could think of nothing to say. An impossibility, really, for he was acutely aware of her at his side, breathing in her rosemary scent, stealing multiple glances at her graceful figure. Moonlight slid through the windows, painting a silver halo atop her dark hair, caressing the curve of her cheek, the hollow of her neck. Her lips pulled into a pout, as if she too wrestled with how to break the sudden awkwardness.

When they finally came to her room, he suspected she was as

relieved as he was. He reached for the doorknob at the exact moment she did, and when their fingers touched, heat against heat, a charge ran up his arm.

She pulled back with a sharp intake of air, her gaze seeking his with questions he couldn't answer.

Even so, he stepped closer, knowing he shouldn't yet helpless to remain apart from her. His hand hovered in the air with an urge to brush back that loose lock of hair, feel its silkiness, feel her. Her luminous eyes locked with his, her lower lip slightly aquiver, not an invitation necessarily, yet neither a denial. Her chest rose and fell noticeably—something he definitely ought not be noticing. There was a line here. A thin one. One he dared not cross.

Should he?

The air between churned with want, need, promise. Yet what could he possibly promise her right now but threat and danger?

He retreated with a small bow. "Good night, Juliet."

"Good night," she said softly, then vanished into her room, closing the door.

The moment the latch clicked, he leaned back against the wall, heart pounding an irregular beat. He didn't have time for this now, and yet here it was, this draw—this irresistible pull—to a woman he suddenly couldn't bear to lose.

He closed his eyes. Hadn't he asked God for help? And Juliet Finch had appeared—resourceful, sharp-eyed, brave. Was she the answer to that prayer or the consequence of his pride?

Because the truth was hard and unforgiving. . .ever since he'd brought her into this, the danger had only grown. More letters. More shadows. Now a man standing beneath her window. This wasn't a solution. This was escalation.

For a moment, he nearly turned on his heel and penned the letter he'd sworn never to write. One word to his father and the man would be on the next ship, walking away from peace and headlong into a storm. But the cost would be more than passage. His father had finally begun to fully live again after his mother's death, to find beauty in the world after years of mourning. No, he could not call him back unless it was truly time—and he wasn't sure if what held him back now was confidence or cowardice. He pressed the heel of his hand to his eyes, suppressing a moan.

Oh God, help me get this right. I cannot afford to fail my father, my sister. . .or Juliet.

Chapter 13

The entire earth was created in six days. Six. And what had Juliet achieved since discovering the patch snipped from Charity's nightgown?

Precious little.

Disgusted with herself, she fiddled with the fur trim on her borrowed pelisse as the coach neared the Bedford Assembly Rooms. All she had to show for the past week was a megrim from scrutinizing the penmanship on a cryptic card.

Farewell to you.

Written in the same nondescript block letters as all the other notes and delivered with flowers for Charity. . .and for her. This time, the boy who'd brought them had conveniently vanished to London, or so Mr. Walton said when she'd enquired—for the young man worked for the greengrocer, after all. And as if that weren't vexing enough, she'd run into Mr. Scather in town, which had sparked yet another pointless row over tinctures and legality.

And then there was Mr. Dankworth. She and Henry had questioned every servant and even trudged to the neighbour's, only for that maddening man to speak about moon phases instead of giving a straight answer—though he did enquire specifically about Henry's sister and seemed to be inordinately interested in her health.

On the cushioned bench next to her, Charity reached over and stilled her hands. "You need not be nervous, Juliet. The only one my brother will be frowning at tonight is me." She arched an indicting brow at Henry, sitting opposite them in the coach.

His scowl deepened, lending him a gothic attraction. "You should have been on that ship yesterday," he grumbled.

The light from the carriage lanterns didn't flicker against his form so much as bow to him. His dark garments—a black coat with silver embroidery on the lapels, a midnight waistcoat and matching trousers—lent him an intensity that stole Juliet's breath. Only the flash of green in his eyes and ivory cravat broke the austere uniformity. Even so, he was an imposing figure, one that commanded attention whether she wished to give it or not.

Charity grabbed the sidewall as the wheels dipped into a rut. "As cochairwoman of the committee that arranged this evening's fundraising soiree, you know I couldn't miss this event. Besides"—she grinned at her brother—"you are too much of a gentleman to drag me to the port kicking and screaming."

Henry planted his elbows on his thighs, leaning forwards. He did not return her smile. In fact, the sharp set of his jaw made it clear he was not playing. "You overestimate me, Sister. If I thought it would work, I'd truss you like a Christmas goose and pack you into a barrel, then load you onto the next dray bound for port."

"Henry, really!" She rolled her eyes.

The passion in his gaze did not relent. Juliet's heart fluttered in response. She had no doubt he would go to any lengths to keep his sister safe. Would to heaven that her own father had felt that way!

Gently, she squeezed Charity's arm. "Your brother merely wants what is best for you, that is all."

"I know." She sighed. "And I will keep my promise. After tonight's gala, I shall take the next ship to Italy. So, no more frowning, agreed?"

The barest hint of a smile played on Henry's lips as he sank back against the cushion. "I make no promises."

With a "Ho now" from the driver, the carriage rolled to a stop. Juliet peered past Charity, catching a glimpse of the Bedford Assembly

Rooms outside the window. How different the stone walls looked by torch flames, so much more regal in the soft glow than in the harsh light of day. Roman columns lined up like soldiers in front of the entry doors, and behind the low-set gabled roof, two upper levels towered above, golden light pouring out the windows.

Henry opened the coach door and jumped down, offering his hand to his sister. Once Charity alighted, he reached for Juliet.

She steeled herself before grasping his fingers—and a good thing too, or she'd have staggered from the twang of his touch through her lace gloves. Just like the night they'd brushed hands at her door, the same heat flashed through her from head to toe. Did he feel the same?

For barely the space of a breath, something sparked in his eyes. Something charged, like the hint of lightning on a stormy night just behind a black bank of clouds. Then, every bit as quickly, it vanished, his expression completely composed as he released her. Had she imagined it?

"Well, ladies, shall we?" He crooked both his arms. Charity took his left. Juliet rested her fingers atop his right, trying not to notice the swell of his muscles beneath his sleeve as he led them into the mix of arriving guests. Inside the lobby, he helped them out of their pelisses and checked their coats, then directed them into the grand ballroom.

Chandeliers glittered like thousands of diamonds over the gathered suits and gowns. Canary-yellow walls added to the enchanting radiance, as did the sconces gleaming along the upper gallery. The hum of conversation filled the room, along with laughter and greetings.

And then—there she was.

Miss Potter, in all her unabashed glory, stood near the punch bowl. Tonight's triumphant hat featured a stuffed owl, an arch of black lace, and what Juliet swore were actual ribbons of spiraled beetroot trailing down like streamers. The woman's audacity knew no bounds, nor did her apparent lack of self-consciousness. Juliet wasn't sure whether to envy her, admire her, or toss the owl a breadcrumb.

The sight drew a reluctant smile, one of the first she'd felt all evening. The familiarity of such an assembly put her at ease, reminding her of better times, whispered praises, the giddy swirlings on a dance floor. This was her element. Her home. A place she'd once commanded with nothing but a smile. . .at least it had been.

But that was in the past now.

She tucked in a stray curl, acutely aware she no longer belonged to this world in her borrowed dress and fake dignity. Were she not accompanied by Henry and his sister, she'd not have been allowed through the door.

"Ahh, Henry. Miss Russell. Good evening." A stocky fellow in burgundy trousers that were far too tight dipped a bow.

Juliet edged behind Henry, allowing them to exchange pleasantries without having to introduce her. Despite the press of partygoers, she hadn't felt this alone in a long time. Perhaps it was the memories crowding her throat that inspired such melancholy. Or maybe it was the fact that once Charity sailed for Italy, she would no longer be needed. Either way, she'd be glad when she could drift off to sleep tonight and escape reality, if only for a few hours.

She scanned the room by instinct, her attention catching on a solitary figure in the corner gripping a glass of blood-red wine that caught the light like a warning. Edwin Parker stood stiff and unsmiling, balanced by his polished cane. Anchored solidly. His eyes locked on Charity with such fierce focus it was as though no one else existed. For a fleeting moment, something unguarded softened the sharp angles of his face. Not calculation. Not disdain.

Longing.

Juliet's breath hitched. Perhaps there was still feeling there—hidden beneath pride and distance. Love, especially when mingled with resentment or regret, could drive a person to strange choices. Whether that made Edwin Parker dangerous was impossible to say—but it was a possibility she could not dismiss outright.

Rising to her toes, she whispered behind Henry's ear. "Mr. Parker is here and has noticed Charity, so be on alert."

The fabric stretched taut across Henry's back, yet his tone gave no hint of alarm as he addressed the man in front of him. "Pardon me, Mr. Hexam. I should not take up all your time tonight."

"Nothing of the sort, my good fellow. I was just about to part ways and visit the punch table. I see Miss Potter and wish to examine her latest millinery conquest. The old girl never fails to surprise."

As Charity bid Mr. Hexam goodbye, Henry turned on his heel, a muscle on his neck standing out like a whip staff. "Where is he?"

Juliet tipped her head. "Over—"

"Henry! I've been waiting for you to arrive." Clara floated over, her ruby earbobs swaying against her stately neck. She truly was a picture, clad in white silk with golden embroidery—her gown a summer day against Henry's winter night. A perfect match to him in every way.

Which oddly chafed.

Clara beamed a brilliant smile, her blue eyes aglow. "Charity, Juliet, you two are heavenly dreams, you look so lovely."

"As do you, Clara." Charity swept her hand from Clara's shoulder to toes. "Your gown is exquisite."

"Isn't it?" She twirled in a graceful circle. The fabric shimmered as it cascaded around her shape, highlighting her curves. "Mrs. Fan did a splendid job, did she not? The most talented seamstress in all of Bedford, I daresay. And oh, Juliet, I had so hoped you would join me for tea after my final fitting, but you"—she turned to Henry with a mock glower—"have been keeping your houseguest far too occupied."

He merely shrugged. "There has been much going on."

"Oh?" Interest curved her lips. "I suppose I haven't been over this week to catch up on all the latest. Nothing bad, I trust?"

"Nothing to concern yourself about." Henry straightened his sleeves as if he hadn't a care in the world. What composure, especially since he had to be itching to confront Mr. Parker.

Charity looped her arm through Clara's, oblivious to any danger. "I really should make sure the silent auction items are in order. Would you like to join me?"

"I would, but the first dance is about to begin and who am I to break the tradition of sharing it with your brother?" She gently pulled away and rested her fingers atop Henry's arm. "Unless, of course, I am presuming too much."

"Well. . ." He paused, then offered a smile to them all. "Far be it from me to dishonour a custom." He glanced at Juliet. "Would you mind accompanying my sister?"

"Not at all."

The lie stuck in her throat like a fish bone. Her eyes lingered on Henry's fine form as he led Clara to the dance floor. Not that she would mind going with Charity to the silent auction, but to see Henry arm in arm with Clara sent a sharp pang of jealousy through her.

More than anything, she wished to be the one at Henry's side.

Henry took his place in the line opposite Clara, just as he had at every other ball he'd ever attended. . .only this time, he wondered what it would be like to take Juliet as his partner. He could, of course, but ought he? Should he indulge in such a pull, or would it only end in ruin?

For him. For her.

And what would his father think—his son, heir to Bedford Manor, publicly admiring a woman society had already cast aside? A woman who'd once poached from their land just to make it to another day. How easily he could overlook that. And wasn't that the trouble? He could hear his father's voice even now, asking if his affections had clouded his judgement. If he'd mistaken recklessness for compassion.

Or perhaps that was his own voice, sharpened by doubt.

The musicians struck the first notes of Purcell, pulling him from his thoughts. He stood at attention while the men on either side of them took a turn. Once they returned to their places, he pivoted around the back of them and then approached Clara.

When they clasped hands, she leaned close. "I trust things have improved for Charity, that there is no more need for her to go to Italy?"

"Actually, she will sail next Friday."

"Oh dear."

He released her fingers, rejoining the line at the opposite end of the set, and when they circled back together, she picked up as if no time had passed. "I thought you had things under control."

He cocked his head. "What things are you speaking of?"

"Oh, you know." She shrugged. "Whatever it is you have Juliet helping you with."

Hmm. A valiant attempt to parry, but he suspected Charity might have told Clara more than he and Juliet would wish. Clara and his sister were best friends, after all.

Once again they joined hands, and he guided her through a series of gentle turns.

"I am sorry, Henry. I know you shall miss your sister greatly." She matched his steps with seamless grace, their movements as comfortable as their friendship. "Is there anything I can do to help?"

Her kindness did much to ease the cynicism that'd been building in his heart. Blast, but he was tired of eyeing everyone with suspicion. "No, but thank you for the offer. You are a good friend."

They separated briefly before she returned to his side.

"I am always at your call, Henry. You have only to ask."

He pressed his fingers against hers, guilt pinching his conscience. After all these years, he took her for granted. She'd been a constant in his life, particularly when his mother had died five years ago, and he was grateful for her. Countless childhood memories bombarded him, from chasing each other about in the garden to sharing secrets beneath the old oak tree.

Loosening his grip, he moved to the outer edge of the formation, then once again returned to the center.

Clara lowered her voice as they came together. "And Juliet? Will you still have need of her once Charity is gone?"

What a dreadful question. He wouldn't have any reason to keep her at Bedford Manor other than that he'd grown accustomed to her smile every morning and conversation at night. "No," he murmured against his will. "She will return to her home."

The thought tasted rancid. Without her, the house would feel unbearably empty. He'd miss her unexpected laughter and—yes—even her bold challenges whenever she did not agree with him. But he could not expect her to stay with him forever.

Could he?

Sympathy flashed in Clara's eyes. "That will be quite a lonely change for you, I imagine."

Indeed—though now was not the time to dwell on such a dismal fact. He forced a smile. "I have plenty to do, what with my father being away. An estate does not manage itself, you know."

Indeed, it didn't, but it wasn't just about keeping books balanced or roofs from leaking. It was about proving himself worthy of the trust placed in him. His father had built the manor into something strong and steady—its roots deep, its reputation untarnished. Henry could not—would not—be the one to falter. He must maintain control. It was his duty. That was what mattered. What defined him. Leastwise he hoped it would.

Because when his father returned, Henry wanted him to find nothing lacking—no cause to regret handing over the reins, and no reason to regret coming home.

Not this time.

"You cannot work all hours." Clara scoffed. "Once your sister is gone, you must come for dinner more often. I will not see you turning into a hermit like Mr. Dankworth."

"You need not worry about me." He offered her a faint smile.

"Of course I shall. You would do the same for me."

Would he? At one time, yes, without question. Yet now his thoughts veered more often to a certain chestnut-haired woman with a defiant tilt to her head. He would always be Clara's friend, but Juliet inspired something much deeper in him. Something that pulled at him with a force he couldn't name, only feel.

Their feet kept time in the final steps, their fingers briefly intertwined before parting. "You are a better friend than I deserve, Clara, and I pray you will meet your match one day."

Her nostrils flared, her fingers flexed—or did he imagine it? Hard to say as they parted for the last time and then reunited as the music slowed to a close. She curtseyed elegantly. He dipped a bow.

Her brilliant smile removed any doubt he'd had about offending her. Clearly she'd taken his remark in stride even though it hinted that his affections lay elsewhere.

"Thank you, Henry. If you will excuse me, I see my mother beckoning me from across the room."

"Enjoy the evening."

"Trust me, I shall." With a wink, she sidestepped him.

Another song began, urging Henry away from the dance floor and the small respite of the normalcy of his former life—the one in which Charity knew no terror. He'd left her in good hands, though. Juliet was as keen to protect his sister as he was—and he still marveled at that. Finding such a woodland sprite that night with one of his bagged grouse had been a blessing in more ways than he'd expected.

Skirting the gathered guests, he strode the length of the ballroom to a set of double-wide doors opposite the main entrance, leading into the silent auction. Three strides past the threshold, his blood turned to ice. Dead ahead stood Charity and Juliet, cornered between a table and the imposing figure of a man in a black suit. The very same one he'd warned away from his sister barely a week ago.

Edwin Parker.

Chapter 14

Gritting his teeth, Henry crossed the room like a storm about to break and planted a hand on Parker's shoulder. Better that than throttling the man. Beyond him, Charity's eyes widened. So did Juliet's.

"Parker." The name flew past his lips hard and sharp. "I would have a word with you."

Parker wrenched away, leaning heavily on his cane, then pivoted. If violence were a foreign language, Henry needed no translation for the hostility darkening his brown eyes. "I require no censure from you, Russell. I was just taking my leave."

"Oh, but I insist." He tipped his head towards the nearest corner.

"Very well," he agreed, though his sucked-in lips looked as if he'd rather keep an appointment with the grim reaper. "I shall humour you, if only to avoid the scene you seem intent on creating."

Without wasting a moment more, Henry strode away. Parker wasn't nearly as quick on his feet, but each of his steps was determined.

"I told you to stay away from my sister," he growled as soon as Parker came within hearing.

Parker planted his feet, staring him down. "I take orders from no man."

"And yet you will have no choice when you are in gaol. I hear turnkeys spare no flying fists when it comes to insubordinate convicts."

"Oh, Russell." Parker shook his head. "I tire of your threats. I have done nothing untoward against Charity, though I can see you do not believe me."

He huffed a snort. "Why should I?"

Parker studied him, an almost-imperceptible twitch tightening his left eye. "If I meant your sister any harm, do you really think I would be stupid enough to be so obvious?"

The thought lodged under Henry's skin like a sliver too far embedded to be removed. Parker's words, his momentary flash of weariness, and the bitterness in his tone didn't add up to a villain bent on frightening a woman to flee her home. And if logic played out and Parker truly did mean ill intent towards Charity, he would likely work harder to remain anonymous instead of approaching her outright at a public function.

Unless he was just trying to throw him off the scent.

No. His fists clenched with a force that trembled up his arms. He could trust no one when it came to the safety of his sister. He wasn't about to lower his guard when so much was at stake.

"I caught you staring at Charity at the Harvest Festival, and now this." He swept his hand towards his sister. "What am I supposed to believe?"

"Believe whatever you like, but do not let your preconceived notions cloud your judgement." Parker advanced a step, the set of his jaw grim. "You may think me many things, but I am no fool. Nor am I an enemy. If your aim tonight is to accuse me, then by all means do so, but I detect there are greater matters afflicting you and your sister."

Henry swallowed. Hard. What on earth had he discussed with Charity and Juliet? Then again, it could be a bluff, a closely held hand of cards that contained nothing but deuces and a useless joker. "Pretty words, Parker, but I do not trust you."

"That is your prerogative." He shrugged one shoulder. "But know this. . .some men are reckless in their anger. I am not one of them. Despite what you or she may think, I would do anything to ensure her well-being."

"Hah!" he spat. "Many a lie is garbed as a truism."

"Then I suppose it is up to you to decide which it is. In the meantime, keep your distance from me or you may find yourself on the wrong side of those bars you are so quick to lock me behind." He rapped the end of his cane against the tile. "And with that, I bid you good night, for I find I tire of this whole charade."

He bypassed him with a swing of his cane against Henry's shin. An accident?

Or a power play?

~

Juliet tensed as Henry strode away with Mr. Parker, the man's uneven gait a detriment to keeping up with Henry's long legs. Henry's steps were measured but not stilted, his voice hadn't rasped, nor his face hardened into a mask of steel. But a layer beneath that reserve? Fury boiled. She sensed it in her gut, unsure whether she ought to admire his restraint or be unnerved by the simmering intensity of it. Either way, there was no denying he was a passionate man...which blew life into a reckless, foreign craving to be the one who evoked that fire.

Then be the one to calm it.

Charity stepped closer to her, the slight rustle of her silk skirts blending with the music filtering in from the ballroom. A few eager patrons filed in the door and, upon seeing her and Charity, strolled to the farthest table loaded with auction items.

"Perhaps," Charity murmured, "we should stop this before Henry does something we are all sure to regret. It's not as if Mr. Parker said anything patently offensive."

"True." She pulled her gaze from Henry. "Yet sometimes the danger lies not in a person's words but in the spaces between them."

Charity bit her lip, one finger brushing absently along the scrolls of a silver candelabra on the auction table. "You don't understand. That's just his way."

"You defend him?" Interesting. Did she harbour feelings for the man? Juliet peered deeply into the woman's eyes, seeking truth. "Do you regret breaking things off with Mr. Parker?"

Charity glanced over her shoulder, clearly seeking the object of their conversation. He stood as a ramrod, face a mask, apparently repelling whatever Henry said with posture alone. At length, she once again faced Juliet. "No. What was between us could not have been. Not then. I did the right thing."

"And now?"

"Now?" She glanced up at the chandeliers as if the answer might be found in candlelight. "No," she whispered, then snapped her eyes back to Juliet. "No," she repeated louder. "I suspect we are very different people than who we used to be, though I confess I don't wish to see him like this."

Juliet watched Parker thoughtfully. He had come upon her and Charity so quickly she'd had no time to steer her friend out of his path, and though he'd said little, the sheer force of his presence had required of her a conscious effort to withstand. "Well, he certainly is bitter. And blunt. He had no right to comment on Henry's choices—or mine. He does not even know me. And how did he hear you were planning to leave for Italy?"

One of her slim shoulders rose, the golden organza on her gown shimmering in the light. "He's always had a way of knowing things about me, which I admit is unnerving. But I don't believe he meant any harm in greeting me here tonight."

"Maybe not, but there's something about the way he speaks—as if everything is a test. I could be wrong, but I can't seem to shake the feeling that he wants me gone. . .or did during our conversation. I think he wished to speak to you alone. Though, I suppose he didn't say any of that aloud. It was more the tone. The way he asked about my presence here. Not suspicious, exactly—just. . .guarded."

Charity laid her fingers on her sleeve, giving a little squeeze. "Mr. Parker enjoys being perplexing. You are giving him more power than he deserves."

Was she? He hadn't threatened her, not directly. And still, the way his voice dropped when he spoke—low, deliberate. Calculated.

It echoed in her mind. . . *"Be careful whom you trust."* That had been his parting remark. It could have been a warning. Or it could've been genuine concern. She didn't know him well enough to be sure.

"I just don't trust him," she said softly. "Not yet. Charity, tell me true, do you think he is resentful enough to be the one behind the letters, the flowers, the threats?"

"Edwin Parker is a complex man. Difficult at times. Imprudent at others. But. . ." Her gaze crept to the two men huddled in the corner, her lips pursing before she continued. "He loved me once—ardently—and a love like that never really fades." She looked back at Juliet. "Does it?"

"Perhaps not, but bitterness can cause love to twist into a distorted version of what it used to be. Something sharp, cutting deeper than any blade." She pressed her hand to her chest as her own words sliced into her. She'd harboured—nay, cherished—bitterness for so long now that it'd carved a hole where a soft heart had once beaten. She'd clung to her father's betrayal, the immense pain of it, like a drowning woman holding to a log, all the while not realizing the very thing she'd held on to might eventually pull her under. Forever. *She* was the one twisted. The one still bleeding from a wound she refused to bind.

But how to break free from that which she'd embraced for so long?

A sigh breathed out of Charity. "I suppose that is why forgiveness is so vital. The worst of us—even Mr. Parker—deserves such mercy, for is that not why our blessed Saviour came to earth in the first place?"

"Oh, how I envy your faith," Juliet whispered, the admission slipping out before she could trap it behind her teeth.

Charity angled her head. "What was that?"

"Nothing." Bah. This strange fire in her chest was far more than nothing. She smiled against the sting of tears. She hadn't felt such a stirring in her soul since before her father's disgrace, a yearning not just to believe in God, but to trust in Him, to surrender and be at peace.

And oh, what she wouldn't give for a little peace.

"Look, here comes my brother." Charity rose to her toes, neck craning. "And there goes Mr. Parker."

Henry swooped over like a bat from a cave, coattails flapping behind. "We are leaving at once."

"Don't be ludicrous. The auction hasn't even begun yet." Charity picked up the candelabra as if her brother required tangible evidence and, after waving it about, gently replaced it. "Besides, it appears whatever you said to Mr. Parker has caused him to flee. Can we not enjoy the rest of the evening?"

"I will enjoy nothing until I know you are safe." He reached for her arm. "Now come along."

Charity flashed Juliet a wide-eyed plea to do something.

But what?

On impulse alone, Juliet sidestepped between the two, staring directly into Henry's eyes. "Dance with me."

The bold request dangled in the air between them, too preposterous to ignore. She might as well have asked him to perform a minuet across a graveyard. He blinked, lips parting as if to reply, yet nothing came out.

And no wonder. She couldn't have said anything more herself if the King commanded it. What had possessed her to suggest such a thing? He was her employer, not some lovesick beau.

"I. . ." He cleared his throat. Whatever he'd intended to say died an inglorious death on his lips, the look on his face completely inscrutable.

"Go on, Henry." Charity's fingers shooed him away over Juliet's shoulder. "I shall find Clara and be well tended. Put your mind on something else."

He stared at Juliet, a slight downturn to his mouth, as if he could not believe he'd been put in such an impossible situation. She ought not even be here pretending to be a lady of status—and they both knew it. But then, surprisingly, the hard line of his jaw softened slightly, as did the intensity of the green in his eyes, though he still said nothing. He was too much of a gentleman to refuse her outright.

Juliet forced her mouth into a smile, though it probably looked more like a grimace. "If you would rather not, I shall be happy to—"

Before she could finish tossing him a verbal lifeline, he pivoted with grace, his elbow crooking. "Would you do me the honour of taking a turn with me on the dance floor, Miss Finch?"

His voice was deeper than usual, more of a rumble. All in all, it was a proper invitation, but one coerced by her own rash tongue. She ought to politely decline and release him from any obligation he might feel. And she would have, were it not for the nudge from Charity causing her to stumble forwards.

Reluctantly, she perched her fingers atop his sleeve, and the moment she did so, he strode off with long steps as if to war. She double-timed to keep up with him, tension radiating off him in waves. His arm was a steel beam beneath her touch. Either her suggestion to dance had irritated him beyond measure, or he was still wound tightly from his conversation with Mr. Parker. Judging by the way he scanned the ballroom with a razor-sharp gaze, it was likely the latter.

The first strains of a waltz filled the air. Couples gathered, ladies' gowns floating across the expanse like flower petals caught in a swirl of water. Henry stopped just past the ring of onlookers, so preoccupied she doubted he even registered the scene—or her.

She squeezed his arm, hoping to draw him out of his dark thoughts. "Be at ease. Mr. Parker is gone."

"Maybe so." His eyes narrowed as he swept the room for a final time before returning his attention to her. "But his threats linger."

Without warning, he grabbed her hand, his other arm snaking around her back, then pulled her into position as if she were a dragon to wrestle. His first pivot swung her wildly around, his grip relentless as he guided her through the turn.

She frowned up at him, fighting to keep her balance. "Do you always dance like a barbarian?"

He peered down the length of his nose at her, a flicker of amusement in his eyes. "You think me a philistine, do you?"

In this moment, absolutely, and she almost recanted of her earlier wish to be the recipient of his passion. But it wasn't her who had incited such harsh behaviour.

"I think"—she paused as he turned her once again—"that you bear the world on your shoulders when it is not yours to carry."

His steps slowed slightly, his palm pressing a little lighter against hers as their alternate arms rose, framing an arch over their heads. "My world holds precious cargo I would not see damaged." His voice was husky with emotion that surely came from a very deep well.

Her breath tangled someplace between her ribs and her heart. Oh, to be the one who inspired such devotion. "Your sister is a lucky woman."

"I do not speak of only her."

Her heart raced at the way he looked at her.

He bent nearer and whispered, "I lied, you know."

"About what?" Oomph. Was that squeak really her voice?

"When I said I would enjoy nothing until I knew Charity was safe." His breath feathered against her neck, spreading a wildfire through her veins. "I am enjoying this immensely."

A soft *humph* snorted out of her. "I bet you say that to all the poachers."

"No." His gaze held steady. "Only you."

Her throat went dry, a nervous laugh barely eking past the tightness. "This might have been a bad idea."

He smiled faintly. "Probably the worst ever."

"And how will we rectify such a mistake?"

His smile deepened, part gent, part pirate. "Perhaps we shall simply have to start over and try another dance."

Her heart banged against her ribs, for there was honestly nothing more she'd rather do.

Once again he led her through a spin, then pulled her close. "Well?" he prompted. "What say you?"

"I say you are very adept at the game of dance floor romance."

He flashed an irresistible smile. "Oh, but I am not playing."

Of course he had to be, but it stole her breath to realize that she desperately did not want this to be a charade. Somehow, despite the difference in their social stations, no matter the fact that she'd been caught stealing the very meat from his table, the pull of this man was more than she could resist.

The music stopped. So did they, but he did not release his hold.

"Henry, the dance has ended," she prompted.

"Has it?" His gaze held hers with promises yet to be spoken.

Whispers shushed around them, those closest questioning the meaning of their ill-mannered refusal to leave the floor. For half a second she considered ignoring them and living forever here in his arms, but for the sake of his reputation, she murmured, "We should get back to your sister."

A sheepish smile crept across his lips. "Yes, I suppose we should."

Spell broken, she followed him to where Charity huddled next to Clara, both engaged in a conversation with a gentleman in a very fine frock coat with buff trousers. His back was towards their approach.

But Clara saw them very plainly, for something green flashed in her eyes. "I was beginning to wonder if you two were going to snub us the rest of the evening."

"And yet," Charity chimed in, "we have been highly entertained in your absence. Allow me, Brother, to introduce a new acquaintance."

The man turned, and when he did, Juliet's blood drained to her feet, leaving her icy cold. She didn't need to hear Charity's introduction, for she knew him intimately well.

Colin Chamberlain.

Her former betrothed.

Chapter 15

"Juliet Finch. Fancy seeing you here."

Juliet clenched her hands so tightly, her knuckles cracked. Of all the horrible surprises, this snake had to show up at *this* ball?

Colin locked eyes with her, a smug tilt to his head, the cleft in his chin more pronounced. He'd always been prideful of that Chamberlain feature. It shamed her now to think she'd once admired it. Admired him. But so had all the other ladies of Cheltenham. He'd made sure of it. And to think she'd fallen victim to that charm.

Henry looked between them. "You know each other?"

"We. . ." She swallowed hard, despising the shrewd gleam in Colin's dark eyes. He was waiting to hear how she'd answer. His words had been nothing but a platter with a sharp knife, poised to slice apart anything she might say.

Well. So be it.

"We are acquainted," she said simply.

"Unfortunately." Colin snorted, almost covering the word.

"Agreed," she whispered. Would to heaven she could travel back in time and remedy that mistake.

"Oh!" Clara clapped her hands, beaming. "A reunion of friends. How lovely. And extraordinary, being that neither of you are from Bedford."

"That is a coincidence," Charity joined in.

"Quite." Colin narrowed his eyes. "What are you up to, Juliet?"

"*Miss Finch*"—Henry stepped closer to her, her name on his lips a shield, a defense, as was the sharp lift of his brow—"is here at my request."

"Your request, eh?"

Juliet's pulse thudded in her ears. That look in Colin's eyes—sharp and almost eager—wasn't new. It was the same look he'd worn when delivering the final blow to their engagement. He'd called it duty to his family's good name, but she saw it now for what it was—a retreat. A carefully measured escape from a match that might have tarnished the shiny facade he took great pains to polish. And yet here he stood, acting as if she were the one who'd wronged him. Her stomach soured. It wasn't enough that he'd abandoned her. Now he meant to destroy her standing with these new acquaintances too. Perhaps especially with Henry. All for spite. Or wounded pride.

Probably both.

Colin faced her with a tug to his cuffs. "How very accommodating you've become." He clicked his tongue with a sad shake of his head. "Just like your father. . .and look where that landed him."

The music restarted, light and merry, nothing like the stormy ire sparking in Henry's eyes. "What are you insinuating about the lady?"

"Lady?" Colin chuckled lightly.

A low growl rumbled in Henry's throat. If she didn't stop this now, fisticuffs would fly right here beneath the crystal chandeliers.

Smoothing her skirts, she forced a light tone to her voice. Quite the feat, that, when she'd rather scream and run away. "Mr. Chamberlain is wont to make cryptic responses. Please pay him no mind. It is a particular pastime of his."

"Much like Mr. Parker." Charity snapped open her fan, cheeks suddenly flushed.

"Intriguing!" Clara turned to Henry. "Will you join in the game as well? Do indulge us. I am all attention to hear what you might have to say."

He didn't spare her the slightest glance. "What I have to say is that I find your comments to Miss Finch to be quite boorish, sir."

Before Colin could respond, Charity's voice cut in, sharp and clear. "I agree. Your remarks, Mr. Chamberlain, are not only inappropriate but entirely uncalled for."

Colin wrapped his fingers around his lapels. "I apologize if I have offended you, Miss Russell, Mr. Russell." He gave a small, stiff nod to each in turn. "But I speak only what is true. Perhaps Juliet has not informed you of her history."

Juliet's heart stuttered, the polished floor feeling unsteady beneath her borrowed slippers. Henry knew her for who she was—mostly—but Charity and Clara had no idea of her disreputable past, nor did she wish them to. "This is neither the time nor place to speak of such things, Mr. Chamberlain."

"And yet," Colin fairly purred, "here we are."

"Indeed, what fate!" Clara bounced on her toes, apparently oblivious to the charge in the air. "I adore it when circumstances converge so curiously."

Henry didn't, not if the rock-hard line of his jaw was any indication. "I am well aware of Miss Finch's history, sir."

"Are you? I wonder." Colin's gaze slid back to Juliet, the dark curls at his temples falling into his eyes. He brushed them back with a swipe, his lips flattening to a malicious line. "The Finches are well known for presenting to the world a sparkling front, when all the while they carry on with their nefarious deeds behind the backs of the unsuspecting."

Fury churned in her belly, at odds with the sweet melody wafting from the dance floor. The accusation, the shame of it all, this was her father's doing, not hers. She jerked her face up to his. "That is quite enough."

Charity stepped closer to her, brows drawn. "What does he mean, Juliet?"

"Nothing of importance," she murmured.

"And so we will leave it at that." Henry's voice cut through the revelry around them.

"Very well." Colin swiped a champagne flute from a passing tray and drained it in one go. "But a word to the wise from a man with experience. This woman is not to be trusted. I should know, for I barely escaped becoming her husband."

Clara and Charity gasped in unison.

Henry turned to her, a tempest of confusion and horror in his eyes. "Is this true?"

"I—" Nausea rose, choking off her words. Suddenly she was thrown back to a year ago, facing the same incredulity, suffering the burn of humiliation. She was a stain upon this society. A black mark everyone wished to erase. Would this nightmare never end?

Pressing one hand hard against her belly, she shouldered her way past Colin and fled the ballroom. A cowardly move to be sure, but wholly irresistible. Cold air slapped her face as she shoved open the door to an empty veranda. No one was out there. And just as well. The hot tears streaming down her cheeks would not be stopped.

She dashed to the railing and held on tight, waiting for the emotion to pass. But it didn't. Shame kept coming in rolling waves, incessant, nothing but distant stars in the black sky to comfort her, for God would not. Nor would she ask Him to. Not again. The fear of not receiving an answer was too overwhelming.

Blast that Colin Chamberlain! She'd tried so hard to run from her past, but here it was like a ghost from a grave, all buttoned up in a bespoke suit.

She gripped the wrought-iron railing, relishing the way the unforgiving metal bit into the palms of her hands. The truth was—she could admit this now that she'd met Henry—she'd never loved Colin. Not really. Nor had he loved her, or he'd not have so casually thrown her aside when her father's disgrace became public. She and Colin had given in to societal expectations, listened to the talk of what a lovely couple they'd made. What a fool she'd been.

Gulping in air, she fought to collect herself. It had been noble of Henry to defend her so boldly, though he'd likely never make that mistake again. Not after Colin's ugly revelation. In hindsight, she should have told him she'd once been engaged. By holding back the full details of her past, she'd completely undermined the trust he'd placed in her. Keeping such a secret would give him the impression she had other dark intrigues to hide.

But it wasn't the dread of Henry's mistrust that sickened her most. No, far worse than that was the knowledge she'd ruined whatever fragile relationship had begun that day he'd caught her in the woods. Since then he'd become her friend, her champion. She'd seen it when his gaze softened on her or his lips curved whenever she chanced to catch him looking her way. She should have stayed in that ballroom, held her head high, met his horrified stare, and shown him she wasn't the awful woman Colin accused her of being. Oh, why hadn't she stayed? A sob ripped past her lips.

She'd fled, just like her father had tried to do when he'd been found out. She was no better than he. She'd wasted the past year scorning the very person she was most like. Her chin dropped to her chest, the realization sapping what little fight she had left. Would that the earth might open up, swallowing her whole, and she could lie down forever. Society wouldn't miss her. Henry probably wouldn't either.

And she couldn't blame him for that.

She inhaled deeply, the cold air an ache in her chest. Would she ever know the peace her aunt spoke of?

Behind her the door opened; music swelled and then muffled as it once again shut. Footsteps drew near—a man's, judging by the deep thud of them. Slow. Deliberate.

She gripped the railing so tightly her knuckles burned. Her heart hoped it was Henry, but it would more likely be Colin come to gloat—the main reason she'd left Cheltenham in the first place, for he'd made life miserable. A coward's habit, she'd later come to realize. Every time he saw her, it reminded him that he'd fled at the first sign of scandal instead of standing beside her as a decent man would. No, a cad like Colin would rather belittle her than admit he'd run off like the scoundrel he was at heart.

Gritting her teeth, she forced her fingers to let go of the iron, determined not to give him the satisfaction of seeing her crumble again. Not tonight.

Not ever.

As much as he hated to admit it, Henry missed his father. Vincent Russell would have known how to handle this situation—how to handle any situation, actually. It was a hard standard to live up to.

But his father was a continent away, unable to advise him now on how to approach the lone woman standing like a cast-off figurine at the edge of the veranda. The bow of Juliet's head cut like a knife. The slump of her shoulders, the defeat and pain pushing her down, squeezed the life out of his chest. And yet with every step closer to her, the echo of Colin Chamberlain's words thudded like an off-key gong.

"She's a conniving vixen, one who will stop at nothing to get what she wants. And if that is you, she will push everyone out of the way to corner you just as she did me."

"She's trouble, Russell. Tainted goods. You'd do best to keep your distance. Had I known she was here, I never would have come."

"Don't say I didn't warn you when she stabs you in the back—and she will. It's a Finch family trait."

Henry stopped a pace behind her, pairing what he'd heard with what he knew of Juliet Finch—and coming up woefully short on how to reconcile the two.

He reached for her, then pulled back his hand as if he might get burned. "What are you doing out here?" The question came out gruffer than he intended.

She spun, eyes wide, cheeks aflame in the light spilling from the ballroom windows. "I—needed a moment. And—you?"

"I needed a moment as well. . .to find out the truth." He paused a beat, praying for wisdom to discern fact from fiction. "I know not

Mr. Chamberlain, and frankly, I do not care to. But I wish you had told me about him. Not because I want to pry, but because I thought we were friends."

"We are! I mean, I hope we still are after. . .well." Once again her head dipped. "I can only imagine what Colin had to say about me after I left the ballroom."

"He had plenty to say all the way to the door, where I deposited him on the front steps."

She jerked her head up. "You escorted him out? Why?"

"My sister and Clara had no need to hear a gentleman berate you. Nor did I." And once again rage fired in his belly. It'd taken all his restraint to keep from throttling the man for the wicked things he'd said about Juliet. "But I must know how much of what he said was true. Were you engaged to that man?"

She bit her lower lip, but even so, she held his gaze. "I was."

The thought of her in Chamberlain's arms—worse, in his bed—hit him like a brick to the head. "I see," he clipped.

"No, you do not." Her pert little nose rose in the air. "I was a different person back in Cheltenham, much like the pampered ladies in that ballroom tonight." She flung her hand towards the assembly hall. "You know society. I played the game and did what was expected of me, as did Colin. There was no love between us."

"Yet you agreed to take his hand?" It was more an accusation than a question.

"I am not proud of what I was, Henry, but yes, I did. Have you never made a mistake in all your life?"

The air chilled, or was that his own shame snaking cold down his back? He'd made plenty of errors, most notably those that disappointed his father. The time he'd trusted a buyer against his father's wishes and incurred a considerable loss on a shipment of Madeira. The year he'd forgotten to inspect the tenant farmers' harvest, and mildew had ruined it all. That one panicked letter in childhood when he and Charity had believed the house to be haunted. In all these things, his father had never voiced his displeasure. He hadn't needed to. His silence had been sharper than any scolding. Since then, Henry had measured every cry for help like it was a coin—and feared spending too much.

And now? He was overdrawn. Again.

He kneaded a knot in his shoulder, chagrined to have pointed out Juliet's faults when his were no less egregious. "So," he said in a softer tone, "did you ever love him?"

She shook her head. "I thought I did, but it turns out I did not."

Thank God. Not that it was any of his business, really, but all the same, her answer surely tasted sweet. The steel in his muscles eased, and he dropped his hand.

Still, something about the man lingered like a bitter draught. He needed to know how deep the wound went. How to protect her from being used in such an ill manner ever again, for of all the things he might fail at, he refused to fail in guarding Juliet the way Chamberlain should have.

"Forgive me for asking," he said quietly, "but who ended it—Colin or you?"

She hesitated but a breath. "He did. He said my name was a liability he could no longer afford to be associated with."

Henry's jaw clenched. "Coward. You deserved better."

She gave a dry laugh. "I have yet to meet this mythical 'better.'"

"Well, you have now."

Her brows rose. And no wonder. It had been bold statement... one he refused to take back.

He stepped closer, searching her face. "Are there any other secrets you harbour? Things I should be aware of? You are, after all, living beneath my roof, and as such, are under my protection. I need to know if there are other men who bear you a grudge."

"No. None. You already know of my father's disgrace, my flight to Bedford, my poverty and loss of status." She looked away then, taking sudden interest in the dark line of hedges beyond the railing. "You have seen me at my worst," she murmured.

"But have I seen it all?" he pressed. "I want to trust you, Juliet, but I wonder if I can."

"I wonder the very same," she whispered, then once again faced him, her tone turning to ice. "I have found that trust is a two-sided weapon."

He flinched at the venom in her words. What the deuce? He'd never given her reason to doubt his loyalty. . .had he? He mulled over the past month, since the day he'd first collared her in the woods.

Nothing egregious came to mind.

He met her gaze head-on, as if by stare alone he could make her see truth. "I would never betray you, if that is what you mean."

A bitter laugh choked out of her. "Would that my father, or even Colin, had embraced the same sentiment."

Ahh. So that was it. The two men she ought to have been able to count on, to provide for her, to protect and cherish her as a priceless gift. He certainly would if given the chance.

Gently, he grasped her shoulders and pulled her close, making sure she could hear the veracity in his voice. "What those men did was wrong, but I am not them."

A soft inhale made her chest rise. "No," she whispered, "you are not."

His focus dropped to her lips, to the very mouth he'd been wishing to taste ever since they'd danced. Had Chamberlain taken such a liberty with her? Had she allowed him to?

"Henry, I. . ." Something vulnerable flashed in her eyes. A glimpse of a little girl who didn't know where to lay her head, wondering who would allow her to shore up against a strong shoulder when she needed it most.

Instantly he sobered, dropping his hold of her—not so much a retreat but rather out of respect. "Come. Charity will wonder where we've gone."

No protest, no hesitation. She stepped into motion beside him, and this time, their silence felt companionable. Not all was mended—neither between them nor within them—but sometimes peace reigned even in a storm.

He opened the ballroom door for her and followed her in, swallowed once more by laughter and candlelight, but something inside him didn't settle.

Trust had been offered. Received. And now it lived in his hands—too warm, too weighty.

Too easily dropped.

Chapter 16

Though it was only half past six, dusk had already crept into Juliet's room, pooling in the corners like spilled ink. Setting down her pen, she turned up the wick in her desk lamp. Twilight was always such a melancholy hour. An in-between, just like her. Too poor to belong to society yet too well bred to fit amongst the servant class. . .a truth she'd been chewing on ever since Colin's appearance at the ball five days ago, reminding her of where she'd come from.

And how far she had fallen.

She picked up her pen with a sigh, leaning over her half-finished letter to Aunt Margaret. She really ought to visit the dear woman instead of sending a stilted note, but there simply hadn't been time. Early Monday morning Henry had received an urgent letter from his father about an upcoming wine exhibition, and he'd tasked Henry with organizing the event, inviting key figures, and ensuring the new Italian blend he'd crafted would be presented to its best advantage. That left Juliet to be Charity's constant companion. Thankfully, no new threats had arisen for Charity—though Juliet herself had not been so fortunate. A cryptic note had arrived, urging her to leave the manor as soon as Henry's sister departed for Italy. But, naturally, none of that could be mentioned in her letter to Aunt Margaret.

Juliet rolled the quill between her fingers, thoughts once again straying to the ball, to Henry—and unfortunately to Colin as well.

His wicked smirk had haunted her ever since yet was tempered by the way Henry had smiled at her that evening. A charge still ran through her every time she relived how he'd danced with her and when he'd held her close on the veranda.

A sharp knock rapped on her door. She jumped, bumping the desk and nearly tipping over the ink bottle. "Coming," she called as she set down her pen and covered the ink.

At the door, Charity's lovely smile greeted her. "I hope I'm not disturbing you."

"Not at all. I was just writing to my aunt." She fluttered her fingers towards her desk.

"Then never mind. You must have forgotten our customary turn about the garden before dinner, but not to worry. I shall be fine on my own."

"None of it. You know your brother wishes me to accompany you while he is tied up with your father's business." Reaching aside, she grabbed her warmest shawl from the peg on the wall. "Off we go."

As she adjusted the wool around her shoulders, she glanced at Charity. "I thought you would be tending to last-minute details for your trip tomorrow. What a grand adventure traveling to Italy shall be."

"Yes, I suppose. I don't know." One slim shoulder shrugged before Charity grabbed the balustrade and marched down the main staircase. At the bottom, she paused for Juliet to catch up. "It's no great secret I don't really want to go, but I know it's for the best. I'm just so. . .tired. And I can't seem to shake off this headache. Why, I don't think I'll eat a bite at dinner tonight."

Juliet frowned as she joined the woman's side. "You didn't eat any of the apple tart or elderberry cheesecake at luncheon, either."

"I have little appetite today." Charity looped an arm through Juliet's and then strolled down the corridor. Though she acted perky, now that Juliet looked closely, she did seem a little pale.

"That gift basket Clara brought me," Charity continued, "was far too charming to waste my time eating, anyway. The travel journal, the writing set, and such a lovely little prayer book. Clara is so thoughtful."

"She is a good friend," Juliet murmured as she held open the back door, though her mind wandered. After the ball she'd found out from Charity that the Whitmore family had extended the invitation to Mr. Chamberlain, though Juliet supposed there was little unusual in that. In their sphere, society was a small world—connections interwoven in ways one rarely saw until it was far too late.

Outside, she and Charity traveled the brick walkway to the garden—or rather what was left of it at this time of year. The boxwood still stood out in its finest greenery, but only a few hardy leaves clung to the rose stems. The bite of a coming frost nipped the air.

Charity picked up a fallen leaf and twirled it between her fingers. "It is my secret hope that once I am gone, Henry will finally listen to his heart and pursue the woman he loves."

A tug pulled at her chest. "I'm sure Clara would be pleased to hear that."

"I love Clara dearly, but that wasn't whom I was referring to. I suspect Henry's affections are directed. . .towards a different quarter."

Juliet blinked.

But before she could press for more information, Charity winced, then dropped the leaf and raised trembling fingers to her temple.

Juliet stepped close to her, pea gravel grinding beneath her slippers, and tugged the woman's shawl tighter at her neck. "Are you all right? Perhaps we should go back in."

"Don't be silly." Charity batted her hand away. "The fresh air is already clearing my head and taking away some of the butterflies in my stomach."

"Are you so very nervous about sailing to the Continent?"

"I guess I am. I have never been so far from home before."

Juliet nodded, inhaling the scent of damp earth and decaying plants. She knew exactly how Charity felt. Bedford had seemed a foreign country at first, especially living in her aunt's draughty cottage so far from town. "It is hard to trade what you know for something uncertain. I surely do not fault you for such feelings. But your brother—"

Charity held up her palm. "I know. He wants what is best for me. He cares deeply for those he loves, and so it is for his sake I am leaving."

Their conversation waned after that, which was just as well. Thoughts of Henry's dedication to his sister crowded out further words, the longing to be the object of such a devotion welling in her throat. Not that her mother and brother hadn't loved her, but to such a degree? Her father had always been too preoccupied with his precious books and ledgers. Of course Aunt Margaret had done her best to make her feel welcomed in her home, but as family, she probably felt it was her duty. An obligation, not a choice.

But Henry, well, there was just something untamed about the way he loved. He was fierce and steady, a solid oak withstanding any storm. What would it feel like to be adored by a man like that, not out of compulsion or shared blood, but for herself alone?

Her thoughts flicked to Charity's earlier words. *"I suspect Henry's affections are directed towards a different quarter."*

Juliet's steps slowed. Had she imagined the look in his eyes the night of the bonfire? Or the heat of his hand brushing hers outside the ballroom—and inside, that waltz? Surely those moments had meant something.

And yet. . .what if she was wrong?

Pah. She kicked at a pebble, watching it skitter into the darkness at the side of the walkway. What an outlandish thought. Despite the small hope she'd harboured ever since he'd spun her around on the dance floor, she—a penniless poacher—didn't stand a chance with a man of Henry's station.

"Juliet." Her name was barely a shiver as Charity pointed a trembling finger.

Tensing, she narrowed her eyes, staring into the shadows where the dark shape of a man stood half hidden behind a towering yew at the edge of the garden. With one quick swipe of her arm, she relegated Charity behind her and picked up a rock. A poor weapon—unless aimed right.

"Who is there?" she asked with more bravado than she felt. "Make yourself known at once!"

The yew rustled as a man sidestepped from it, the hem of his coat pulling a limb along for the ride. It was too dark to make out the details of his face—particularly since he wore a hat pulled low over his brow. He didn't advance any closer, though, thankfully. He just dipped his head. "Miss Finch. Miss Russell."

She knew that raspy voice. Her grip on the rock loosened. While she remained on alert, at least the panicky race of her heart calmed down. "Mr. Dankworth, what are you doing here?"

He ambled a step forwards, boots silent on the grass. "Came by to speak to Mr. Russell...about that wine shipment of his father's. Found him occupied. Didn't seem right to interrupt. A bloom unbidden heralds ruin."

"Then why not wait inside?" Juliet pressed.

Mr. Dankworth's lips curled at the edge—not quite a smile, though. "Walls stifle truth. Folk talk freer when they think they're alone. And the night listens better than any servant." His gaze lingered on Charity. "You learn more in shadow than you ever will in candlelight. That's where the real things whisper."

Juliet's stomach turned. "Enough riddles. State your business or be gone."

"Not an *or* but an *and*. Two birds, you know." His voice dropped low, his gaze fixed on Charity. "But here's a thought for you to chew on—when the crow leaves feathers on your doorstep, is it a gift... or a warning?"

Charity edged closer to Juliet. "Let's go back to the house."

Juliet clenched her jaw. "Next time, Mr. Dankworth...announce yourself."

He tugged his hat lower. "But then the story's already written. I prefer to turn the page when no one is looking. Good night, Miss Finch, Miss Russell." His gaze lingered on Charity to the point that Juliet opened her mouth to confront such boldness.

But then he retreated, melting into the night like he'd never been there at all.

"I don't like the way he looked at me," Charity whispered.

Juliet faced her with a cheerful smile, hopefully easing some of the woman's anxiety. "Do not fret. I have found Mr. Dankworth to be quite harmless."

A correct enough statement, for now. People changed, some for the better, others for worse. Even if it were true that he took interest in a wine shipment, why had he been here in the garden, watching them stroll along?

"Well." Charity clutched her shawl tightly to her neck. "I am going in."

She bypassed Juliet, her steps crunching gravel. Juliet stared long and hard into the darkness, making sure Mr. Dankworth hadn't doubled back for any nefarious reasons. Nothing good ever crept out of the gloom, so she kept hold of the rock.

"Oh!" Charity's cry mingled with a hard crunch of pea gravel.

Juliet ran down the path and, when she rounded a corner, stopped in front of Charity, who lay sprawled in a heap on the gravel. "Charity!" She dropped to her knees, wildly assessing the woman. "Are you all right?"

"I am fine, just—" She pressed her fingers to her side, brow tightening.

"You are a very pretty liar. Let me help you up." She slid an arm around Charity's shoulders, lifting her to her feet.

"Thank you." Charity pulled away, brushing crushed leaves from her skirt.

"Here, let me do that." Finally dropping her makeshift weapon, Juliet shook away the debris. "You are lucky you did not twist your ankle with such a fall."

"Clumsy me. I should have watched my feet instead of staring into the darkness, dreading another glimpse of that man."

"Be at peace. He is gone." She gave the fabric one last brush-over with her palm, then tensed when she neared Charity's hem. There on the ground lay a green ribbon, one side of it still tied to ankle height on the branch of a lavender bush, its lingering sweetness a macabre contrast to the horror racing through Juliet's veins. After untying it, she rose, clutching the frayed strip.

"What is that?" Charity's brow puckered. "Your hair ribbon? I... I don't understand. Is that what tripped me?"

Juliet swallowed, throat thick. "I am afraid so."

Charity paled, shaking her head slowly. "But. . . ? Surely you didn't. . . ?"

"Never! I swear it."

Charity pressed a hand to her chest, voice barely a whisper. "I didn't think so. But it *is* your ribbon. I think. . ." She blinked rapidly. "Come, Juliet. Henry should hear of this. There must be an explanation."

She moved forwards, glancing back once as if wishing none of this could be true.

So did Juliet.

Reluctantly, she followed, strangling the life from her ribbon, thoughts scrambling.

Someone had taken this ribbon from her room.

Someone had set her up as an aggressor.

Someone wanted her gone.

Blast!

Henry slammed down his pen, disgusted by the blot of ink ruining the pristine contract he'd been labouring over for the past hour. Another mistake. Another sign of disorder. One disaster after another had plagued his whole day. Nay, more like the whole week.

Lacing his fingers behind his head, he leaned back in his chair, the creak of leather competing with the pop of wood in the fireplace. He stared at the paneled ceiling, weary of numbers and meetings and failure.

Father had entrusted him with the soon-to-arrive shipment of his new blend, and he had yet to arrange a venue and finalize his list of possible investors. It was his responsibility. His test. And he was floundering. He ought to be spending his time keeping an eye on Charity until she departed for London tomorrow instead of burying his head in paperwork.

But it wasn't just the wine or the investors or the endless contracts. It was the feeling that no matter how many tasks he completed or fires he stamped out, he was still falling short—just as he had after Mother died. They'd all mourned, naturally, but Father took it hardest. Oh, he had tried to draw his father back to life—inviting friends, managing the estate, keeping everything just so. But nothing reached through the fog. His father had left for Italy not out of whimsy nor fully because of business. It was a retreat. A quiet resignation that Henry hadn't been able to stop. He hadn't known what to say back then. Still didn't.

So he worked. He filled the silence with duty and deadlines, hoping to earn back the confidence he feared he'd lost. And now, with so much hanging in the balance—with Charity's safety, Juliet's trust, the estate's future—he couldn't afford to come up lacking again. He huffed a long breath. Failure never came easy.

Would to heaven it might never come at all.

A scurry of footsteps entered the study. Charity stood, pale of face, clutching tightly to the shawl gathered in puckers at her neck. Juliet followed, as wide-eyed as the night he'd caught her in the woods.

He rose at once, his chair scraping harshly against the wood flooring. "What has happened?"

"Forgive our intrusion, Brother, but there is something you should know about." Wincing, Charity pressed a hand to her side, slightly swaying on her feet.

He frowned, concerned, but before he could go to her, Juliet shored her up with an arm about her shoulders. "Charity, please sit. We can explain everything just as well from a chair."

"Wise words." He ushered them to the sofa in front of the hearth. Charity sank as if exhausted. Juliet perched on the cushion next to her, set to take flight if spooked.

He took the opposite chair, gripping its arms, the room steeped in foreboding. "Now then, what exactly is it you are to explain?"

Charity plucked at the tasseled hem of her shawl. "I asked Juliet to take a turn in the garden with me before dinner, as has been our habit of the past week. All was well until I saw a man near the shrubbery."

He shot to his feet. "What man?"

"No need to charge off." Juliet wound a dirty green ribbon into a tight coil as she spoke. "It was only Mr. Dankworth, and he has since left the premises. He said he called at the house for business with you but that you were too occupied to see him."

Interesting. Henry rubbed the back of his neck. "I was not informed of his arrival, though now that I think on it..." His words trailed off as he recalled the harsh reprimand he'd handed the footman the last time Woodley had interrupted him. "However, it is not out of the realm of possibility Woodley turned him away. Yet even were that the case, why was Dankworth in the garden?"

"I asked as much." Juliet jutted her jaw. "He claimed the benefit of evening air and not wishing to disrupt your train of thought, though he was quite cryptic about it as usual."

He snorted. A flimsy account if ever he'd heard one. He'd have to pay the man a call in the morning and ask him exactly what he'd been about.

Charity leaned forwards slightly. "Henry, I didn't like the way he looked at me." She winced again, untangling her fingers from the fringe and pressing her palm against the side of her abdomen.

Alarm settled sickly in his gut. "Are you unwell, Sister?"

She shook her head. "It's nothing. Just a cramp I've had on and off all day."

Henry stiffened. Oh. Women's things. A subject he was loath to broach. Instead, he turned to Juliet, unable to stop a glower from tightening his brow. "Why did you not call for me immediately?"

She straightened as if ready to do battle. "Do you really think you would have heard me in here all the way from the garden? Besides, I was perfectly capable of managing the situation. Mr. Dankworth is singular to be sure, but he is not a threat."

"A man does not hide for innocent reasons." A growl rumbled in his throat. He *would* speak with the fellow on the morrow.

Juliet folded her arms, boldly staring him down. "I shielded your sister the entire time. He would have had to plow me over to get to her."

"And I am supposed to feel good about that?"

"Calm down, Brother." Reaching across to him, Charity squeezed his knee before settling back against the sofa. "It is true I could have run to safety if Mr. Dankworth had advanced, but nothing of the sort happened. It is what took place after that which I thought you should know."

"There is more to this?" His voice rose.

And the women flinched in unison.

Exhaling deeply, he pinched the bridge of his nose, fighting to collect himself. Bullying these two would get him nowhere. He dropped his hand while lowering his tone as well—though the strain in his voice likely betrayed him. "Forgive me. Continue, please."

Charity shifted uncomfortably on the cushion. "After Mr. Dankworth left, I told Juliet I wished to return to the house. I didn't wait for her reply, and as I hurried away, I tripped over something." She side-eyed Juliet.

Juliet held up a ribbon, tightly wound in her hand.

Henry's brow furrowed. "I don't understand."

"My hair ribbon was stretched low across the path," Juliet explained. "Tied at ankle height."

His chest tightened. Someone had deliberately set a trap—for Charity? For Juliet?

He stared at the ribbon as though it might explain itself, mind spinning, not with suspicion of Juliet—for he could not believe that—but with fury that someone had entered her room and used her belongings. Violated her space. Threatened his family.

Again.

"You're certain this is your ribbon?" His voice came low and tight.

Juliet nodded. "It must've been taken from my dressing table. I had not noticed it missing."

Hmm. A convenient excuse. The tiniest doubt niggled at his mind. Pushing it away, Henry exhaled through his nose and forced himself to think. "So. . .whoever set this snare wanted it traced back to you."

Juliet's mouth trembled. "It appears that way."

Beside her, Charity pressed her hand again to her side, her face drawn and pale. "If you've no objection, Brother, I—I believe I'll lie down for a bit."

At once, Henry moved to her. "Of course. Let Mrs. Hamby fetch you a sleeping draught."

Charity offered a faint smile before rising and quietly slipping from the room.

Henry waited until the door latched behind her, then turned back to Juliet. His fists clenched at his sides. "Juliet, you swear you. . ." The words snagged on his tongue. No, she would never. Involuntarily, he shook his head ever so slightly, then took a beat to shift direction. "You realize what this means? Whoever it is that's doing such things is not only toying with Charity—he is now trying to cast blame on you."

"Perhaps." She swallowed hard—blast it, she'd seen his moment of doubt—but kept her composure. "Which means this isn't only about Charity anymore."

He turned towards the fire, heart hammering. "And—things are escalating."

Skirts shushed behind him. "Henry. . ." A light touch landed on his sleeve. "Believe me, I want to find whoever's doing this as much as you do."

"I know," he said hoarsely.

His gaze flicked towards the doorway where Charity had gone. "I suppose it is one thing to be angry, and quite another to be frightened."

"And. . .you're frightened," Juliet whispered.

"For both of you," he admitted.

They stood there in fragile quiet for several breaths before Juliet murmured, "Then let us continue to work together to end it."

Henry exhaled slowly, his anger cooled by her calm strength. He gave her no answer, though, for in truth he was beginning to wonder if he should cut her free to escape whatever danger might be coming their way next.

"Henry? You do want me to stay, do you not?"

Before he could speak again, the door burst open and Mrs. Hamby hurried inside, wringing her hands. "Sir—you must come at once!"

Henry's stomach clenched. "What is it?"

"It's Miss Charity." The housekeeper's voice trembled. "She's fainted."

Chapter 17

Three long days. Three longer nights. . .and this one wasn't even over yet. Juliet yawned large and long as she swung around to the corridor leading to the kitchen. A stout spot of tea would be just the thing to keep her awake the rest of the night. Hopefully.

A slight glow crept out of Henry's study as she walked past. Apparently Molly had forgotten to bank the fire, which would make it harder for the young maid to refresh it in the morning. Juliet backtracked, then hesitated. Should she go ahead and do the task herself, or did Henry hold his study as sacrosanct?

And why was she even considering carrying out such a duty as if she herself were the maid?

She pressed her hand against the doorframe, taken aback by just how much she'd changed over the past year. Menial chores didn't seem degrading anymore, but rather a mark of endurance, of a strength she would not have known she'd possessed had she not been forced into such a situation. Maybe this change—this situation, even—was not an obliteration of who she was but rather a foundation of who she might become.

"Juliet?"

She froze at the deep voice. "Henry?" Tentatively, she stepped past the threshold, holding out her lamp.

The master of Bedford Manor slouched in a chair near the hearth, his long legs stretched towards the flames. Spare light flickered across his features, riding the sharp cut of his jaw and accentuating the furrows carved into his brow. His shirtsleeves were rolled to his elbows, skin and muscle exposed. Stubble darkened his face, the weariness in his eyes even darker. His tousled hair caught what little light there was, the golden strands painting a halo.

Her breath caught in her throat, and it took several tries to get words out. "Why are you sitting in the dark? You should be abed by now."

"So should you." He rose like a panther, silent and sleek, jabbing at the fire with a poker until flames licked upwards. After tossing on several logs, he lit a thin twig of kindling and then set the candles to life on each side of the mantel mirror, significantly brightening the room before dropping back to his chair. "Come. Sit with me a moment. I would speak with you."

She took the small sofa opposite him, wary as she settled the folds of her skirts. They'd hardly said a thing to each other since that horrible night when, in spite of his words, she'd read flickers of doubt in his eyes about her green ribbon, and Charity had taken ill with bilious fever. He'd never accused her of anything outright, but even if he'd wanted to, there'd simply been no time. When he wasn't sitting with his sister, she was. They were two ships merely passing in a sea of worry over Charity's welfare. What prodded him to seek her out now?

He steepled his long fingers beneath his chin, his grey-green eyes solemn as a clergyman's. "I wanted to thank you for caring so tenderly for my sister. You have gone beyond anything I have asked of you."

She blinked. Gratitude was the last thing she expected from him. "I want to see Charity recover every bit as much as you."

"I believe you do."

"Do you?" Heat crept up her neck, spreading to her cheeks. "I thought perhaps you might not trust me anymore, I mean since the ribbon incident, and. . .well. . .I suppose you have reason not to, considering how we met."

"You had cause," he said gently. The fierceness in his eyes softened enough to disarm her.

"I am sorry, you know." She shifted on the cushion, gown rustling, leather creaking. "I do not remember if I told you that yet, but regardless, it was wrong of me to steal from you. From anyone, actually. I should have. . ."

Words stalled on her tongue, tasting like ashes. She should have what? No answer had come to mind when her stomach churned with emptiness this past year, nor did any solution present itself now. A huge sigh deflated her. "I do not know what else I could have done, but I should have figured out something other than resorting to thievery."

He rose, cracking his neck one way and the other, then strode to the small cart near the door. Lifting a carafe, he directed a raised brow at her and, at the shake of her head, poured only himself a drink and returned to his seat. "So, tell me. Why the sudden change of heart? About poaching, I mean."

"Honestly? It doesn't feel sudden to me. Deep down I always knew I ought not, but. . .well, desperation and all that, you know." Aimlessly, she trailed her finger in loop-de-loops on the arm of the sofa, the action giving her time to collect her thoughts. "I suppose what it comes down to is that being here with you and Charity this past month has reminded me what it is like to live with integrity—the kindness and friendship both of you have offered, seeing how you look out for your sister, how you strive to do what is right despite the difficulty of doing so. . ." Her eyes lifted to his. "You make me want to be a better person."

Something unreadable flared golden in his eyes, something that vanished with a quick shake of his head. "Not me, Juliet. Anything good in me—any strength or virtue—comes from God alone. Without Him, I would not even try to do what is right. And that is the thing. . ."

Gripping his glass in both hands, he planted his elbows on his thighs, firelight casting his face in an amber glow. His unwavering gaze bored into her, like a warrior seeking to breach a wall. "The truth is none of us are good on our own. Every last one of us falls short. I know that better than most. And I suppose such is the whole point of forgiveness, though I admit I have my own dragons to slay in this respect."

Her whole frame went taut as her father's face the last time she'd seen him came to mind. Oh, he'd been sorry enough to have been caught, but had he ever really felt bad about ruining their family? Ruining her? How could she possibly forgive someone who had knowingly committed such a heinous act? Of course she knew she must. . .she just didn't know how. She looked away from Henry's all-seeing eyes, the hollow ache in her throat making it hard to breathe.

At length, she whispered, "I know."

For a long while silence reigned, broken only by the occasional snap of the fire and soft clink of Henry's glass as he set it down. Thankfully he didn't push her for any further elaboration.

Eventually, his voice came low and soft. "Those demons you are wrestling, Juliet—they can be vanquished. You don't have to carry them alone. All you need do is relinquish them to God."

Hah! Did the Reverend St. John not say as much every blessed Sunday? She jerked her face back to him. "But what of you? You speak of relinquishing burdens as if yours are neatly packed away. I have seen the weight you carry. Yes, you press on—but you do so by sheer force, not surrender. You don't ask for help. You command it. There's a difference."

She leaned forwards, fingers laced tightly in her lap. "I may be a poacher with no claim to wisdom, but I know a thing or two about traps. And the worst kind are the ones we set for ourselves."

His brow furrowed, gaze flicking to the fire—away from her.

She let her voice soften. "You can't protect Charity, or this house, or even your own soul, if you're the only one standing guard."

He didn't speak, but something in his posture shifted—shoulders loosening, the rigid line of his jaw easing just a fraction—as if her insight had pierced some hidden armour.

But she wasn't finished.

She crouched in front of the fireplace, holding out her hands on the thin pretense of warming them, though the real heat burned in her chest. "There's something else. About your sister." Her voice stayed low, steady. "Please let me go to my aunt tomorrow. I mean no disrespect to Dr. Branch, but all his cupping and bloodletting is doing Charity no good. I think you should dismiss him."

"He is the most respected doctor in all of Bedford."

"Maybe so." She glanced over her shoulder. "Yet that does not mean his practices are helping your sister. Rather, I see the life draining from her. I have also seen what my aunt's remedies can do. She has the wisdom of generations. At least give her medicinals a chance."

His lips flattened, and for several beats he said nothing. Not surprising. Dr. Branch had a certified education to back up his methods, while all to recommend her aunt was a lifetime of tending the sick and injured with roots, leaves, and flowers. Minds such as Henry's discarded ancient remedies as old wives' tales.

Finally, he nodded. "Very well. But I am not discharging Dr. Branch. Administer what your aunt recommends, but he will still oversee her care."

A concession, but not enough. She rose, spreading her hands. "But Charity will not thrive if her life seeps away by fleam and blister!" Her voice rang overly passionate in the small room, but so be it. She'd watched her brother slip from this world by just such atrocious means. She would not see a woman she'd come to love suffer the same cruel decline.

"Henry, please." She dropped to her knees at the side of his chair, skirts pooling around her. "I have seen the damage bloodletting and cupping accomplish. My brother, cut down by disease, wasted away by such treatments. Do not let that happen to your sister. At least give my aunt's remedies a solid try. You have met her. You know she is keen of mind. She doesn't guess—she simply knows, after so many years tending the sick."

Late-day stubble roughened his jaw as he pressed his mouth into a tight line. A battle raged behind those green eyes. Good. At least he was considering it.

Loosening the cravat from his neck, he unwound the fabric as if he couldn't breathe, then balled it into a wad. "Three days. That is all. I shall ask Dr. Branch to hold off on his practices until we see what your aunt's tonics bring about in that time, but hear me well. If Charity worsens, I will dispense of those tonics immediately. Understood?"

She grinned. "Yes. Thank you. And with that, I shall bid you good night." She pushed up, victorious, but before she could gain her feet, Henry's grip on her arm stayed her.

"Wait." His command was quiet, soft almost, but the weight of it cut through the shadows like a sharp blade. "There is something else."

Her recent triumph faded into unease. Wary, she sank back to her place beside him. "What is it?"

His thumb brushed along her sleeve, though she doubted very much he felt the fabric—or her. The glaze in his eyes hinted that the man inside was miles away. Without so much as a word, he released her arm and collapsed back in the chair, dragging a hand over his face in what appeared to be utter exhaustion.

What was it he couldn't bring himself to say?

~

This was a mistake. A full-blown, wholly avoidable catastrophe. What on earth was he doing?

Henry tensed, resentment flaring—at himself most of all. He'd made a vow, hadn't he? To rise to the measure of the man who raised him. To act with reason, not sentiment.

And yet there sat Juliet, every soft breath of hers doing strange things inside his chest. How could a small woman affect him in such an enormous way?

He scrubbed his face, again and again. Certainly he had been consumed with the torment his sister had suffered and now the very illness she fought against, but instead of distracting him from Juliet, as he thought it should, it only seemed to highlight her every action—her compassion, her tenacity, her determination, even her willingness to risk his ire if she believed something was for the best, such as arguing for her aunt's tonics. Surely this was madness, he'd reasoned, brought upon him by the strain of all that had been happening. Avoid her and the feelings would go away. So, he had buried himself in his work. Except that only fed his admiration, as she took his preoccupation in stride, shouldering extra burdens to let him work in peace. Then seeing her here tonight, lamplight kissing her face. . .

He shot to his feet and strode to the mantel, gripping the solid oak until his fingers went numb. Better that than lose himself in those beguiling sage-tinged eyes that seemed to breach every defense he could construct. Should he go down this road with her or not? The consequences were dire, like jumping off a cliff, unsure how deep the fall or how hard and rocky the landing would be. Blast! He'd been plagued since the night he'd first laid eyes on her.

"Henry?" Her voice was a shiver. "You are frightening me. Please tell me what troubles you so."

He closed his eyes, a sigh draining out of him. This was it. The moment he cut open his chest and allowed her to see the heart that beat for her inside. . .or pleaded fatigue and sent her away—only for his anguish to continue in secret. Hanging his head, he kicked his toe against the brazier, watching sparks spit into the darkness. Either he summoned the nerve to speak his heart here and now, or he let it go. Let *her* go. Bitter laughter caught in his throat. What an impossibility!

He swung around before he changed his mind, spilling words before he could stop them. "You are not the same person I found in the woods. Wild. Reckless. Headstrong. And I cannot reconcile it." He flung out his arms. "You kneel before me to plead for my sister's welfare and that change in you, well. . .it—it humbles me and I cannot help but admire you."

She sank back on her heels, a slight shake to her head. "I. . .do not know what to say other than I *am* changed. Having the weight removed from my shoulders as to where my next meal will come from, seeing my aunt on the mend because of good food and good care. . . I do not think you realize what you have given me. A chance to breathe. A chance to be. To stand still long enough to see the world in a different light. To see *you* differently as well."

Her words hung between them, delicate but strong with promise . . .altogether dangerous for his current frame of mind.

"You do not understand." In two strides, he grabbed her arms and pulled her up more harshly than he intended. "I want to be angry with you. I want to hold on to my doubts because to do so is easier than trusting someone who—"

He clamped his mouth shut. No. He could not finish this. He never should have said anything to begin with. This *was* a mistake!

"Someone who what, Henry?"

"Never mind. It is late. I will bid you good night now and leave you to my sister." He turned.

Only to be pulled back with a tug to his shoulder.

"No. If what you say is so"—Juliet's sage eyes blazed into his—"then tell me why you cannot trust me."

"Because you have the power to undo me!" He flung the words like a dagger through the air, cross at himself for admitting such a weakness, crosser still that it was true. In all his years no woman had moved him so much as this tangle-haired vixen who'd robbed him of game and heart.

"Undo you?" She angled her head, her fine brow creasing. "How?"

Now there was a loaded question, one that could blow them both apart. . .one he had no power whatsoever to resist. He pulled her close, raw instinct governing against reason. His voice dropped to a hoarse whisper, his breath blending with hers. "You make me desire things I have no business desiring."

She swallowed, visibly, but no fear flashed in her eyes. Only questions and. . .could it be? A reflection of his own want and need?

"What do you mean?" she breathed, unsteady yet firm. "I would have the truth."

Would she?

Truly?

Could she take the whole of him—the damage, the wanting, the truth, or would his confession break them both?

"The truth is this." Without another thought, he pulled her close and brushed his mouth against hers.

And was instantly made whole, never even realizing he'd ever been only part man. Barely living. Barely knowing. Until now. Fire licked through him, fusing them together, the heat of their union a blaze that scorched and healed.

"Juliet." He spoke against her lips, more of a moan than a name. "I fear you undo me altogether."

She grabbed handfuls of his shirt, clutching him nearer, clinging as if he were the only fortress she would ever seek. So. She felt this too.

The thought thrilled, heightening every sense. His heart thundered against his ribs, his mouth trailing over the curve of her cheek, down the softness of her jaw, the maddening velvet of her neck. She fit so well against him, like God had made her as his very own. And he for her, as she surrendered, moulding against him.

But a heartbeat later, she stiffened.

Broke away.

Sucked in a breath then slapped him with a hard crack to his cheek.

He gaped, stunned, confused, horrified by the accusation thick on the rush of air she exhaled.

Tears welled in her eyes, the shimmer of them orange and red, each drop threatening to spill down her flushed face. Her chest rose and fell unevenly, as if she could no longer breathe.

Before he could say a word, she rushed past him, skirts aswirl, and vanished out the door. He stood completely at a loss, thoughts tightening into a black snarl. Should he go to her? Apologize? Drop to his knees and swear never again to accost her in such a reckless, unthinking fashion?

Instead, he lifted a shaky hand to his cheek and collapsed into a chair as if the life had been drained from him. His arms, so recently filled with her warmth, now hung useless and cold.

"What have I done?" he whispered into the flames. "Oh God, what have I done?"

Chapter 18

By the time weak morning light painted a thin line on the horizon, Juliet was halfway through the woods to Aunt Margaret's. Leaves crushed beneath her pounding steps. The sting of an October mist against her cheeks was a welcome annoyance. Better to focus on the cold than relive the taste of Henry or the feel of his warmth, as she had done all through the long night. What a trollop he must think her! Had she not cleaved to him? Matched him passion for passion? Allowed his advances when she knew she ought not?

But oh, how she could have spent eternity there in his arms.

Bah!

She upped her pace, putting as much space between herself and Bedford Manor as quickly as possible. Her fingers curled into tight fists, nails digging crescents into her palms. She would not—would *not!*—bring them to her lips again, touching in wonder where his mouth had so perfectly pressed against hers. Not again.

Pausing at the cottage gate, she held herself still, every muscle taut, thoroughly vexed with herself. With Henry. With the mess she'd allowed to happen. Stars above! Had her life not been complicated enough?

And now this.

She yanked open the gate, surprised at the easy give and nearly losing her balance because of it. Pulled from her morose thoughts, she gaped at the freshly painted fence. There was now a neatly curving cobblestone path leading to the front door—the *new* front door with a brass knocker. Recently glazed windows sported lacy white curtains on the inside. The eaves had been repaired, without great gaping pieces missing. And over it all was a tightly shingled roof with nary a spot of moss or mould. Many a happy fairy tale could be written about this snug little house, all dressed up with crisp whitewash.

Juliet pressed her hand to her heart. My! No longer was this a shack of desperation but a cheerful haven, one that promised warmth and laughter, not chills and dread. Henry was to thank for this.

The very man she'd struck full in the face.

Heart aching, Juliet made her way to the door, faintly knocking before letting herself in. If Aunt Margaret were yet asleep, she'd not wish to startle the old dear. She'd simply put the kettle on and have some hot tea ready for when she awakened.

"Juliet?" Seated at the table in front of a worn Bible, Aunt Margaret glanced up. Her brows furrowed. "It's barely morning, child. What are you doing here so early? Is all aright?"

"All is fine with me." She smiled, the fabrication prickly on her tongue as she shrugged out of her pelisse and hung it on a peg. A new rug adorned the floorboards, soft beneath her feet as she crossed the room to buff a light kiss against the crown of Aunt Margaret's head. "And you. . .are you well?" Retreating a step, she studied her aunt's face. Her skin, once pale and pulled tight over sharp bones, was now vibrant, her cheeks plump and rosy. Juliet's smile grew into a large grin. "You look like a new person."

"I feel like one too. Actually"—Aunt patted her belly—"I feel like a stuffed sausage what with all the good food I've had of late."

"I am happy to hear it." Juliet beamed, gratitude welling towards a man who had every right not to speak to her again. . .but better not to dwell on that right now. "Shall we have some tea?"

"That would be lovely. There are also plenty of eggs and bacon to be fried. Will you stay for breakfast?"

"I would like to, but I cannot tarry long." She strode to the hearth, thoughts straying to the basket of tinctures she ought to be packing for Charity right now. She couldn't afford to chat overlong, but oh how good it was to see her aunt so hale and hearty.

Grabbing a densely woven cloth, she removed the kettle and poured two cups, then returned to the table. "Here you are." She set down Aunt Margaret's steaming brew before sinking into the adjacent chair. Cupping her hands around her mug, she peered at her aunt over the rim. "I was wondering what you would recommend for bilious fever."

"So, there is a purpose to your visit after all. Who suffers such an ailment?"

"Charity Russell. I have three days to prove that your remedies are superior to Dr. Branch's bloodletting." Setting aside her mug, she squeezed Aunt Margaret's knee. "Which I know they are."

"Hmph! I should say so." The old dear lifted her nose in the air. "We shall pack you a basket after our tea and put Miss Russell back to rights without spilling any of her blood."

"I knew I could count on you." Juliet saluted her aunt with her mug. For several cozy moments, she enjoyed the warmth of the tea, the crackle of the hearth, and the fact that no more draughts crept in through the windows. But deep down, turmoil mixed with her drink. She needed to return to Bedford Manor and not only see to Charity but also face Henry.

She set her mug down, then said with a smile, "You would have howled to see Miss Potter at service last Sunday. I swear her hat had half the parish garden atop it—berries, blooms, even what looked like a velvet turnip." She gave a soft laugh. "If eccentric millinery were a weapon, that woman could conquer armies."

Aunt Margaret chuckled, the sound like a balm.

But the smile faded from Juliet's lips almost as quickly as it had come. The image of the hat disappeared beneath the weight of memory and regret.

Aunt Margaret angled her head, her sharp eyes narrowing. "How are things at the manor? Is your. . .*business*, as you call it, with Mr.

Russell nearly finished? Not that I wish to take you from him if you are yet occupied, for he has been overly gracious in fixing up this old place and providing for my needs, but. . .well. The truth is I miss you."

"I miss you too." She reached for her aunt's hand, pleased to feel life pulsing beneath the older lady's skin. "I wish I could give you an answer, but I—I do not know how much longer I shall be there."

Especially not after last night's kiss in the study.

Heat flushed her face at the memory. Pulling back, she reclaimed her mug and stared into the brew, anything to keep from fingering her lips yet again.

"Hmm." Aunt Margaret studied her as if she were a puzzle to be solved. "What troubles you? And don't say nothing. Your chin always quivers when you are unsettled. Is it Mr. Russell? He has not harmed you, has he?"

Charity jerked up her head, alarmed her aunt would even think such a thing. "No! He has not harmed me at all. Rather. . .I—" She shot to her feet, the chair wobbling from her abrupt departure, and paced the small room. Cowardly, yes, but the only way she could admit to her abominable behaviour. "*I* struck *him*, Aunt."

"You what?" The older lady gaped—then burst into laughter, sloshing tea onto the table.

Alarmed, Juliet circled back to her. "Aunt Margaret! Have you gone mad?"

Her aunt waved a hand in the air, tears dampening her cheeks as she tried to catch her breath. "Oh, Juliet, my impetuous girl. Forgive me. It's just that the image of you slapping that poor man is too much."

"It is not funny." Juliet stamped her foot. Churlish, but not to be helped. "I have made a complete wreck of things, I'm afraid."

"Now, now. It cannot be all that bad." Pulling out a handkerchief, Aunt Margaret dabbed at her eyes while patting the vacated chair. "Come. Tell me what happened."

Huffing a long sigh, Juliet sank and then tossed back the rest of her drink for fortification. "He kissed me. Last night."

"Did he?" Aunt's smile faded, replaced by an inquisitive pinch to her lips. "Was it unwelcome?"

Unwelcome?

She choked. She'd never felt so whole as she had in Henry's arms, like she'd been broken all her life until his embrace had mended and moulded her into a new being. He'd stolen her breath, her heart, and given both back in ways she couldn't begin to describe. This time she couldn't stop the press of her fingers to her lips, a vain attempt to hold in the taste and feel of him.

"No," she whispered. "It was not."

Aunt's face softened with compassion, a faint smile curving her lips. "Then why did you strike him, child?"

"I. . .I do not know. There were so many feelings, so many thoughts." She hung her head, even now unable to sort through the snarl of emotions balled up in her chest. Having been courted before by Colin Chamberlain, she should be no stranger to such a wild flux of passion.

But Colin had never moved her so deeply.

At length, she peered up at Aunt Margaret. "Henry said I undo him. I cannot begin to understand what that means. Is it good? Bad? He sounded angry but then he pulled me into his arms."

A twinkle lit Aunt's eyes. "Oh, my dear, it means the man is in love with you."

"Love?" She blinked, her hand rising to her chest. The word voiced aloud hit harder than she expected, stirring a whirl of emotions she wasn't ready to name.

"Why such surprise? You are a lovely young lady, but more than that, you are a determined survivor, a woman capable of enduring hardship without breaking. That kind of strength is irresistible."

"I am a thief who stole game from his grounds!" She slammed her mug on the table, rattling her aunt's in the process. "I am not of his station."

Aunt Margaret chuckled. "The heart does not care about society's limitations. I am certain Mr. Russell forgave you the night you were caught, or he would not house you beneath his roof."

"But I slapped him, Aunt Margaret. How could he ever forgive such an affront?"

"You underestimate the power of a sincere apology. . .that is, if you are sorry."

She folded inwardly, shame curling through her like smoke. "I am," she mumbled. "But I doubt he will believe me. He barely trusts me as it is."

Aunt Margaret's hand rubbed up and down on her arm, as if she might soothe her angst by touch alone. "If Henry Russell is half the man I suspect he is, he will respect your repentance and match it with forgiveness. But the first step is for you to take, my dear. The question is will you?"

She bit her lip, the tea in her belly churning at the thought of facing him again after such heat, such intimacy. . .such a blow. Her head sank even lower. "I suppose I owe him that much."

Hah. What an understatement.

She owed him her life.

Pinching the bridge of his nose, Henry blew out a long breath. Stars and thunder! He was tired, not to mention practically cross-eyed. The varied and minute details on the customs and excise forms were enough to drive a man insane. But if he didn't fill in all the proper information, his father's shipment would be delayed at port, resulting in fines, or worse. . .confiscation. Which would never do. He would *not* fail his father. Not again.

He leaned back in his chair, fighting against a flicker of memory that nudged him. How easily his father had forgiven him years ago. Forgiven what Henry had never quite forgiven himself for.

Bah! He shoved the thought aside. It had no bearing now.

Not when he was failing his sister in exposing her tormentor.

And especially not when he'd failed Juliet as he had last night.

He glanced towards the hearth, unable to keep his eyes off the spot where he'd held her in his arms and kissed those sweet lips of hers. Blast! What a cad he was. She'd had every right to strike him. If any man had taken such a liberty with his sister, he'd have run the scoundrel through with a sword. He'd gone to her room at first light to tell her as much and apologize, but she'd not answered his knock or his pleas through the shut door. So, he'd buried himself in here the moment Dr. Branch had arrived, desperately seeking to forget Charity's feverish face and the fire in Juliet's eyes last evening.

But he would never—ever—forget that kiss.

A light rap tapped on the doorframe, drawing his attention. Juliet stood on the threshold, looking so lovely it hollowed out something deep inside him. She gripped a basket filled with bottles and brown-paper packets, her doe eyes blinking warily. "May I have a moment?"

Was this it? Would she leave the basket with him and say goodbye forever? He rose slowly, unsure if any words would make it past the ache in his throat. "Of course. Come in."

She took the seat in front of his desk, her blue gown a summer sky against the deep brown leather. But she did not hand over the basket. She clutched it in her lap like a barrier between them.

He sat on the edge of his chair, tense beyond measure. "I—em—I was wondering if we were still on speaking terms. Apparently we are. . .unless you have come to tell me goodbye?"

Her shoulders squared. "Is that what you would like me to do?"

"No!" The word flew out like a cannonball, and she flinched. Pah! Why could he never maintain control around this woman?

Kneading the back of his neck, he softened his tone. "No, it is not what I want."

For a few breaths she said nothing, just sat there hugging the basket all the tighter. Then, something steeled in her, as if she'd come to a hard-won decision. "I wish to say I am sorry for striking you last night, and I hope you will find it in your heart to forgive me."

Forgive her?

He sucked in a breath. He'd been the one to pull her body against his, claim her lips as if he had some sort of right. Yet she sought *his* forgiveness? Unbelievable.

Once again he rose, driven to kneel at her feet, to take her hands and rub small circles into the softness of her palms, but that would be a mistake. Instead, he crossed to the front of his desk and planted his hands behind him against the tabletop. Better that than make a fool of himself again. "I am the one who should be apologizing to you, Juliet. I never should have taken such a rude advantage, and I am sorry I kissed you."

"I am not." Rosy red flared on her cheeks, but she did not look away.

He swallowed—hard—trying not to gape. First an apology and now an admission she'd welcomed his advances? He would never understand women! Even so, a slow smile lifted one side of his mouth as he ran his knuckles over the very cheek she'd so thoroughly walloped. "You certainly have a singular way of showing your affirmation."

Her lips quirked. "My aunt calls me impetuous."

I call you beautiful.

He clenched his teeth lest those words spill. Too much too soon would scare her off. Better to take small steps than plow her over with the full force of the passion pounding in his chest.

"So," he drawled. "How do you wish to navigate"—he waved his hand between them—"whatever this apparent connection is?"

Her teeth toyed with her lower lip for a moment. Only God knew what went on behind those sage eyes of hers. Silently, she rose and circled the chair, resting her basket on the rise of the back.

"For the time being," she began, "I suggest we continue our employer-employee relationship. I came here because of your sister, making a promise to you—and myself—that I would help you find whoever it is that torments her. And now, especially with Charity having taken ill, I think she should be foremost in both of our minds.

If whatever feelings you and I have are real, time will not diminish them."

He clutched the edge of the desk, grateful for the support behind him, for the sacrificial sentiment behind her words knocked him quite off balance. Slowly, he shook his head. "You are a remarkable woman, Juliet Finch."

She blushed again, maddeningly adorable. "Well, you have given me three days to improve your sister's health, so I had best be about my business." She whirled, skirts swishing as she strode to the door.

"Juliet?"

She glanced over her shoulder. "Yes?"

"Is your aunt certain those medicinals will help Charity?" He nodded towards the basket.

"As certain as one can be. But I know you are a man of faith, so a little prayer would be welcome as well."

And just like that she was gone, leaving behind her ever-present scent of rosemary and crushed leaves.

Henry rounded his desk and dropped into his chair, spent. Had he done the right thing in allowing her to administer such tonics and powders to his sister? Dr. Branch certainly hadn't agreed with him. The man's righteous indignation at being asked to pause his ministrations still burned his ears.

Yet if he could not trust Juliet—the extraordinary woman who'd snared his heart so thoroughly—then what future could they possibly have?

Chapter 19

For the first time in five days, Juliet fully relaxed against the soft cushions of the sitting room chair. . .but that did not stop her from keeping a watchful eye on Charity. It was, after all, the woman's first excursion from her bedroom since taking ill. She appeared of fair colour, sitting so prettily on the sofa in a ray of afternoon sunshine, and for that, Juliet's heart smiled. How good it was to see Henry's sister back amongst the living. Her light laughter at whatever Clara had whispered was sweet to Juliet's ears.

Shifting on the cushion, she allowed the bulk of her fears to melt away. The past days had blurred into a collection of sleepless nights and endless ministrations of Aunt Margaret's tonics. Thankfully, after the grueling first twenty-four hours, Charity's fever had broken. She'd steadily strengthened since then, so much so that today she'd ventured downstairs.

Henry stood near a writing desk, eyeing his sister. It hadn't been easy on him, fretting over her while working to carry out his father's business, but he'd done so without complaint.

Clara perched next to Charity, hands folded in her lap. While she chatted about the latest fashion, Clara kept her own sort of vigil, studying Henry's sister as well. Clara appeared as polished as ever, but beneath it all, Juliet sensed her concern too.

When Clara's conversation lulled and the room fell silent, Charity tilted her head, gaze bouncing between them. "All right, you three. While I appreciate your care, you must stop it. Every one of you."

Clara pressed her fingers against Charity's sleeve. "Stop what, darling?"

"You are all looking at me as if I shall break into a million pieces right here on the sofa. I assure you I am fine. A little fatigued, perhaps, but otherwise of sound mind and body."

Juliet smoothed her skirt, caught in the act but not repentant. "It was not so very long ago you were lying abed giving us a fright. In light of that, you shall have to put up with our furrowed brows for at least several more days."

"Juliet is right." Henry took the chair adjacent the sofa. "We are happy to see you up and about but do not wish you to overdo it."

Charity shook her head. "I cannot overdo anything beneath your watchful eye, Brother. But I appreciate the sentiment."

"Ahh, but it is not my eye you should fear. Juliet was most diligent this past week. Administering tonics. Mixing powders. Spoon-feeding you and dabbing away your fever with a cool cloth. Your illness did not stand a chance under her tender care." A flash of appreciation sharpened the green in his grey eyes. "Remind me, Juliet, to call upon you next time I take ill."

Her mouth dried, her tongue lying fallow. How was she to speak when he looked at her that way?

Clara rose, rounding the sofa while running her finger along the back of it. "Indeed. Juliet's hidden talents are enviable. Though I daresay I have spent more than my fair share of time in my mother's sickroom the past month, what with her horrid megrims. I don't know how many trips to the apothecary I've made. But. . ." Her lips quirked. "Do be careful, Juliet. Henry just might devise an ailment merely for the attention."

Henry chuckled. "Now there is a capital idea. Perhaps I shall take to my bed."

Charity reached for a nearby pillow and hugged it. "Let us have no more talk of sickness, though I admit lying about gave me much time to think. And in that time, I came to a conclusion. . .that there was no place I would rather be than here at Bedford Manor with all of you. Please don't get the wrong impression. I love Father and dearly wish to see him, but he will eventually return, and I shall see him then."

Henry straightened, tension creeping into his frame. "You may be out of the woods fever-wise, but there is still danger here for you."

Clara glanced sharply over her shoulder. "What danger are you talking about?"

Henry tugged at his collar. "What I mean to say is that there is still the fact that a holiday—particularly now—would do my sister good."

Charity shook her head, her golden curls—once so vibrant—now limply swinging against her neck. "I am quite adamant about this, Brother, so do not vex me."

"He has a point, though, darling," Clara said. "The Italian weather is far more conducive to healing than this chill and damp. Why, I have a brilliant idea!" She clapped her hands. "Since I cannot accompany you to Italy, why doesn't Juliet travel along? Then you would not feel so lonesome. There. Problem solved."

Juliet's gaze shot to Henry. Would he send them both away, make her Charity's guardian on the journey? To leave Bedford Manor now, to leave him, well. . .the very thought made her heart sink.

Henry's jaw flexed. His gaze flicked from Juliet to Charity, and finally to Clara, before he looked away as if weighing something that refused to settle. His mouth opened, then shut again. A breath. Another glance at Juliet. Finally with a sudden squaring of his shoulders, he spoke. "No. It is out of the question." His arms folded, his wide lips pinched. "Juliet shall remain here."

"Oh? Not even to be considered, is it? Hmm." One of Clara's brows arched as she glided over to him, graceful as a swan. She lightly brushed her fingers over his shoulder, barely grazing the fabric of his frock coat. "I assure you I am every bit as helpful as Juliet."

Juliet tensed. Clara was everything she was not. A lady of good standing, as poised as the Queen herself, and from a well-respected family. Not to mention beautiful. A ragged sigh passed her lips. Oh, she cleaned up well enough, she supposed, but how could she compete with such a woman?

And yet. . .she'd been the one Henry had kissed.

Clara smiled brilliantly. "But if you will excuse me for a moment, I should like to freshen up—and I shall also check on some tea for us all."

Charity faced Clara, her shawl falling to the back of the sofa. "That would be wonderful. Thank you."

As Clara swept out of the room, Henry rose and snugged Charity's wrap around her.

His sister peered up at him. "While I appreciate the gesture, I am not made of porcelain, you know."

"Says the one who was flat on her back this past week." He smirked as he reclaimed his chair.

"Yet here I sit now before you," Charity parried. "So, you may stop playing nursemaid."

Juliet smiled at the banter. "Your brother means well, Charity."

"I know. As did you, forcing me to drink such awful brews. You are quite the tyrant." She winked as she set aside the pillow. "I am not sure if it was your aunt's medicinals that did the trick, or if my ailment was simply frightened into submission by your determination."

Juliet laughed. "I make no apologies."

"As well you should not." Mischief laced Henry's tone. "Though I think Dr. Branch might still be expecting a measure of contriteness for having abandoned his usual procedures."

"Well." Charity huffed. "He won't get it from me. I was the one poked and bruised by his methods."

Juliet's humour faded. She'd seen the signs of Dr. Branch's treatments, the ugly purpling on Charity's arms where the cups had sucked the blood to the top of her skin. The many scabs peppered on her flesh from the incisions. Even now the thought of those images sparked a righteous anger. "Beast," she murmured, then louder, "you did suffer, Charity, but I think the doctor's ego may have seen the gravest injury of all."

"Thanks to you, Juliet," Henry cut in. "It takes a strong spirit to challenge the esteemed Dr. Branch—and me—yet you did so without flinching." He fixed his gaze on her, the lines on his face softening, as did his tone. "You are an exceptional woman."

Heat rose up her neck and spread across her cheeks. "I only did what I thought was right."

"Not everyone has the backbone to do so in the face of resistance." Undeniable admiration smouldered in his eyes.

Her heart stuttered in response. My. Was it warm in there? She pressed her hands flat against her skirt to keep from fanning herself, but all the same, fire burned her face.

Charity cocked her head, the angle of it not only amused but curious. "Pardon me, but did I miss out on something while I was abed?"

A slow grin spread over Henry's lips, as if he was reliving that kiss all over again. The rogue.

Juliet squirmed, mortified. No way would she admit to that scandalous moment in Henry's study.

"I did miss out." Charity's eyes widened. "Do tell!"

Juliet froze. How could she possibly explain the magnetic draw of Henry when she'd barely had time to analyze it herself?

Clara strode in then, clearly having heard Charity's plea. "Seems I returned just in time. Tell what?"

Henry turned towards her with a casual toss to his head. "Nothing. You know my sister. Inventing tales where there are none."

"Perhaps." Clara took the chair nearest Henry. "But I can practically smell the intrigue in the air."

Juliet forced a weak smile, her heart thudding against her ribs.

Let it go, Clara. Please let it go!

Thankfully the footman arrived bearing a large silver tray. He placed it on the table nearest Juliet, then retreated to take up a post near the door.

Clara, mercifully distracted by the scent of souchong tea, clasped her hands primly in her lap. "Ahh, tea at last. Juliet, would you mind?"

Her? She flexed her fingers, startled by the request. Usually Charity would serve, being the lady of the manor, which naturally would be too much to ask of her during her recuperation. But then Clara—being a long-standing friend—should have enjoyed the privilege. Why would the woman abdicate? Then again, with the bottle of Aunt Margaret's tincture on the tea tray, it only made sense that she'd know how many drops to use.

She smiled. "I would be happy to."

She poured the first cup, the strong scent of a very dark tea wafting to her nostrils. As such, she only filled the cup by half, then added a liberal dose of the tonic. Crossing over to Charity, she handed her the brew.

"Thank you." Charity smiled as she took the saucer.

"Oh, darling, your shawl. Let me adjust it." Rising, Clara set aside Charity's tea then fussed with the woman's wrap.

Juliet returned to the tea table, and by the time she poured the next cup, Clara had resumed her seat near Henry.

"Thank you, Juliet." Clara gracefully accepted her tea, her lips pursing ever so slightly as she blew away the steam.

When Juliet passed a cup to Henry, his fingers brushed like a whisper against hers, and a thrill charged up her arm. A knowing gleam lit in his eyes.

She turned away, determined to keep her composure. After pouring herself a cup, she returned to her chair, but one sip was all it took for her to set it aside for now. It was far too hot. She preferred her brew tepid—a trait that often earned her teasing from Aunt Margaret.

Charity sipped her tea diligently, while Clara rested her cup and saucer in her lap, leaning towards Henry. "So, how is the business for your father coming along?"

"Slower than I would like." His shoulders slumped somewhat from the weight of his responsibilities; then he slugged back the rest of his drink and set it down. "I am sure my father is having fits over the delays—not to mention Charity's illness—but neither could be helped."

"But that is all in the past. Your sister is clearly on the mend, and I am certain you shall be victorious no matter the amount of heel dragging from shippers or warehouses or whatever else it is you are dealing with." She fluttered her fingers in the air.

While Henry and Clara continued conversing, Juliet absently stirred her tea. Though she hated to admit it, Clara's encouragement had seemed to lift some of Henry's burden. Truly, she ought not feel jealous.

But she did.

Charity's teacup clinked against the saucer, drawing her attention. Henry's sister sat very still, and though her grip appeared loose on the cup, her knuckles paled. Egads! Her face seemed more drained as well.

"Charity?" Juliet set her spoon aside and leaned forwards. "Are you all right?"

A small smile ghosted her lips. "I am fine."

Soothing words, but Juliet suspected them to be a lie. She studied the woman, Clara and Henry oblivious to what was only a gut feeling inside Juliet. Was Charity on the verge of a relapse or was she merely becoming fatigued?

Charity swayed aside, setting her saucer down overly harsh, the porcelain clattering on the small table.

That did it.

Rising, Juliet crossed to the sofa and sat beside her. "Now that you have finished your tea, how about I see you back to your room?"

"Not yet, I think." Charity pressed a hand to her belly. "I should like to rest here a bit and digest my drink before going up."

"Very well," she acquiesced, though she determined to stay by Charity's side.

The footman appeared, bowing politely. "Finished with your tea, miss?"

Charity nodded slightly, eyelids fluttering as if she could barely keep them open.

"Yes, she is, thank you," Juliet answered for her, alarm a prickle down her spine. "Charity, I fear you have overdone it today. Let me ask Henry to help you upstairs, hmm?"

Charity's head lolled. "Yes, I think that would be—"

She collapsed against the sofa, body going slack.

A strangled cry eked out of Clara. "Oh dear! She's swooned."

"Charity!" Henry shot from his chair as Juliet bent over the woman, pressing the back of her hand against her brow.

Henry dropped to his knees beside them, collecting one of Charity's hands, her skin ashen against the life pulsing through his. "How is she?"

Juliet pulled back, frowning. "No fever, but she is clammy."

"Call Dr. Branch at once!" Henry barked over his shoulder at the footman.

"Yes, sir, but I suggest I also fetch the constable."

A stunned silence sucked the air from the room. They all turned to Woodley, Henry's brow a dark line not to be crossed. "What did you say?"

Woodley hesitated only a heartbeat before lifting the amber bottle from the tea tray and presenting it in his gloved hand. "Just in case she may have been poisoned."

Poisoned?

Poisoned!

What madness was this?

But there was no time to think on it. Charity's fingers were impossibly cool against Henry's skin. His sister needed help. Now.

"Go!" he bellowed to Woodley. "Dr. Branch cannot be far off as he left only recently. Send him at once, then. . .get the constable."

He could hardly believe those words had passed his lips, but better to have the law nearby if needed.

Oh God, please do not let it be needed!

Juliet pressed her hand against his sleeve. "We should lay her down. Keep her head elevated. Then—"

"Then what, Juliet?" Clara's voice cracked, fearful. "How much of that tonic did you give her? Furthermore, what was *in* that tonic?"

Juliet recoiled as if slapped. "I did nothing untoward!"

"I–I'm sorry," Clara whispered, wringing her hands. "I don't know what I'm saying. It's just—she was perfectly fine until then."

Henry's gut twisted as doubt rose like bile to the back of his throat. Clara was right. Juliet had served his sister. Could she have miscalculated the dosage?

Great heavens! What was he thinking? Surely Charity had simply overdone it today.

He pulled away from Juliet. "I shall tend my sister."

"Henry, let me help. I need to assess her symptoms and send them to my aunt straightaway."

"Surely that's not wise." Clara's voice quivered. "We don't yet know what happened." She took a step forwards, reaching a trembling hand towards Juliet but not touching her. "You've done everything you can, Juliet. Let Henry and Dr. Branch see to her now."

Juliet looked from Clara to him and back, disbelief bright in her eyes. "But you don't actually think I gave her the wrong amount of tonic."

"No, no—of course not," Clara whispered. "I only mean. . .there's no sense making things worse if we don't fully understand."

"Enough." Henry shot up his hand. "My sister is my first concern right now. Juliet, please move so I may make her more comfortable."

"Very well." She stepped back, lips pressed tight.

He could feel her wounded gaze upon him as he turned back to Charity. His sister's skin was cold as marble. "Charity, can you hear me? It's Henry." He shook her gently. "Give me some sign."

Only shallow breaths answered him. Her eyelids fluttered, but her head lolled lifeless again.

"Where is that blasted doctor?" he growled.

Behind him, Juliet's voice softened. "Try to keep her as still as possible."

Clara drew closer. "Henry. . ." Her voice was lower now, coaxing. "Think carefully. Juliet means well, I'm sure—but if something was given to your sister in error, even with the best intentions. . ." She trailed off, her words hesitant, as if she hated even to suggest it.

"I gave her the correct amount of tincture!" Juliet burst out. "Gentian root. Chamomile. Yarrow and peppermint. Nothing lethal. An overly large dose would make her stomach sick and create a mild disorientation, not. . .this. Oh, Henry, at least loosen her collar so she may breathe easier."

With shaking fingers, Henry worked loose Charity's lace. "Come back to me, Sister," he whispered, his forehead resting lightly on hers.

Her lashes flickered.

Hope surged.

Then her head dropped limp again.

He staggered backwards, helpless.

The door opened. Mrs. Hamby swept in, skirts whispering. "Molly told me, sir. I've brought smelling salts."

Juliet rose, but he stopped her with a small wave and accepted the vial from the housekeeper. "I will administer it."

He cracked open the top and waved it gently beneath Charity's nose.

Nothing.

"Please, Sister. Fight." He hovered closer.

Still nothing.

Clara let out a breathy gasp. "Oh, Henry. She was fine until the tea." She dabbed her eyes. "Juliet, perhaps something was mixed by mistake. That happens, doesn't it?"

Juliet straightened, face pale but steady as she shook her head. "I did not make any mistake. The medicine was taken from the same bottle I used this morning." She swept her hand towards the tea tray at the bottle in question.

The doctor finally arrived, followed closely by the constable. Rain still clung to their coats.

Henry exhaled, his shoulders sagging. "Thank God."

The doctor's examination was swift and thorough, going so far as to collect Charity's cup and swirl his finger around the liquid remains. After that, he collected the bottle and sniffed it, his tongue darting out for a wisp of taste before a great scowl darkened ominously on his brow. He faced them all with a stern set to his lips. "Laudanum and, if I don't miss my mark, oil of ether."

The constable spoke before any of them could respond. "Who put that in Miss Russell's tea?"

Henry's gaze shot to Juliet, barely comprehending what was going on.

"I did," Juliet said, her voice steady despite the trembling of her hands. "But I added only what I believed to be my aunt's tonic, not laudanum or oil of ether."

Henry turned on the doctor. "Are you certain?"

"As far as I can be without further analysis. And with a mixture this strong, your sister has a hard fight ahead of her." He handed the bottle to the constable, who swiftly pocketed the evidence.

"Then by your own admission, miss," the constable said, advancing on Juliet, "you'll have to come with me."

"Wait!" Henry darted between them. "Is that truly necessary? Can you not question her here? Miss Finch has done nothing but care for my sister. . .up until now." He hated himself for those last words, yet they couldn't be stopped.

"Mr. Russell." The constable folded his arms, a bull not to be moved. "I understand this is difficult, but with the doctor's witness of the residue in your sister's cup, Miss Russell's apparent state of unconsciousness, and Miss Finch's own confession of administering the substance found on the tray, it falls to me to act on what is presently before me. The evidence warrants immediate custody. I am afraid this is nonnegotiable, so please step aside."

"I did not poison Charity!" Juliet cried. "Anyone could have added those ingredients to my aunt's tincture. I certainly didn't!"

The constable cleared his throat. "The household staff will be questioned in due course, miss. But respectfully—you prepared the dose and delivered it to Miss Russell. That places the burden squarely at your feet until proven otherwise and constitutes sufficient cause for detention pending further enquiry."

All the blood drained to Henry's feet, leaving him cold as a winter wind. Fury. Fear. Confusion. There were too many things to sort through to stop this. He spun to Juliet, horrified, then sickened even further as he took in the trembling of her fingers as she pressed them to her mouth. Tears shone in her eyes, yet did not spill, for she was ever the strong pillar. . .lovely in her fierceness, heartbreaking in her vulnerability.

A slight moan came from the sofa, pulling his attention to Charity. His sister. His own flesh and blood. There was no denying she had been poisoned.

The constable stepped closer, his voice low but firm. "Mr. Russell, God willing your sister will recover. But deliberate or accidental, the law requires that I secure the person most immediately connected to the act. The sooner I have Miss Finch in my custody, the sooner we may learn the truth—and ensure no further danger comes to your family." He paused, then added with quiet finality, "And if you hinder me, sir, I will be obliged to consider such action as obstructing a constable in the course of his duty—a charge I would sorely regret bringing against you."

Henry gritted his teeth until his jaw cracked. Though it killed him in every possible manner, he had no choice but to step aside—and he did so without a backwards glance at Juliet, for if he did, it would surely break him.

"Very well, sir." The words barely made it past his closed throat. "Do as you must."

Chapter 20

Betrayed. Again. By another man she loved. How was such a nightmare to be borne? Juliet curled into a ball on the wooden cot, trying hard not breathe in the stench of sweat and blood woven into the thin blanket pulled up to her shoulders. Not that it did much good. The threadbare piece of wool was more a memory of a blanket than any real guardian against the chill of the damp cell. And the reek of this place! It would take a blistering bath to rid her skin of it. . .*if* she ever had the chance to bathe again.

A sob choked past her lips. What was to become of her?

"Quit yer cryin' and get some sleep!" the woman on the other side of the wall barked. "Don't do ye no good, nor none o' the rest of us."

"Caw! Leave her be," a man's voice rumbled in the darkness. "Fine lady like 'er ain't accustomed to sleepin' where rats play in the dark."

Another man hooted. "Ain't no rats hereabouts, Jackie. They'd starve a'fore their chompers could graze any flesh off yer skinny bones."

"Better scrawny than stinkin' like a mule's backside," Jackie shot back.

"Everyone shut yer gobs!" her neighbour shouted. "All this racket is keepin' me from me beauty sleep."

"Beauty? Hah! That's a howler." Jackie whooped, his coarse laughter harsh on Juliet's ears. "T'aint no amount o' shut-eye that'll fix what God din't finish on yer face."

"Keep it up, Jackie, and I'll come over there and finish what the Almighty started with yer rotten teeth!"

A crude curse ripped out of the man. "I'd like to see ye try, luv."

Enough!

Juliet sat straight up on her cot, covering her ears with her palms. "Stop squabbling! Is it not bad enough in here without quarreling amongst yourselves?"

Everyone chuckled then, loud enough to be heard past her stopped-up ears.

"Well, well." The bass words were muffled. "Looks like Queenie got her a spine after all."

"Aye, luv. Day or two more and ye'll be snappin' like the rest o' us."

She sank back to the cot, the wobbly legs creaking, trying hard not to lose her composure once again. Her eyes already stung from so much crying. It seemed anger kept desperation at bay, so better to hold on to her irritation at her gaol mates than give in to tears. Like the woman next to her had said, it didn't do any good anyway. Weeping wouldn't unlock her cell door or clear her name of the taint of poisoning Charity.

She scrunched her eyes closed, trying to pretend she was beneath the cozy counterpane of her bed at Bedford Manor. But no. All she saw on the inside of her lids was Henry, his mouth pressed tight, his left eye twitching, fear and shock and other emotions crossing his face so swiftly she could hardly name them. In the end, though, doubt had reigned.

Right before he'd turned his back on her and told the constable to do as he must.

She'd fought that man's grip like a rabbit caught in one of her snares, kicking, wriggling, screeching of her innocence. If she lay on her other side, she would yet feel the pain in her bruised bicep. But that didn't hurt nearly as much as Henry's betrayal. Did he honestly think she had poisoned his sister? Had she not tenderly cared for Charity during her illness? Stood side by side with him in trying to free the woman of her tormentor?

Had she not kissed his lips with all the passion he'd stirred within her?

She turned her face to the wall, ashamed she'd thought that kiss had meant something to him. For all his pretty words, clearly it had not, for how quickly he'd tossed her aside.

Worse than that, though, was the death knell to her hope. How stupid she'd been to think he had seen her at her worst—a lady fallen from status, a poacher, a nobody—and believe that he'd accepted her for who she was. . .determined, capable, trustworthy. She gritted her teeth. No. He'd chosen to doubt her instead of trust. Ahh, yes, she could understand his loyalty to his sister, but to think of her as someone who would willfully poison her?

And if Henry couldn't believe her, who on God's green earth would? There was Aunt Margaret, of course, but the word of a poor widow would carry no weight in court.

Chill seeped into her bones, and she shivered. She would end up like her father, godforsaken in these walls of doom and despair.

Unless, of course, they hanged her first.

That thought went down like a mouthful of rancid meat. Oh, that Charity would live! Not for Juliet's sake alone, but because the mere thought of that sweet woman's life coming to an end at such a young age just wasn't right. If Henry's sister didn't make it, her death would destroy him. Juliet pressed her knuckles to her mouth, pushing back another sob. Despite how much he must doubt her now, no matter the pain he'd caused by casting her in here, she could not bear the thought of him enduring such a grief. . .for well did she know the pain of losing a sibling.

A bond that, once broken, could never be rejoined.

She sank into an exhausted sleep, surrendering to hellish images and darkness so thick, it lived. How long she lay in such torment, she could not say, but when her eyes did open, night yet reigned, only now it was accompanied by the snores and heavy breathing of her gaol mates.

Driven by an urgent need she could no longer put off, she rose and wrinkled her nose at the bucket in the corner. She'd avoided the horrid thing, but it was inevitable she would have to give in to such an indignity. Likely better now, under the cover of shadow, than when eyes might witness her shame. Her empty stomach heaved at the thought, and it took all her fortitude to take the first step towards it.

But as she did, her foot slipped on something. Frowning, she caught her balance and, ever so tentatively, crouched to see the cause. A small square of white paper lay stark against the filthy stone floor.

A paper that had not been in the cell when she'd first been so roughly shoved inside.

Glancing about, more from habit than from actually expecting to see anyone, she swiped it up and unfolded the tiny note. Thankfully, the author—whoever it was, for no signature graced the bottom—had used a very dark ink. Holding the paper up to her eyes, she read the few words twice over in the spare light of the torch flickering outside her cell.

And tried to ignore the gooseflesh rising on her arms.

Trust is dangerous, so beware.
Near the old stone gate, truth lies buried where lies take root.

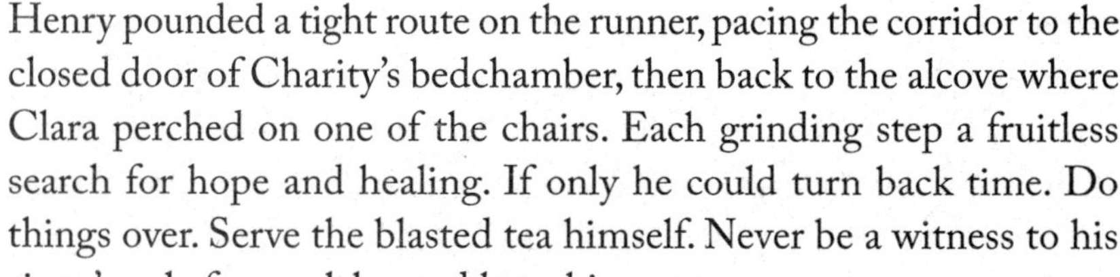

Henry pounded a tight route on the runner, pacing the corridor to the closed door of Charity's bedchamber, then back to the alcove where Clara perched on one of the chairs. Each grinding step a fruitless search for hope and healing. If only he could turn back time. Do things over. Serve the blasted tea himself. Never be a witness to his sister's pale face or laboured breathing.

And especially not have agreed to allow Juliet to be hauled off to gaol.

"Sit down." Clara reached out, snagging his coattail. "Working a rut into the floorboards will do your sister no good."

Did she think he didn't know that? Would to God there were something he *could* do that would help Charity!

Exhausted, he dropped into an adjacent chair, rubbing his palms along his thighs. "The doctor has been in there a long time," he grumbled. "Too long."

Tipping his head back, he stared at the ceiling. He'd been so determined to shoulder everything on his own. To prove he didn't need his father's guidance or interference. That he was capable. He could handle it.

And now. . .now he couldn't shake the fear his pride might be the thing that killed his sister.

Leaning aside, Clara stilled one of his hands with a firm grip. "Actually, I believe it is a good sign he's still in there. If things were going terribly wrong, Dr. Branch would have been out here by now."

A small amount of relief pulsed through him—a very small amount—yet for that he was grateful. He flipped his hand over, giving Clara's fingers a little squeeze before releasing her. "Thank you for staying here tonight."

She pulled back, tucking an imaginary swath of hair behind her ear, for no curl ever broke rank from her perfect coif. Clara was always polished, poised, so unlike. . . He swallowed hard, stopping himself before he could finish that thought.

"I will always be here for you, Henry. That's what friends are for. Besides, I sent word to Mother so she will not worry, leastwise about me. I have no doubt she will be praying for Charity every waking minute."

A comfort, that. He'd take all the prayer he could get on his sister's behalf. He forced his lips into what he hoped was some sort of smile. "I appreciate how your family stands with ours no matter what."

She shook her head, her tone resolute. "No gratitude needed. I would do so even if the past generations did not bind us together. You must know you mean the world to me." She paused a beat. "And Charity, of course."

Admiration shone in the brightness of her gaze and the blush on her cheeks, making him feel. . .nothing whatsoever. What was wrong with him? Any man would be moved to some degree to receive such an adoring look from a beautiful woman. Naturally he cared for Clara. He had ever since they played together as children. Yet she'd always—and ever would be—naught but another sister to him. A very loving sister, yes, but nothing more. Guilt settled over his shoulders like a cloud of black smoke. It would kill him to disappoint this woman, but he could not return any other affection than the brotherly sort. No. This faithful friend of his deserved better.

He jolted to his feet, itching to move, yet settled for raking his fingers over his scalp as he gazed down at Charity's bedroom door. "I just wish I knew what was going on in there."

"I can tell you." Clara's voice sharpened dramatically. "Dr. Branch is doing everything in his power to counteract the damage inflicted by Juliet Finch. You never should have trusted her. None of us should have. To think it was her all along."

"What do you mean?" He wheeled about.

She merely blinked. "Well, surely this proves Juliet was the one who's been tormenting your sister."

So. His suspicions had been correct. His sister had shared her woes with Clara. And here he and Juliet had been so careful not to expose too much information, for Charity's sake. A bitter laugh ripped out of him. "To what end?"

"Oh, Henry, there are wicked people in this world, those who will do anything to secure what they want. And make no mistake about it, Juliet wanted you. I saw it in her eyes. So, what better way to win you over than to appear as a redeemer of the one you love most—your sister. Think about it. Someone begins tormenting your sister. Then Juliet shows up in your life at just the right time, conveniently skilled. That's quite a coincidence, don't you think?"

"That is ridiculous!" He fisted his hands so tightly that his arms shook.

Despite his vitriol, Clara showed no offense. "Do not be so humble, Henry. Your name is well known. You are a man of wealth and position, and a handsome one at that. Juliet may have sought you out because of those things, orchestrated this entire scheme to secure a very comfortable life for herself."

He shook his head, trying to make sense of her logic. "Are you implying Juliet poisoned my sister—and is responsible for all the other torments before that—simply to win me over? That is insane!"

"Not to win you over, Henry, but to make herself a place by your side. She's a lovely woman, and beguiling. With enough proximity, what man could resist such charms?" She rose, landing a light touch on his shoulder. "I know this is hard for you, but think about it. The letters, the personal items moved or broken, the feeling your sister had of someone watching her? And then, just when Charity was to leave and end her place in your home, Juliet used her skill in medicinals to keep Charity here. To make herself essential to you. Because a sick sister needs a companion—and a distraught brother? Well, he needs someone to lean on. You see now, don't you? Why could it not have been Juliet? She had every opportunity, especially when you invited her into your home."

He wrenched from her touch as if burned. Had he truly allowed the very one he'd sought to vanquish live beneath his roof? Sup at his own table next to his sister?

Still. . .Juliet's sentiments and actions did not add up. She never had explained the green ribbon his sister had tripped over. Her knowledge of the manor grounds was as intimate as his own. And—God forgive him—she had certainly welcomed his kiss, despite the slap that followed.

These truths went down like wormwood. But no. He could not accept it. These things might sanction what Clara said, but the confirmation was too abhorrent to even consider.

For if Clara spoke truth, not only would he be a fool, but Juliet would be a monster.

He scrubbed his jaw with his knuckles, over and over, the rasp of whiskers harsh against his skin—an annoyance he relished, for to take on the anguish of accepting Juliet as the villain would drive him to his knees.

And yet. . .a small voice in the back of his mind refused to be silenced.

If she were playing a part—if all of this had been some elaborate game—why the poaching? If she were responsible for the torment from the beginning, why choose such a dangerous method of bringing herself to his attention? Why risk arrest? Exposure? She couldn't have known he'd spare her.

Blast it, he couldn't think straight. Not while Charity's life hung in the balance. Not while guilt and dread pulled him in opposite directions.

Later. He would sort it out later. When he had his wits about him.

If it wasn't already too late.

The quiet swoosh of a door against carpet cut the silence. Henry spun about the moment Dr. Branch stepped into the corridor, then took off at a good clip to meet the man but a few strides from his sister's room. "How does she fare?"

The doctor's brow condensed into an ominous line. "I am sorry to say that Miss Russell has yet to regain consciousness. If she'd not already been weakened by her previous illness, she may have rallied by now. The laudanum and ether she ingested has reduced her breathing to a hazardous degree, and I am afraid I have done everything in my power to neutralize the effects of such a dose. As such, she will require a constant vigil tonight. Shallow or not, if she continues to breathe until morning, then I think we will have turned a corner, and she should improve dramatically."

"*If* she continues to breathe?" The walls closed in on him, the world turning black at the edges. No. No! This could not be happening.

God, please!

"Of course she will recover." Clara's voice sailed resolute, a lifeline in this sea of horror. "Your sister is strong."

"Mmm." Dr. Branch removed his spectacles, rubbing the glass with his handkerchief for a good while before tucking away the cloth. "She is resilient, no doubt." He reset the glasses on the bridge of his nose, hooking the ear pieces securely. "But," he said with a sigh, "to be perfectly honest, I fear Miss Russell's vital functions have been significantly impaired. I have done my best with friction, bleeding out the impurities, and continued administrations of smelling salts, but you must understand, Mr. Russell, that there is no antidote."

Henry shoved his hands into his pockets to keep from shaking the man. "Can you truly do nothing more for her?"

The doctor wagged his head. "It has been a delicate battle, one which I have fought with all my resources, but your sister is in God's hands now."

Chapter 21

Three days in the belly of a fish. Three in a cold stone tomb. Juliet hunched listlessly on the wooden cot, note dangling from her fingers. Despair wrapped its arms around her. Again. It was her constant companion now—one she welcomed, for at least it was familiar. Was this how Jonah had felt when he'd been trapped in the dark and deep? How Jesus had suffered when bearing the load of sins that were not of His own making? Mirthless laughter caught in her throat. Who was she fooling? She was not a prophet or a saviour.

She was just a girl in a cage awaiting a fate she was powerless to stop.

So she clung to the only thing she knew: bitterness. And why not? It was all she had left. But it gave no relief, not a shred of it. She was sinking, hard and fast. Hardly able to breathe for want of release.

She crumpled the paper into a tight wad and threw it against the wall, sick to death of this wallowing, this unfair hand she'd been dealt. Had her father never ruined their family, she wouldn't be in this situation!

And yet where had her anger gotten her?

She huffed a long sigh. Oh, it had worked for a while, she supposed. Her fury had protected her from facing every lie he'd spun, each promise he'd broken, the scars he'd carved into her heart, but here? Now? It did no good. So much pain filled her chest it was a wonder her lungs worked at all. The rage that had been her armour seemed as confining as this cell. It hadn't saved her from anything. Not from poverty or hunger. Not from Henry's doubt and betrayal. And it certainly hadn't freed her from this wretched place.

She pressed her fists to her eyes, shoving back the tears that burned, but they slipped through anyway. She just couldn't contain it anymore.

"You ruined everything!" she rasped. "I hate you! Do you hear me?" She lifted her face and howled at the mouldy ceiling. "I hate you!"

She froze, stunned by her own venomous words, unsure if she were crying out to her dead father or to God.

"Shut yer yappin'!" Jackie barked from down the line.

She barely heard the man's voice over the rush of blood in her ears and the echo of her own wicked confession. Is that what she'd become? A hater of man and God? Trapped in a snare of her own making?

Shaking started in the pit of her belly and spread, so violently she grasped the edges of the wooden cot and held on for dear life. She had to, or she would break.

But it was too late.

She slumped over, unable to bear the weight of her own deception any longer, pushed down by a truth so heavy it was impossible to raise her head. She had never truly hated her father. Not really. She'd merely wanted him to love her as a father should, to care for her more than himself, and when he hadn't, when he'd rotted in that gaol cell unrepentant towards both God and her to the very end, she'd clung to bitterness instead of that painful truth.

Still, was she not following in his footsteps? She'd ruined herself as thoroughly as he had. No, worse. He'd never blamed her for his sins, yet here she was accounting to him all her woes.

She bit her bottom lip until she tasted the salt of blood. Jonah had given in to God and gone to Nineveh. Jesus—despite shouldering the sins of the world—had submitted to His Father's will. And here she sat in a damp prison, clutching an anger she never should have clung to in the first place. What a fool.

Her head hung even lower. "I—"

The whisper stuck in her throat like a hot coal, one she would either have to swallow forever or spit out and be rid of for good.

Perspiration prickled cold on her brow, and she tried again. "I forgive you, Father. Do you hear me, God?" She lifted her face, tears burning her cheeks. "I forgive him. I forgive all of it. The betrayal. The lies. Everything. He was a broken man, as misguided as I have been. Oh, Lord, pardon my own transgressions."

For a long time, she sat there. An eternity, it seemed. The air just as damp and reeking of unwashed bodies. The chill seeping through the fabric of her gown and pores of her skin. The door did not magically swing open to offer her a way out.

But despite all that, ever so slowly—yet steadily—the tightness in her chest loosened, enough so she could breathe again. Then more. Something much more. A strange lightness, long forgotten, replaced the strangling tide she'd swum in for so long.

Peace.

Delicate and fragile but growing with every breath she took.

Straightening, she wiped her eyes, bewildered by the profound change. Not a blessed thing was different behind these bars of steel and hard rock walls, but inside. . .she gasped. The hollow in her heart that'd whistled with nothing but cold air now pulsed with warmth.

She collapsed against the wall, face to the heavens, a bittersweet smile lifting her lips. Why had she not done this long ago?

Screeching hinges barged into her holy moment, followed by the clap of boots against stone. The turnkey—a burly fellow with a pockmarked face—stopped in front of her cell. "Look lively, Miss Finch. You've got a visitor." He turned his face back towards the door he'd come through, gesturing with a wiggle of his podgy fingers. "Come along. No one here's going to bite ye."

"Hear that, boys!" Juliet's neighbour on the other side of the wall squealed. "Queenie's got herself a caller."

"Hope he brought flowers," Jackie hollered back. "Might knock down some o' yer stink."

A foul curse ripped the air. "I'm a bucket o' posies compared to yer reekin' carcass."

The turnkey grabbed his club. "Quiet down, or I'll have you all muzzled like the pack of yapping curs you are." He stomped down the row, banging the bars with his bludgeon.

Juliet rose, tentatively peering as far as she could into the corridor. Had Henry recanted his doubt and come to release her? Or maybe by some great miracle Aunt Margaret had rallied to plead for her discharge?

The crisp cadence of expensive shoes clipped along the passageway. Long legs encased in finely pressed trousers entered her view, topped off by a lean torso and the unmistakable shape of a horse face. The man's spectacles reflected hellish glimmers from the wall torches.

Her brows rose. She never expected this. "Mr. Scather?"

The apothecary stopped in front of her door, head dipping in a curt nod. "Miss Finch."

This made no sense whatsoever. Surely he didn't think she was peddling her aunt's tonics in here. And even if he did, what could he possibly do about it? She was already in gaol!

She pursed her lips, thoroughly confused. "But. . .why have you come?"

Before he could answer, the turnkey planted himself next to the man. "You've got five minutes." A few drops of brown tobacco juice dribbled out the side of his mouth, but he did nothing to swipe the mess away. "I'll be waitin' by the door." He shuffled off, slapping his club against his palm.

Mr. Scather's gaze followed the hulk for a beat before looking down the great length of his sloped nose at her. "I came to see the reckless woman who once again threatens to ruin my business."

"How can I possibly accomplish that while locked in here?" She snorted.

"It is not what you are doing so much as what you have done. Poisoning a lady of society!" He spread his hands. "Have you lost your wits?"

Dread coiled in her stomach, and she pressed her fingers to her lips. "Has. . .has Miss Russell died?"

"No. I hear she fares well, no thanks to you and your evil intent."

Relief flashed through her, followed by a wave of righteous fury. "You have no right to accuse me of such a wicked crime."

"I have every right," he growled as he stepped closer, his wafting breath pungent with cloves. "Do you think your actions have not cast suspicion on all who deal in pills and remedies? There is already a noticeable downturn in my business."

"What have I to do with that? I am no apothecary, as you have repeatedly pointed out." She paced a small circle, trying to make sense of his words. "I fail to see how my imprisonment affects your sales."

His upper lip curled slightly. "The people of Bedford make no distinction between a street peddler such as yourself and an upstanding man of the trade like me. Remedies are remedies to them. What you did stains my name as well."

Juliet folded her arms like a shield against his accusations. "I have done nothing other than to be accused, through no fault of my own."

He chuckled, the sound hollow. "That is beside the point. Gossipmongers care nothing for the truth. My bottles are being looked upon as liquid death, all because the woman who sold tonics on the street has poisoned a gentlewoman. . .with laudanum and ether, no less."

He advanced, grabbing the bars with his long fingers, his voice lowering to a deadly tone. "And I think it may be no coincidence that recently a substantial amount of laudanum has gone missing from my stock, not to mention some oil of ether. What have you to say to that?"

She gaped, hardly believing the gall of the man. "Are you accusing me of theft, sir?"

He glanced from left to right before settling his dark gaze back on her. "I don't see anyone else in here who has the know-how and capability to overdose an unsuspecting victim to the point just shy of death. So"—his head cocked—"how did you do it? Pay a light-finger to snatch a bottle here and there when my back was turned? Or did you somehow sneak in at night? And what are you planning to do with the rest of it now that you are behind bars?"

Her old friend fury sparked into life, burning a trail up from her belly. Had she not suffered enough indignities that she now must bear this man's indictments?

She dropped her arms, hands curling into fists at her side. "Perhaps you ought to speak to the constable, Mr. Scather, because I have no idea where your missing laudanum could be."

"You and your silver tongue." He sneered. "You think you're so cunning, but this time your scheming is at an end. It appears you have ended up where you belong."

She propped her fists onto her hips. The man ought to be grateful bars separated them, for she'd really rather pop him in the nose. "Did you come all this way to gloat, Mr. Scather? Or is there a point to your visit?"

He adjusted his spectacles, his dark eyes narrowing behind the glass. "The point is this, Miss Finch. If you truly are as innocent as you claim, then clear your name quickly, because if you do not, more than your own reputation will suffer."

She flexed her fingers, frustration a living animal caged inside her chest. Did he not realize she'd like nothing better? "Then help me do so," she challenged.

A humourless chuckle rumbled in his throat. "That is not my burden to shoulder. You are a clever woman. More than resilient and highly intelligent. I am sure you will think of something. You always have in the past."

"Look around you." She flung out her arms. "I have no resources to use in here. No power to do anything other than sit on that rock-hard cot." She jabbed her finger over her shoulder at the hated wooden frame.

"You have a mind, do you not? Use it. Think! If you did not poison Miss Russell, then who benefits from making you look the guilty party? Who stands to gain from such a ruse? Identify the culprit and outmaneuver them. And do so quickly, for both of our sakes." He retreated a step, readjusting his black hat with a sharp clap to the top of it. "Good day, Miss Finch."

She barely registered his departure, his voice still echoing inside her head.

"Who benefits from making you look the guilty party? . . . Identify the culprit and outmaneuver them."

She grabbed on to the bars to keep from swaying, so stunning was the simplicity of the words. She'd been so busy mucking about in self-pity, too preoccupied with anger towards Henry, her father, and—God forgive her—the Almighty Himself, that she'd not given a second thought to who really poisoned Charity.

She stumbled to the corner and swiped up the note, then dropped to the cot and unfolded it. Smoothing out the wrinkles, she stared at the words with fresh eyes, then jerked up her head at the clank of the heavy door slamming behind Mr. Scather.

"Who benefits?" she whispered. "Well, sir, I suppose I will just have to find out."

October afternoons were made for sitting in front of the fire, a dog at your feet and a cider in your hand, with nary a care in the world to weigh you down. Henry smirked at the flames in the sitting room hearth. Well, he had fire, at least. One out of four would have to do.

For the hundredth time he glanced over at Charity. She lounged comfortably in one of the wingbacks, a lap rug tucked about her legs. Idly she traced her fingers over the embossed letters on the cover of a book she had yet to crack open. He frowned. Her bones were far too sharp beneath the soft fabric of her day gown, and those dark crescents beneath her eyes had yet to lighten. She'd come a long way since that eternal night when any breath might've been her last, but she was not her bonny self, either. A concern, that.

Would to God it were his only one.

He shifted on the sofa, giving up on reading the newspaper he'd already folded and refolded into oblivion. When he wasn't anxiously attending his sister, his head was filled with worry for Juliet. She'd been in that horrid gaol for three days now. How did she fare? He ought to call on her, demand answers to the questions that'd gnawed his mind raw, but Charity had needed him here. Leastwise that's what he kept telling himself. The truth was—God forgive him—he couldn't bear the thought of facing Juliet, looking into the depths of those sage eyes, and witnessing guilt instead of innocence.

Absently, he drummed his finger against the paper, ignoring the headlines. He'd questioned every one of the staff about the poisoning, twice over for Woodley and the kitchen servants, which had gotten him exactly nowhere. It still appeared Juliet could be guilty of slipping that laudanum into Charity's cup. . .and yet, something about it refused to settle.

If this had been her grand scheme all along, why hadn't she played her hand more carefully? Surely she could not be responsible for the tormenting notes and flowers, for she had no reason to believe he would take her in as an assistant rather than have her hanged for poaching. And after he had done so, well. . .why poison Charity? Why risk her place, her future, with something so sloppy—so obvious?

Blast it all! He pinched the bridge of his nose mercilessly. If only he knew the truth!

Outside, hoofbeats pounded against the gravel drive. He snapped up his head, glad for a diversion, and tossed the paper aside. Striding to the window, he pulled the sheers back with a sweep of his hand and peered through the wavy glass. A man in a black riding coat dismounted from a sturdy bay, landing strongly on his right leg. Though the visitor's back was turned, Henry's gut tightened. He didn't need to see the face.

He knew.

Wheeling about, he dashed from the room, making it to the front hall the same time as Mrs. Hamby's dark skirts swished into view from the opposite corridor.

He waved her away. "Thank you, but I will handle this."

One of her brows arched in curiosity, yet she dipped her head. "As you wish, sir."

By the time he reached for the knob, she'd already vanished down the passageway. Exhaling sharply to maintain control, he yanked open the door and then widened his stance on the threshold. The man would have to take him down bodily if he tried to enter.

"Parker," he said through clenched teeth. "What are you doing here?"

"Ever the gentleman as usual, I see." Edwin Parker leaned on his cane, his deep-set eyes raking over Henry, assessing him as he might a head of cattle to be purchased. . .looking for weaknesses. "But since you insist on forgoing manners and coming to the point, I shall play along." His chin angled like a man spoiling for a brawl. "I am calling to see how your sister fares."

Despite the astonishment washing over him, Henry kept his tone even. "My sister is no concern of yours. I believe she made that clear to you last year before you trotted off to the military."

Parker winced ever so slightly.

Ahh, a direct hit—one that should feel as a victory. So why the sudden shame squeezing his chest?

Parker squared his shoulders, a bull about to charge. "That does not negate the fact that I still care for her, which is no crime."

"No, but it is curious that after being home these past three months, you are suddenly so interested in her health." Henry sucked in a breath, an ugly realization stealing the air he sought. "How the deuce do you know anything about my sister's health?"

"Word travels." Parker shrugged a shoulder, completely nonchalant. "And Dr. Branch is my physician as well."

"He breached confidence with you!"

"Calm down. All your Russell secrets are still intact. It was merely conversational, I assure you. But enough was said from him—and other contacts—to know Charity may have been poisoned, and even now Miss Finch is behind bars because of it."

Henry gripped the doorjamb. Of course tongues wagged. Always did and always would. But to think of his sister's and Juliet's names being bantered about in a pub like yesterday's news did not go down well.

Parker shook his head, a slight smirk twitching one side of his mouth. "Come, now. Not even you are above gossip. But that is beside the point. How is Charity?"

"Why do you not ask Dr. Branch?" He huffed. "I am sure he will tell you."

"Do you never tire of chewing on sour grapes? I am here in goodwill, nothing more." Parker held his gaze, unflinching.

He was a bold man, Henry would give him that. One who apparently still harboured affection for his sister despite past circumstances . . .just as he could not seem to banish his feelings towards Juliet. A tiny tendril of empathy broke through the hard ground of his heart. Perhaps he was being a bit of a brute. "Pardon me, Parker. I am. . . out of sorts. It has been a grueling week."

Hah. What an understatement. The past several months had been taxing.

"Believe it or not, I understand. We all have our crosses to bear." A gust of wind caught the man's hat. Leaning heavily on his cane for balance, Parker clapped his free hand atop it before the thing flew away.

Shame burned in Henry's belly. Here he stood solidly on two legs when Parker had made the effort to ride over here hindered by a war injury. All the fight drained from him, and he softened his tone. "My sister is on the mend. She is weak, but getting stronger every day, thank God."

"I am happy to hear it. May I—" Parker's voice cracked, and he cleared his throat. "May I see her? Just for a moment?"

Henry inhaled deeply, the scent of an upcoming storm heavy on the air. Dark clouds gathered in the east. An ill omen warning him not to allow Edwin Parker anywhere near his sister?

Or all the more reason to invite the man in?

"Very well." He stepped aside. "But only for a minute."

Parker bypassed him, fumbling in his pocket. Once inside, he pulled out a pocket watch, golden chain dangling from his fingers, and offered it on an upturned palm. "Should you like to time me?"

Henry rolled his eyes. The man's humour was as dry as the brown leaves that'd blown in onto the carpet. "No need. This way."

He strode from the hall, the rhythmic thump of Parker's cane keeping time with his steps. Hopefully he wasn't leading a wolf to his sheep.

Charity looked up as they entered, her expression freezing the instant she saw Parker.

"Edwin?" His name was barely a breath as she straightened in the chair.

Folding his arms, Henry leaned his shoulder against the wall near the hearth, close enough to guard his sister if need be, while at the same time allowing Parker space to speak with Charity.

The man pulled off his hat, setting it on the side table before dipping a deep bow. As he rose, his brow creased when he took in her frail form. "Good afternoon, Miss Russell. I will not intrude on you for long. I merely came to see with my own eyes that you are well. I. . ." His Adam's apple bobbed, his hard swallow audible in the quiet room. "I feared the worst."

"That is unexpectedly kind of you, but as you see, I am recovering beneath my brother's watchful eye." Her gaze flicked to Henry then back to Parker, her fingers playing with the hem of the lap rug.

"I would expect nothing less, though you must understand I had to put my mind at ease." The sharp line of his shoulders relaxed, a rare smile softening the harsh planes of his face. "I am happy to see you no longer languish."

Charity's eyelashes fluttered, a dusky rose spreading over her cheeks. "I appreciate your concern." She twiddled all the more with the blanket fringe.

Henry hissed a quiet breath between his teeth. Since when did his sister fidget like a schoolgirl in this man's presence? While he appreciated the life seeping back into her flesh, it irked him for Parker to be the cause. She'd suffered enough when she'd anguished over breaking things off with him, and even more when he'd played the part of the spurned suitor all over town to gain sympathy.

"All right, Parker. I can only assume your curiosity has been sated." Henry stepped away from the hearth, one arm sweeping towards the door. "I shall see you out now."

"Henry!" The landing of Charity's book on the floor clapped as sharply as his name from her lips. "Don't be so boorish."

A glimmer of amusement sparked in Parker's dark eyes. "He is only being protective, which is reasonable. I would do the same were I in his shoes. Besides, I do not wish to tire you."

Henry tensed as the man closed the distance between him and Charity, ready to spring if Parker tried anything untoward.

But Parker merely retrieved her book and—ever so gently—set it on her lap. "Should you have need of anything—anything at all—simply send me word. Despite our. . .past, I would do all in my power to help you."

Charity nodded ever so slowly as she clutched the book to her chest. "I know that, and I appreciate it."

He dipped his head, then pivoted with aid of his cane and collected his hat. With a last bow to them both, he bid good day, then clapped on the beaver-felt top hat and hobbled to the door.

Henry followed him into the corridor, jaw tight, undecided what to make of the exchange between his sister and this man.

Parker didn't so much as glance over his shoulder. "Don't worry. I won't pilfer any silver on my way out."

Henry gritted his teeth, trapping a frustrated retort. The man could try the patience of a saint, and God knew he didn't come close to that title.

When they reached the front hall, Parker turned to him, face unreadable but his tone a challenge. "Take care of her, Russell. I would not see her suffer any more than she has."

Sincerity swam just below the surface of those words, catching Henry quite off guard. "Nor would I," he murmured. He'd taken every measure in his power to see to Charity's well-being, yet each had proved insufficient. No, he could not resent the man for caring for his sister. By his own admission he had loved her once.

And likely still did.

Without another word, Parker snugged his coat tight at his neck and opened the door, then stepped out into the first spasms of what promised to be a drenching rain. Henry watched him swing up to his mount with a wince, disregarding the drops of water pelting his own face. Had he been wrong about the man?

He closed the door against the chill and wandered back to the sitting room, unsure what to think about anything anymore. Charity hadn't moved a whit, the book still clutched to her chest, her face fixed on the orange glow of the fire.

Alarm throbbed in his temple, and he pressed his fingers to it. Had Parker's visit been too much too soon? He crossed the rug, dropping to her side. "I shall see you back to your room now."

"Not yet." She didn't even glance at him, just stared at the fire with a wistful purse of her lips. "It is so cozy here by the hearth."

Henry leaned back on his haunches, doubting very much it was the warmth of the crackling logs pinking her cheeks. "Do you care for the man. . .Parker?"

She hugged the book all the tighter, her voice fairy light. "We were friends."

Friends?

A loaded word, that. What did it really mean? He thought he knew, once, but now? He stalked to the mantel, trying to make sense of it all. Swiping away one of the candlesticks, he spun it slowly between his fingers, studying his sister. "It was my understanding that Parker wanted more, and you did not."

"Mmm." At length, her gaze lifted to his. "People change, Henry. Not everyone is the villain we make them out to be."

His fingers stilled on the candlestick. Ever since spying Parker on the street corner near the bakery, he'd thought the man a scoundrel—the potential tormentor, no less! And yet had he not come here today, was even now riding home in a buffeting rain, not to cause trouble or distress but to simply assure himself of Charity's well-being? Henry white-knuckled the brass stick. How could he have been so wrong about him? And worse. . .*oh, dear God.*

If he was wrong about Parker, what about Juliet?

The candlestick clattered to the slate tiles in front of the hearth, chipping off the corner of one and sending it flying.

"Henry!" Charity cried.

He swiped up the brass holder and set it harshly on the mantel, rattling the other trinkets. Perhaps he'd been too caught up in emotion when Charity had swooned that afternoon. Maybe he'd been too eager to agree with the constable, allowing him to haul Juliet off without first giving her the benefit of the doubt. He exhaled sharply through his nose. Clara had painted a portrait of Juliet as a schemer, orchestrating everything to secure his favour. But poaching? That wasn't clever. It wasn't calculated. It was reckless. Desperate. If Juliet had come to Bedford Manor with motives, she would've played the part of a lady. But she hadn't. She'd risked everything for food, not affection. That was not the mark of a schemer.

It was the mark of a survivor.

He pressed his hands to his head, squeezing in frustration.

What *was* the truth?

"Henry?" Charity's voice crept up his spine like a shiver, her fingers whisper light on his shoulder. "Are you all right?"

"I am fine." He forced a measured tone and turned with a fake smile, then guided her back to the chair and retucked the lap rug about her legs. "Now, you rest here, and I shall have Mrs. Hamby bring you some tea. There is something I must do. Something I should have done long before this. Promise me you shall stay right here until I return, hmm?"

"Of course. But what is it that is suddenly so urgent?"

He clutched the back of Charity's chair as if clinging to life itself. "I must find the truth."

Chapter 22

Trust is dangerous, so beware.

Juliet fingered the note in her pocket as she paced a route around her cell. She didn't need to see the scrawled ink anymore. The words were seared into her mind. And likely would be forevermore.

She chewed on her thumbnail as she swung into another circuit, which honestly didn't take long, so small was the cell. Ignoring the stench of her own unwashed body—ahh, but she'd give her left arm for a rose-scented bath—she focused on the message. Was this a broad warning or a specific threat about a particular person? Probably not the former, because who would bother to deliver such a vague note? And if the latter, did it mean she'd misplaced her trust in someone she'd thought an ally but was really working against her?

A shiver lifted gooseflesh on her forearms, but not from the chill of the stone walls. If that line of thinking were correct, there remained precious few people to beware of, for she'd allowed her heart to trust only Aunt Margaret, Charity, and. . . She chewed her thumb more furiously, not wishing to admit the last person.

Henry.

Her step hitched, the thin soles of her shoes so damp her toes squished inside them. Logically, Aunt could do nothing in her condition. And Charity was the victim in this whole scenario. So that left. . .him. The man who'd held her in his arms, claiming she undid him. The one who'd looked at her as if no other woman existed.

The one she'd given her heart to.

Wind howled through the cracked window high up on the wall, but the mournful sound might as well have slipped out of her own throat. What a fool! She deserved to be in here for being so naive.

Juliet whumped down on the hard cot, teeth juddering. Better to move on to the next part of the note than dwell on such a hideous truth.

Near the old stone gate, truth lies buried where lies take root.

Clutching the coarse blanket to her chest, she hugged the filthy fabric, thoughts awhirl. She knew exactly where the old gate was, but what truth lay beneath the dirt there? Something to prove her innocence? Something that revealed Charity's true tormentor?

She cast the blanket aside, shoulders slumping. For all she knew it could be naught but a cruel jest. Or worse. A trap.

Yet was she not already trapped?

Her head dropped to her hands. She would never know the answer unless she got out of here. She *had* to find what lay near that gate! But how could she possibly do so while locked in a prison of iron and stone?

"What do I do, God?" The prayer was little more than a whisper—one that startled. One that felt like breathing. How easily her petitions flowed now that the floodgates of her spirit had been opened.

Or maybe she was just too exhausted to fight on her own anymore.

"Oh, Lord." She exhaled shakily. "How can I possibly find what is buried when I am trapped behind these bars? Or—" She jerked up her head, sucking in air as a realization hit her hard. "Is this yet another thing I must surrender to You?"

The only answer was the scrape of an iron latch and creak of hinges. Heavy boots thudded against stone, the jingle of keys whapping against the turnkey's thigh as he came into view. "Pull yourself together, Miss Finch. You've another visitor."

He tipped his head towards the door, signaling for whoever it was to enter.

"Hear that, Jackie? Queenie's holdin' court again." The woman in the next cell over cackled at her own jest.

"Hope it's one o' her knights armed with a battering ram," Jackie bellowed back. "A big hole in the wall would do us all good."

Juliet rolled her eyes as the hefty guard once again pulled out his club and lumbered off, banging the bars and threatening the inmates. Such behaviour was becoming as routine as the mealy porridge served twice a day.

She rose, not even bothering to smooth the wrinkles from her gown. If Mr. Scather wished for another session of gloating, why bother trying to mould herself into some semblance of propriety? The man would never respect her anyway. She folded her arms, prepared for battle.

But nothing could have prepared her for the silent figure standing tall in the gloom—one that stole the breath from her lungs.

Henry's dark coat clung to his broad shoulders, his collar turned up against the cold. Wet hair curled beneath his black felt hat, torchlight flickering against the droplets like the sky had wept over him. He said nothing as he approached, his jaw fixed as his gloved fingers wrapped around the bars. Never once did his gaze stray from hers. He was a handsome, brooding spectre, one she loathed to admire so much.

She dropped her arms, her fingers flexing, unsure if she ought to curl them into fists or cover her face and weep, for far too many emotions churned in her belly. Part of her—the traitorous part—wanted to run into his arms. The other longed to spit in his face. How dare he show up now, after three endless days of cold and want and fear?

Even so, the very sight of him—drenched and haggard, unmistakable pain in his grimace—squeezed her heart. She planted her feet, unwilling to take a step towards him, for yes. She *was* a fool. She was a stupid, blind-eyed namby when it came to this man.

And that infuriated her more than anything.

He worked his jaw, struggling for words as if they'd turned to stone in his mouth. Good. Let him struggle. It was but a mere taste of the melee her life had been this past year.

"Juliet." A thousand heartbreaks lived in that one, throaty word. "Are you—" He drew in a stuttered breath. "Do they treat you well?"

She bit the inside of her cheek to keep from scoffing. What sort of question was that when he could see the black mould on the walls and hear the scathing skirmish going on between Jackie and the turnkey at the end of the passageway? She lifted one shoulder nonchalantly. "As well as any gaol, I suppose, though I haven't much former experience to compare this with."

He pressed his forehead against the cold iron, his eyes closing, lines of grief etching deeply at the sides of them.

Juliet's brow crumpled. What was this? Why such sympathy from the man who'd sent her here? "Why have you come, Mr. Russell? How fares your sister?"

"Charity is on the mend. I. . ." He closed his eyes for a moment, and when they reopened, red rimmed the whites. "I need to know the truth, Juliet."

"Well, you surely seemed certain of it when you allowed the constable to escort me to this fine establishment." She flung out her arms, indicating the rough wooden cot in one corner and horrid waste bucket squatting in the other. "I am here because you believe me the villain!"

A muscle jumped on his jaw. "I know you are angry but—"

"Angry? Angry!" She stomped to the bars, facing him nose to nose, and lowered her voice to a guttural tone. "You underestimate the depth of my fury, sir."

"Please." His breath puffed hot against her brow. "I want to believe in you. I truly do, but surely you admit the evidence against you does not bode well."

"I could say the same of you."

"Me?" He reared back his head. "What do you mean?"

"You told me you would never betray me." She stabbed him in

the shoulder with her finger. "You said it out loud, right to my face. Yet here I am, by your hand, your own words branding you a liar."

"No." He shook his head violently, droplets of water hitting her face. "I would never willingly betray you."

"Nor would I poison your sister. I am not the monster everyone makes me out to be!" Her voice—harsh and crackly—bounced from wall to wall like a mad woman's. She retreated a step, breathing ragged, hating the awful sound of it, hating even more that this man could drive her to such unbridled passion.

Henry whirled, slapping his open palm against the opposite wall. His head hung as if she'd whipped him.

Bootsteps thundered their way, the smack of the turnkey's club against her bars a lightning bolt down her spine.

Henry turned back swiftly.

The grizzly turnkey merely hitched his thumb towards her. "She giving you trouble, Mr. Russell?"

"No." Henry scrubbed his palm over his face, the motion rough with fatigue. "I would appreciate a moment more with Miss Finch, if you please. Alone."

"Aye." The big man gave a nod. "As you wish. I'll wait near the door, then." He ambled off, but not before he directed a dark look her way.

Slowly, Henry approached her cell, the lines of his jaw hardening. "Will you swear before God you are innocent? Think very carefully before you answer." His voice lowered to a menacing whisper. "Do you swear it?"

She searched his face, her gaze flicking between each of his grey-green eyes. Oh, but she was desperate to read what went on inside this man, to know that he would believe her if she but said the word . . .but would her word alone be enough? Was *she* enough for him?

She pressed her lips tight.

Oh God, please let him believe me.

Inhaling deeply, she stepped up to the bars and grasped the cold metal. "Yes, Henry. I vow before you and God that I never have done—and never will do—anything that would harm your sister. And now I must ask the same of you."

She lifted her face to his. "Will you swear before God that you believe me?"

Henry stood at the very tip of a precipice, teetering above a black abyss waiting to swallow him whole if he answered no. . .or yes. Either promised dire consequences. Again, he spun away from Juliet's beseeching eyes. A cowardly move, perhaps, but altogether necessary. This was no small question. He must bear the weight of it without allowing himself to be swayed by the sight of a woman worn thin by three days in this wretched place.

A woman who still had the power to squeeze his heart.

He retreated to the solid wall beside her cell, just out of her line of vision. Sliding his back against the cold stone, he sank into a crouch, revisiting every memory he had of the untamed Juliet Finch. She was a wild one—or could be—but she was also a refined lady, one with nothing to gain by harming Charity. Nothing financial. No negative history or vendetta. She'd even risked herself to try to help him find his sister's tormentor.

He tipped his head back, eyes fixed on the blackened ceiling, though he saw none of it—all he could picture were her fiery eyes, burning into his soul as she vowed her innocence. Would she dare swear such a thing before God if she were guilty? No. Juliet was many things—impetuous, headstrong, passionate—but never once had she given him cause to believe her a liar. Even when she'd been caught with a grouse in her bag she'd put up no defense. . .which pointed to her veracity now. So, either he believed her, or he didn't. There was no in-between. It came down to faith. Faith in her. Faith that no matter how dark things might appear, she was worth holding on to.

He rose, expelling the past three days of angst in a great whoosh of air, then returned to Juliet, heart banging against his ribs like a war drum. She stood as he'd left her, clutching the bars, knuckles white, face even whiter, shoulders a stiff line.

He met her gaze head-on. "I believe you, Juliet." He swallowed, conviction coating his throat. "I swear it."

She drew in a shuddering breath, a barely audible "Thank you" passing her lips when she released it.

And just like that, the heavy load he'd carried the past three days lifted, replaced by a lightness he hadn't felt in a long time. Hope. Not simply because truth had won out, but because he finally could move forwards without doubt dragging him down.

She studied him, likely calculating his sincerity, and when apparently satisfied, she reached into her pocket. "If we are to trust one another, then I think there is something you should know."

She pulled a small paper from her pocket and held it out.

He unfolded the creased note, paper nearly ripping from having been handled so much, and read: *Trust is dangerous, so beware. Near the old stone gate, truth lies buried where lies take root.*

Interesting. But what did it mean?

Cocking his head, he waved the paper in the air. "Where did you get this?"

"Someone slipped it under the bars the first night I was here. I can only guess it was the guard, though he admits to nothing. I suspect someone paid him to pass it along to me."

"Why?" He fingered the paper. "What truth does it speak of?"

"I wish I knew, but perhaps it is something that will prove my innocence." She stepped closer to the bars, hesitation clear in the working of her jaw. "Will you go there? To the old stone gate? Will you look for what is buried?" She pressed her lips tight, a sign that her pleading had cost her some dignity.

"No." He shook his head, a slow grin teasing across his mouth. "We will go there together."

She snorted. "That might be a bit difficult for me at the moment."

"Then I shall have you released at once." A smile lifted his lips, then faltered as his gaze passed over her. Shadows hung like sharp sickles beneath her eyes. Her chestnut hair had lost all lustre.

Exhausted hollows stood out in stark contrast to her cheekbones. This was his fault. All of it.

Gently, he pried her fingers from the bars, enfolding her cold hands in his own. A bird couldn't have felt more fragile. Ever so tenderly, he chafed warmth back into her skin, aching at the smallness of her hands and the way she trembled beneath his touch.

"I never should have allowed you to be brought here in the first place." Regret stuck in his throat.

"No, you shouldn't have." She huddled closer to the bars, a sudden sheen of tears glistening in her eyes. "But, as much as I hate to be here, it has worked out for good, for I have finally found peace."

Emotion clung to her lashes, but her poise never faltered.

His brow scrunched. "How so?"

White teeth flashed as she nibbled her lower lip, almost as if the action would summon the right words to the surface. Eventually, she peered up at him, a new confidence in the set of her jaw. "The truth is that for too long I have allowed myself to be bound by the past—by bitterness, fear, the need to survive on my own. It all caught up to me in here, and I. . .well, I suppose I finally realized I do not have to define myself by the measure of what has been done to me, but by the measure of what God has done for me."

"Oh, Juliet." He shuddered. "I should have been here at your side, fighting this battle with you, not against you."

"You cannot stand between me and God. This was something I had to work out alone with Him, and I fear I never would have had I not been forced into captivity." A radiant smile broke across her lips, so brilliant it outshone the torches lining the walls. "All is well now, truly. I mean that."

He believed her without question, for there was a new light shining in her eyes—and it wasn't from the flickering flames. Somehow, like Job himself, she'd found peace from God. A gift, despite being on the wrong side of the bars.

While the true villain yet roamed free.

He pulled away, exhaling sharply. "Then let's get you out of here, shall we?"

"You mean—?"

He pressed a finger to her lips, the softness nearly driving him mad. "I mean I was a fool to ever doubt you, and I will never make that mistake again." His hand brushed her cheek, lingering for a moment longer than necessary. "I shall speak to the magistrate at once and return posthaste."

Without another word, he whipped around, his boots thudding against the stone as he strode to the turnkey. Minutes later, he remounted his horse and rode for the magistrate's house, despising the rain that slowed him.

Despising even more when the magistrate's butler told him the man had gone to London and would not return until late that night. Blast. Juliet, already worn by three days in that stinking cell, would have to suffer another eternal night.

Gripping the reins tighter, he turned towards home, determined it would be her last night in that rathole. Ever. If that note were true, he could prove her innocence and possibly unveil the tormentor at last.

By the time he reached Bedford Manor and fetched Carver, he was soaked through, his coat a second skin. But so be it. He had a mission to accomplish. The wind howled through the trees, branches rattling like bones all the way to the southeast corner of the estate where the crumbling remnants of moss-covered stone pillars were all that remained of a forgotten gate. He swung off his mount and grabbed his shovel before Carver caught up to him.

Working together, scoop after scoop began to scar the earth. Over and over again. Rain filled the hollows. Mud splattered them both from head to toe.

And they found nothing.

Enraged, he dug all the more furiously, churning up muck and stone until his muscles quivered. Minutes stretched to hours. And Carver, God love him, plugged away at his side.

But still nothing. All he unearthed was a massive load of frustration.

Until at last, he hurled aside his shovel and howled up at the stormy sky.

Had someone else already been here and dug up whatever truth that note had hinted at? He dropped to his knees, pounding a fist into the mud. Someone had been here. Someone knew. And now the hope of finding whoever was behind all this mess was gone.

Chapter 23

Strange how life could change in twenty-four hours. One day your heart soars with hope, then lies broken and bleeding the next. Juliet sat on the rock-hard cot, twisting the fabric of her skirt into little puckers. Fretting the material. Fraying her nerves. Why had Henry not yet returned? He'd said he believed in her innocence, and she believed that he did.

So where was he?

The question consumed her. She'd expected him to return last evening. When that didn't happen, she'd hardly slept for anticipation of an early-morning release. That was ages ago. Furiously, she wound the cloth one way then another, questions swirling in her head. Had the magistrate refused her discharge? Or worse, had Henry not even visited the man and instead first sought the buried evidence—then found something damning against her? Another vial of laudanum, perhaps? A torn bit of one of her gowns? Maybe even a written confession forged in her own penmanship? Clearly whoever had been tormenting Charity was not above such a dastardly deed, wishing not only Henry's sister gone but her as well.

And if Henry had unearthed supposed proof of her guilt for a crime she didn't commit, did that mean the next face she'd see would be a hangman's?

She shivered, and not just from the bone-chilling cold—then her spine snapped straight as the iron latch on the admitting door scraped open. Hinges screeched. Boots thudded. Heart racing, Juliet shot to her feet. He'd returned. Henry had returned! She flew to the bars.

Only to see the turnkey standing there, club ready at his side—the *only* thing at his side. Henry did not accompany him. She pressed her fist to her belly, gutted.

The man eyed her as if she were merely one more item on his daily task list to tick off. Which she probably was. He reached for the key looped to his belt. "Looks like you've been dealt a new hand, Miss Finch."

"Ho, ho!" Jackie called from farther down. "Queenie's got herself a pardon."

"Careful there, yer highness." The woman in the next cell cackled. "Don't let that door hit yer royal behind on the way out."

Ignoring them, Juliet smoothed her shaky hands along her skirt, working out the twists she'd inflicted. "What does that mean?" she asked the turnkey.

He swung her door wide open. "You're free to go, miss."

She blinked, hardly daring to believe his words. If that were so—*oh, God, please let it be so*—then where was Henry? She gazed past him, murmuring, "On whose order? Who freed me?"

The big man shrugged. "I just do as I'm told. All I know is I'm to let you out. What happens after that is up to you, I suppose." Hooking the key ring back on his belt, he turned away.

"Ye better hustle along, Queenie, a'fore that bounder changes 'is mind. . .lessen ye'd like to skip down here a'ways fer a good-bye kiss," Jackie hollered.

"Don't do it, luv! Ye're sure to catch a crawler o' a disease from that barker."

Gathering her skirts, Juliet dashed after the turnkey, glad to be free of such unending waggery, and reached the door just as he did. She followed his blue coat up a set of spiraling stairs, the air fresher with each tread. With a final turn, they emerged into the receiving area of the Bedford gaol.

When she'd first been hauled in, she'd cringed from the intimidating starkness of the place. The black beams overhead had pressed the air from her lungs. The pockmarked desk near the windowless front door stood empty now, as the guard was at her side, but the sight of it still sent shivers down her spine. That's where she'd been indelibly marked as a criminal in the ledger. Next to it was the scarred wooden bench, stained with the sweat and despair of countless criminals—herself included—as she'd waited for her imprisonment.

But now it all seemed a cheery haven compared to what she'd endured belowstairs.

Only one other door graced the west wall. The warden's office, where two men conversed in low tones, both with their backs towards her—one of which sent her pulse into an erratic beat.

Henry's black coat fell in crisp lines over his broad frame. He stood rigid, fists flexing at his side, hinting at restraint. Had it been such a battle for her release? Warmth wrapped around her shoulders. If it had been a struggle, he'd fought it for her.

"Here she is, Mr. Gabbert." The guard nodded at the warden, then apparently washing his hands of the whole business, strode to the chair behind the desk and plopped down, wood creaking.

Henry spun at her approach. It took everything in her not to run into his arms and pretend none of this had ever happened. But the moment she gained his side, his scent of bay leaf and leather wrapping around her like an embrace, she could finally breathe again. She peered up at him, knees shaky. "I was beginning to wonder if you would return."

A sultry smile curved half his mouth, and for a breath-stealing moment, she wondered if he would pull her against him. He did not reach for her, but his husky tone caressed her all the same. "I will always come for you."

Behind him, the warden cleared his throat. "See that you keep the terms of her release, Mr. Russell."

"No need for a reminder, sir." Though he spoke to Mr. Gabbert, his gaze did not stray from her face. "I shall not be letting her out of my sight." He crooked his arm, his tone softening. "Come."

She pressed her fingers against his sleeve, allowing him to steer her towards the door. "What terms?"

He glanced down at her as he led her outside. "I will explain it on our way home."

Home.

Her breath caught. How lovely the sound of that word. Even lovelier was the scent of rain-washed streets mixed with chimney smoke. A whirlwind of leaves swirled at her feet as Henry stopped near the carriage and helped her up. She sank onto the velvet cushion, the softness of it something she would never again take for granted. Oh, how thankful she was to be out of that hellish place!

Henry climbed in beside her, rapping on the wall for the driver to move on. When the carriage lurched forwards, his thigh bumped against hers. A thrill charged through her, but even so she eased away, putting space between them, painfully aware of how wretched she must look—and smell.

"So"—she faced him—"what are the terms of my release?"

"It took me all morning to persuade the magistrate, Mr. Trumbill, but..." A roguish grin spread over his wide lips. "You are to be under my custody until the true cad who poisoned my sister is caught."

So. He did still believe her—and the thought squeezed her chest. She smiled in full. "How did you manage that?"

"I reminded Mr. Trumbill that I never actually signed any papers for your arrest, that no formal charge had been made, and that holding a lady without solid evidence would reflect poorly on how he carries out his duties. I also may have mentioned that when my father returns, he would not appreciate learning a guest of his household had been left to rot in gaol while the real criminal ran free." One of his brows arched. "And my father happens to be the reason Mr. Trumbill holds the magistrate position to begin with."

"Ahh, I see. You employed a veiled threat."

"If you will." He rubbed his chin. "I prefer to think of it as creative persuasion. Besides, I needed you out of there posthaste. It turns out you do me no good behind bars."

"Is that so?" She smirked. "And what if I should decide to run off in the night and flee this custody of yours?"

His smile faded, his voice dropping to a low murmur. "Then I would follow you, for I will never lose you again."

She swallowed hard as his gaze met hers—almost reverent, as if she were a priceless gem he valued more than life. Would that time might stand still, for she could live forever in such a look of devotion.

"Thank you," she whispered. "For all you have done."

"I only wish I could have done more." He reached for her hand, rubbing little circles on her palm, quiet for a moment. "But. . ." he said at length, "I fear I do not bear good news."

While his touch felt delicious, she pulled away, acutely aware of the grime on her skin and not just a little nervous about what he might mean. "What is it?"

"I went to the old stone gate." With a sigh, he kneaded a muscle at the back of his neck. "Carver and I dug half the night, but we found nothing."

"Hmm." She stared out the window, unmindful of the oranges and yellows blurring past. Why would someone have troubled to write that note if Henry had searched the area and uncovered nothing? It had been so specific. *"Near the old stone gate. . ."*

A jolt shot through her.

"There are two gates!" She twisted to face Henry with her whole body.

He frowned. "What?"

"There is—I think—another gate. Or I mean there was. It is nothing but an ivy-covered lump in the southwest corner near Mr. Dankworth's property line. I know because I tripped over it one night, scraping my shin on the rock beneath." She leaned towards him. "Take me there! Take me there now."

He reared back his head. "But what about a bath and change of gown first? Are you not—"

She held up her hand. "I am sure you suffer more from my filthy state than I do. An hour or more longer will not make a difference to me."

Henry shook his head. "But we have no shovels, nothing to dig with."

"The ground is surely soft from yesterday's rain. A stout branch ought to do, leastwise to poke about and see if there is any hint of something buried." Lightly, she squeezed his arm. "Please?"

He exhaled hard through his nose. "Fine. But if you swoon from exhaustion, I will not be held accountable, is that clear?"

She grinned. Victory!

"Such a minx." He chuckled as he let down the window and hollered the new route to the driver.

For the rest of the ride, Henry filled her in on how well his sister had slept last night—unlike him—though he'd left too early to see how she fared this day. No doubt she was even stronger and would be glad to see Juliet. While Charity still had many questions and doubts, she bore her no real malice, for like him, she refused to believe Juliet guilty of such wicked intent.

Juliet let him talk, soaking in the comforting bass of his voice and the warmth of his presence beside her.

Sometime later, the carriage rolled to a stop. Henry helped her out, ordering the driver to wait for them; then they both dove into the trees. It was a slog through the greenery in her gown, the brush and bramble still heavy with yesterday's rain. Despite it all, she pressed onwards, Henry at her side, her breath quickening as they neared the property line.

She slowed her pace and narrowed her eyes, scanning the autumn foliage.

"There," she whispered, then louder with a point of her finger. "Over there. Just beyond those alders."

Henry's brow wrinkled. "There is nothing but more overgrowth."

"Exactly." Quite unladylike, she hiked her skirts and plowed ahead. A faint rise of land loomed ahead, appearing as nothing more than a great mound of ivy—exactly what she'd been looking for.

She dropped when she reached it, crouching low and feeling about. Slivers of bark dug beneath her nails, and with a bit more rummaging, she pulled out a sturdy branch and began stabbing it into the soil. It sank with great mucking sounds, until finally it smacked against something hard. Rock hard.

The old gate.

"Here!" she cried.

Henry joined her, his trousers taking a beating as he dropped to his knees. They both poked about, she working with her stick, he scooping up dirt like a dog. Earth churned. Leaves and bits of vines flew into the air in a frenzy. Her puffs of breath mingled with Henry's in the crisp air, the effort of their labour glistening on his brow and warming her cheeks.

And on her next pitch of dirt, a piece of filthy cloth took flight.

Juliet gasped. "Henry, look."

Henry glanced up just in time to see a dirty scrap of linen land atop a web of overgrowth near his knee. In one quick swipe, he snatched it up and worked to untie several knots in the twine wrapped tightly around it. Gold glimmered inside. He inhaled sharply as he pulled out a bracelet and raised it to eye level.

For several heartbeats, he stared, mind sluggish, unable to comprehend how he could possibly be fingering such a valuable piece of jewelry. This was no ordinary trinket. It was worth a small fortune. A family heirloom. . .only it did not belong to his family.

He crushed it in his fist, eyes closing, unwilling to look at the bauble any longer.

"What is it?" Juliet dropped next to him, her skirts snagging on the bramble.

"A bracelet." He heaved a huge sigh, voice dropping. "Clara's."

"Clara's?"

The sharp snip of her name set a cluster of rooks to flight, their harsh cries echoing through the cloudy afternoon as they wheeled skyward.

"Why is her bracelet buried out here?" Juliet leaned closer, holding back her thick hair with one hand as she studied the gold. "Could Clara be behind all that has happened?"

He shook his head. "Clara may be persistent, even overbearing at times, but she is not the sort to do something so underhanded." He tucked the bracelet in his pocket and rose, brushing his hands together to remove the grime.

Juliet stood beside him, not even bothering to shake away the crushed leaves clinging to her hem. "We should at least question her. It is her bracelet, after all."

"Agreed, yet I will do so on my own. You have been through enough these past days." He turned to her then, offering his hand. "But let us go to the manor first. I really ought to see how Charity fares, and I suspect you would appreciate a warm bath."

"More than you can know."

He led her through the trees, back to the waiting carriage. It wasn't a far ride to the house, but long enough that Juliet's head eventually lolled against his shoulder, her eyes fluttering closed and her breathing even. His chest squeezed. No wonder she was exhausted. Four days in gaol was enough to drain the vinegar from even the tartest of souls, and then to go tromping about in the woods? She was a plucky little sprite.

He shifted carefully, sliding one arm around her shoulders and tucking her closer. He might not have the answers to all the questions plaguing him, but of one thing he was sure. . .she belonged here in his embrace.

And he reveled in it all the way home.

The carriage rocked to a stop on the gravel drive, stirring Juliet. She jerked away from him, tucking her hair behind her ear. "I. . .I beg your pardon. I suppose I dozed off."

"You surely did, but no apology required."

He swung down and helped her to the drive, then escorted her to the front door and pushed it open. Warmth greeted them, along with the swishing skirts of Mrs. Hamby as she swung into the front hall.

Her dark little eyes widened. "Oh my. Miss Finch! Poor dear. Such a state. I shall have Molly draw a bath at once." She fluttered around Juliet while gazing up at him. "There is something you must—"

"Whatever it is can wait." He shrugged out of his coat. "I should first like to see my sister."

Mrs. Hamby lifted her chin. "I should like to as well."

He froze. "What do you mean? Is she not in her room?"

"No, sir. I called on her not an hour ago, but her bed was empty. I assumed that somehow I missed your arrival, and you'd escorted her somewhere."

"Impossible. It has taken me all day to secure Miss Finch's release." He strode off, gut twisting, and took the stairs two at a time. Juliet's skirts rustled behind him all the way to Charity's room.

He pounded his fist against the door. "Charity? I am coming in."

He didn't wait for an answer.

The door banged against the wall as he stalked inside.

But as Mrs. Hamby had said, the room was vacant.

He wheeled about, nearly crashing into Juliet in the corridor. She stumbled. He righted her with a grasp on her arm.

And a deep voice stopped him in his tracks.

"Henry?"

He turned towards the stairs, where a broad-shouldered figure ascended. Silver streaks winged back at his temples, but time had done little to soften the man's commanding presence. His travel-creased suit spoke of days on the road, and as he approached, a faint scent of basil and cinnamon hung about him. His face was golden, kissed by a foreign sun, his gaze keen and assessing.

Vincent Russell, Esquire.

Henry immediately straightened his shoulders.

Of all the times for his father to return home.

Chapter 24

If Henry were a panther, this man was a wolfhound in comparison. Instinct drove Juliet back a step. His stride was unrushed and methodical, that of a man accustomed to obedience without a snap or snarl. His presence alone commanded respect. He held his head high as he approached, bearing the same angular jawline as Henry, every bit as strong and resolute. This was a man not to be crossed. Yet despite all that, she got the distinct impression he was an evenhanded gentleman—open to reason and compassion—and would not bite without due cause.

But when he did, he would not let go.

"Father." Henry's head dipped in greeting. "I was not expecting you."

"Yes, I can see that." Drawing close, his father clasped Henry's shoulder. A brief touch, yet significant. Obviously they held a close relationship, for affection gleamed in the green streaks of the man's hazel eyes. All in all, he was not an unkind-looking fellow, but neither would he be one to tolerate foolishness.

He pulled away, his gaze flicking between them. "The two of you appear more travel weary than I am."

Her hand flew to her hair, smoothing and tucking. Pointless, really. One could not instantaneously craft a bird's nest into a sleek swath of satin. Nor could she do a thing about her filthy gown.

Or—most unfortunately—her stench.

Henry stood straight as a church spire. "I will explain, Father, but first allow me to introduce you to Miss Juliet Finch." He swept his hand towards her, pulling her up to his side. "Miss Finch, my father, Mr. Vincent Russell."

She dipped a curtsey, despising the caked mud on her hem. "Pleased to meet you, Mr. Russell."

"You as well, Miss Finch." He gave a sharp nod, then arched a brow, humour twitching his lips into a grin. "I can only hope your current state has nothing to do with my son."

She returned his smile, deciding that despite his quiet dominance, she liked him. "It was a joint effort, sir."

He turned to Henry. "And am I to find Charity so disheveled as well?"

Henry tensed—she could feel it even though she stood apart from him. "I certainly hope not."

"Well, I should think you would know." His smile faded. "When I arrived not long ago, Mrs. Hamby informed me your sister was with you."

Henry shook his head. "Mrs. Hamby was incorrect."

"Then where is she?" It was not an angry question, not harsh or condemning in the least.

But all the same, Henry flinched. "I. . .am not sure, sir."

Mr. Russell's brows raised to the rafters. "Am I to understand while you and Miss Finch were apparently rolling about in the great outdoors, that your sister has gone missing?" His eyes bounced between them, sharp as a tailor's pins, and Juliet suddenly longed for the floorboards to develop a sense of mercy and swallow her whole.

Henry inhaled sharply, the sound striking a protective chord in her heart. All this time he'd borne the responsibility of caring for his sister in a most noble fashion. There was no way she could stand here and allow his father to think otherwise.

She pressed her palms along her skirt. "I assure you, Mr. Russell, that Charity has been your son's utmost concern. Besides, we do not know for sure she is missing, and that is what we were investigating."

A low sound rumbled in his throat, not a growl so much as a statement somewhere between doubt and disapproval. He stared at her then, his keen eyes pinning her in place, his thoughts unreadable. She forced her gaze not to falter, her muscles not to move, for any show of weakness might attract an attack.

Perhaps she should have let Henry defend himself.

"If I may ask, Miss Finch." His voice was smooth as a calm sea, but with an undercurrent of skepticism. "What are your qualifications in such matters? What exactly is your association with my son and daughter?"

"I..." Her throat dried. How was she to answer that? She couldn't very well say Henry had caught her poaching on his land.

Henry stood tall at her side, every line of his frame a silent declaration. "I hired her, Father. Juliet is under my employ."

And custody.

She clenched her teeth to keep from grimacing. Admitting such a thing would not go over well.

Mr. Russell narrowed his eyes. "What sort of mayhem has been happening under my roof during my absence?"

Henry hefted an enormous sigh. "A lot, I fear." Then he glanced at her. "How about you go freshen up? I think my father and I have much to say."

She nodded, a cowardly act, and yet her feet itched to flee. She'd heard of powder kegs going off before. The boom of explosion. The devastation left behind. All from one little spark at the wrong time. She did not wish to be the flash that set these two at odds, and she *really* didn't want to be around should such a thing happen.

"Father." Henry indicated the stairs with a tip of his head. "Shall we retire to the study?"

"Finally, something that makes sense. I look forward to your explanation, Son."

As they fell into step, Juliet pivoted and dashed down the corridor with as much dignity as she could muster. Never had she been so glad to reach her chamber door. Once inside, the sweet scent of lavender greeted her.

So did Molly, who glanced up while pouring a final bucket of steaming water into a washtub. "Here ye be, miss, and just in time too. Water's nice and warm, it is." She smiled as she gathered the other empty bucket. "Is there aught else I can get ye?"

Juliet could have swung the woman around, so happy was she to even think of stepping into that basin and scrubbing away her grime. "No, there is nothing I want more than a long soak. Thank you, Molly."

The young maid bobbed a quick curtsey—a bucket in each hand—then quietly exited, leaving behind blessed silence save for the crackle of a fire. Juliet smirked. Funny, before spending four days with Jackie and the rest of the inmates, she'd never appreciated how wonderful stillness could be.

She quickly peeled off her dirty garments and sank into bliss. It was nearly indecent how much she adored the kiss of water and soap. For a long while, she closed her eyes, allowing the warmth to soak into her skin and make her a new person.

But even in that state of heavenly surrender, she couldn't help but wonder how Henry fared. What was happening in the study? Sharp words and barbed looks? Or weighted brows and repentant shoulders? Either way, at least his father was there, talking to him. Caring enough to demand answers. Her father would never have done such a thing. He'd always been too tied up with ledgers and contracts, the accounting of money far more important than a daughter who longed to be noticed.

She rose and grabbed her robe, surprised that such a thought didn't sting nearly as much as it used to. After rubbing off the moisture in front of the fire, she dressed and ran a comb through her hair until every tangle straightened itself out. She'd lingered here long enough. With Henry hopefully still occupied, she'd have time to poke about Charity's room for any clues as to where the woman might be.

She rapped on the door, hoping for a response, but when none came, she entered anyway. Inside was just as she remembered. The bed sat at center with an embroidered counterpane atop, unwrinkled. The hearth sputtered with the last of a fire that'd likely been set earlier that day. Late-afternoon shadows haunted the corners. Juliet trailed her fingers over the furnishings as she circled the room, then stopped as she glanced at the rug near the desk. A folded paper had fallen. She scooped it up immediately.

Dearest Henry,

I have decided to go to Italy after all. As you said, it will be good for me. I shall write to Father and let him know, so there is no need for you to act on my behalf. I will send you a note when I arrive.

All my love,
Charity

Juliet frowned. This couldn't be right. Why would Henry's sister drag her feet all this time about going to Italy, then suddenly leave with nothing but words penned on paper? And that so quickly on the heels of barely recovering from her illness and a poisoning?

This did not add up at all.

She tucked the note in her pocket and sped to the stairs. No matter what Henry and his father might be discussing, they needed to see this.

But the moment she stepped into the front hall, she froze.

Mrs. Hamby stood at the front door, conversing with a beam-shouldered man in a blue coat. A blue *constable* coat.

The same man who'd hauled her out of here days ago.

"Ahh, Miss Finch." His moustache rode the rise of his lips as his dark eyes settled on her. "Just the woman I was looking for."

Henry sank into the leather chair adjacent the hearth, keenly aware of the man standing across from him. This was his father's domain. No matter how long Vincent Russell had been away, he reclaimed his place the moment he stepped through the door. Henry had merely been a steward, a placeholder.

A little boy pretending to fill his father's shoes.

Not that his father need say as much. Authority clung to him like a well-fitted coat. It always had.

His father studied him a moment, the flickering light of the fire sharpening the angles of his face. Henry knew that look. It wasn't mere curiosity—it was an assessment.

"So, that woman. . ." His father's tone was casual, yet not to be brushed off. "This Miss Finch. I notice you are on a first-name basis with her and that she is residing here at the manor." He paused, smoothing a crease in his trouser leg. "What is the nature of her 'employment,' as you put it?"

Henry shifted on the cushion, leather creaking along with the crackle of wood in the grate. Several answers sprang to mind. None of them any good. How could he possibly explain the enigmatic Juliet in a way that would endear her to his father just as she'd captured his affections? His father would want facts, not the merits of a headstrong woman who'd charmed him against his better judgement. There was nothing for it but to be honest. . .and to start at the very beginning.

He met his father's gaze head-on. "Remember when, shortly before you left for Italy, Carver informed us he suspected a poacher was nicking our game?"

"I do." He wagged his finger. "But do not think to change the subject."

"I wish I were." A humourless chuckle rumbled in his throat. "Juliet is—or was—that poacher."

"A woman?" His father's brows drew into a stern line before he stepped away from the hearth. Languidly, he strolled to the drinks cart and pulled the stopper off a decanter, then glanced over his shoulder. "Do you expect me to believe that?"

Henry shrugged. "She was caught in the act. Ask Carver if you like."

Liquid poured into a glass. The stopper clinked into the bottle.

His father's footsteps shushed over the rug, the cushion on the chair across from him whooshing as he sat. For a long while he said nothing, just swirled the liquid in his glass, watching the tiny whirlpool. Then, quiet as dusk in a graveyard, he spoke. "So, you invited a thief to reside in our home. Had I known your judgement to be this skewed, I never would have left the estate to your care."

Henry flattened his lips, trapping a frustrated groan. That stung. Not just because it was a slight, but because it confirmed his deepest fear. Ever since his father had left for Italy, he had questioned himself on each decision, second-guessed every choice, all in an effort to prove his worth. To show his father—and the world—that he'd raised an honourable man.

And yet he'd fallen short.

He ought to hang his head and beg for pardon, but self-pity would do Juliet no good. Despite the regret burning beneath his skin, he answered with quiet steel. "Juliet is no common thief, Father. She hunted on our land to stay alive, taking only what was needed. Margaret Brewster, the widow in the woods, is her aunt. There are too many details to go into at the moment but suffice it to say they both fell on hard times—life threatening, actually."

His father tossed back his drink in one great swallow, then set the glass on the low table between them. "That still does not explain why she is at Bedford Manor now."

"I have a feeling you are going to like this even less," Henry murmured as he rose. What he must say next would be better spoken without bearing the weight of his father's gaze.

He paced to the desk and gripped the edge. "Several months ago—four, I believe—Charity began receiving cryptic notes, then flowers, followed by more sinister means of communicating a threat."

He blew out a low breath. Even now he could hardly believe he'd let such a travesty go on for so long. "Someone wished her gone." He turned, leaning against the solid wood for support. "I tried to convince her to come to you while I sorted through who the tormentor might be, but you know Charity. She can be so. . .obstinate."

"Yes. Like your mother, God rest her." Planting his elbows on his thighs, his father steepled his fingers. His jaw stiffened, though it was hard to tell if it was from concern or a stifling of grief. "Why did you not inform me of this? I would have returned home at once."

"Which is why I did not. You left me to manage things here, and I—" His voice caught, and he swallowed. "I did not want to be the reason you had to come back. Not again."

His father hissed a breath. "I thought we were beyond that childhood incident. You learned your lesson. You have proven yourself responsible, or I would not have left you in charge."

The words settled over his shoulders like a blanket Henry didn't know he needed. His father thought he had been doing a good job. That he'd learned and grown.

But the man's next words popped that rising elation. "Yet it appears you have taken this too far the other way. You were not meant to be God, Henry."

Be God? Is that what had happened here? Had he shouldered responsibilities that were not his to carry? He shoved his hands into his pockets, conscience thoroughly pricked. "Perhaps you are right," he said slowly, "but what else was I to do? When Mother died, everything shattered. You lost yourself in grief. Charity drifted. And I. . . I thought if I just kept things running—the estate in order and the books clean—it might ease your sorrow. Might bring you back to the land of the living."

His father said nothing, just waited. The fire crackled in the grate, and for a moment, he saw himself then—barely more than a boy—trying to mimic the way his father sat in this very chair, handling correspondence with ink-stained fingers too small for a man's pen.

"Then you left," he continued, "and I was certain it was because I failed. So, when things went wrong again—when the letters started coming and Charity grew frightened—I could not bear to call you. I thought, if I could fix it this time, maybe it would prove I was capable."

"Oh, Son. There was nothing for you to prove." His father let out a long breath. "Apparently, this conversation is long overdue. Henry,

I am proud of you. You have grown into a fine man. I thank you for all the care you have shown those around you, and I know the estate will be well managed when I am gone. But being responsible does not mean refusing to ask for help. It is knowing *when* to ask and learning to let go of what isn't yours. Otherwise, you are in danger of shutting out the very ones you wish to help."

Henry pressed his knuckles to his mouth, the truth hitting him harder than expected. Because that was exactly what he had done, to Juliet most of all. When she needed belief, he'd given suspicion. When she offered help, he'd kept her at arm's length. He sat back heavily, the chair groaning beneath him. "I thought I was protecting everyone, but. . .maybe. . .I was only isolating myself. Even from God. Because as you've pointed out, I was carrying burdens that were never meant to be mine alone."

"Then perhaps it is time to set them down."

The words loosened a knot inside him. His father was right. He *didn't* have to do this alone. And now that he thought on it, he hadn't been. God had been there, providing help even when he'd been too stubborn to ask for it, all bundled in a wild sprite of a woman.

He blew out a steadying breath. "Despite my failure to contact you, Juliet came along at the right time. Her tracking skills are impeccable, and she knows the grounds hereabouts better than Carver. So, instead of pressing charges, I made a deal with her to help me find who was after Charity." Yet how often had he hindered even that providential aid with his doubts and second-guessing? All because he assumed Charity was *his* sole responsibility.

And she wasn't.

A sigh deflated him. "That went a bit sideways, though, as I now fear whoever has been tormenting Charity is trying to scare off Juliet as well."

His father trapped him with an all-knowing stare. "You care for this woman."

Care? No. That was too small a sentiment. Something far too unmatched for the way she had somehow become his very breath.

Juliet challenged him in ways he'd never imagined. Infuriated him like none other. Broke him and remade him with nothing but a smile.

But he couldn't very well blurt that out—not to the man who'd schooled him in duty since he could walk in straight lines.

So he offered the truth, trimmed and tidy. "I do."

The words hovered, not loud, but loud enough. Like thunder far off—distant, inevitable. Whether his father brushed them away like lint or let them settle into his bones, it made no difference. Juliet had already taken root.

Henry squared his shoulders, voice steady. "But I vow I have not let my feelings stand in the way of caring for Charity, especially not when she was ill."

"Ill? Blast it all, Henry!" His father jumped to his feet, pounding to the door and back, eyes ablaze. "My daughter has been ill, and you did not tell me of it? You take things too far!"

"I *did* send word about her contracting bilious fever. I suspect, however, that you left Italy before the message arrived. Furthermore, you need to know that she was also—"

A sharp rap on the door cut him off. Mrs. Hamby stepped in, face paling. "I beg your pardon, Mr. Russell, Master Henry"—she nodded at each of them in turn—"but you must come at once. The constable is in the sitting room with Miss Finch, and—"

Henry didn't wait for the rest. He dashed past her, heart in his throat, striding down the corridor with clipped steps. Juliet had only just received her release hours ago. Surely the man wasn't here to shove her back into that wretched rathole?

Was he?

He stormed into the sitting room where Juliet stood near a chair, more lovely than she had a right to be with her posture picture-perfect and demeanor calm despite the rough-and-tumble Mr. Fisk pacing before her.

Henry stationed himself a step in front of her, a human shield that Fisk would dare not cross if he knew what was good for him. "What is this about?" The question flew out strident and harsh.

"Henry." His name was a growl on his father's lips as he trailed Henry into the room.

In a much more pleasant tone, his father approached the big constable, extending his hand. "Good afternoon, Mr. Fisk."

The constable gave him a hearty shake. "Afternoon, Mr. Russell. I didn't know you were back in town."

"I only arrived a few hours ago." A wily smile curved his lips. "I trust you kept lawlessness from reigning in my absence."

Fisk chuckled. "I do my best."

"Well then." His father retreated a step. "To what do we owe your visit?"

The constable worried his hat with his fingers as his glance flicked amongst them all. "Mr. Scather reported quite a few bottles of laudanum have gone missing. He mentioned Miss Finch's name in association and that it could be linked to your daughter's recent poisoning."

Henry sucked air in between his teeth. He hadn't gotten to that part yet.

And his father signaled his horror in the magnificent scowl he directed Henry's way. "You did not tell me about that."

Henry squared his shoulders. Better to go down bravely. "I was about to when Mrs. Hamby came in."

Beside him, Juliet breathed a small groan.

Sensing the tension in the air, Fisk retreated a step. "I will let you sort this out in private, then. I've gotten all the information I need from Miss Finch." His gaze narrowed on her as he clapped on his hat. "But remember, I shall be keeping a close watch on you."

She didn't so much as flinch, God love her. "I would expect nothing less, sir."

Shaking his head, his father exhaled sharply. "I will see you to the door, Mr. Fisk."

The constable dipped his head as a parting gesture, then followed the man out.

The instant they were alone, Henry turned to Juliet, barely able to keep from pulling her into his arms. "Are you all right?"

She nodded, but her lips pressed tight as she retrieved a paper from her pocket. "You need to see this."

He unfolded the small square of paper, and the meaning of the words sank like rocks to his gut. "This cannot be true!"

Her brows raised slightly at his outburst, her voice a calm sea in comparison. "That is exactly what I thought."

He clenched the paper in his fist. The penmanship was shaky, but the message had undeniably been written by his sister's own hand. She was gone. To Italy. Could it be true?

Or was it a deception?

Chapter 25

So. Henry agreed with her. The notion hung in the air like the final note of a lullaby, softening the room's gathering dusk. Juliet allowed a small smile at the triumph, although not an actual grin. The dismal situation did not sanction such mirth. She'd barely been out of gaol for a few hours and already the constable was sniffing about, just waiting to pin something else on her. Drat that Mr. Scather!

A scuffling of feet entered the room, Mrs. Hamby leading the charge. Behind her, Mr. Carver hustled in the footman, Woodley looking for all the world like he'd seen a spectre. Or maybe an entire host of them, so ashen was his face.

"What the deuce is this about?" Henry boomed beside her.

"I should like to know as well." His father's tone was no less harsh as he strode into the room.

Mrs. Hamby aimed an accusing finger at Woodley. "The instant I mentioned that the constable Mr. Fisk was here, this bodger made a run for it out the back door. I wasted no time in asking Mr. Carver to haul him right back in." Her eyes narrowed at the footman. "I refuse to speak poorly about anyone if there is no outward cause, Mr. Woodley, but dashing off like that just wasn't right. I cannot abide such questionable conduct. What you did was untrustworthy and outright defiant, ignoring me like you did." Her gaze shifted to Henry and his father. "I thought you might wish to question him about such odd behaviour before I turn him out."

"Well done, Mrs. Hamby." Henry's father nodded at the woman. "You are entirely correct. My son and I will handle the matter from here."

Carver pushed Woodley into a chair. "You want me to stay, sir?"

Henry shook his head. "That will not be necessary." He turned to the footman, his expression ice and steel. "Woodley will not do anything foolish, will you?"

The footman white-knuckled the chair arms. "N–no, sir."

"Right." Carver tipped his head. "But all the same, forethought spares regret." He pulled out a length of rope from his pocket and made short work of fastening Woodley to the chair.

After jerking on the knot, Carver straightened and tugged his forelock at the Russell men. "I shall be but a call away should you require a little muscle."

Mr. Russell stayed the man with a touch to his arm. "Why don't you go fetch the constable, just in case there is need. He can't have gone far."

With an "Aye, sir," Carver strode from the room, Mrs. Hamby following.

They had barely exited before Henry turned on Woodley. "What have you done?"

His father laid a hand on Henry's shoulder. "Allow me."

But his line of questioning didn't go any better. Oh, Mr. Russell's tone was deadly calm, all right—but deadly all the same. Woodley looked positively green seated before the two imposing men. Even were the footman inclined, Juliet doubted very much he could put two words together without swooning.

She stepped closer, studying the man. Fear twitched his lips, his nostrils flaring with each ragged inhale, but she sensed instinctively it was not only the Russells causing such a visceral reaction. He was terrified of something—or someone—else.

"Pardon me, gentlemen." She rounded the tea table, facing Henry and his father. "If I may have your permission, I should like to ask

Mr. Woodley a few questions of my own."

Mr. Russell's brows rose.

Henry's furrowed. "What could you possibly ask that we have not?"

"I mean no disrespect." She smiled sweetly. "Your queries are spot on, and yet I would like to give it a go."

Mr. Russell retreated a step, gesturing with an outstretched arm. "Be our guest, Miss Finch. Women are not without their merits when it comes to getting a man to speak."

She gave her own gesture—towards the door. "Thank you, but I ask that you two step out of the room while I do so."

"No." Henry's dismissal rang sharp. "If Woodley made a run from the constable, there is no telling what he might do if left alone with you. I will not have you in danger."

A sweet sentiment, but one wholly misplaced. She laid a light touch on Henry's sleeve. "I am not asking you to leave the premises, merely to stand outside the door. Besides, he is tied up." She glanced at the footman. "But even if you were not, you would not harm me, would you, Mr. Woodley?"

He shook his head vehemently. "No, miss! I would never do such a thing."

She peered up at Henry. "There. And I do not think I need to remind you that time is of the essence concerning your sister, do I?"

His jaw ticked. A cord rose along his neck. For a moment, she thought he would argue further.

But then—he stilled.

A flicker of something shifted in his expression. Thought. Memory. Decision. She could almost see the war waging behind his eyes.

And then his posture changed. Less braced. Less rigid. "I don't like this, Juliet," he murmured. "But I trust you."

He looked to his father, who gave a sharp nod, then turned to Woodley, dropping into a crouch with the weight of a threat. "Don't give me reason to regret that trust. Understood?"

Woodley swallowed and nodded, paling by degrees.

Without another word, Henry stood and backed away. After a final glance at her, concern still etched in every line of his face, he and his father stepped out into the hall.

She pulled over a footstool, placing it squarely in front of Mr. Woodley, then sat, a little lower than eye to eye, which would hopefully give the illusion she was no threat. Unbidden, a snort begged for release, but she pressed her lips tight. Who was she fooling? She was no threat at all, so she would simply have to shoulder her way through this dangerous charade, a skill she'd honed in many a ballroom to avoid unwelcome advances.

"It is just you and I now, Mr. Woodley. This is your one—and only—chance to confess all to me. I may look the part of a woman of no consequence, but I assure you I have far deeper connections than you can imagine. From what I have seen these past two months of observing your service here at Bedford Manor—and trust me, it is no coincidence I arrived when I did—I do not believe you own a criminal nature. Rather, I suspect you may be a victim of circumstance."

His jaw dropped, his mouth contorting several times before words escaped. "How could you possibly know that?"

"Because as a casualty of the very same injury, I can spot it in others."

"You?" He spluttered. "But you are a lady of high standing."

"Mmm." She stared him down. "We are not all as we appear, are we?"

He jerked his face aside, cursing under his breath. Dark hair fell over his eyes, yet he said nothing more.

So. She'd struck an exposed nerve.

But what was he hiding? Who was Mr. Woodley? If he was indeed a *Woodley* at all. He could be operating under an assumed name, yet was surmising such a risk worth taking?

"Your name is not Woodley," she said matter-of-factly.

He snapped his face back to hers, a storm brewing in his eyes. "What else do you know?"

"Enough to have you arrested," she bluffed. "But if you are frank with me, I shall be lenient. Now"—tipping back her head, she stared down her nose—"tell me all."

A low breath dragged out of him, followed by a look of determination. "Fine, but I'm not naming any names. I'm not that sort."

She did not flinch. "Go on."

"I hail from Porthcurno," he said, "where smuggling is a way of life—a life my mother, a former lady's maid, wished me no part of. She made sure I knew how to live amongst the gentry. When I came of age, the local squire took me in as a hallboy, where I learned to serve in a fine house. I was trained in more delicate duties—how to carry a tray, wait a table, and address my betters. Enough to pass as a footman, which I aspired to. But my father never let me forget what stock I came from. Smugglers like a man who can slip between the cracks. So, I learned the hard way how to live in both worlds... until a deal went bad."

Juliet tapped a finger to her lips. "A deal you knew about," she murmured.

"It wasn't me who peached to the revenue men, I swear it! But I got the blame all the same. And with a price on my head, I ran."

"To Bedford," she drawled, his situation becoming clear. "With whatever money you had in your pocket and some forged papers to present here at the manor."

He nodded.

Rising, she circled the footstool, thinking hard. Cornwall was far away, and the man had already resided beneath Bedford Manor's roof for nigh on three years. So, why such fear now?

She stopped, biting the inside of her cheek, as if she could chew through the problem itself.

Think. Think!

Maybe, like her, someone else had found out about this man's past and threatened to tell his former associates where he was. Someone who could then use him as a pawn for their own nefarious deeds...

Unless, of course, Woodley was the tormentor.

She frowned. That didn't ring true. He had run from trouble, not sought it. A man desperate to disappear wouldn't stir up attention. And what would he stand to gain by prodding Charity away from her home?

Still, there was some sort of connection here. She could feel it in her belly. "What have you to do with Miss Russell's tormentor?"

His face hardened. "I'm not going back, and she can't—"

He clamped his jaw tight.

Juliet cocked her head. "She who?"

He took sudden interest in his shoes.

"Are you speaking of Mrs. Hamby?"

The name garnered no response. Of course it didn't. If the housekeeper had known of the man's past, she'd have sent him packing long ago.

Juliet paced away, something niggling at the back of her mind, an unease that'd been rattling around since she and Henry had discovered Clara's bracelet in the woods. A wealthy woman like Miss Whitmore had no reason to be wandering that stretch of trees so far off the beaten path. And now here was Woodley, a man clearly dreading to name the woman he feared.

A woman with secrets and power.

He didn't like this. Not one bit. Henry hovered near the open door of the sitting room, instinct urging him to go back in. But he stayed put.

Juliet's voice carried—steady, sure.

He exhaled hard. Trusting her meant stepping back. Trusting God meant believing the Almighty could guard what he could not.

So he stayed. Silent. Still. Letting both of them do what only they could.

His father leaned against the paneling, fumbling about in his waistcoat pocket and finally producing a silver cheroot case. He flicked it open with ease, one eye on Henry. "Let me get this straight. Someone has been tormenting your sister in hopes of getting her to leave the country, then she took ill, and then someone poisoned her."

Henry gritted his teeth. "Yes," he ground out.

His father produced a single rolled cigar, running it beneath his nose as he tucked the case away. "Is there anything else I should know?"

Henry shook his head. "That is the whole of it, Father."

"And your suspicions of this villain are. . . ?"

"At first I thought it might be Edwin Parker, for he returned home around the time this all began. And you know he did not leave on good terms with her."

"He did not." His father tucked the cheroot between his lips, then pulled a small tinderbox from his coat pocket and struck flint against steel. A tiny spark caught in the char cloth, and he coaxed it into a flame before touching it to the cheroot's end. "Though I fail to see why he would wish her gone from Bedford."

"Originally, I thought revenge. Spite for her refusing his hand, wishing her banished as he had no doubt felt banished." Henry hefted a sigh. Though he still did not trust the man completely, Parker had shown no reason to question his integrity. "But recently I have come to the conclusion that did not suit."

His father circled the rug, a curl of smoke wreathing his head from a mighty exhale. "All right, if not Parker, then who else?"

"Carver has spied Mr. Dankworth poking about the grounds at odd hours. He also had contact with Juliet and Charity under odd circumstances, and seems to take particular interest in Charity."

"That old hermit?" His father stopped near the grand staircase, resting one arm casually against the balustrade. "If—as you say—he's been interested in your sister, then what could he possibly gain by chasing her off?"

"You know he has not been right in the head since the death of his wife and daughter. Perhaps Charity reminds him too much of his loss."

Though if Dankworth were going to come unhinged, it would have likely happened years ago when the two women in his life had perished in a carriage accident. Henry held up a hand before his father could speak. "Yes, I know, not likely, but I have had to consider every possibility."

"Indeed." His father nodded. "Outside of you failing to write me sooner—a misunderstanding I presume we have now cleared up—it sounds like you have done all you could. I would not have done better if I had been here."

The words struck deeper than praise—because they named the ache he hadn't dared admit. All this time, he hadn't needed to prove himself. He'd just needed to stop bracing for disappointment.

"Any other leads?" his father prompted.

He sidestepped to the console table, aimlessly picking up a recent calling card from Miss Potter. "One more. Woodley," he murmured, thoughts turning dark. Dropping the card, he spun towards the sitting room, itching to march in there and shake the man until intelligence tumbled out. "That footman is clearly hiding something!"

"He is." Juliet crossed the threshold, one brow arched in amusement. "Mr. Woodley hides a sordid past, one that involves smuggling on the Cornish coast, but I do not believe he is Charity's tormentor. I think the honour goes to Miss Whitmore."

Henry's hand drifted to his pocket, his fingers curling around the gold bracelet. Clara's bracelet. The metal warmed beneath his touch, a heated reminder there was still much mystery to solve.

"That is absurd." His father aimed the burning end of his cheroot at Juliet. "The Whitmores have been family friends for generations."

Juliet took up a post in front of the gilt-framed mirror, her hair yet damp and curling down her neck. "Things change over time, whether we like them to or not."

Henry stifled a snort. "But why? What reason would Clara have to frighten off Charity?"

She speared him with a piercing stare. "You."

"How ridiculous." A denial, but even so he stilled from the probability of it.

"Is it?" She launched away from the mirror to stand in front of him. "If Clara got Charity out of the country, she would have you to herself. But then I came along, which necessitated she get rid of me as well, hence my incarceration." Her voice lowered to a dire tone. "And now your sister is missing, Woodley is terrified, and the only person who benefits from all this is Clara."

His father took a last drag on his cheroot, then crossed to the table where they stood, and ground it out on a silver salver. "She has a point."

She did—but it went down like a fish bone in Henry's throat. "Are you seriously asking me to believe that my childhood friend, the woman who has been nothing but kind to our family, has orchestrated all this?"

"Clara has been patient, which is not the same as being kind. She has been lying in wait for her chance to get you alone and persuade you there is no other woman for you but her."

The explanation made more sense than he cared to admit. He'd always known she'd admired him, but he'd written it off as nothing more than platonic. Now that he thought on it without blinders, though. . .the flattering words, the way she always seemed to stand too close for propriety and spoke of his future as if she were a part of it. How she looked at him not as a man with his own choices but as one she could steer to her own will.

His gut clenched. Had she been plotting all this time to ensnare him, body, mind, and soul, and he'd been too naive to recognize it?

He tugged on his cravat, fighting for breath while he strode to the front door. "I need some air." He yanked it open.

Only to see Edwin Parker, one hand clutching his cane, the other raised to grasp the brass knocker.

Amusement flickered in the man's dark eyes. "Taken to answering the door yourself, Russell? Times are strange indeed." He strolled past him, doffing his hat and shaking the mist off the felt. Then he spied Juliet and his father. "Mr. Russell, I had not heard you had returned home. Good afternoon, sir, or what is left of it, at any rate." He sketched a bow and then turned to Juliet with a dip of his head. "And Miss Finch, good afternoon to you as well. I hadn't realized you'd been released from gaol."

"As you see, I have been." She curtseyed.

Henry's fingers curled at his sides as he studied the man. "Why have you come?"

"Don't panic. I won't stay long." Parker set his hat on the table. "I merely learned some curious information in town and thought I'd stop by to see if it were true."

Henry narrowed his eyes. "What sort of information?"

Parker glanced at the sitting room, obviously expecting the conversation to be had in the comfort of a sofa and chairs, but when none of them made a move for such trappings, he merely stationed himself with a shoulder against the wall. "I had business at the livery stable—my horse needs shoeing—so I spoke with Mr. Toll, the stable master. During our conversation, he let something slip that I didn't think much of until I returned home. Another horse was taken out just after daybreak, one that also needed a shoe. Mr. Toll wasn't keen to let it go far, but apparently a wealthy lady who'd ordered a coach early this morn insisted there be no delay and wouldn't wait for the blacksmith. She argued the point until another carriage arrived."

"Who was this woman?" his father cut in.

"Mr. Toll did not identify her, and I did not ask. At any rate, a driver and a nurse debarked this new carriage, assisting an unsteady, veiled lady whom they delivered into the coach the woman had hired. The wealthy woman herself did not join them, nor did the driver. That coach departed with the veiled woman and the nurse, bound for Tunbridge Wells."

Such gossip. Henry snorted. "I had no idea you fancied yourself a society matron."

"We all have our weaknesses." Parker smirked. He paused a beat, his fingers drumming on the handle of his cane. "When I returned home and had a moment to think on the matter, the less sense it made. Why would a wealthy woman hire a public carriage instead of using her own? And why send an ailing lady to Tunbridge Wells when

Cheltenham is closer and far more fashionable? And then it struck me. The only lady I know of with health concerns is Miss Russell."

His fingers stilled, and his voice lowered. "So tell me, has Charity taken a sudden turn for the worse?"

"Blast!" Henry paced across the rug and back. "It *is* worse. Charity is gone."

Parker gripped his cane with both hands. "What do you mean, gone?"

His father straightened, stepping away from the balustrade, his entire frame going rigid. "My daughter is missing, and I suspect you have just given us some valuable information."

Parker blinked. "So that *was* Charity? But you did not send her?" His eyes widened. "Are you saying she has been abducted?"

Juliet stepped up to Henry so quickly, her skirts swirled around her legs. "Do you still believe Clara innocent? She certainly qualifies as a woman with means to hire a coach. She probably coerced Woodley to help her and sent your sister to some undisclosed place where she will not be found."

Parker snapped his fingers. "But I know just the place. Bellamy House, a private nursing institution in Tunbridge Wells. I was meant to go there when my leg failed to heal after being wounded by one of our own men, but the home was at capacity, so I was diverted to Bath instead."

Henry stilled, sickened, as all the pieces fell into place. "If this is true, then the driver of that carriage this morning was no doubt Woodley—and he'd better confess if he knows what's good for him."

He stormed into the sitting room.

Only to find the chair empty, a rope pooled at the legs, and the curtains billowing in like ghosts from an open window.

Chapter 26

As town houses went, Clara Whitmore's was no more or less outstanding than any other Juliet had ever visited, which was oddly off-putting. While she and Henry waited for the butler to answer, Juliet glanced at the large sconces on each side of the door, their flickering candle flames alive in the fresh dark of early evening. The dim light licked over the polished brass knocker just like every other house on the street. A residence like this did not belong to a villain.

Or maybe that was the most villainous thing about it. The polished veneer. . .just like Clara herself.

"Stop that." Reaching aside, she stilled Henry's hands, preventing him from wringing the life out of his leather gloves. "Wishing you were throttling Mr. Woodley's neck will not make it so."

His gaze flicked to her, then to the street. "I should have gone with my father and Carver to find him."

"Yet you were the one who insisted I not confront Clara alone." Her lips twisted into a smirk. "Though it would have been a pretty spectacular catfight."

He frowned down at her. "That is exactly what I am here to prevent."

The door opened to a hook-nosed man clad in black. "Good evening, Mr. Russell. Miss Whitmore did not inform me you would be calling tonight."

"This is an unexpected visit on my part, as well. Is she available?"

"I believe she is tending Mrs. Whitmore, but you may wait in the sitting room while I enquire." He allowed them entrance into a spacious front hall, a modest chandelier casting golden light over the black-and-white-tiled flooring. Shutting the door, he assessed her with a measured eye while speaking to Henry. "Whom shall I say is calling?"

Henry gripped his gloves with both hands. "Simply inform Miss Whitmore I am here. I will not detain her for long."

"Very good. The sitting room is already lit with a fire." He swept his hand towards a door with a golden glow spilling out.

"Thank you." Henry strode away without waiting for further invitation, his shoulders rigid, his step clipped and stilted.

Juliet caught up to him just past the threshold of a green-and-cream-painted sitting room. The warmth of the fire couldn't touch the storm simmering in his posture. "Give me those gloves before you wear holes in them. You are working yourself into quite the lather." Not that she blamed him, but still. . .their interview with Clara would have to be handled delicately—with calculated thought, not emotion.

He shoved the gloves into his pocket. "There. Happy?"

"No." She squeezed his arm. "Not until we find your sister, but I am certain Clara knows something."

He huffed a sharp breath. "Yes, but the real question is how much will she admit to?"

"I got Mr. Woodley to talk. I think I can—"

"Henry!" Clara flew into the room on a cloud of jasmine perfume, her silk skirts billowing. She was all smiles and bliss, her eyes twinkling with love and life. "What a surprise! How lovely to see—oh."

Her smile froze as her gaze landed on Juliet. Her chin lifted a fraction, just enough to claim superiority. "Miss Finch. I had not heard of your release from gaol."

Juliet savoured the victory before curving her lips into a pleasant smile. "I would be surprised if you had."

Clara's left eye ticked a moment before she diverted towards the drinks cart. Her hands hovered over the crystal decanters. "May I offer you both some—"

"No refreshments required." Henry's harsh tone rang like an unexpected gong. "Only information."

Clara hesitated a moment longer, then turned around, her smile sliding into place as the consummate hostess. "As you wish. Please, won't you have a seat?" She gestured towards an emerald-and-gold damask sofa, lowering herself into a matching chair across from it. "Now, what is it that you think I can tell you?"

"Where my sister is." Henry sat as stiff as a weaver's beam.

Clara blinked. "What?"

"You heard me."

Juliet shivered from the ice in his voice. And he'd worried she'd be the one with claws out at this inquisition? She folded her hands in her lap, softening her tone in contrast. "What he means is do you happen to know where Charity might be?"

Clara's brow furrowed. "I did not know she was gone."

"You are her dearest friend." Henry snorted, his skepticism more than apparent. "Surely she would have said something to you."

"She has been ill, Henry. . .which makes this all the more disconcerting." She traced a well-manicured finger along the arm of the chair, lips pursing for a moment. "Wait a minute." Her head tilted. "You do not think she is here, do you? Because I can assure you she is not."

"I do not know what to think!" Henry jolted to his feet, striding to the mantel and bracing his hands against it as if he might rip it from the wall.

Juliet smoothed her palms along her skirt, his frustration seeping into her bones. They were getting nowhere asking direct questions, so perhaps it was time to dangle some bait instead of casting empty lines. She speared Clara with a sharp look. "There was a note in Charity's room, saying she'd gone to Italy."

"Well." Clara leaned back with a tinkling laugh. "There you have it. Why the concern?"

Henry spun, folding his arms over his chest like a shield. "You said yourself she has been ill. Do you not find that incongruous?"

Her smile faded. "Yes, I suppose it is." Her eyes widened slightly, and she pressed a hand to her chest. "Oh, Henry, are you thinking someone *made* Charity leave? What an awful thought! Something must be done, and I will be glad to lend any aid I can. What can I do?"

Hah! She'd done quite enough already. This woman belonged on a Drury Lane stage.

Henry shoved his hand into his pocket and pulled out the bracelet, holding it up so that lamplight glittered off the gold. "You can start by telling me why I found this in the woods."

Clara gasped. "*Oh!* I thought I lost that ages ago. . . I didn't realize it was still on the grounds. Thank you, Henry."

She jumped up, hand outstretched.

Henry merely tucked it back into his pocket, face inscrutable. "I will hold on to this for now. I would not wish for you to lose it in some other obscure place."

"But. . ." Clara's brow twisted. "I don't understand."

Juliet stood as well. "Why was your bracelet on the manor grounds?"

Clara turned, eyes flashing. "I visit there often enough. I ride with Charity—or at least I did when she was fit to do so. How dare you question me so rudely in my own home?"

"There is nothing rude about Juliet's question." Henry stepped away from the hearth, planting his feet wide. "So, answer it."

"I have given you a perfectly plausible answer." She closed in on Henry, lightly rubbing her fingers along his arm. "I understand you are upset over your sister's disappearance, but pray do not take your frustration out on me. I only—ever—mean the best for you. Do not be angry."

Juliet folded her arms. "Who do you know in Tunbridge Wells?"

Clara glanced back at her. "No one. Why do you ask?"

"What about any connections with Bellamy House?" Henry's gaze sharpened on her.

She frowned, her brow furrowing slightly. "I do not know what you are talking about. Truly. Of course I am worried about Charity, and I will do all I can to help you." She stepped towards the bell-pull, her fingertips reaching for the scarlet cord as she faced them both. "But for now I am afraid I shall have to ask you to leave. My mother is upstairs with a raging megrim, and I must return to her side. I hope you understand."

Aha. The megrims! Clara had the perfect opportunity to pocket extra laudanum every time she visited Mr. Scather's shop for her mother's medicine.

"So, tell me, Clara." Juliet crossed the rug, studying the woman's perfectly painted face. "Just how much laudanum did you—"

"I beg your pardon, Miss Whitmore." The butler strode in before she could finish—and before Clara had even rung the bell—a cream-coloured envelope with a gold seal in his outstretched hand. "A message arrived for you, miss. Marked urgent."

Clara retrieved the note and, without so much as a glance, held it behind her back. "Thank you, Graves. My guests were just leaving." She turned to them as he took up a post near the door. "Now, as I said, I have pressing matters to attend, so I bid you good night."

Henry shook his head, red creeping past his collar. "I will not leave here until—"

Juliet grabbed his arm, digging in her fingers to make a point. She only had one shot at this—and that was now. "Come, Henry. Clara is clearly preoccupied."

He glowered. "But—"

She shot him a sharp look, silently pleading for him to trust her. Would he?

His frown deepened, but at length, he gave a barely perceptible nod.

Juliet flashed Clara a smile as she led him forwards. "Thank you for your time."

"Of course. Good night."

Hardly a step past the woman, Juliet lunged sideways. Her hand shot out. Fingers grasping. Snatching at the note. Yanking it away.

Clara's blue eyes blazed. "How dare you!" She dove.

Henry blocked her.

Juliet ripped open the note.

And when the meaning set in, she gasped.

Henry whirled at the sudden intake of air from Juliet. The stunned look on her face lifted gooseflesh on his arms. He plucked the paper from her fingers just as Clara shoved past him.

"Give me that!" Clara swiped for it, her usually composed features twisted into desperation.

Stretching his arm high, he held the missive far from her reach and narrowed his eyes at the black ink.

> *Dear Miss Whitmore,*
>
> *As per your request, everything is in place for the new arrival, and I shall do all in my power to carry out your wishes.*
>
> *Thank you for your generous donation.*
>
> *Dr. Robert Floodstone, Director of Bellamy House*

Clutching the paper, he whirled on the woman he'd trusted all his life. His friend. His confidant.

His betrayer.

"Why?" His voice boomed to the rafters but so be it. Let it thunder to the heavens if that's what it took to shake the truth from her. "Why would you be informed by the director of a recovery home in Tunbridge Wells—a place you claim you have no connections with—of a soon-to-arrive patient? Is this where you have sent Charity? *Is it*, Clara?"

Clara froze, her mouth deformed into a big O, her eyes seas of glass, looking for all the world like Lot's wife taking a last glance at Sodom and Gomorrah.

Just before she became a pillar of salt.

And then she folded, falling into a chair, palms pressed to her cheeks. Tears came. Buckets of them. Washing over her fingers, her lips, her chin. A woman racked by sorrow, sucking in stuttering breaths.

Henry scowled. He should feel some measure of pity, but no. He would not grant her that. And yet—though she didn't deserve such a kindness—he mechanically thrust a handkerchief towards her. A lifetime of training was too hard to break. "Here." The single word was like gravel in his throat.

She snatched it, pressing the fabric to her eyes. "I. . .only wanted . . .to help," she sobbed.

Juliet flung out her hands, scoffing. "Drugging a woman and shipping her off against her will is a strange way to help her."

Clara dragged the handkerchief across her face, her voice warbling between gasps. "Everything has been too much for Charity. I only wished her to receive the tender care she deserves. You have been blind, Henry, buried in your father's affairs. I don't blame you, but someone needed to act on your sister's behalf. So I did."

Henry's gut seized. Was that what she told herself to justify such a wicked act? That she'd been the righteous one in all this? That she was some sort of saviour?

"What a load of claptrap!" Juliet's voice lashed through the air, cutting right through Clara's pretense. "You tormented Charity." She stabbed her finger through the air. "You poisoned her with laudanum you stole from Mr. Scather. You set me up to bear the blame for it. And now, on top of it all, you have kidnapped Charity."

Clara's head snapped up, handkerchief balled on her lap, tears pushed away by a blazing mask of fury. "The only thing I have done is care about my dearest friend in all the world. My dearest friends." She jerked her face towards Henry, eyes wild. "Look at me, Henry. Look! I have always been here for you. For Charity. We have known each other since our time in leading strings. You cannot believe I would be so wicked as to do what this woman accuses me of."

Henry studied her face, then advanced a step and stared deeper. Beyond her facade. Past any charade. Seeking for truth.

But he might as well have been gazing at a marble statue.

"What I see"—his voice cracked, so loath was he to admit aloud what he barely wished to ponder in secret—"is a woman who believes she is justified in her crimes. A woman who would go to any lengths to attain what she wants."

Juliet turned on her heel, striding towards the butler, who yet lingered at the door. "Call the constable."

Clara surged to her feet, crimson blotches staining her cheeks. "Do not presume to order my staff about, Miss Finch."

Henry rubbed the back of his neck, once again forced to choose to commit a woman to gaol. . .only this time he spun towards the butler without hesitation. "Do it."

The man gave a sharp nod and left the room.

Clara whirled to him, hands outstretched, lower lip quivering. "Henry, you cannot be serious about this. Think of all the times we have shared, how I have proven my loyalty to you and your family. You cannot let this upstart drive a wedge between us. She has poisoned your mind!"

"And you have poisoned my sister."

Clara winced as if struck. Her mouth opened, perhaps to deny or maybe to beg, but she never got the chance.

The butler reappeared, his brows oddly knit. "Pardon me, sir, but the constable is already at the door."

Henry cocked his head. So soon? He exchanged a glance with Juliet before marching out to the front hall, the women's skirts swishing behind him.

Indeed, there in the front hall the constable waited, imposing in his calf-length blue wool, flanked by three bloodied men.

Henry's father, Parker, and Woodley.

Chapter 27

Juliet raced neck and neck with Clara as they followed Henry to the front door, using every ounce of self-restraint not to elbow the woman into the wall. Clara deserved it for what she'd done to Charity. But this was, after all, her home—for now. If Juliet had any say in the matter, the constable would haul her to the very cell she'd left empty earlier that day.

"What the deuce is going on here?" Henry boomed as she caught up to him, Clara gaining his other side.

Juliet pressed a hand to her chest, barely comprehending the sight in front of her. Mr. Russell's cravat hung like an unraveled noose around his neck, the right sleeve of his coat torn. A smear of blood darkened the corner of his mouth.

Beside him, Mr. Parker didn't fare much better. His waistcoat was splattered with mud and a fresh cut bloomed red at his temple. He leaned heavily to one side, propped up by his cane, the set of his jaw betraying a pain he refused to acknowledge.

And then there was Mr. Woodley.

He stood in the center of the bedraggled group, just in front of the constable. Blood matted his hair above one ear. His lower lip was split. A darkening bruise spread along his jaw. There was a crooked hump misshaping his nose, and one of his eyes had nearly swelled shut. When his good eye landed on Clara, he paled to a deathly grey, stumbling back and smacking into the constable. His lips parted in a silent oath.

So. He did fear Miss Whitmore.

Juliet dropped her hand, her fingers absently trailing along her skirt. She'd been right all along.

The constable—not Mr. Fisk but every bit as burly—nudged Woodley forwards. "This man's life was saved by the quick action of Mr. Russell and Mr. Parker."

Henry's father pulled out a handkerchief and dabbed at the blood near his mouth. "Once we left Bedford Manor, Parker here used his military skills to track Woodley to the livery—or nearly so. We can only surmise he intended to hire a horse and make a run for it."

"Only a rather bullish thug ended that plan." Mr. Parker rolled his shoulder as if shaking off the lingering effects of the fight. "It was quite the skirmish, one I admit I rather enjoyed. I haven't seen that much action since my men and I held the line at the Chindwin River. I'm afraid, however, the devil gave us all the slip." He directed a sheepish smile at Henry. "Your father called for a constable while I revived Woodley."

Juliet stepped closer to the footman, head tilted as she studied his battered face. "Who did this to you?"

Surely Clara couldn't have known he'd been trying to flee and arranged for someone to stop him in such a brutal fashion.

The footman's good eye darted wildly between the gathered faces before finally landing on Clara. Sure enough, he aimed an accusing finger at her. "She did. But"—he sniffed a trickle of blood seeping out his nose—"how did you know?"

Clara turned her attention squarely on the constable instead of Mr. Woodley. "I have no idea what this man is speaking about." Her words were smooth enough, but Juliet didn't miss a quick swallow before she continued. "I have been in my mother's bedchamber all afternoon, tending to her needs. My staff will vouch for it. But even if I had not been at home, it is ludicrous to suggest I could have wrought such havoc on this strapping man."

She flung a dismissive hand towards the footman. "When you two came upon Mr. Woodley, was it a woman who was besting him? Who bloodied the both of you in such a fashion as well? Do you seriously think I could have done such a thing?"

Balling up his handkerchief, Henry's father glowered. "Of course not. Parker already said it was a bullish thug."

"There you have it, then." Victory—or was it venom?—dripped from her confident tone. She pinned Mr. Woodley with a cancerous look, her voice sweet as molasses but twice as thick. "You are a liar, sir."

Juliet peered at the woman on the other side of Henry's broad frame. "And you are very quick to defend yourself."

A murderous red crept up her neck. "I—"

Henry slashed his hand through the air. "No one wishes to hear any more of your alibis, Clara." He turned back to the footman, words like steel on stone. "Tell us, Woodley, how you know Miss Whitmore suspected you'd talked with us."

His Adam's apple bobbed, and he tugged at his collar, his grey pallor deteriorating to a pea-soup hue. "She's the only one with reason to send someone after me."

Ahh. Juliet bobbed her head, the details fitting together like puzzle pieces. Since Charity was neatly tucked away and Juliet was supposedly in gaol, Clara had no more need of the footman. He was only a liability to her now.

"So." Juliet faced the sorely beaten man. "It was one of your Cornish connections who found you. You think that Miss Whitmore informed your prior associates of your location and they'd come to enact retribution?"

Clara laughed, the sound brittle in the stuffy hall. "Oh, please. Do you really think I would know such details about a footman in another house?" She turned to the constable, squaring her shoulders. "Now, if you will pardon me, I have other things to attend. I suggest you take this party down to the station and sort this out."

"No!" The footman's bark came out raw, a man on the edge of

madness. He lurched forwards, then staggered, his hand flying to his throat. "You're the one who—" He sucked in a great gasp of air, clawing at his collar. "You said to keep my mouth shut or I'd"—another ragged inhale—"regret it and—"

His head swayed like a rabid dog's, breathing erratic. Panic spasmed across his battered face as he realized his own body was about to betray him. "She made. . .me do it," he rasped.

Juliet stepped forwards, straining to hear his weakening voice. "Made you do what, Mr. Woodley?"

"She—" He wobbled, his mouth opening and closing like a fish aground. Something gurgled in his throat as his pupils shrank to pinpricks. His face twisted in agony and one hand slapped his chest. The other flailed wildly about.

Then, like a marionette whose strings had been severed, Mr. Woodley collapsed to the tile.

Could things get any worse? Biting back a *blast it all*, Henry dropped to a crouch and pressed two fingers against the footman's neck. The constable held no such restraint and spat out a curse as he hunkered down next to him.

Opposite, Juliet knelt, worry pinching her brow. "Is he going to be all right?"

A weak pulse beat beneath Henry's fingers. Barely. He glanced at the constable. "This man needs a doctor."

"Indeed he does." The constable rose, arms outstretched. "Everyone step back. Give the man some air."

Henry straightened out Woodley's legs while Juliet swiftly shrugged out of her spencer and balled it up. Without hesitation, she tucked the fabric beneath the footman's head.

"Perhaps we should carry him into the sitting room," Parker suggested.

Clara sniffed. "No need. I shall see that my butler calls Dr. Branch immediately."

She whirled.

Henry lunged, grabbing her arm. "Oh, no. You are not going anywhere."

She wrenched away—or tried to. He held tight.

"Henry!" She glared at his fingers clutching her sleeve. "Unhand me this minute."

"And let you get away?" A mirthless chuckle rumbled in his throat. "Not on your life."

Clara swiveled her head, her blue gaze petitioning his father as if he were God. "Mr. Russell, I appeal to your better sense, as clearly your son has taken leave of his own. The Whitmores and Russells have been family friends for generations. You cannot doubt my loyalty. And where would I run? This is my home!"

His father rubbed his knuckles along his jaw, a favourite thinking stance of his.

Henry gaped. Surely he wasn't considering this.

At length, his father tucked away his handkerchief, straightening to his full height. "Let her go, Henry. This is not how civilized people behave."

It was a command, not a request—one that chafed.

Henry shook his head. "There is nothing civilized about Charity being shipped off against her will."

His father advanced, stopping inches from Clara, his face hewn like stone. "Clara will not flee." Each word was a proclamation. A demand. A challenge for her to go against it and find out what sort of brimstone would rain down upon her head.

Clara trembled beneath his grip. Good. Let her feel the full weight of what she was up against.

Henry released her.

Juliet let out a breath as if she'd been holding it the entire time, then turned from the spectacle to the constable. "We believe Miss Whitmore—along with Mr. Woodley's aid—arranged for Charity Russell's abduction and had her taken to Bellamy House in Tunbridge Wells. For such a crime, she should be placed into custody at once."

"Preposterous!" Clara stamped her foot. "I will not tolerate such accusations in my own home. Though it pains me to do so, I ask all of you to leave at once, for I must attend my mother posthaste. Even now she lies abed suffering." Her fingers fluttered towards the main staircase leading to the first floor.

Henry gaped. "And what would you have us do with Woodley here? Roll him out the door for the doctor to attend him on the lawn?"

"That is not my concern. My mother is of foremost consideration at the moment." She sashayed melodramatically to the bellpull, an unnecessary act. The butler yet hovered just down the corridor.

Henry turned to the constable. "I agree with Miss Finch. Miss Whitmore should be taken into your custody immediately, and here is proof to back up that statement." He handed over the wrinkled paper.

Sniffing, the constable squinted at the note. His lips twitched one way then another before he gave a little shake to his head. "All this proves for certain is that Miss Whitmore gave a generous donation to Bellamy House and that she evidently has some sort of acquaintance with a Dr. Floodstone. That is hardly call to lock her in gaol. Without evidence of foul play, I cannot simply arrest a lady because another is missing."

"Pah!" Parker rapped his cane against the tiles, the sharp crack splitting the air. A volcanic shade of red crept past his collar, his temper near the breaking point, and Henry didn't blame him a bit. "Station an officer here and come with us to Tunbridge Wells to rescue Miss Russell; then you shall have your evidence."

The constable wagged his head. "That's out of my jurisdiction. In order for me to accompany you, paperwork must be filed and—"

"Blast the paperwork!" Parker cut in, his voice like the crack of a whip. "My men and I suffered on the battlefield for harebrained negligence such as this." He stepped forwards, his cane now gripped like a weapon. "I ride for Tunbridge Wells tonight. Who stands with me?" His fierce gaze shifted from face to face.

Henry glanced at Juliet, then his father, resolution carved in both their expressions.

"We do," he agreed. "If the law will not act swiftly, then we shall." For while Charity might be the responsibility of the Almighty, that did not mean he had to stand around and do nothing.

He turned to Clara, stepping close enough that only a breath of air separated them. "But"—his voice dropped to a treacherous bass—"do not think to flee. If you are responsible for this, you'd best pray I find Charity alive and unharmed."

Chapter 28

Eyes heavy, Juliet stared out at the darkness beyond the carriage window, too tired to think straight. The glow of a nearly full moon illuminated the countryside, casting eerie shadows over the hedgerows and open fields. It'd been five hours—maybe six—since they'd left Bedford, so it had to be after midnight.

Her head bobbed with the rhythm of the wheels against the road, making it hard to stay awake. She shifted against the squabs, determined to keep her eyes open. Across from her, Mr. Russell had dozed off miles ago, leaving her to stand vigil—or sit, as was the case. Not that she needed to, but it seemed the right thing to do, especially since Mr. Parker and Henry were deprived of even lolling their heads against the inside of a carriage wall.

Mr. Parker's horse trotted slightly ahead of them, his silhouette black and stiff in the saddle. Henry hung back a bit, riding alongside the carriage, his greatcoat billowing around his horse's flanks. He rode like a man holding himself together one breath at a time. His head dipped every now and then. He had to be as weary as she. But he pressed on, a commanding pillar atop his mount. Unshakable and solid. The kind of man she could trust with her life.

The kind she wanted to belong to.

"You love him, do you not?"

The question crept out of the darkness, quiet and startling. Her head whipped towards the opaque outline of Henry's father. How could he have possibly seen the longing on her face at this witching hour? Could he even now detect the dark red that was surely blooming on her cheeks?

She clenched her hands in her lap, willing her head not to duck or turn away. "You are very bold, Mr. Russell."

"I would not be a successful entrepreneur if I were not." Amusement laced his voice.

"Nor would I be a well-bred lady if I were to answer you, though I suppose that status could be called into question, being that I am currently traveling unchaperoned with four gentlemen." Her lips quirked into a smirk.

"I see why my son is attracted to you." His teeth flashed white in the gloom. "Yet I cannot help but ask what it is about him that draws you?"

"Henry is. . ." Unbidden, her gaze slipped back to the very man they spoke of. How to finish that? Noble? Stubborn? So handsome it stirred something reckless inside her?

"He is stalwart and loyal," she said simply, knowing full well the description didn't cover even a tiny portion of his virtues.

"Mmm," Mr. Russell rumbled. "I should say Henry is too self-sacrificing for his own good, condemning himself for things outside his control. Though he tries, he is unable to right the wrongs of this wicked world."

She turned to him, eyes wide. "Surely you do not fault him for Charity's situation? He has done nothing but do his best to protect her in your absence."

"No. I find no fault in that, but rather. . . Well, I suppose I should say he is given to a certain well-meaning habit. One that's been ingrained in him since he was a child."

Aha. There was a story here. She leaned forwards. "Does this have to do with the time he called you and your wife home from a business trip?"

He gave a grunt that might've been a chuckle. "He told you

about that night, eh?"

"Just the broad strokes. As I recall, a hedgehog and some loose shutters were involved."

"And a supposed ghost haunting the manor." He looked out the window, silent for several moments. "My wife and I came home from France expecting chaos. Instead, the night I arrived I found two frightened little souls under one blanket, shivering in the parlour like leaves in a storm. Henry's arms around his sister, eyes big as moons. I'll never forget the way he looked up at me, like he'd failed somehow. . .like it was his job to keep the darkness out."

Juliet's throat tightened.

"After I explained away his fears to nothing more than circumstance instead of supernatural activity, he felt ashamed. I told him all was well, that no harm had been done. But somehow he believed I was angry." Mr. Russell's voice deepened with emotion. "He couldn't have been more wrong. I was grateful."

Juliet tilted her head. "Grateful?"

He gave a soft huff of breath. "My son's letter didn't pull me from something important. It *was* the important thing. I came home, not because I had to, but because it reminded me why any of it matters. My children needed me. And when I found them under that blanket, so frightened. . ." His throat moved up and down as he swallowed. "That was the first time I realized my son had a protector's heart. He was just a boy, but by heaven, he would've taken on the world for his sister."

Juliet's breath caught.

"He's never quite shaken the guilt of that night, has he?" the elder Russell said with a faint smile. "Thinks he wasted my time. But what he really did was show me the kind of man he was becoming. I've never been prouder of him than in that moment."

"He is a good man, Mr. Russell."

"That he is." Turning aside, Henry's father stretched out his long legs at an angle and thus, evidently more comfortable, fell back into silence.

But not for long. Soon thereafter, the driver called, "Easy now, girls," and the carriage slowed to a halt.

Juliet frowned. "Why are we stopping?"

Mr. Russell chuckled. "The horses need to rest, and so do you."

"But Charity needs us!"

"She needs us in fine form, not stumbling from fatigue." He reached for his hat on the far side of his seat. "Do not fret, Miss Finch. If I know my son, this respite will only be a few hours, so I suggest you make the most of it."

The door opened. Henry helped her down, watching her with quiet intensity, and his hand lingered on hers even after she alighted. "How are you holding up?" he asked.

She smiled. How like him to concern himself with her comfort when he'd been the one bumping along in a saddle. "This carriage ride is making me soft. I am used to tromping through woods at all hours of the night."

He returned her grin, his thumb brushing over the curve of her cheek. "Minx."

An ostler collected his bay. Another began unhitching the other horses.

Henry offered his arm. "We are only here long enough for the animals to rest, so I suggest you get what little sleep you can. Parker's already arranging a room for you."

His father joined their side, one brow arched. "What about for me?"

Henry's mouth twisted into a smirk. "I was recently told I took on too much responsibility. Thought I'd give delegation a try. You are clever, Father. You shall figure something out."

"Splendid. I'll go make up a stall." With a theatrical sigh, his father turned on his heel and marched towards the yard, tossing a dismissive wave over his shoulder.

Henry merely chuckled.

Juliet shook her head, half amused, half bewildered. These Russell men—equal parts charm and cheek.

A night mist curled around them as Henry led her to the front door of the black-timbered coaching inn. The White Hart, according to the placard hanging overhead.

Inside, nothing but vigil lamps lit the public room. Mr. Parker stood near a counter, speaking in low tones with a man in a stained white apron. At Juliet and Henry's approach, they both looked up.

Mr. Parker nodded at her. "Your room is ready, Miss Finch. First one at the top of the stair on the left." He faced Henry. "You should get some sleep too, Russell."

"As should you, but not too much. We leave before dawn." Henry placed a firm hand at the small of her back, guiding her to the narrow staircase. How Henry's broad shoulders would manage the climb without rubbing holes in the fabric of his greatcoat would be a miracle. The wooden planks groaned behind her at his heavy steps.

When they finally located her room, he reached for the knob, then hesitated. "You will sleep, will you not?"

She shoved down a yawn and forced a smile instead. "Only if you do."

He grumbled as he shoved open the door, then retreated a step.

She ought to go in. Common sense cried for her to take every advantage of the blessed relief a soft mattress would bring to her weary bones. But she didn't move. Couldn't. Not when he stood there looking like that—like a man fraying at the seams, stitched together by duty and running low on thread. She'd do anything to lift even a fraction of that burden.

It wasn't much, but soft as a feather, she rested her palm on his cheek, her fingers grazing the stubble on his jaw. If nothing else, she would offer him hope. "We will find her, Henry. Your sister knows you will come for her, and God will take care of her until then."

Hope—and fear—flashed in his eyes. "And if she is not in Tunbridge Wells? If this is all some wild-goose chase?"

She jutted her chin, resolute enough for both of them. "Then we will keep looking until she is safe."

For several moments, he said nothing, just stared into the depth of her soul as he wrapped his fingers around her hand. Ever so slowly, he turned it palm up and pressed his lips gently against her skin. "I do not deserve you," he breathed.

Inside, she melted, craving to nestle into the warmth of his arms. But this was not the time or place. Not yet. Though it killed her in a hundred possible ways, she pulled back.

Then curved her lips into a saucy grin. "Well, you had best make yourself worthy then, Mr. Russell—and I have no doubt that tomorrow you will."

By the time they reached Tunbridge Wells, everyone was out of sorts. It was to be expected. Save for the animals, Henry doubted any of them had truly rested when they'd stopped last night. . .and that was eleven hours ago. He'd snapped at his father when they changed horses. Parker had grown powerfully taciturn, his usual quips nonexistent. Not even Henry dared poke that bear. His father had nearly rubbed his temples raw from frustration. And then there was Juliet. . .sweet, beautiful woman—stubborn as a field of thistles. Despite his coaxing, she'd barely eaten two bites the entire journey, and she was already painfully thin from her stint in the Bedford gaol.

Yet he appreciated that determination of hers as she entwined her fingers through his on their march to the front door of Mrs. Bellamy's Private Home for Rest and Recuperation.

It was an unassuming building, the kind that might house a dowager keen on living the rest of her days in Kent's pastoral countryside. Wisteria vines hugged the stone walls, nothing but the most stalwart of leaves clinging to them this late in the season. White lace curtains hung in every window, and a sculpted boxwood sat on each side of the front entrance.

His father heaved a sigh as he pulled alongside. "At least it is a respectable place, so there's that."

"I don't like it. Feels too quiet." Parker rolled his cane between his palms. "Either they don't expect trouble, or they're ready for it. And there is only one way to find out." He reached for the brass knocker.

Henry beat him to it, restraining himself from banging a hole through the door.

Juliet squeezed his hand, peering up at him with a sad smile. "This will soon be over," she whispered.

Before he could answer, the door flew open to a bulgy-eyed matron, a scowl pulling her brows into an ominous dark line. "May I help you?"

It was more an accusation than a question.

Henry stepped forwards, ready for battle. "We are looking for Miss Charity Russell and request that you take us to her at once."

The woman's lips pursed, making several dark whiskers stand out at the sides of her mouth. After thinking a moment, she shook her head. "I am sorry to disappoint, but there is no Miss Russell in residence here."

"Please." Juliet stepped up beside him. "If you would but look at your records. Miss Russell would have arrived yesterday with an attending nurse. She is my height but with golden hair and blue eyes."

The woman pressed her fingers against her ample belly, pulling her shoulders back.

"As I said, there is no record of a Miss Russell—or an attending nurse—on the books. And I should know, as I am Mrs. Bellamy. I oversee all those who are admitted."

No. Unacceptable. If Charity were not here, then not only had they wasted all this time, he had no idea where to look next. She *had* to be inside.

And just like that, the last of his patience snapped like an over-drawn bowstring. "Blast your books, madam! Let us in at once."

A firm hand landed on his shoulder, pulling him back, steady and unyielding. His father's voice followed, cold yet calm, as quietly threatening as a knife pulled from its sheath.

"Pardon my son," he said evenly, his unrelenting stare sizing up the woman. "We are all a bit overwrought, but this is an urgent situation. My daughter is missing, and we have cause to believe she is here. Now, if you would please step aside."

He stopped right there, omitting a threat if she did not comply. But he needn't elaborate. His father might be in his sunset years, but there was no denying the power in his stance.

Mrs. Bellamy's chin quivered slightly, a hint of sympathy wavering on her lips. But then she drew herself up, smoothing her hands along her black skirts as if brushing away any soft emotions. "I am sorry to hear of your distress, sir. I would like to help you, but I cannot. Bellamy House policies allow for no strangers to be admitted under any circumstances. The convalescents residing here require perfect peace and quiet."

Once again she reached for the doorknob. "I wish you all the best in your search for this Miss Russell of yours. Now, if you'll excuse me, I have patients to attend."

She swung the door.

Parker swung his cane, catching the space between wood and frame.

Then pried it open wide to a mottle-faced Mrs. Bellamy.

"As a former officer," he began with the smoothest of tones, "I understand your concern for those beneath your care. In fact, I recuperated in just such a residence as this, and many of my fellow soldiers can even name this establishment as their first step towards recovery. While I respect your discretion, I know from experience that not every patient is admitted by choice. Some arrive unconscious. Some drugged. And some, I daresay, are delivered under questionable circumstances. I would hate to see Bellamy House associated with such a scandal. If word got out"—his tone dropped to a dangerous growl—"and I assure you, it will, then those government contracts you rely on for your income would vanish overnight."

Her nostrils flared. For the first time she looked truly rattled. Henry drew a deep breath, thanking God for Parker's military connections.

But then, just as suddenly, Mrs. Bellamy's face hardened to granite. "By all means, sir, fetch a constable. I shall have the lot of you arrested for trespassing!"

She gave his cane a swift kick and slammed the door shut.

Parker wobbled.

Henry grabbed his arm, shoring him up while exchanging a knowing look with the man. Good. Judging by the fire in his dark eyes, they were on the same page.

"So." He let go of Parker's sleeve. "On three, I ram it open with my shoulder, and you employ that blade of yours?" He nodded towards Parker's cane.

Parker bobbed his head, a rakish tilt to his lips. "She can't say we didn't give her a chance. One. Two."

"Wait!" Juliet dashed to the door to stand spread-eagle in front of it. "You are not seriously considering such a move, are you?"

His father advanced, hand stretched out to her. "This time, Miss Finch, I am inclined to agree with such a foolhardy measure. Come. Let us step back."

"No." She shook her head, eyes wide. "I learned long ago the only way to capture the prey you are after is to take it slow and quiet. A bull in a china shop only alerts every teacup to its doom."

Henry exhaled sharply through his nose. "Clever words will not find my sister."

She met his gaze, calm and unwavering. "And neither will charging in blind. Give me five minutes. Let me circle the grounds—see if I can spot where they're keeping her. Then you'll have direction instead of guesses."

Henry bristled, jaw tight. Everything in him screamed to act, to crash through that door and shake answers from the walls. But her words struck true. Charging in blind could cost them everything. He looked at her—really looked—and saw no fear, only focus. Determination. She'd faced worse than this. She'd survived worse than this. And she wasn't asking to do this for glory.

She was asking because she knew how.

His hand came up, raking the back of his neck as if he could scrub the fight out of his spine. His gut twisted, every instinct at war.

And then—he stepped back.

"If the room's upstairs," he muttered, "you'll break your neck."

Juliet arched a brow. "Then I suppose I'll aim for a soft landing."

The corner of his mouth quirked. She slipped away without another word.

And he let her go. Not because he was helpless.

But because, at last, he wasn't.

Chapter 29

Well. This was new. Scouting by the light of day was a whole different animal than slinking about in the night. And in a gown, no less. Hiking her skirt in one hand, Juliet crept close to the foundation of Bellamy House, every sense heightened. One slipup could alert the staff, at which point she had no doubt Mrs. Bellamy would make good on her threat to have them all arrested.

A fate she'd much rather avoid.

Rounding the front of the building, she left behind the low drone of the three men. Henry was likely still bristling about his decision to let her go off alone. His father probably paced like a tethered tiger. And if she didn't return soon, there was no telling how much damage Mr. Parker would do with that cane of his.

Which was exactly why she had to be the one to do this. Now. While Mrs. Bellamy was peeking out the front draperies, keeping an eye on the trio.

Ahead, part of a curtain hung out from a window. Keeping one eye on the ground lest she snap a downed twig from one of the nearby hawthorn bushes, she crouch-walked onwards and stationed herself just below the sill.

Inside, a rocking chair creaked a rhythmic song. Soon it was joined by the sharp clip of women's half boots echoing against the tile.

"Come now, Mr. Groffit." A woman's voice. "It's teatime, sir. Let me help you to the dining room."

A muffled grunt followed, then a man's voice. "What about my laudanum?"

"Not yet. Doctor says you've had enough for now. Up you go. There's a good man."

A groan. The fast wobble of the chair before it died off. Footsteps then, this time more of a shuffle, slow, methodical, and growing fainter.

Juliet rose slowly until her eyes cleared the sill. This wasn't Charity's room, but it did belong to a patient, which would give her an idea of the layout. In the corner nearest the door stood an iron-framed bed, neatly made up. The rocking chair she'd heard occupied the corner on the other side of the door. A wardrobe graced one wall and—if she rose a little higher and craned her neck—a cabinet with medical equipment was just to the side of the window. It all smelled of vinegar and liniment.

Good information.

Lowering, she continued on to the next window, this one closed. Either a sign the room was not occupied or that its resident required absolute quiet and privacy. . .meaning someone dreadfully ill or someone whose presence was meant to remain undetected. Like Charity.

Ever so slowly, she eased herself up to peer in—and her heart sank.

The bed was empty.

Still, there were many more to scout. And she did. Juliet worked her way around the big building until she'd nearly circled the expanse—leastwise until there were no more windows to peer in. Defeat tasted like too much salt in her mouth. Returning to the men empty handed would only inflame them all the more.

She paused at the corner of the stone wall leading to the front and glanced upwards, not only asking for some heavenly guidance, but also studying the upper-level windows, where more curtains billowed out. Charity could be up there. She *had* to be.

So. There was nothing for it, then.

Juliet retraced her steps to the rear door, where a particularly thick cluster of wisteria grew, probably watered by a scullery maid too lazy to carry her dish bucket any farther. If the maid or any other staff member came outside right now, there'd be no hiding.

With all haste, she grabbed the hem of her skirts and twisted the fabric into a knot just above her knees. Bulky—and scandalous—but it would do.

After one last peek at the mountain she must climb, she grasped the woody trunk and hefted herself up. The vine scratched against her palms, rough and gnarled, but it held—for now. Hopefully when she reached the decorative ledge, that would hold her weight as well so she could sidestep from window to window. All the while, she forced herself not to look down and contemplate how it might feel for her bones to shatter.

As she neared the overhang, she narrowed her eyes, clinging tightly to the vine while considering the best way to manage once she no longer had such a handhold. Other tendrils spiraled out, embracing the entire house. Some looked promising. Others looked as weathered as windblown old lace. Would they bear her weight? Or—

She cocked her head, listening hard, all thoughts of technique flying from her mind. She couldn't be sure, but she thought she'd heard a weak voice of protest.

Again, words fluttered out through the nearest open window, as soft and determined as a hummingbird's wings. "Let me go. I want . . .to go home."

"Now, now, miss." A stronger voice, female, this one carrying an air of authority. "All is as it should be. You must focus on resting, hmm?"

Juliet's heart raced. It could simply be some patient complaining.

Or it could be Charity.

Determination sparked inside her like flint against steel. She reached for the next handhold, fingers wrapping around the bark, and pulled herself up. Then she stretched for another. Grasped it. Pulled. Repeated. Only three more feet to the ledge when something cracked.

Then tore.

The vine gave way.

She swung wildly, the sudden drop jerking her arm and wrenching her shoulder as she hung one-handed. Midair. Feet scrambling for purchase.

And finding none.

A cry strangled in her throat.

Henry snapped shut his pocket watch, shoving it into his pocket with such force that the stitching gave way with an audible pop. Juliet should have returned by now.

Stifling a growl, he tugged his lapels, frustrated. He never should have let her go off alone in the first place.

"Juliet's time is up." He turned to Parker. "We will flank the building and meet at the rear. I'll head east, you west. If you come across Juliet, send her here where my father will be waiting."

He glanced at his father. "Agreed?"

The elder Russell didn't hesitate. He gave a single sharp nod. "And if none of you return in five minutes, I shall break down the door."

Judging by the vinegar in his tone and grim set of the man's jaw, Henry had no doubt his father would do exactly that. He'd do the same were he not on the hunt for a certain wild-haired, independent woman.

He stalked off, heels grinding into the gravel path circling Bellamy House. No green-gowned woman caught his eye as he swept the grounds. Thankfully, no staff members caught his attention either.

The path wound past clipped hedges and an occasional gnarled hawthorn bush. He scanned along the stone walls, also taking note of open windows—which would be a far easier entry than the heavy front door, though it would no doubt frighten an unsuspecting inmate. Above, more windows opened to the fresh air. Any one of them could belong to Charity. . .or to Juliet, if she'd already scaled the walls in one of her reckless attempts to help. Despite a spark of fury, his lips twitched into a small smile. She was an untamable force, that woman.

Near the rear corner of the building, a flicker of movement snapped his gaze upwards. Just a loose vine flapping in the breeze. He exhaled sharply, rolling his shoulders before cracking his neck one way, then the other. If he did find Juliet clinging to a ledge like some lawbreaking street urchin, he'd throttle her.

After he made sure she was safe, of course.

He rounded the back of the house, jaw clenching tighter with each step. No Juliet in sight.

Parker was already there, leaning on his cane near the back door. He shook his head at Henry's approach. "No sight of Miss Finch. Did you find her?"

"No, I—"

A cry choked above them.

Henry's stomach plunged as he jerked back his head to see Juliet dangling by one hand, her feet scrambling against the stone, every kick useless.

Parker uttered an oath beneath his breath, backing up with a stilted limp. Henry dropped into a crouch, arms outstretched, calculating the distance. The thought of her falling—of those clever hands slipping, that lovely neck snapping if he missed.

No. He tensed. He would catch her!

God, please let me catch her.

Her half boot found purchase. A desperate push, a wobble, and then—

She was climbing again.

The breath shot from his lungs, fury fighting with relief. "Juliet," he whisper-growled. "Climb down here at once!"

She didn't even glance at him. She simply held up one finger, shushing him.

And then climbed higher.

Chapter 30

This might be a bad idea. Maybe her worst ever. But something niggled in Juliet's gut, urging her upwards. The weak protests floating out the open window had to belong to Charity. She'd stake her life on it—and in fact might just be doing that very thing by clinging to this rickety vine. Still, this was the only way to know for sure. Besides, if she did fall, Henry's strong arms would catch her.

And then he'd blister her ears with a scolding.

Taking great care to avoid such a fate, she tested each handhold with a little tug as she climbed onto the ornamental ledge. The carved limestone seemed solid enough beneath her half boots, but not so strong that she'd give up her grip on the wisteria. Plus, it wasn't that wide. She edged sideways on the balls of her feet, fear a constant hum at the back of her mind. Thankfully, prayer no longer felt like a desperate plea—it was simply the air she breathed, steady and sure. Her trust certain that no matter what, God held her soul securely in His hands. Oh, how much she'd changed in the past few months!

She inched her way to the window.

Inside, a broadsided nurse in a light grey gown and white apron stood in front of an iron-railed bed, her back to Juliet. Her ample hips blocked the patient from view, but Juliet could make out the restless shift of movement beneath the white sheet.

She leaned closer. *Come on, Nurse. Move!*

A sharp whisper rose from below. "Juliet!" Henry grumbled. "Get down here this instant."

She winced. He wouldn't be put off much longer. Knowing Henry, she wouldn't be surprised in the least if he was contemplating how to scale the wall to drag her back down.

Still, she held her ground. The west wind picked up, sending a stray curl whipping over her brow. It tickled her lashes, blurred her vision, but she dared not brush it away. Instead, she blew a quick breath upwards, blinking as her eyes watered.

Below, Henry growled another warning.

And then—at last—the nurse shifted, her heavy heels scritching across the floor as she turned towards the medicine cabinet.

Juliet's breath caught. The woman in the bed came into view—golden haired, wrists bound to the iron rails, blue eyes fixed on hers in startled recognition.

Charity.

Her mouth opened, poised to speak, but Juliet pressed a quick finger to her lips. If Charity warned the nurse now, that window would be slammed shut before she had a chance to get inside.

A sharp movement below drew her gaze. Henry watched her, his face a thundercloud, his arms crossed tight.

She met his glare, mouthing an exaggerated "I found her."

He pointed firmly to the ground, his meaning unmistakable.

Yes. Climbing down would be a wise idea. She'd accomplished what she'd set out to do. A proper lady wouldn't even be in this situation to begin with.

And yet…

She gnawed on the inside of her cheek. Now that she was so close, the urge to help pushed her onwards—a decision she'd no doubt hear about later.

With a sharp shake of her head, she grasped the side of the window and hefted her leg over the sill, praying that the nurse still busied herself at the cabinet. She landed on light feet.

But not light enough.

The nurse glanced over her shoulder, and when she locked eyes on Juliet, she whirled with her fists on her hips. "I don't know how you got in here but get out. Now!" She flung her arm towards the door.

"If you value your employment, madam, you will not say another word. Nor will you stop me. This woman is here against her will, and I intend to see her released." She strode to Charity and began untying the bindings on her wrists, all the while keeping an eye on the nurse. "Now, if you please, go down to the rear door and see that it is unlocked at once."

The woman's eyes narrowed to slits. "I don't know who you think you are, ordering me about like the King himself, but Mrs. Bellamy will hear of this!"

She spun on her heel, marching to the door—

Which burst open before she reached for the knob.

A gust of cold air swept through the room as Clara stormed in, a wild-eyed tempest. Gone was her usual flawless composure. Her hair was mussed and hanging in a loose braid over her shoulder. Deep wrinkles marred her gown. Dried mud clung to the hem. The lace on one sleeve hung limp, as if she'd fought her way here—through carriage doors, brambles, or worse. All in all, she was a wreck.

One that Juliet could barely comprehend. What was she doing here?

A lethal shade of red darkened Clara's face as her gaze landed on Juliet. "You!" She spun towards the nurse, voice shrill as broken glass. "Get this woman out of here! She is mad."

The matron hesitated but a breath before nodding. "I will call for an orderly at once."

"There is no time for that," Clara snapped, the whites of her eyes too large, too unhinged. "Must I do everything myself?"

Clara shoved her hand into her pocket and pulled out a small—but deadly—pistol.

Then aimed it squarely at Juliet's chest.

Blast that woman!

Henry barely suppressed a roar as Juliet disappeared through the window. He had to get up there. Now. Even if it meant breaking down the door and alerting everyone inside.

Bah! He fisted his hands, forcing down the reckless urge to barge inside like a raging bull. Getting himself detained by some hulking orderlies wouldn't do Charity or Juliet any good.

Get a grip, man. Use your head.

Sucking in a calming breath, he reached for the knob.

Parker beat him to it.

And the door swung open freely.

What? No lock? No resistance whatsoever?

He hesitated for half a second, exchanging an arched brow with Parker. Then he tore off, thanking God for small miracles while pleading for larger.

He took the rear stairs two at a time. Parker's gait laboured behind him. It couldn't be easy for the man on this narrow servant stairway. Still, Henry gave him credit. By the sound of it, Parker wasn't too far behind.

Clearing the last step, he lunged into a passageway lined with doors. A maddening puzzle. One he had no time for. He'd just have to—

A woman's scream punched the air.

Second door down.

He sprinted, floorboards groaning beneath his weight. Reaching the door, he threw his shoulder into it, sending it careening into the plaster wall with a deafening crack.

And his breath slammed to a halt at the sight before him.

Charity sat up in bed, rubbing her wrists, face pale as a gravestone. A nurse hovered next to her, hands twisted in her apron, eyes wide with horror.

Directly in front of him, Clara Whitmore clutched a flintlock pocket pistol—six inches of deadly force—aimed directly at Juliet's heart.

Juliet didn't move. Didn't flinch. But he did.

Without hesitation, Henry veered around Clara and stepped between them. His entire body became a barrier, his arms lifted, palms out. Not because he feared confrontation, but because a head-on attack might get someone killed—and as such, he kept his voice low and deliberate. "Clara, stop this madness."

She blinked, her expression distant, dazed. Like a cracked porcelain doll with the pieces barely holding together. "Henry?" The gun held firm, but her voice wavered. "What are you doing here?"

Every muscle in him screamed to rush her. But one glance at the pistol told him it wouldn't take much. A twitch. A gasp. One wrong word. He needed to buy time, to reach her heart before she pulled that trigger. "The real question is—what are *you* doing?"

"Don't you know?" Confusion flickered over her face. "Everything I do is for us."

He saw it now. Through the cracks in her resolve, the trembling beneath her icy poise. This wasn't villainy. It was delusion. And that made her even more dangerous.

"Put the gun down," he said softly, "and explain it to me."

For a second—just a second—her grip slackened.

But then, as if snapping back into place, she straightened. "Of course you shall have your explanation. I would give you anything you ask, for we are lifelong friends, are we not?" Her voice turned almost wistful. "The simple truth is you have spent so much time doting on your sister that you had no time for me. So, she had to go. It was never personal—not really. She's a sweet enough girl. I merely needed her out of the way."

It was a struggle, but he kept his tone even. "So you deliberately tried to frighten her away?"

"I needed to. I knew she wouldn't leave of her own accord. Always clinging to you. Needing this. Wanting that. So—" Her eyes glimmered. "I enlisted Woodley to help me scare her off."

"But how? Why? No man would willingly. . .ahh. You must have paid him well."

"Hardly. Didn't cost me a thing." She chuckled, the gun wavering in her hand. "Remember when I went off to visit my cousins in Cornwall shortly after finishing school? They rubbed shoulders with the local gentry, so I spent a fair amount of time at the home of Squire Eldon, who happened to employ a hallboy named William Wood—or as you know him, Woodley. Some time later, my cousin wrote to me of a scandal involving smugglers. Many were arrested, and all blamed your illustrious footman for ratting them out. It seems he used to be one of them. I simply used that information to persuade him to help me pocket items from Charity's room, set up trip lines, and the like—or I'd let those angry smugglers know his location. His unique skill set proved invaluable—he even had experience in hiding his footprints."

Henry narrowed his eyes. "And the poison? Was that Woodley too?"

"Heavens no! The man's too thick for something that delicate. That was me. I simply uncorked Juliet's precious little tonic and added a hefty dose of laudanum and ether before Woodley brought it in. Simple. Neat. Traceable—to Juliet."

"And devastating," he said under his breath.

But apparently loud enough for Clara to hear, for the gleam in her eyes turned to ice. "She needed to go too. She's like a leech, always near you, yet *I* am the one who is supposed to be at your side! Not your sister, and certainly not that trollop behind you."

It took every ounce of will not to let anger betray him. This particular knot required a deft touch. A slow, careful unraveling. Not brute force.

Behind her, Parker slipped in, silent as a ghost. He crept towards Clara. Just a little longer.

"You are right, Clara," Henry murmured. "We are friends. And that's exactly how I know you do not want to hurt anyone."

Her focus skittered to the pistol, her brow folding as if she couldn't understand how in the world her fingers came to be curled around such a weapon. "I don't mean to harm you."

"Then don't." He took half a step closer. Every heartbeat thundered in his ears, but he didn't flinch. He couldn't. Calm and steady—not power or cowardice, but control. He pressed on. "You do not want to do this."

A tremor ran down her arms. "You don't understand. Those women have ruined everything. I had a plan—a future—for us! They stole it from me."

One more breath. One more inch. Parker nearly there. Slowly, he shook his head. "No one stole anything, my old friend."

Unnatural red splotches blossomed on her cheeks. "Do not tell me I am wrong!"

She raised the pistol higher.

This was it. The moment. He didn't move. One step, one startle, and she might fire. But if he kept her talking a breath more, a heartbeat longer. . .

So he held his ground, gambling on his resolve for a win. "I am not saying you are wrong, just—"

Parker lunged.

His cane clattered to the tiles as he seized Clara's wrist and twisted sharply.

She shrieked, the sound feral. Her elbow snapped back, catching Parker in the ribs.

The gun flew—a shot cracking on the air.

Time splintered. Juliet screamed. Or perhaps Charity. Hard to say.

Parker grunted, stumbling back, barely catching himself against the wall as blood bloomed on his waistcoat.

Henry surged forwards, locking both arms around Clara, crushing her flailing limbs against his chest. She bucked like a wild animal, shrieking, her nails raking at his forearm, her heels kicking his shins. "Let me go!" she howled, twisting, her breath hot and ragged against his collar.

But he held fast, every muscle straining as she fought him.

The nurse rushed to Parker's side, pressing her hands to the wound to staunch the bleeding.

Juliet flew to Charity, gathering her into her arms, stroking damp hair from her face. Charity whimpered, eyes glassy with confusion and lingering fear.

Then came the pounding of feet.

The room swarmed with movement—orderlies storming through the doorway, Mrs. Bellamy gasping at the chaos, Henry's father stepping inside, sharp-eyed and unreadable.

"It's over, Clara," Henry rumbled into her ear, tightening his hold as he wrenched her arms behind her back.

She sagged in his grip. "Nooo," she wailed, her head snapping back against his shoulder. "I only ever wanted you to love me!"

His jaw clenched, his voice hard as iron. "I doubt very much if you even know what love is."

Her breath came in shattered gasps. But there was no fight left in her.

The orderlies stepped forwards, their hands closing over her arms.

And Henry let go.

Chapter 31

Juliet sat stiffly between Henry and Aunt Margaret, her gloved fingers entwined tightly in her lap. This was it. The culmination of twenty-seven days of depositions, enquiries, and fending off gossip ever since Clara's arrest. Though it had barely been a month, the ordeal seemed like a lifetime ago now.

Thankfully Charity and Parker had recovered well enough. He'd suffered a rather nasty wound on his rib cage, but the shot miraculously missed anything critical. Charity had regained her vitality, though her nightmares yet lingered. Henry and his father spent alternate evenings calming her when they hit hardest.

Juliet had returned to Aunt Margaret's cottage, which was so different from when she'd lived there before. A cozier little home could not be found in all of Bedford, with its picket fence, scalloped white soffits, and neat brick walkway. . .all thanks to Henry's thoughtfulness.

And then there was Henry.

She peered at him, studying the unyielding set of his jaw as they waited for the judge's sentence. The betrayal of his childhood friend had taken a toll. New creases lined his brow, and those shadows beneath his eyes might be permanent smudges. Not that she minded. They were a testament to the compassionate soul that lived inside.

Sensing her perusal, he reached for her hand without so much as a glance. It was like that, now. Unspoken gestures. Endearments that need not be whispered for her to hear them. To feel them. Theirs was a love forged in trial, steady and certain, needing no words to make it known.

The gavel rapped, and she faced forwards. Ahead, a white-wigged judge sat ensconced on his elevated platform, his faded blue eyes surveying the prisoners below him. Woodley stood in the dock, wrists clapped in darbies. Clara sat to the side of the wooden enclosure, eyes usually vacant but sometimes sparking with cognition—and it was for those moments that a strapping guard stood next to her. At times she understood the gravity of the crime she'd committed, but more often than not, Clara Whitmore had retreated to some faraway land in her mind. Not only had she lost Henry, she'd also lost herself.

"William Woodley," the judge began, "after hearing the evidence brought before this court, I find you guilty of abduction and conspiracy to cause harm. You aided in the unlawful detainment of Miss Charity Russell. Furthermore, you concealed information in the act of poisoning, causing the unjust incarceration of Miss Juliet Finch. For committing such crimes, I hereby sentence you to transportation for seven years of hard labour at His Majesty's penal colony in Van Diemen's Land."

Murmurs rumbled through the courtroom. To his credit, Woodley stood straight-backed and impassive. A pang of sympathy twinged in Juliet's chest. He was a strong man, though. There was every likelihood he'd endure. And at least he'd be out of reach of the vicious smuggling band that'd tried to drag him back to Cornwall.

"May God have mercy on your soul." The judge banged his gavel once more, a signal for the two guards flanking Woodley to lead him away.

"Now, for the decision on Miss Whitmore." He adjusted his wig as he leaned forwards. "Are you able to stand, miss?"

Clara rose with dignity, nose in the air, her bravado an indication she was lucid. Behind her in the gallery, Mrs. Whitmore held a handkerchief to her eyes, dabbing furiously. How hard this had to be for her.

"Very good." The judge shuffled some papers on his desk, held one up to his eyes, and then methodically set it down. "Miss Clara Whitmore, you have been charged and found guilty of abduction, false imprisonment, and the attempted murder of Miss Charity Russell."

"No!" she shrieked, her hands waving frantically. "I never tried to kill Charity. She is my dearest friend!"

The gavel cracked. "Order!"

The guard nearest Clara clamped her arm, holding her steady as her breath came in frantic gasps.

An uneasy silence settled over the courtroom.

The judge pulled off his spectacles and pinched the bridge of his nose before continuing.

"Normally, for committing such crimes, you, Miss Whitmore, would be sentenced to death or transportation. However, given your fragile mental state and upon the testimonies of Dr. Branch and Dr. Yeats, you are deemed unfit for traditional penalties. Therefore, you are henceforth committed to the Bedford Lunatic Asylum, where you will remain for the rest of your days."

Mrs. Whitmore swooned in the bench behind her daughter, the gentleman beside her fanning her face in a frenzy.

Clara whirled towards Henry. "Stop this! Tell them I belong with you. You *know* I belong with you. I did this for you. For us. You love me. You owe me!" Her words choked into a garbled wail as she thrashed in the guard's grip.

Henry remained motionless, his expression flint.

The gavel struck again, the report of it sharp as a shot. "Take her away," the judge boomed. "Court is dismissed."

The judge rose, his black robe billowing as he departed for his chamber. Others stood as well, chatter breaking out as the guard hauled Clara off, her wails a pitiful sound.

Juliet leaned towards Henry, who sat as if his spine were a rod of steel. "Are you all right?"

He gave a sharp nod; then finally, his body uncoiled as he faced her. "I am glad it is finally over."

Next to him, Charity broke from her father's embrace, tears in her eyes. What an ordeal this had been for her—for them all.

Juliet squeezed Henry's arm gently. "My aunt and I shall meet you outside. Take a moment to be with your family."

His jaw worked, emotion rippling below the surface in those grey-green eyes of his. With a quiet exhale, he covered her hand with his own. "Thank you, Juliet."

She nodded, then turned to her aunt. "Shall we?"

"Yes, dear. It has been an eventful few days, and I am more than ready for a quiet evening by the hearth." Her aunt pushed up, swayed a bit from sitting so long, and then edged her way along the bench to the aisle. Save for some random aches and pains, and that she tired easily, Aunt Margaret was back to her normal self, going so far as mixing up a new batch of tonics from the last of her herbal reserves.

Out in the lobby, the horse-faced Mr. Scather waved and approached, blocking their exit. Out of habit, Juliet tensed.

"Ladies." He dipped his head. "I will not detain you long as I know this has been very trying for you both. That being said, allow me to come directly to my point. Mrs. Brewster"—he peered at Aunt Margaret over the rims of his spectacles—"I should like to offer you employment."

Juliet reared back her head. Of all the things she'd expected him to say, this did not even make the list.

Her aunt reset her hat, coaxing it to a jaunty angle. "Thank you for your offer, sir, but I am not in need of employment."

"No, no. Of course not." Mr. Scather tugged at his cravat, his overlarge Adam's apple bobbing. "What I mean to say is I should like to offer you a partnership of sorts."

"What sort?" Juliet narrowed her eyes.

The apothecary lifted his pointed chin while wrapping his fingers around his lapels. "I should like to take you on as a partner, Mrs. Brewster, if you will have me."

Juliet's jaw dropped. "Why would you even consider such a thing?"

His dark eyes shifted her way. "Because your aunt's customers are as loyal as they come. Actually"—he turned back to Aunt Margaret—"they trust you. They believe in your knowledge and your remedies. And after the laudanum incident. . .well, I'd be a fool not to admit that I have some things yet to learn."

Juliet blinked.

Aunt Margaret did not.

"So, you want my aunt to rescue your business?" Juliet shoved down a bitter laugh. "This from the man who once threatened to have me arrested—"

"Juliet," her aunt said gently, patting her sleeve. "Let's hear him out." She leaned closer and whispered, "I'm not getting any younger, you know. This might be a wise move."

Juliet pinched her lips tight, holding in a retort. She hated to admit it, but her aunt had a point. Her days of scrambling through underbrush with a basket and a spade were numbered. Maybe—just maybe—this arrangement had merit.

"Very well." She adjusted her gloves with deliberate care. "I shall leave the two of you to discuss your business. But mind yourself, Mr. Scather." She stepped nose to nose with him. "See that you treat my aunt with respect, or you and I shall have words. Words I promise you will not enjoy."

He gave a small, sheepish nod. "Duly noted."

She veered around the man, hardly knowing what to think about the whole conversation, and stepped outside to a brisk November breeze. Gunmetal clouds scudded overhead. Winter would call before anyone knew it. She pulled her coat tight at the collar.

Across the green, Miss Potter was about to enter a carriage, her latest millinery marvel a towering swirl of navy silk, cascading peacock feathers, and a delicate birdcage veil dotted with tiny sapphire beads. It was part sculpture, part spectacle—utterly ridiculous and yet somehow. . .surprisingly magnificent. Honestly, Juliet rather admired it, both the woman and the hat.

"Psst."

She jerked her head aside, unsure if she'd really heard something.

Could be just the wind.

"Psst, Miss Finch!"

Definitely not the wind.

She trotted down the few steps and approached a nearby grouping of boxwoods.

Branches rustled. Several leaves fell to the ground. A breath later, out stepped Mr. Dankworth.

Her brows rose to the sky. "Why are you in the shrubbery, sir?"

"Too many people." Nonchalantly, he brushed cobwebs off his shoulder. "So, how did it all turn out?"

She clapped a hand to her hat before it flew off in the next gust. "Mr. Woodley is to be transported for seven years, and Miss Whitmore has been committed to the asylum."

"Did the bracelet help bring about her conviction?"

"Yes. Well—" She hesitated, then shook her head. "Not on its own. But it did corroborate the rest. It wasn't the linchpin, but it helped unravel the lie."

She bit her lip. "Wait a moment…" Her eyes narrowed on him. "You found it, did you not? You buried it. And you sent me that cryptic note as well. I might have known!"

A sly smile half curved his lips. "Generally, I despise riddles, but sometimes they are the only way to speak the truth without shouting."

"Why did you not simply go to Mr. Russell?"

"I do not trust men in power, Miss Finch. Nor the law." He paused, the toe of his boot kicking at the dirt. Then he looked up. "I do not expect you to understand my reluctance."

There was something familiar in his words, something that resonated deep in her soul. She knew what it was like to have a hefty mistrust of others, especially those in higher society, and how it felt to be overlooked, to be told she did not belong. Perhaps Mr. Dankworth had experienced the same, for reasons she could only guess.

She met his gaze, her voice softening. "And yet, perhaps, I do. At least somewhat. You know what it is to be an outsider, as do I."

He swiped a podgy hand over his brow, nodding. How a man

could sweat on a blustery day like this was beyond her.

"And Miss Russell?" He cocked his head, glancing up at the courtroom entrance, almost as if the mentioning of her name might make her appear. "How does she fare now?"

"Very well. I have no doubt she will soon put all this behind her."

Mr. Dankworth slowly nodded, saying nothing, his shoulders bowed from some unspoken misery. She had assumed his interest in Charity stemmed from a peculiar quirk of his solitary ways, but maybe it was something that ran deeper.

She stepped closer. "I am curious, sir, why do you take such an interest in her?"

He looked away, staring into the boxwoods. For a long while, he said nothing. Eventually he murmured, "My daughter would have been her age, had she lived. Same honey-spun hair. Same eyes. . .so blue you could see eternity in them."

Sorrow lay heavy in his words, a weight from which no mortal could crawl out from beneath. So. This was why he holed up in that house of his, living in memories, wallowing in grief. Likely he grasped at the past because the future held nothing for him.

Juliet's heart broke for the lonely man. "I am sorry for your loss."

"So am I." He heaved a great sigh.

Juliet reached for him but pulled back before touching his sleeve. She sensed that he needed his sadness, for without it, he wouldn't know what to do. Who to be. And to be cut adrift without any identity was a quick way to lose the will to breathe.

She forced a small smile. "And what will you do now?"

"Disappear, as I always do. A man can hide quite well when no one is looking." He retreated into the boxwood, his voice barely a whisper. "But should you require a friend in the shadows, Miss Finch, you need only call."

The courtroom, though emptying, still buzzed with low murmurs and the scrape of boots against the wooden floor. Benches creaked as spectators filed out. Henry stood in the aisle with his father and sister and, for the briefest of moments, gave in to the pity rising from his gut for the broken woman who'd so disrupted their lives. Clara was gone now, led away by two hulking guards, but her cries still remained. . .and would haunt him for many nights to come. How could a mind become so shattered, seemingly without warning? Had there been signs he'd missed? Would to God he'd noticed them sooner—would to God any of them had—and all this could have been avoided.

With a final look at the side door out which Clara had been led, he tucked away those thoughts and turned to his sister and father.

"So." Relief curved his lips. "It is finished."

Charity let out a long breath, her head bobbing slightly. "It is, and I am glad for it."

Father, ever stalwart, nodded solemnly. "At last justice is served."

Henry's gaze traveled past his sister to a white-haired woman, shoulders stooped, face folded in mourning. Mrs. Whitmore. Beside her stood a woman in a dark blue pelisse, her hand supporting the grieving mother's elbow. A short distance behind her stood a man in black with the bearing of a sentry. Her solicitor, likely, hovering close for any last-minute legal needs. Henry's chest squeezed uncomfortably, making it hard to breathe. What a horrid day for her.

Catching his father's eye, he tipped his head towards the sight, and with a confirming nod, he collected Charity's arm, and they approached the woman as a family.

His father bowed formally, his voice deep but gentle. "You have my—our"—he swept his hand towards Henry and Charity—"condolences, madam. We can only imagine the sorrow this day has brought you."

She lifted her face with a hint of Clara's defiance, yet the red in her eyes spoke an entirely different story. "Thank you. As a parent, I am sure you understand this is an impossible sorrow to bear."

Henry swallowed the knot in his throat. "And yet, Mrs. Whitmore, even in such sorrow you are not abandoned, not by God or by the

Russells. I hope you know you can call upon us should you have need."

"Indeed." Charity hesitated a moment before reaching out, offering a gentle touch to the woman's sleeve. "If there is anything we may do to ease your burden, please send word."

Mrs. Whitmore's eyes filled with a glassy sheen. Her mouth worked, but it took several tries before a papery-thin voice whispered, "Thank you."

"Come now, Mrs. Whitmore. It is time I see you home." The lady next to her dipped her head at them before leading the woman away.

Clara's mother seemed so small, so. . .breakable as she shuffled next to the blue-coated woman, her steps unsteady. Clara was her only child, her sole comfort in old age.

And now that was gone.

Beside him, his father sighed. "How I hate to see her that way."

Charity pressed her fingers to her lips, drawing in a shaky breath. "So do I."

Footsteps scuffed the floorboards nearby, the measured but uneven gait drawing their attention. Parker pulled up before them, an odd gleam in his dark eyes. "Well, Russells, it seems the last page of this tragedy has been written."

His father inclined his head. "For which we have God—and you—to thank."

Parker smirked at Henry. "As it turns out, I wasn't half the rogue you thought me to be, hmm?"

A dry chuckle escaped him. "Surely you cannot expect me to admit to such in a court of law."

Charity batted his arm. "Behave yourself, Brother."

Parker's amusement faded, his expression changing to something more serious as he tugged at his cravat. "I. . ." He exhaled sharply. "I realize this is not the time or place, and yet after witnessing the tragic turn of Miss Whitmore's life, I think we all may appreciate how suddenly the unexpected can happen. That being said"—he turned to Charity—"I should like the honour of courting you again, if you are at all agreeable, Miss Russell."

Henry's brows lifted as he stared at his sister. After her history with this man, would she cut him off as she'd done once before?

Or had she—and Parker—changed so thoroughly that she'd give him another chance?

A smile ghosted her lips, faint but there all the same. Those blue eyes of hers swam with all sorts of emotions—surprise, hesitation, amusement—and finally settled into twin pools of admiration. "I—" She cleared her throat before letting out a little laugh. "I agree, sir, your timing is rather odd, but my answer is yes."

Parker's whole face smiled, but still his lips pressed tight. Joy suppressed, for now. Gripping his cane in both hands, he pivoted to their father. "Have I your permission as well, sir?"

His father stroked his chin, no doubt weighing what had recently happened. Through it all, Parker had proved himself a man of integrity. And after what Charity had endured these past months, did she not deserve the joy now shining in her eyes? Apparently Father thought as much, for after a brief moment of further silence, he nodded.

"I hope, sir"—Henry directed a pointed stare at his sister—"that this go-around results in a better ending than the first time."

Parker flashed an impish smile. "So do I." He turned to Charity with a crook of his arm. "Shall I see you to the door, Miss Russell?"

Her smile bloomed like a flower facing the sun, radiant and beautiful. "I can think of nothing better, Mr. Parker."

As they strolled away, Henry's father eyed him. "Well?"

Henry frowned. "Well, what?"

His father shook his head with a knowing smile. "Parker's right. You never know when the unexpected will happen. I think we have all learned that clinging so fiercely to control cannot prevent tragedy. Life is not a matter of careful planning but of faith. And yet you stand here, waiting as if for a signed decree granting you permission to be happy."

"But I am happy." His brow scrunched. "All has turned out well for Charity. Better, in fact, than I imagined."

"I was not speaking of your sister." His father clapped him on the shoulder, lips twisted into a wry smile. "Son, it is time you loosen your stranglehold on responsibilities and instead pursue a certain woman who appears to be your match in every way. Go." He nudged him with a little shove. "Track this poacher of yours before she decides you are not worth the trouble and flies away."

His father's words sank deep. Glorious. Taking root.

And he needn't be told twice.

"Sage advice." With a wink, he strode off, urgency propelling him past the clusters of lingering court attenders. This had been a long time in coming—too long.

He burst through the courthouse doors, a crisp gust of November air slapping his skin. He welcomed it, drinking deep, clearing his mind.

Juliet stood near the boxwoods, her figure framed against the stark November day. Windblown hair escaped her bonnet, flying like a banner in the breeze, much like the first night he'd caught her in the woods. Wild and unapologetic. He'd never tire of such a sight. She belonged here, in the open, part of the brisk air and boundless sky, as untamed as the elements around her.

But more than that, she belonged with him.

His steps quickened, confidence a fire in his belly as he closed the distance between them.

She turned towards him, eyes bright with curiosity, lips already parting to speak.

He didn't let her.

He caught Juliet around the waist, pulling her flush against him, and kissed her. No words. No explanations. Just a physical statement of how things were.

And what was to come.

She melted against him, grabbing handfuls of his coat and pressing ever closer.

When he finally pulled away, they were both breathing hard.

One of her brows rose, amusement quirking her very red lips. "What was that for?"

"You." He grinned. "And us."

"Us?" Her nose wrinkled, her confusion so adorable it slipped past every defense he'd ever built.

"Yes, us." He dropped to a knee, tugging off one of her gloves and guiding her hand to press against his chest. "Though I admit I'm taking a bit of a risk here. Last time I kissed you without warning, I got slapped."

A laugh burst out of her.

"This time, however," he went on, "I thought I would try following it up with a proposal, because I'm not just asking for a future. I'm asking for you. All of you. Forever."

Her mouth opened, but no words came out. Just a little puff of air that misted in the cold. Then, slowly, delight dawned on her face, her mouth curving into that familiar smile that undid him every time.

"Are you proposing marriage to a poacher, sir?"

"I am." He grinned. "To the woman who trespassed onto my land and made off with my heart."

"Then my answer," she said, voice light with joy, "is yes."

Chapter 32

Six months later, May 1821

Juliet paused just below the rise, silent as the beech trunk she hid behind. Overhead, brilliant green leaves, fresh from their buds, shushed in the morning breeze. She lifted her nose, sniffing the air. Hawthorn blossoms, sweet but musky, almost almondlike, blended with the earthy scent of moist dirt beneath her feet. Both lovely, but not what she wished to inhale. Had she been wrong?

Crouching, she studied the ground. Ahead, a branch lay snapped in half. A yard in front of that was a flattened patch of wood anemones, their white petals crushed by a heel. Her lips quirked. Perhaps she wasn't as far off as she thought.

She pressed onwards, upwards, landing each step as quiet as a fox on the hunt. Stopping at the next tree, she pressed a hand to her belly, pushing back a sudden grumble. This time, on this quest, the hunger pang was of her own making, so unlike last year. Bother! She should have at least grabbed a piece of toast on her way out of the manor. Maybe she should turn back. It wasn't as if this pursuit was of life-or-death importance or—

She jerked up her head, inhaling sharply. There. A hint of bay leaf. The musty tang of old leather and aged paper. Faint, yet unmistakable.

Appetite forgotten, she crept up the remaining stretch of ridge, then hesitated as she spied her prey.

Henry stood with his back towards her, surveying the vast fields in front of him, looking every bit the lord of the manor as he had that night she'd first encountered him in the woods. Strong. Steady. So handsome it ached deep in her ribs.

And completely unaware.

Grinning, she left behind the trees, easing each step soundlessly into the soft spring growth. The thrill of catching him off guard sent a charge through her.

Then died a quick death as his low voice carried on the next waft of breeze.

"Juliet," he said simply.

Dash it all!

She stomped up to him, a pout to her lips. "How did you know I was there?"

He turned to her, chuckling. "I always know when my wife is nearby."

She huffed. Saucy bounder. But even so, she shoved down a smile. "What are you doing out here brooding so early in the day?"

He shook his head, wind tousling his hair. Which was completely unfair. She ought to be the one running her fingers through it.

"I am not brooding but rather counting my blessings."

She arched a brow. "And you cannot do that inside the house?"

"No. I am far too distracted when you are within arm's reach." A sultry gleam glittered in his eyes, one that never failed to inspire a twinge low in her belly.

She wagged her finger. "I know exactly what is on your mind, sir, and do not think to—"

He lunged.

She shrieked.

Then was instantly quieted by the press of his mouth against hers.

As always, she leaned into him, thoroughly captured by the depth of his love for her. This man. This moment. She would never tire of such a God-given gift.

It wasn't until she was breathless that he pulled away with a rakish tilt to his head.

She poked him in the chest. "You do not play fair."

"No," he drawled while snatching up her hand and planting a kiss on the tip of her finger. "Then again, neither do you."

He wrapped his arm around her shoulders, pulling her against his side, pivoting slightly at the far-off sound of hoofbeats.

Down in the valley, two riders sped along. A black-coated man brought up the rear, mounted on a magnificent ebony stallion. Ahead of him, not by much, the blue skirts of a woman rippled against the flanks of a bay, her laughter as bright as the May morn.

Leaning her head against her husband's strong shoulder, Juliet glanced up at Henry. "Do you think Edwin allows her to win every race, or is your sister truly that good a horsewoman?"

Amusement rumbled in his throat. "Charity is an excellent rider, though I know firsthand a husband is wont to please his wife."

She melted against him with a sigh.

The breeze carried the scent of wildflowers, and somewhere nearby, a lark sang. She closed her eyes, committing it all to memory—the warmth of her husband's hand, the strength of his embrace, the promise of the road ahead.

Long ago, on a day of dust and wind, she had been reborn into a hard-cracked survivor. Yet here, now—with her husband's lips at her temple and the future spread vast before them—she was something more. Not merely existing but truly living.

And loving.

And home.

BIBLIOGRAPHY

Adkins, Roy, and Lesley Adkins. *Eavesdropping on Jane Austen's England: How Our Ancestors Lived Two Centuries Ago.* Abacus, 2014.

Anderson, Robert Tuesley. *Jane Austen's Table.* Thunder Bay, 2021.

Cashman, Bernard. *A Proper House: Bedford Lunatic Asylum (1812–1860).* North Bedfordshire Health Authority, 1992.

Fullerton, Susannah. *Jane Austen & Crime.* Jones Books, 2006.

Miller, Thomas. *The Poacher, and Other Pictures of Country Life.* Kessinger, 2009.

Mortimer, Ian. *The Time Traveller's Guide to Regency Britain.* Penguin Random House, 2020.

Pfeiffer, Carl J. *The Art and Practice of Western Medicine in the Early Nineteenth Century.* McFarland, 1985.

Trench, C. C. *The Poacher and the Squire.* Longmans, 1967.

Willes, Margaret. *Country House Estates.* National Trust, 1996.

HISTORICAL NOTES

Poaching in Regency England

Taking game from private lands was a serious crime in Regency England. If the poacher was caught armed or in a group, particularly at night, the 1816 Game Act called for an immediate sentence of death. For lesser offenses, such as trespassing to hunt or trapping without violence, offenders were often sentenced to seven to fourteen years transportation. That meant they were shipped off (literally) to Van Diemen's Land, a penal colony in Australia. . .which was really a life sentence, unless you were lucky enough to survive the awful conditions and hard labour.

Bedford Assembly Room

Most Regency assembly rooms served as venues for social gatherings such as balls, concerts, or public meetings. These rooms were central to the town's social life, providing a space where residents engaged in cultural and recreational activities. Probably the most famous are the Bath Assembly Rooms, known for their elegance and association with fashionable society—and, of course, Jane Austen.

The Waltz

The waltz originated in Austria and southern Germany, making its way to England around the 1790s. At first, it was considered quite scandalous because of its intimate nature in the way partners held each other in such a close fashion. Those more conservative condemned it, but in 1814, the Prince Regent himself endorsed it, and this dance then grew to be a staple in ballrooms all across England.

The Apothecaries Act of 1815

The Apothecaries Act of 1815 was a significant piece of British legislation regulating medical practice in England and Wales. It established professional standards for apothecaries (early medical practitioners akin to general physicians) and aimed to ensure public access to qualified medical care. It specifically required anyone practicing medicine to have a license issued by the Society of Apothecaries. Candidates had to undergo formal training, including attending lectures, obtaining apprenticeships, and passing an examination. This helped differentiate medical professionals from untrained practitioners, who were seen as quacks, mountebanks, or charlatans.

Bilious Fever

Bilious fever was a broad term used in the eighteenth and nineteenth centuries to describe a variety of illnesses that presented with symptoms such as fever, nausea, vomiting, diarrhea, and abdominal pain, often associated with bile or digestive upset. It was thought to be caused by an imbalance of the "humours," particularly excess bile, as per the medical theories of the time. The term was used broadly, encompassing conditions we now recognize as gastrointestinal infections, malaria, or other febrile illnesses. Treatments at the time were purging, bleeding, rest, and diet. Most cases resolved in a few days to a couple of weeks, though it could become life threatening depending on what the "real" issue was.

Tunbridge Wells

Spa towns were all the rage during the Regency era. Most notable is Bath, brought to the forefront by Jane Austen, but there were others. Tunbridge Wells' notoriety as a spa town dates back to the early seventeenth century, when an iron-rich spring was discovered. This led to the town becoming a popular destination for those seeking the health benefits said to be gained by drinking that water. While its popularity as a spa town declined with the advent of sea bathing, Tunbridge Wells remains proud of its spa heritage and continues to be a point of interest for tourists.

ACKNOWLEDGEMENTS

First, a tip of the hat to the amazing team at Barbour who make my books shine brighter than a freshly polished teapot. Annie Barkley and Shalyn Sattler, you deserve an extra sprinkle of confetti for your endless patience when there's a fire to put out.

To my incredible agent, Wendy Lawton—thank you for championing my words even when I second-guess every single one of them.

To my brilliant critique partners and fellow word wranglers: Kendall Hoxsey (for providing Ghost Block as needed), Tara Johnson (fellow emotional roller-coaster rider), Julie Klassen (historical genius), Shannon McNear (research queen), Ane Mulligan (who always knows just what to say), Chawna Schroeder (story alchemist), and MaryLu Tyndall (pirate-hearted encourager). I couldn't have done this without you. For reals.

To the readers who keep me going, cheer me on, and remind me why I love telling stories: Gene Gwennap, Almira Kline, Margie Swearingen Mijares, and Janet Shillam-Day—you're all gems in this giant treasure chest of a writing life.

Special shout-out to Charity Henico. . .who gets the cutest tongue-tied fangirl award. Yes, my readerly friend, I *did* name Henry's sister after you.

And finally, to my husband, Mark Griep—you are the best plot twist that ever happened to me.

ABOUT THE AUTHOR

Michelle Griep's been writing since she first discovered blank wall space and Crayolas. She is the Christy Award–winning author of historical romances that both intrigue and evoke a smile. An Anglophile at heart, you'll most often find her partaking of a proper cream tea while scheming up her next novel. . .but it's probably easier to find her at www.michellegriep.com or on Facebook, Instagram, and Pinterest.

And guess what? She loves to hear from readers! Feel free to drop her a note at michelle@michellegriep.com.

OTHER BOOKS BY MICHELLE

Lost in Darkness
Man of Shadow and Mist

The House at the End of the Moor

The Thief of Blackfriars Lane
The Bride of Blackfriars Lane
The Sleuth of Blackfriars Lane

The Bow Street Runners Trilogy

The Captive Heart
The Captured Bride

Once Upon a Dickens Christmas

Praise for *The Bird of Bedford Manor*

What a great premise! An impoverished gentlewoman poaches game on a handsome gentleman's estate and soon finds herself helping him hunt down the menacing stalker tormenting his sister. Danger, intrigue, and romance ensue. Don't miss *The Bird of Bedford Manor* by talented author Michelle Griep.

—Julie Klassen, author of *Whispers at Painswick Court*

Michelle Griep is the Queen of Historical Romance Mysteries! Her novels never fail to entertain, intrigue, and warm my heart. If you're looking for a story that contains a slew of fascinating characters, a swoon-worthy hero, a feisty heroine, a heated romance that only dreams are made of, and a mystery that will keep you guessing until the end, then *The Bird of Bedford Manor* will not disappoint!

—MaryLu Tyndall, author of award-winning
Legacy of the King's Pirates series

The Bird of Bedford Manor captured me from the first, finely wrought line. Michelle Griep's fast-paced, unpredictable storytelling shines brightly in this Regency novel that is as clever as it is colorful. The lush English setting is another coup. Bravo!

—Laura Frantz, Christy Award–winning author of *The Indigo Heiress*

What a thrilling tale! Full of witty banter and clever prose, Griep delivers yet another engaging story with enough sigh-worthy romance and thought-provoking mystery to keep readers eagerly turning the pages. Highly recommended for readers who love quick-paced, low-spice Regency romances.

—Sarah E. Ladd, bestselling author

With charm, mystery, and a heady dose of romance, *The Bird of Bedford Manor* is sure to steal your heart as effectively as our poacher-heroine stole the hero's and whisk you back in time and straight into their story. I could scarcely put this down! An intriguing concept, characters you'll soon call friends, and impeccable writing combine to make this one unforgettable.

—Roseanna M. White, Christy Award–winning,
bestselling author of *The Imposters*

Michelle Griep is a master of her craft. Her details delight, her emotion enthralls, and her whimsy woos the reader. The story world of *Bedford Manor* is rich in intrigue, peppered with delightful characters, and the romance. . . whew! I might need my smelling salts!

—Erica Vetsch, author of the Of Cloaks & Daggers series

Michelle Griep is at her finest in this toe-curling romance of forbidden love and intrigue. With a huntress, a wealthy landowner, villainous foes and spine-tingling danger, *The Bird of Bedford Manor* is a story I will revisit over and over again. Readers won't be able to put it down.

—Tara Johnson, Carol and Christy Award nominee of *Engraved on the Heart*

With her signature flair for vivid storytelling, Michelle Griep delivers a breathtaking tale of passion, peril, and impossible choices. *The Bird of Bedford Manor* sweeps readers into a world of a single-minded poacher, a dashing landowner, and enemies lurking in the shadows. Brimming with intrigue, heart-stopping moments, and a romance that sizzles against all odds, this is a book that demands to be read—and savored again and again.

—Ane Mulligan, author of the award-winning Georgia Magnolias series

Juliet will go to any length to provide for her ailing aunt, even if that means poaching on a neighbour's land. Henry will go to any length to protect his sister and track down her mysterious tormentor, even if that means hiring the young woman caught in a criminal act, herself a lady fallen on hard times. This story will have readers rooting for both, as *The Bird of Bedford Manor* carries on Griep's brand of the brave, plucky heroine and the honorable hero who sometimes gets in his own way.

—Shannon McNear, 2014 RITA® nominee, 2021 SELAH winner, and author of Daughters of the Lost Colony series

Taunting with clues and whispering with doubts, *The Bird of Bedford Manor* intertwines mystery and romance, luring you ever deeper into a maze of riddles and questions. This is a story that does not easily release its prey.

—Chawna Schroeder, author of *Illuminary*